T0089042

PENGUIN CLASSICS

POET'S PUB

ERIC LINKLATER was a Scottish writer born in Penarth, Wales, on March 8, 1899. Although Linklater initially studied medicine, he later became interested in journalism. Much of his writing is based on his experience in the military and his extensive travels of the world. During World War I, he served as a sniper with a Scottish infantry regiment, and after suffering a severe head injury he was hospitalized for several months. In the 1930s he became a full-time writer, publishing novels, poetry, short fiction, satires, travel pieces, children's books, war histories, and two volumes of autobiography. The satirical *Juan in America* examines the catastrophe that was Prohibition, while *Private Angelo* humorously recounts the postwar reorganization in Italy. His children's novel *The Wind on the Moon* was awarded the Carnegie Medal. *Poet's Pub* was adapted into a British comedy film in 1949.

NANCY PEARL is a literary critic, a librarian, and the author of *Book Lust: Recommended Reading for Every Mood, Moment, and Reason*. She is a regular commentator on NPR's *Morning Edition* and the 2004 winner of the Women's National Book Association Award.

ERIC LINKLATER

Poet's Pub

Foreword by
NANCY PEARL

PENGUIN BOOKS

PENGUIN BOOKS

Published by the Penguin Group
Penguin Group (USA) Inc., 375 Hudson Street,
New York, New York 10014, U.S.A.
Penguin Group (Canada), 90 Eglinton Avenue East, Suite 700, Toronto,
Ontario, Canada M4P 2Y3 (a division of Pearson Penguin Canada Inc.)
Penguin Books Ltd, 80 Strand, London WC2R 0RL, England
Penguin Ireland, 25 St Stephen's Green, Dublin 2,
Ireland (a division of Penguin Books Ltd)
Penguin Group (Australia), 250 Camberwell Road,
Camberwell, Victoria 3124, Australia
(a division of Pearson Australia Group Pty Ltd)
Penguin Books India Pvt Ltd, 11 Community Centre,
Panchsheel Park, New Delhi – 110 017, India
Penguin Group (NZ), 67 Apollo Drive, Rosedale, Auckland 0632,
New Zealand (a division of Pearson New Zealand Ltd)
Penguin Books (South Africa) (Pty) Ltd, 24 Sturdee Avenue,
Rosebank, Johannesburg 2196, South Africa

Penguin Books Ltd, Registered Offices:
80 Strand, London WC2R 0RL, England

First published in Great Britain by Penguin Books Limited 1929
First published in the United States of America by Jonathan Cape & Harrison Smith 1930
This edition with a foreword by Nancy Pearl published in Penguin Books 2012

ISBN 0-978-0-14-310666-1
CIP data available

ALWAYS LEARNING   PEARSON

For Elspeth Mary

Contents

Foreword

You are about to begin one of the most delightful novels I've ever read. I first encountered Eric Linklater's *Poet's Pub* when I was working at Yorktown Alley, a wonderful independent bookstore in Tulsa, Oklahoma. In 1985, Penguin, as part of the celebration of its fiftieth anniversary, presented to booksellers boxed sets of facsimiles of the very first ten Penguins ever printed as a thank-you for their longtime support. (In addition to the set of books, our sales representative also presented me with a stuffed animal—a penguin—that I named Howard Slutes, in his honor. It still graces my fireplace hearth today.)

In the 1930s, Allen Lane, an editor at Bodley Head (a major British publishing company), was given the responsibility of selecting the first books considered of literary quality to be reprinted in paperback ("penny dreadfuls" were already available in paper editions at the time). Due to the popularity of these new paperbacks, Lane was able to spin off Penguin as an independent publisher, rather than have it remain an imprint of Bodley Head. The original paperbacks Lane published were all branded as Penguin Books on the cover, along with the logo of the eponymous penguin. He succeeded beyond all expectations in his mission of making good books more accessible (and less expensive) than they'd been before. (Jeremy Lewis's *Penguin Special: The Story of Allen Lane, the Founder of Penguin Books and the Man Who Changed Publishing Forever*, is an excellent biography that vividly captures Lane's outsize personality.)

The ten titles that Allen Lane chose to be published under the Penguin imprint are fascinating to consider. I'd love to have been at a dinner party with Lane at the time so I could have asked him, Why *this* book by that author and not another one? And why indeed *this* author at all, rather than that one? Taken together, the books constitute an amalgam of what was on offer to serious readers in the early decades of the twentieth century. These first ten Penguins include novels by authors still read and enjoyed today, as well as others who are now much less known (if known at all). Eight of the first ten were novels, one was a biography, and one was an autobiography.

The famous (or infamous, depending upon your opinion of Lane's choices) ten are Ernest Hemingway's *A Farewell to Arms*, Dorothy L. Sayers's *The Unpleasantness at the Bellona Club*, and Agatha Christie's *The Mysterious Affair at Styles*. (The popularity of these is such that someone is probably reading them even at the moment I write this sentence.) Included as well were *Ariel*, a biography of Percy Bysshe Shelley by André Maurois; *Carnival*, a memoir by Beverley Nichols; four little-read-today novels by Compton Mackenzie, Mary Webb, E. H. Young, and Susan Ertz. And, of course, *Poet's Pub*.

The hero of *Poet's Pub* is Saturday Keith, the seventh son of his parents. He was, to be sure, born on a Saturday. (His eldest brother had been born on a Sunday, second-eldest on a Monday, and so on, but they were given more usual names. It was only when the seventh baby seemed eager to enter the world late on Friday night that Saturday's father, intrigued with the notion of having a child born on every day of the week, encouraged his wife with these words: "Hold him, my love, hold him! There's an hour to go yet. Be brave, my dear, this is the last one, I swear.") Saturday attends Oxford, where he wins a rowing blue, awarded for high achievement in university sports (although to his sorrow he loses the most important race, against Cambridge). He also writes spectacularly abysmal poetry, although he rather likes his own work (several cringe-worthy examples are included in the novel). After his most recent collection, *February Fill-dyke*, has appeared to scathing reviews, the very dejected Saturday realizes he quite possibly is in need of a new career.

Luckily, he's offered the job of running a newly refurbished

pub called the Downy Pelican, soon to become known as Poet's
Pub by its guests. Though it's far from the civilized world of
London, the pub (think small hotel) caters to wealthy visitors,
especially Americans.

In addition to Saturday, "mine host," the delectably quirky
characters who people the novel include a learned professor
("who was famous in academic circles for his vigorous championship of the eighteenth century") and his attractively intelligent daughter; a dubious but ravishing chambermaid named
Nelly Bly, who just might be a Russian spy; Quentin, Saturday's best friend and a novelist by trade, who assures Saturday
that one can "always find human nature near to the surface in
a pub, however expensive, and human nature is coarse enough
for the most modern novelist"; an American entrepreneur,
whose solemn face "looked a badly carved oak"; a suspiciously
nonbookish book collector; a family of professional travelers,
recently returned from Turkestan; a portrait painter named
Angela Scrabster; a literary critic who despises Saturday's
poems; the critic's wife; a long-distance sailor; a race-car adventurer; a mother/daughter theater-producing team; and Lady
Porlet, "who had never written anything (for she had rheumatic finger-joints) and never read anything (for she had no
brains) and never been out of England, for she had no interest
in foreign parts." Throw into this brew as well Holly, the pub's
bartender, whose greatest accomplishment is that he's created
a blue cocktail. (For eager imbibers there's also a description
of a little-known—but real—drink known as "lamb's wool," a
favorite of Saturday's.)

The destinies of all these characters intertwine over the course
of the novel and culminate in one of the funniest car chases
ever to be found in the pages of a novel. I will tell you only that
it involves a charabanc, a buslike vehicle that one doesn't usually associate with chases over hill and dale. (Coincidentally to
the reissuing of *Poet's Pub*, Britain's *Guardian* newspaper reported that the lexicographers at Collins—publishers of a well-
regarded dictionary—had declared that the word "charabanc"
was in imminent danger of extinction: nobody was using it

anymore. If this sad fact is not a call to read *Poet's Pub*, and a not-so-subtle entreaty to make "charabanc" part of your everyday vocabulary, I don't know what is.)

Eric Linklater was quite a prolific writer. Over his lifetime (1899–1974) he published almost two dozen works of fiction, including two books for children, as well as biographies and memoirs. These days his best-known work is probably not *Poet's Pub*, which was his second novel, but rather his third, *Juan in America*, published in 1931, two years after *Poet's Pub*. Reviewing this lively tale of the last years of Prohibition as seen through the eyes of a British traveler, *Time* magazine's critic decreed that it provided "many an authentic bellylaugh."

I suspect that the pleasure you'll take from reading *Poet's Pub* will not—quite honestly—involve belly laughs. This isn't a slap-your-knee-and-chortle-loudly sort of book. If I'm not mistaken, however, you'll find yourself chuckling sotto voce at least once or twice on each page. The joy in reading *Poet's Pub* derives from Linklater's ability to find humor in the quirks and foibles of human nature, as well as to write excruciatingly bad poetry on behalf of his main character.

I've now read *Poet's Pub* four times between 1985 and 2011 and enjoyed it immensely each time. I hope you do, too.

NANCY PEARL

FOOL: If a man's brains were in's heels,
    were't not in danger of kibes?
LEAR: Ay, boy.

Poet's Pub

CHAPTER I

The storm gathered and its thunder broke the fantastic idyll. The female centaur, ink-stained, with blown grey hair and the end of a cigarette in her mouth, faded like a Cheshire cat. The hunted poet Hylas stood up, weak as water because of the rape he had eluded, and vanished before his knees could knock again. The thunder became nearer, clearer, and increasingly wooden in tone. A square of daylight opened into the forest and made everything evident—the end of the bed, blue and grey jugs on the washstand, a crumpled coat, red toes that stood up from beneath the ruffled nether hem of a sheet.

Saturday Keith was awake.

"All right," he shouted, and there was no more knocking.

"It's eight o'clock," said a female voice.

Not that it was a woman who wrote it, thought Keith. Women never write in the *Literary Supplement;* or at any rate no oftener than they preach from other pulpits. But I've never dreamt of anything so like a critic as that she-centaur. The engulfing female. The shy poet lost in a marsh of explanation. Centaur, censor, ride a cock-horse to Banbury Cross. And I'm damned if "The Blue Scarf" is like the Boat Race.

He reached for his glasses and the crumpled copy of *The Times Literary Supplement* which lay on the floor at his bedside. He had reached Betterton the night before after walking thirty-two miles—which made a hundred and eight in four days—and found, with some trivial mail, three reviews of *February Fill-dyke.* Two of them were like the reviews of his first poems. The third was worse. He read it again.

"No serious poet can to-day afford to work without a theory." (It sounds like an advertisement, he thought. Equip your library with our special rot-and-blot-proof theories. Warmly recommended by the leading poets. Easy payments arranged. You can earn while you learn.) "It is no longer enough to sing, no longer permissible to soar with beautiful and ineffectual wings into a luminous void. The poet must state, and what he states must be selected, significant and individual. It must have visible roots in actuality and growth in personal experience. Mr. Keith, indeed, realizes this—or appears to realize it—in such poems as 'The Blue Scarf,' where his long service with the Oxford University Boat Club finds an echo in lines which apparently reproduce the obedient rhythm of a crew with ears agape for the coach's next remark.

> 'Then through the wood the wind came with a shout,
> And like blue wings her long blue scarf flew out,'

writes Mr. Keith, and we may pardonably think of such a couplet as the response to an injunction to 'Give her ten'—though Mr. Keith exceeds his instructions and gives us twenty."

He threw the paper away, viciously, and got out of bed to retrieve it. Because he had three times stroked a University crew to defeat they would never take him seriously. There had been a cartoon in the *Daily Day* the morning after his last race, in which three British heavyweight boxers, all well known for their habit of being knocked down, were shown writing him a congratulatory letter; dictating a message of sympathy from a prone position; telephoning, prostrate, an invitation to meet them. A photograph of him that made his face longer than it was, saddened beyond nature by horn-rimmed spectacles, had appeared in every illustrated paper beside the smiling, dentifrice-advertisement, curly-haired picture of the victorious Cambridge stroke. And now the critics were determined to perpetuate the memory of his Blue—the darkest Blue in history—in facetious comments on his poetry.

He looked at the review again. They had given him two-thirds of a column, which was generous, and the reviewer had praised a lyric beginning

> "My love is young and very fair,
> The sunlight will not leave her hair,
> And in her lightly-laughing eyes
> I see my own twin destinies."—

which was illogical for a man who deprecated unaugmented singing. But his last remark hurt. He quoted a few lines:

> "The earth was white and windless in the morning
> Like Leda with her plumage spread for Jove,
> And in the evening Jove went down the sky
> In sunset gold to Danae,"

and added, "Mr. Keith is, as he always was, indomitable. But here he is bucketing badly and a long way from Mortlake—or Parnassus."

It was for this that he had thrown up his job with Butterworth, Lackaday and Company, the Shippers, Brokers, Exporters, East India Merchants and God knew what. Butterworth and Lackaday collected Old Blues as other people collect Old Masters, and used them for their own ends. Saturday Keith had never been able to discover the precise nature of those ends—for he lacked the commercial instinct—and his two years in the City had seemed like two years among white mice in a revolving cage. He knew that Butterworth and Lackaday made money for themselves and some for their shareholders, and he realised that their business spread over all the lines of communication of Britain's commercial empire. He was willing to admit that their work was valuable to many different kinds of people. But he could not understand why they wanted Old Blues in their office, and he could not find an individual purpose in his own work there. It bored him and puzzled him. And when *February Fill-dyke* appeared he grew momentarily elated, for his publishers had done their work well, and told young Stephen Lackaday (who was hard and ageless and not really young) that he was leaving the firm.

"Why?" asked Lackaday.

"I don't quite know," said Keith, meaning that he didn't quite know how to explain his reasons to such a successful man as Stephen Lackaday.

"You're making a mistake. A man with a good athletic record, any man with a Rowing Blue, can do well in this house if he cares to pull his weight."

"Damn my Rowing Blue," said Keith. "I'm sorry. But I've made up my mind. Good-bye, Mr. Lackaday."

"Good-bye," said Stephen Lackaday.

Keith had then taken a train from Paddington to a station with a green-painted wooden fence and "Welcome" done in white letters on the opposite embankment. There he bought a toothbrush, wrote to his rooms asking that his letters should be forwarded to "The Feathers" at Betterton, and walked cheerfully towards three trees that stood by themselves on a round green hill. He walked seventeen miles the first day and bought a shirt, a collar, and a pair of socks. The next day he did thirty-four miles and bought another pair of socks; on the third day twenty-five miles and washed his original shirt (which he carried economically in his pocket); and on the fourth day thirty-two miles, arriving at "The Feathers" as the new moon disappeared behind it. He ate cold beef and five tomatoes, drank two bottles of beer, read his three reviews, a letter from his mother, and a telegram saying "Meet you at Betterton Friday—Quentin Cotton"; and went to bed with blistered feet and a dismal apprehension that he was a fool to write in private what men could rail at in public.

His feet were still sore. Each little toe, flattened between shoe and neighbour toe, was puffy with a half-broken blister. He sat up and rubbed them softly. He was wearing the shirt he had bought at the end of the first day, a vulgar thing with broad purple stripes. There was a picture of "The Retreat from Moscow" on one wall, and "The Broken Square"—mop-headed Sudanese hurling themselves at heroic bayonets—decorated another. Through the window he saw a red and white cow and the corner of a haystack. Were these significant? he thought. Here, perhaps, if he could express it with personal emotion, was a microcosm that reflected the macrocosm; individual, raw poetry of the twentieth century; with his ego as the nucleus here was the necessary yolk of experience. Could he state it, arhythmically, tonelessly, flatly but significantly, so that it would be recognized as poetry? He thought not, and lay down again, pulling the sheet to his chin.

He was awakened for the second time by louder knocking.

"All right," he said.

The door opened and a man who looked curiously like Sir Peter Lely's portrait of Wycherley came in—Wycherley without his curls, Wycherley dressed in a smooth-fitting, powder-grey suit, powder-grey shirt, collar, and tie, that is.

"Hullo, Quentin," said Keith, "you're early."

"You lazy dog," said Quentin, and sat down on the bed.

Quentin Cotton was the son of Sewald Cotton of Cotton's Beer, and Lady Mercy Cotton, the second daughter of the late Marquis of Bealne. Cotton's Beer, when old Sewald married, had slaked the thirst of a county and two modest market towns. But Lady Mercy had changed that. Now it was poured, in a glittering amber stream, from gigantic bottle to gigantic glass high over Piccadilly at night. "Is Ninepence Dear for *Cotton's* Beer?" said the white-and-amber sky-sign. And promptly another glass was poured, golden-full and silver-topped with electric foam. Now Cotton's Beer was drunk in every county in England, in mining villages and seaside towns and industrial capitals, in Birmingham and Rhyl and Tunbridge Wells and Newcastle and Stoke-on-Trent and above all in London, the heart of the Empire. Now it was exported—with chemical preservatives, though these were not advertised—to India and Kenya and Malay and other places as thirsty. It was advertised on hoardings, in the air, in penny papers and Sunday papers, and always in *Punch*. It was securely established as Britain's Best Beer; or at any rate as One of Britain's Best Beers. And all this was due to Lady Mercy whose aristocratic blood was inspired with an almost divine energy. Old Sewald Cotton was a quiet man, content to live on two or three thousand a year, happy enough to be known with respect in two small towns and their not-important neighbourhood. But the business mind and the aptitude for commerce which have become so pronounced a feature of England's peerage found their sturdiest, loftiest-reaching flower in Lady Mercy, and Lady Mercy, marrying Sewald Cotton because she liked him, gave Cotton's Beer a place beside the nation's daily bread.

Quentin Cotton's first novel, *A Nettle Against May*, was to some extent re-action against this activity, though he and his mother remained very good friends.

"You lazy dog," he repeated, and straightened the crumpled pages of *The Times Literary Supplement.*

"They've picked out the worst lines in the book to write about," said Keith.

"They always do. A reviewer must amuse his public, and good poetry's dull stuff. I like the bit about bucketing."

"Damn you," said Keith, and got up.

He was tall and broad, six feet and thirteen stones, and his purple-striped shirt came down no farther than was strictly necessary.

"I'm going to look for a bath."

"You can't go out like that."

"I'm not as naked as I feel in *The Times*," he answered and shut the door behind him.

"And no more naked than your Highland ancestors when they walked abroad," said Quentin agreeably.

Saturday Keith's family history was, in some of its aspects, almost common knowledge. Gossip-writers of two generations had been fond of it and historians had mentioned its remoter stages with respect. His father, Sir Colin Keith, had been famous for four things. As a young man he had insulted, amusingly and dramatically, an Austrian archduke. As a grown man he had drunk his two bottles a day when all Scotland was becoming sober and serious. As the father of seven sons he had insisted on the youngest being christened Saturday. And at the age of sixty-one he had taken a battalion of the Royal Scots to France and been killed, beside one of his sons, at the second battle of Ypres.

The archduke had been insulted, because Sir Colin found him, a guest of the family, trying—and very nearly succeeding, for an archduke is, or was, an archduke—to seduce one of Sir Colin's sisters. Hapsburg *savoir-faire* saved the immediate situation and later Hapsburg magnificence suggested that Sir Colin's anger might be appeased by the gift of two polo ponies. The ponies were sent with an admirably worded expression of the archduke's gratitude for such charming hospitality.

Sir Colin shot them, quite humanely, and ordered the carcases to be sent back. As the archduke had by that time returned to Vienna the ponies had a long way to go, and their conveyance excited wide-spread interest. The story of their killing and the reason for it got about, at first discreetly, afterwards amplified and penetrating to more vulgar ears, and nearly caused a diplomatic incident.

The birth of a seventh son is a notable event in any family, and it was more notable in Sir Colin's because Colin, the eldest, had been born on a Sunday, Ranald on a Monday, Iain on a Tuesday, Patrick on a Wednesday, Malcolm on a Thursday, and Alasdair on a Friday. When Lady Keith became pregnant for the seventh time Sir Colin's excitement grew with every month.

"He'll be born on a Saturday," he said, "and that will make a good deed for every day in the week. I've worked harder than God, for He rested on the seventh. If the boy's dropped on a Saturday I'll call him Saturday, By God I will!"

His agitation became pitiable when Lady Keith's pains set in on a Friday afternoon, and it was said that he stood outside her door and called to her, once or twice, "Hold him, my love, hold him! There's an hour to go yet. Be brave, my dear, this is the last one, I swear."

It was ten minutes past twelve when the boy was born, a strong baby with black hair on his head, and Sir Colin had a dozen of the oldest Château Margaux brought up. He christened the child, still wet from the bath, sprinkling his forehead with claret and solemnly saying, "In the names of your mother and myself and God the Father I call you Saturday Keith." Another glass he gave to his wife, and to the remainder he and the doctor, as soon as the latter had finished his work, sat down in the library. They finished the dozen by breakfast-time and went out, Sir Colin with a gun, for it was September, and the doctor with his stethoscope ready for the next patient.

When War broke out Sir Colin bullied and cajoled, intrigued and read his drill-books, shouted here and flattered, there, until he was given command of a Kitchener battalion of his old regiment. He drank a last bottle, toasting the king, his wife, and the prospect of wilder fighting than the world had known for a long time, and sent the remainder of his cellar to a newly-opened War hospital in Edinburgh. He and three of his sons were killed, one on land, one in the air, and the second eldest at Jutland. Colin, except for a leg that he left on the Somme, became Sir Colin and sat at home contentedly enough. Malcolm and Alasdair were farming in East Africa. Saturday, too young for the war, impractical and a natural athlete though hampered by astigmatism, went to Oxford.

He had inherited his gift, or fancy, for poetry-writing from his mother who, poor woman, had occupied the inactive months of her repeated pregnancies with composing verses, some of which were published in gift books for her friends. When Saturday was a little boy she became more active, and walked over high hills with field glasses through which she observed, carefully and cleverly, the habits of nesting birds and migrating birds and birds that were comparatively idle.

"I have always been so fond of them," she said. "But I could never reach them. I so rarely had the time or the figure for much walking."

She began to contribute articles to the *Scottish Field* and other periodicals interested in wild, though not human, life, and her pen found a strength that it had not known in verse. Her occupation with nature, which is intentionally beautiful and deliberately cruel, had protected her a little against the shock of losing her husband and three sons. Or perhaps she had taken her sorrow to the hills where no one could see it. She appeared to be happy.

Saturday re-entered the bedroom with a towel round his middle instead of the purple-striped shirt.

"I'm useless as a shipper, exporter or broker," he said, "and not much good as a poet. What shall I do?"

"Have a drink," Quentin suggested.

"I can't make a profession of that."

"Why not? You boast about your palate. You can tell the difference between a tenpenny Médoc and a Lafite. Be a wine-shipper."

"I haven't a ship."

"Then keep a pub."

"I would, if I had one."

"Keep my mother's newest one. She's just bought 'The Pelican' in Downish. It's going to be the most expensive pub in Britain. Come in as her manager."

"Do you think she would like me to?"

"I'm sure she would. She wants someone like you. She has romantic ideas, though she's business-like, and the idea of a poet permanently in her pub would delight her. And you're a Blue as well—"

"Does she collect them too? Butterworth and Lackaday did."

"But mother's discriminating. She refuses to hear of lacrosse, for instance. Now be serious. This is the seventh old inn she's bought, and the best. It's going to be the best pub in the world. England's glory, an echo of coaching days, tantara, tantara, mine host in a red waistcoat—you're getting fat enough for a red waistcoat—and thirteen private suites for rich Americans."

"I know the recipe for lamb's wool. They'd like that."

"You're the man my mother is looking for. Have you heard about 'The Pelican'?"

Quentin, irresistibly captured by any idea that came to him swiftly and spontaneously, was enthusiastic over his maturing suggestion.

Saturday shook his head.

"It's four hundred years old with a bear-pit and a central courtyard where strolling players used to act. They call it 'The Downy Pelican' now, but that isn't its original name. It started as 'The Tabard.' Then the three dullest poets of the seventeenth century happened to live in Downish—Fabian Metcalf, Philip Goode, and Martin Stout—and they drank in 'The Tabard' and recited their ridiculous mock-metaphysical verses to each other and to the landlord, who had literary aspirations. He thought well of them, for they spent their money there and they wrote verses of a kind which he couldn't, though he wanted to, and in their honour he re-christened his inn 'The Downish Helicon,' which so far as I know was his one literary excursion. But Philip Goode died, and Martin Stout and Metcalf and the landlord died, and no one remembered them, and the inn sign grew battered, and the villagers thought nothing of so strange a name and could never learn to pronounce it. So when the eighteenth century was nearly finished a new landlord had the sign repainted and lettered with what he took to be its proper name, 'The Downy Pelican.' And that's what it is called to-day."

Keith had heard something of Lady Mercy's inns, as every newspaper reader had. "The Prince in the Sun" at Bromley, "The George" at Molton, and three or four others had become famous again since she bought them, tactfully re-conditioned them (preserving what was good and building new bathrooms) and re-created their reputation for serving honest English food—which meant Scotch beef and French sauces—and honest English drink—which meant Cotton's Strong Ale, Cotton's March Beer, and Cotton's noble Audit Ale. She put wine in the cellar—wine bought from dispersed and nobler cellars—and a discreet American Bar in the buttery of such inns as had a buttery, so that in three or four years what had been a hobby, an amusing pendant to the brewery, became a highly profitable concern and Lady Mercy was elected a Vice-President of the Hotel-keepers' Association.

Keith walked about the room absent-mindedly dressing himself. The idea attracted him. He was interested in food. Its names were to him like the names of far countries to passionate travellers, and minestrone, macédoine, caviare, bortsch, sucking-pig, celery and goulasch sounded in his ears as sonorously as Chimborazo and Cotopaxi. He had thought, more than once, of writing a Gargantuan epic of food, of inventing a young Gargantua who should eat his way through France and Eastern Europe to Russia, and thence to enormous feasting in Central Asia where whole sheep were stewed in a massive pot, scenting the mountain winds with unimagined sweetness and savoury strength. . . . A gastronomic Tamburlaine, flinging bawdy wisdom about him as he tossed aside the bones, cracking jests as loudly as marrow-bones, catching at Truth and floating dumplings with greasy fingers. And regretfully he had put the thought away, feeling incompetent to undertake so huge a task without a Marlowe's vigour; feeling, too, a little ashamed of even vicarious greed. He had so often been hungry—for training diet is Spartan-simple though sufficient in calories and such—that his dreams turned naturally to exotic and mountainous meals.

Though Gargantua-Tamburlaine were too great a figure to draw he might cut a fair enough landlord, he thought. He might even be a good landlord, and a good landlord is a good citizen of any state except the forty-eight west of the Atlantic.

> "'For malt does more than Milton can
> To justify God's ways to man,'"

he said aloud. "I'll do it, Quentin, if your mother will take a risk. But I know nothing about the business side of it."

"That doesn't matter. We'll have a chartered accountant or somebody like that to arrange the profit and loss. You're the landlord, and all you have to do is to look hearty and remember the recipe for lamb's wool. I shall probably live with you for a time. I came down here, as a matter of fact, to propose a holiday together. I want a more vulgar environment for my next novel. They tell me that *A Nettle Against May* is a little precious. I may find a coarse enough note at 'The Pelican.'"

"When it's going to be the most expensive pub in England?"

"You always find human nature near to the surface in a pub, however expensive, and human nature is coarse enough for the most modern novelist."

A feeling of unreality took possession of Keith. A hundred and eight miles in four days had tired him; he had been bitterly disillusioned by *The Times* review, for he had hoped foolishly, building great castles of optimistic stone and beams of spacious imagining—so well had his publishers done their work; and now the whimsical proposal to manage a pub for Lady Mercy Cotton elated him the more because of the weariness and smarting disgust which it had banished. He sat down and laughed tremendously, so that the bed creaked beneath him and the red and white cow under his window looked up and said "Mooooo," in a voice that was mildly interrogative.

"Come and have breakfast," said Quentin.

CHAPTER II

"The Downy Pelican" stood in the main thoroughfare of
Downish, a little past the square. What it showed to the street
was small in comparison with that which lay behind. Two steep
roofs, one a yellowish grey and the other a yellowish red; in a
pointed stone doorway an oak door grimly embossed with
ninety-six large iron nails and two iron hinges designed to represent *fleurs-de-lys;* a row of diamond-paned windows; the
enormous sign, white and green with antique lettering in gold,
that slowly creaked below a ponderous iron bracket; and at one
end—unobtrusive but sufficient, for common folk have a keener
nose than their betters—a little sign that said "Bar." Most important of all was the spacious archway that led into the courtyard, for "The Pelican" like a true philosopher looked inward
rather than outward, and its courtyard was cool and comforting, with shadows broken prettily by pink roses, with an oak
gallery running round it so that guests could look across at
other guests, or downwards to see the Boots chatting pleasantly with a maid, and reflect that here even the servants had
leisure to live as human beings should be allowed to live.

Comfort and dignity—strange bedfellows—slept together
as if in the Great Bed of Ware, and thought drowsily of ancient
history. Once there had been a monastery here. Henry VI, a
wretched fugitive from someone or other, had found refuge in
it and repaid the hospitality of the monks by taking a mad fit
and babbling of hell, the English constitution, and the marrow-
bone pie which he had had for his supper. An alchemist in
Henry VIII's time, after the monks had been disestablished,
hanged himself here and left a paper saying that he had hidden
the recipe for the philosopher's stone in the cellar; which, although it was manifestly improbable, had resulted in half the
building being pulled down and three townsfolk killed by a
falling beam before it was decided that the alchemist had been
joking; though indeed they did discover directions for "appar-
elling Malmsey" beginning, "If you have a good But of Malmsey and a But or two of Sacke that will not be drunke," to
which the whimsical scholar may have referred.

There was an excellent scandal about Queen Elizabeth and the Earl of Leicester, who had been indiscreet enough to stay a night here; the same night, though, it was protested, on opposite sides of the courtyard. Later, much later, Sheridan got notably drunk here after having left London to recuperate from a drinking bout. A highwayman or two had business with the place, but the Vicar of St. Saviour's in his history of Downish, is unimpressed by this connexion. And Mr. Gladstone after speaking in Downish gave a signed photograph of himself to the landlord, which the landlord, after Mr. Gladstone had gone, very spiritedly burnt in the middle of the courtyard.

As to the appointments of the inn, they were in keeping with its history; mixed but interesting. There was an oak room with a Gothic timbered roof and hammer beams; and there were delightful but unobtrusive plumbing arrangements which Lady Mercy had caused to be installed. Sanitation had modestly compromised with the splendid past and "The Downy Pelican" was a bird to be proud of.

It was six months since Saturday Keith had been summoned to interview Lady Mercy Cotton; six months since she had said to him, without preamble: "So you're going to manage my new pub for me Mr. Keith? That's delightful of you. Mr. Owens— Grieve Owens, you know—asked me for it, but he's only a Soccer Blue and I was very doubtful about giving it to him. I have one other Rowing Blue, a Rugger International, two Hockey Blues, and an exceedingly good Hurdler at the 'Prince in the Sun.' They're all doing ever so much better than 'The George' which is managed by Mr. Salmson. He was President of the Union, wasn't he, Quentin? I thought so. People don't take to him as they do to a man with a public record. But sit down, Mr. Keith, and we'll talk it over."

Lady Mercy was a tall, very charming, slightly untidy woman with a greyish, horsey face. One eyebrow rose higher than the other and her lips moved in such a way that it was difficult to tell whether she was laughing at herself, at the world in general, or being entirely serious and sensitive to the exact meaning of her words. Her hair, a streaky black and white, was artistically cut, and an episcopal-looking ring ornamented her right forefinger.

"I know your poems, of course," she went on. "There are two in *February Fill-dyke* which delighted me. So many people look in ponds nowadays and write graceful biological verses about small things in them that one is a little tired of aquarium poetry. But your water glittered and your weeds honestly grew. I think you are a poet, Mr. Keith. Your mother writes too, doesn't she? And your father had one of the only five palates in Scotland. I bought the remainder of his cellar after the war. Yes, I know he gave it to a hospital, but the Superintendent told me that he simply hadn't the heart to use it. So very Scotch, I thought. And of course the soldiers did like beer better than Clos Vougeot. So there it was on his hands, practically intact, and I bought it quite cheaply. I'm glad that I didn't pay much for it, because the money went into a most tasteless War Memorial. A drinking fountain, Mr. Keith. Rather insignificant, don't you think?"

Lady Mercy's right eyebrow rose to a dizzy height and her mouth set forbiddingly.

Keith laughed and said, "I'm glad that you think I can be trusted to look after 'The Pelican.' I have a lot of ideas about food and several about drink—"

"I knew you would. Poets are really the most practical people on earth so long as they are allowed to do what they like. It's only when they're driven along uncongenial paths that they become woolly and distrait. I wish Quentin could write verse, but he persists in experimenting with the most shapeless kind of novel."

"My dear mother," Quentin protested, "my novel was at least different from every other modern novel. They assume that all the world is hard and put their heroes in the middle like a soft core in a green apple. My hero was hard, and his trouble was that the world about him was soft. I had nothing about timid virginity, the trials of adolescence, or the rupture of innocence in the whole ninety thousand words."

"But you didn't know what to do with your hero at the end, did you?"

"I left him with dignity."

"In an impossible situation, Quentin. Now let me talk business to Mr. Keith."

Gradually, in the following months, Keith became aware of Lady Mercy's ability. He and "The Pelican" were advertised together, tactfully, pleasantly, in social paragraphs and semi-literary journals. His Blue was remembered without the circumstances attending it and he grew to understand its commercial value. His poems were frequently mentioned and often his publishers reported that another copy of *February Filldyke* had been bought. Even his first volume, the pretentiously named *Micomicon*, reappeared and sold a dozen or two. People agreed that he was a poet, though they did not know his poetry. And one day a journalist who had dined—or said he had dined—with Lady Mercy, wrote charmingly of her poet and her "Pelican" and called it, laughingly, "Poet's Pub"; scarcely realizing as he did so the adhesive quality of happy alliteration. For the new name began to dispossess that on the swinging white and green sign, and passing motorists would say to the wives, "'Poet's Pub,' my dear," when they saw "The Pelican" on the board; and charabanc parties on their way to the Roman baths at the north end of Downish would stand up in their chariot and peer curiously at the inn ruled by one who wrote verses. "Poet's Pub" grew famous and its thirteen suites were full; or about to be full.

Saturday, sitting in his office, read the list of his guests. Mrs., Miss Diana and Colonel Waterhouse, whose exciting travel story, *A Hunter in Turkestan*, had been so well received—an autographed copy lay on Saturday's desk; Angela Scrabster, who had been in China painting the portraits of Chiang-Kai-shek and Feng Yu-hsiang; Sigismund Telfer, who wrote *Polyphobion*, which was called the "New Poets' Bible"; his wife Jacquetta, who had sailed a fourteen-foot boat single-handed round the Baltic; Sir Philip Betts, the racing motorist who had been forced to go to the Iraq desert to find a level stretch long enough to let his car have its head; Jean Forbes and her mother Tommy Mandeville, whose joint revue, *Peace in Our Time*, was in its sixth month; Lady Porlet, who had never written anything (for she had rheumatic finger-joints) and never read anything (for she had no brains) and never been out of England, for she had no interest in foreign parts.

Thank God for Lady Porlet, thought Saturday. Does all the

world write—except Lady Porlet? Does everyone go to Central
Asia or Pekin? Old Waterhouse's book is the twenty-fourth
autographed copy I've been given in six months. You read mine
and I'll read yours. They might at least cut their pages first.
And listening to them is like a geography lesson. I believe I
have the only sensible job in the country, for I stay where I'm
wanted and I haven't written a word for a week.

He pulled out a drawer and lifted from it a pile of untidy
manuscript, reading a line or two here and there.

"It's damned good. I swear it is," he said aloud. "I'll start
typing it to-morrow."

He went back to the visitors' list. The last comers were Mr.
Aesop R. Wesson and Mr. Theodore van Buren, both Americans. Professor William Benbow and his daughter would arrive that afternoon.

Mr. van Buren was a man in the middle sixties, a man with
a battered-looking face, heavy and humorous and deeply lined.
From the inner ends of his eyebrows creases ran diagonally
upwards and outwards on his forehead, so that he seemed to
have two pairs of eyebrows. A gash like a sword-cut—but it
was wry laughter that had made it—seamed his cheek. He had
a pendulous lower lip and he wore a bowler hat a little too
small for his head. He was a bulky man and his overcoat hung
shapelessly from his shoulders as he walked.

His compatriot, Mr. Wesson, was a mild gentleman with
curious eye-glasses and a placid white face. He looked like a
professor, but he had told Saturday that he was a book-
collector, which few professors can afford to be.

Professor Benbow, on the other hand, looked—as Saturday
knew, for he had heard him lecture on Hakluyt—more like an
admiral than a professor. A kind of eponymous admiral, perhaps, for his name had probably moulded his character, his
character dictated his habits, and his habits exerted their influence on his appearance. He was famous in academic circles for
his vigorous championship of the eighteenth century—"a gentleman's century," he declared—and he had been offered a
knighthood for his official War History of the submarines, of-
fending a few by his refusal of it and insulting most of his Uni-

versity friends by his dedication, which read: "To the officers and men of the British Navy who served us in the depths of the sea. I like them better than dons."

A maid tapped at the door, opened it, and announced "Professor Benbow, sir."

Keith went down to meet him.

"So you're Mr. Keith, are you? Let me congratulate you."

"Why?" asked Keith.

Professor Benbow's voice rose from a rumbling bass to a tone of stentorian clarity.

"Because you have found a useful job. If every pub in England were run by a man of character and education, this would be a country to be proud of—prouder, I mean. Joan, my dear, this is Mr. Keith."

Joan Benbow said, "I've seen you before, of course."

To a casual glance she was one of those attractive young women who are so common in Great Britain; moderately athletic, with excellent complexion, the appearance of perfect health, good legs, and features just sufficiently different from type to give a semblance of individuality. The more curious eye found other things of interest in her. Her features were better than a passing glance suggested—delicately better, not obtrusively excellent—and her temper was an alternation of shyness and scepticism, momentarily composed, perhaps more often ingenuous. She looked slimmer than she actually was, standing in front of the enormous bowed shoulders of her father.

Saturday Keith had been unable to acquire, in six months, a proper manner of professional reception.

He said, "I'm glad you've come. I always wanted to meet you," and looked with some embarrassment from one to the other.

"Don't ask me about your poetry," said the professor. "No good ever came of discussing poetry."

Joan, on the verge of a remark, thought better of it and kept silent.

"Come and talk to us after dinner if you have time," suggested the professor.

The three hours till dinner-time seemed curiously long to

Saturday, and it occurred to him that he had told, unintention-
ally and without even noticing it at the time, a mild untruth
when he stated that he had always wanted to meet Benbow.
He had never felt such a wish, he decided, and certainly he
had not entertained it as a permanency. Nor had he lately pretended to it out of wanton politeness. He sighed, for he was
intelligent and the obvious reason presented itself. And he admitted that Joan Benbow was not commonly but uncommonly
attractive.

There was the wife of the man who was exploring in Brazil,
and the daughter of the man who wrote about Jeremy Bentham, he thought. Each of them put me off my work for a week.
But I wrote a good sonnet about one, and I could have written
a better about the other if it hadn't seemed so cold-blooded.
Therefore I'm a bad publican and a bad poet too, for a good
publican ought to be a little above life, a little bit enthroned,
and a good poet ought, I think, to be just a step or two below
life; polite life, I mean. . . . It's a quarter to nine.

The Elizabethan hall was full of his guests, and though no
one sat on the oak settee the logs crackled most successfully in
the huge hearth and two of the pictures looked remarkably
like Holbeins. Talk, distributed over two or three little groups,
made a soft conversational symphony in which it was possible to make out occasionally the individual themes. Now and
again there was a little too much brass when Jean Forbes's voice
became animated, and once or twice Sigismund Telfer beat
loudly on the drum of his criticism.

Mr. van Buren, it seemed, had met Professor Benbow in America during the war, when the former was inventing new engines
of destruction for Allied use and the latter was lecturing on the
righteousness of the Allied cause. They were now renewing these
bonds of sympathy.

"Come and sit down, Mr. Keith," said van Buren. "The professor and I are old friends. We met in the Yale Club in New
York just after he had made the best speech I have ever heard."

"And possibly the most untruthful. The war was a blessed
time for us older men in that we could tell more lies with more
assurance of telling the truth than at any other period since—"

"Since the war before the last," suggested Keith.

"I suppose so. It's only in years of national peril that we're able to feel really confident."

"Peace is too exciting to be sure about anything," said Joan.

"You've said it, Miss Benbow. Peace *is* exciting, because when the country's at peace its citizens can think for themselves, think selfishly, and have adventures of their own. When there's a war no one has time for anything but the national adventure."

Mr. van Buren looked solemn, and when solemnity settled on his face it looked like badly carved oak. In the lull that followed his sententiousness they heard occasional phrases and motifs from other parts of the room.

"Feng was the most fascinating person I've ever painted," Miss Scrabster was remarking. "He made improper proposals to me through an interpreter. They call him the Christian general. . . ."

"There was a Chinese governor in Kashgar"—this was Colonel Waterhouse—"who lived in mediæval state and had executions every morning. I saw the heads. . . ."

"She's a good actress of course, but she sleeps with her understudy. I'm not old-fashioned but I do believe in being natural. . . ."

"Mrs. Mandeville—forgive me interrupting you again—but did you say this was Wednesday or Thursday?" Lady Porlet had been expecting a letter all day and was a little restless.

"He was a picturesque old ruffian with a bodyguard dressed in rags, mounted on scrubby ponies. . . ."

"No, I didn't have much rest. Nasty, steep little waves you get in the Baltic. . . ."

"We ought to learn from the pointillistes. Put, your colour on pure, in spots, and you get a luminous spectrum in verse as well as in painting. . . ."

"I was going to do Chang Tso-lin as well, only of course he got murdered. . . ."

"Perhaps Chang would have seduced her without an interpreter," said the professor thoughtfully, and Mr. van Buren laughed heavily and wheezily. Then he said, "I beg your pardon, Miss Benbow."

"Why?"

"Well, I suppose we were being coarse for a moment."

"Father has taught me to think of coarseness as a character-istic of good writing."

"I've taught you to recognize mealy-mouthing as one of the signs of bad writing, you ungrateful rig. I've taught you to be suspicious of girls' school enthusiasm for pure-minded, thin-lipped, lady-like editions of the great authors. I've taught you—no, I'm on holiday and I refuse to think of literature as a task. It ought to be an adventure. Either the adventure of sailing your own ship or the adventure of exploring the islands that greater minds have discovered for us."

"But no-one would remember poor dead authors if people like you weren't paid to talk about them."

"She's calling you a vocal gravestone, professor."

"A perpetual injunction to 'Absent thee from felicity awhile,'" said Keith.

The professor's bushy eyebrows leapt up like white flaps. "You're in the majority," he said, "till I'm dead too. What have *you* been writing?"

"Satire," said Keith.

"Satire in a pub? Merciful God!"

"Have you ever drunk lamb's wool?"

"Can you make it?"

"Yes. I owe you an apology. Come and share a bowl of lamb's wool instead."

They went, all four of them, to the American Bar which was in the buttery. It was deserted except for a white-faced, white-coated little man who stood behind the gleaming counter, with eyes that shone more brightly than silver or polished mahog-any or crystal beakers, and stared with a wild surmise at two glasses on the board. One shone with a liquid palely blue as April skies, the other more nobly glowed with a darker hue, the colour of darkest blue-bells in a wood.

"I've done it, sir," said the little man in a hoarse, self-wondering voice. "Oh, Mr. Keith, I've done it. I've done it twice, both of them different."

"Done what?" asked Keith.

"Blue cocktails," said the little man. "Nobody's ever made

one before, not proper blue, like these. Mr. Keith, I'm an inventor!"

Mr. van Buren solemnly shook hands with him. "I know the feeling," he said, "it's worth living for."

"Congratulations, Holly," said Keith. "I'll raise your salary from to-night."

"Thank you, sir, but it isn't that so much—though I thought you would—it's just the feeling of having done it, if you understand me."

"They're like butterflies," said Joan, holding one up in either hand. "Can I taste them?"

"A cocktail after dinner? Certainly not." Professor Benbow was indignant at the suggestion.

"Please, sir, just this once," pleaded the inventor. "It isn't likely the lady will form a habit, as it were, and this is the only notable thing that's happened to me since I was bayoneted by a Prussian Guard on the 25th of September, 1918, sir. I'd like to celebrate it, if you don't mind."

Joan sipped first one, then the other. "I feel as though I could eat another dinner," she said. "I think you ought to call the light one Heaven."

"I thought of calling them Butterfly and Bluebell," said Holly diffidently, "but perhaps you think that a little bit too sentimental, sir."

"How did you discover the secret?" Saturday asked.

"It was like this, Mr. Keith. All my life I've collected cigarette-pictures, and you'd scarcely believe what I've learnt from them. British Birds, and Birds' Eggs, and Railway Engines, and How to Mend a Burst Pipe, and Aeroplanes, and Regimental Crests, and all kinds of things. Cigarette-pictures have been one of the greatest powers of education that this country's ever known, and when I was in hospital I set to work to cultivate my mind with them, and I've done it, sir. If ever any of you gentlemen want to know anything about the Little Crested Grebe, or the Snow Bunting, or even how to put down linoleum properly, I can tell you. Why, they're just like a University, sir, if you collect them seriously. I've got two sets of every series that's been issued, one pasted into my albums face up—that's with the picture showing—and one with the letter-press, so to speak. I learnt a good lot about printing-terms from them too—"

"But how did you get hold of the idea for these blue cock-tails?"

"It was out of Native Wild Flowers. I don't want it spread abroad, as it were, but I can trust you gentlemen and you too, miss, can't I? Well, there's a flower called the Blue Gentian, and the information on the back of the, picture of it—like a little essay, you know, sir—said that a harmless vegetable dye could be made out of it. So I went to a chemist and he had it right there on his shelf. I bought a bottle—it only cost eighteenpence—and then I set to work. Some kinds of gin took the colour right out of it, but I wasn't going to be beat, so I experimented, and ex-perimented—I got more help from a series that told all about the solar spectrum—and at last I got it, sir. And now won't you gentlemen try one?"

"I certainly will," said van Buren. "I've just finished work on a formula for synthetic fuel myself—automobile fuel, not man fuel—and I can share your feeling."

"And I've just finished a new book of verse," said Saturday.

"What the devil's that?" asked the professor. "No, not verse. I know what it is, worse luck. That slithering and rub-bing at the door."

Keith opened it.

A mild, a little startled, ivory-pale face appeared. It had light-coloured eyes vaguely blinking behind silver-rimmed eyeglasses, and beneath it were a tie and collar such as dissent-ing clergymen wear. A tallish stooping figure sidled into the room.

"Why, Wesson," said van Buren, "you've come at the right time."

"I was looking for a . . . I thought of having a drink," said Mr. Wesson gently.

"You're on the point of it. Miss Benbow, Professor Benbow, let me introduce a compatriot of mine to you: Mr. Æsop Wes-son, who collects books."

"I always wondered where they all went to," said the profes-sor gravely.

"Not modern books, professor. Nothing is of much interest to me until it is—oh, quite old. And then almost everything is interesting. Isn't that curious? I bought Hepplewhite's *Cabinet-maker and Upholsterer's Guide* last week for £60, because it was printed in 1789. I don't care much about cabinet-making, of course, though I did some fretwork when I was a boy, but I think old things are interesting. And the Comte de Buffon's *Histoire Naturelle des Oiseaux* a gift copy of the author to Helvetius—I paid £80 for that on the same day."

"Holly, here, gets his information on birds rather more cheaply," murmured Keith.

"Oh, it wasn't for information that I bought it. Indeed, I can't read French. But the date of it is 1770 and it is very rare."

"Mr. Wesson," said the professor firmly, "we have two duties on hand. One is to drink the health of our friend Holly, who has just invented a new kind of cocktail, and the other—against which the former may unhappily militate—is to exercise our judgement on Mr. Keith's brewing of lamb's wool, a respectable drink at one time much in vogue in England."

"Mix enough for half-a-dozen, Holly," Keith directed. "Which shall it be, the light or the dark?"

"The dark," said Joan, "The Oxford blue. We're not going to drink Cambridge in your pub, whatever we do outside."

"And there they are christened for you, Holly. Oxford and Cambridge are good enough names for them, aren't they?"

"Anything that a lady like Miss Benbow suggests is all right, sir," said Holly politely; and deftly poured measures of this and measures of that, crystal clear, faintly yellow and richer orange, a glass delicately poised with the rising meniscus unbroken, a drop, two drops of wormwood, a fluid ounce of sweetness and an ounce of twice-distilled strength . . . gravely, intent on his task as an alchemist seeking the elixir, the aurum potabile, Holly poured his chosen liquors into a long silver shaker, added broken fragments of ice, screwed down the top, and, like a man with the palsy, shook. His hands were clenched on either butt, his muscles were taut, his face set like a mask. And all this time his audience watched him silently as if a conjuror were at work, and where paper flags had gone in the doves of peace might emerge. Then the rapid shaking changed to a long swinging movement like an old-fashioned concertina-player swinging his instrument to spread its melody wider, more powerfully. And at last he was done. He set six glasses on the bar and poured into each a liquid, at first cloudy-blue like the sky at morning, that slowly cleared to a hue ineffable and serene.

"To you, Mr. Holly," said the professor, "I drink, for the only time in my life at such an hour as this—and I shall suffer for it—a cocktail *honoris causa*. Joan, my dear—gentlemen: Mr. Holly, for his contribution to the art of life."

Solemnly they drank and Holly watched. His mouth was a little open, the lips were nervous, he flushed and grew pale again. His eyes were very bright. Joan had an uncomfortable feeling that he was going to cry. He did indeed mutter something that ended in a sniff; he blew his nose with uncommon intentness; and then he remembered the sixth cocktail that stood on the bar, and drinking it off he immediately became calm and assured. "Thank you," he said, and was not without dignity.

"Now it's your turn, Keith," the professor reminded him.

Saturday said, "I shall want assistance. I wonder if you—?"

"Why of course," Joan replied, and went with him.

"Been busy since you landed?" said Mr. van Buren to Mr. Wesson.

"Well . . . yes, in a quiet way I suppose I have. There were the two books I already mentioned to you. And I bought some other things. A note-book of Garrick's with copies of poems and letters in it. And a lot of letters written to him by different people. Doctor Johnson, and . . . oh, contemporaries, you know."

"What letters are those?" asked the professor.

"Personal gossip; letters such as we all write. From Johnson, and Sir Joshua, and . . . but I have scarcely had time to examine them."

"I thought that Johnson's letters were all known."

"These may be unrecorded. But I have hardly looked at them yet." Mr. Wesson laughed, a little throatily, and lit a cigarette. Professor Benbow stared at him in a way that Mr. Wesson found embarrassing. "They are at my bank," he said, and turning to van Buren asked him, smiling: "and how is your work progressing? Yours is real work, unlike my dilettante book-collecting."

"It's done," van Buren said shortly.

"Ah!" said Mr. Wesson.

"One of the few books I have which would be of any interest to you, Mr. Wesson—I can't afford finery," said the professor, "and I don't know that I want to—is a first edition of Donne's Poems. The 1683 edition, you know, with the two original blank leaves. What would you give me for it, supposing I was willing to sell?"

Mr. Wesson coughed. "It's difficult to say, offhand. So much depends on, oh, the condition it's in."

"It's perfect."

"Well. The 16—?"

"The 1683 edition, with the two blank leaves."

"Of course. The two blank leaves. Would you take, say—"

"Would you give me £100 for it?"

Mr. Wesson played with the stem of his glass and stared hard at a globule of blue liquid that still rolled stickily in the bowl. "I should have to think that over," he said at length.

The professor laughed. "Don't worry. It's not a serious offer. I should hardly like to exchange old Donne for a cheque. I'm frightened of what he might say, if I ever meet him across the Styx."

Saturday and Joan returned with a bowl that perfumed the room and made all mouths water with its rich October smell. Lamb's wool is a mixture of hot ale, the pulp of roasted apples, a little sugar, and a little spice. Much depends on the quality of the apples; more on the ale. Saturday had discovered that even the best apples and the oldest ale are improved by an egg or two beaten up in thin cream with enough whisky to counteract the fatness of the cream. His lamb's wool was drunk in silence, the silence of appreciation, the quietness of content. The professor, indeed, smacked his lips and meditatively said "Yes," as if answering at last the doubt which he had harboured. The wonder in van Buren's face changed perceptibly into an expression of perfect happiness. Only Mr. Wesson sipped hurriedly at his glass and seemed troubled by the silence. He misunderstood it and construed it as the consequence of his unwelcome presence.

He was on the point of saying good-night and leaving them when the professor said, "What is it that you have been working on, van Buren—if I may ask? You said something about synthetic fuel."

Mr. van Buren hesitated and covered his hesitation by offering the professor a cigar. Then he said,

"Civilization depends on transportation, as your Mr. Kipling once pointed out. And more than half of our present transportation depends on petroleum, so that if the oil wells went dry, or if they passed into certain hands, many of us would be awkwardly situated. So certain people, from time to time, have tried to find a substitute for petroleum, or to make petroleum themselves without having to tap the earth for it. I have attempted, in my own way to solve that problem."

"And how did you go about it?" asked Mr. Wesson.

"That at present is my own affair," said van Buren gruffly.

Mr. Wesson apologized. "I realize the value of secrecy," he said. "A book collector appreciates the need for discretion as well as anybody. I remember once—"

He described a perilous campaign to secure a copy of Castiglione's *Courtier*, but his story excited little interest, and Mr. Wesson discovered that he was feeling sleepy.

"I don't like him," said Joan when he had gone.

"He's a fool of a book collector," said the professor.

"Is he?" asked van Buren with interest.

"I laid two traps for him. I don't know why, except that I suspected him of crass ignorance when he began to talk about Johnson's letters—I don't believe he has found any new ones; he doesn't deserve to—and I hate to see good books or even good letters handled as if they were stocks and shares. He fell into both traps."

"I didn't notice them myself," admitted van Buren.

"But Wesson should have seen them if he has any real interest in his job. I talked of Donne's Poems as having been published in 1693. They came out fifty years before that. But Wesson didn't query my date, so he knows nothing about John Donne. And I maintain that bibliophile worthy the name ought to know something about him. The second trap was in the price I mentioned. A copy of the Poems went for £150 last month—a keen book collector would surely have noticed that—but Wesson flinches at a mere hundred."

"I met him on the *Loretania* a week ago," said van Buren. "I put him down as harmless. He's inquisitive and he's got money. He told me about his own business and he wanted me to tell him about mine. But I didn't encourage him. I decided that he was one of those people who don't need encouragement."

"He's an American citizen, isn't he?" asked Saturday.

"He is," admitted van Buren, "and I suppose there are some British citizens that you aren't particularly proud of. I expect that Wesson knows something about the books he has bought, but is in fairly complete ignorance of the million he hasn't. He may be a genuine collector though he isn't a scholar. Don't think I'm defending him though, because I'm not. I don't like him any better than a bad smell."

"He hasn't an American accent," said the professor.

"I guess a man who spends his time among old books will lose any kind of a human accent," replied van Buren.

CHAPTER III

Quentin Cotton got out of his car and walked into "The Downy Pelican."

"Good morning, George," he said to the Boots. "Is Mr. Keith in his office?"

"I think he's in his sitting-room, sir. I'll find out."

"Don't bother. I'll go up and see."

He ran briskly up the shallow stairs, turned right, and facing him in the corridor saw an extremely pretty girl with red hair, an expression of humorous unconcern, and an attractive uniform—frilly about the cap and apron, cut roundly in the neck—of white and green.

"Hullo," he said, "who are you?"

"I'm a maid," she replied coolly.

"Then you're defrauding my sex—no, don't go. I want to talk to you. I'm always talkative in the morning. You haven't been here long, have you?"

"Long enough to learn my way about. Good-bye."

She continued her way, which Quentin had halted, and Quentin, turning to walk beside her, explained, "I'm a friend of Mr. Keith's—"

"A man in his position must have all sorts of acquaintances, I suppose."

"And so many compensations. Where are you going now?"

"Why do you ask?"

"My general interest in humanity is narrowing to a focus on you."

"I don't pose for strangers," she replied, and went up a staircase which, as it was steep and unobtrusive, apparently led to the servants' quarters.

Quentin walked thoughtfully towards Saturday's rooms.

Saturday was playing with unapt and hesitating fingers on a typewriter. Little metallic rushes, sudden jars and a tinny discord told that another couplet of "*Tellus* Will Proceed," his new poem, had been translated from an inky, scribbled-on, drawn-on piece of notepaper to moderately accurate typescript. He was making a single copy only, for carbon paper puzzled him and (as he used it) generally repeated the lettering on the back of the original sheet.

Quentin looked over his shoulder and read from the page that stuck, like a letter too big for the letterbox, out of the top of the typewriter:

> "And like a racing cloud that runs around.
> On stark Helvellyn, his beard was blown about
> In the wind, but louder than the wind his shout
> Daunted the sea: 'How goes it, Twinkletoes?'
> Then, like the bell of St. Hospice in the Snows,
> So clear and silver-thin, the Star replied.
> 'What ship is that?' And the great Dutchman cried
> 'The *Tellus* out of Chaos; Captain—God!'

And laughed again with ribald hardihood
As blacker waves leapt on the labouring bows. . . ."

"You haven't told me about this," said Quentin. "What does it all mean?"

Saturday, staring glumly at almost indecipherable manuscript, looked up, searched, and handed him a page on which, under the title, was written, "Ship *Tellus* will proceed to Apogee for orders."

"You see?" he asked.

"Tellus is the earth, so far as I remember, and Apogee sounds reasonably like a port on the West Coast of Africa. But I don't understand about the captain."

"The captain is the Flying Dutchman; a sort of cosmic Flying Dutchman; sometimes he thinks he is God."

Quentin looked grave. "And the passengers?" he asked.

"The hold is full of rats."

"Talking rats?"

"Yes. Damn you, don't be so confoundedly sceptical. I'm sick of doing piddling little things. I'm bone-weary of microscopic, pedantic, analysed-emotion-and-synthesized-effect. I'm trying to do a big thing. I may have made a fool of myself—no, I'm damned if I have—or if I have I didn't expect you to be the first to say so."

"My dear old fellow, I'm saying nothing of the sort. But we— you and I and all of us—have got into the habit of looking sideways at anything deliberately ambitious. We're inclined to go slow, in this year of grace, and count our steps and watch the next man's expression and chop logic small enough to be sure that there aren't any bones left in it. We've given up epic and satire on the grand scale and throwing our caps over the moon. But if you can do it—or if you have done it—I think Tellus and the Dutchman is a splendid idea. Especially the rats."

Saturday grunted, "I'm bloody sensitive about it."

"I know. Just like a mountain would be if it really produced an elephant after getting accustomed to ridiculous mice."

"Do you mean *February Fill-dyke?*"

"I've said the wrong thing again. But you're suffering from

poet's itch. Forget that manuscript and tell me who is this new
pretty girl you have here."

Saturday's expression changed. The unhuman grief of au-
thorship lifted and he looked eager, happy, interested in things
beyond the seed of his mind.

"Where did you meet her?" he asked.

"In the corridor as I was coming along. I spoke to her and
she answered flick! like a schoolboy's catapult."

"That doesn't sound like her. She's rather quiet. And she
doesn't impress nearly so much at first sight as when you have
studied her a little. She's reticent, like a shop window with one
necklace or one hat in it. But you know there's more behind."

"A delicatessen shop with three pepper-corns in the window
is what I would compare her to. She isn't your type at all, Saturday. You like the receptive kind, the chalice woman; the tactful underliner of what you say."

"I don't. I like independence more than anything else. But a
girl can be independent without contradicting everything she
hears."

"Not if she's honest. People talk such rubbish. Anyway this
red-haired lily of the ballet wouldn't agree with me."

"Red-haired! But Joan hasn't red hair."

"Then who's Joan? The one I met is as red as a new penny."

"Joan is Joan Benbow, old Benbow's daughter."

"I might have known. You're so damned above stairs in
your fancy. I'm democratic. The girl I have been talking about
is a maid of some kind. How many copper-crowned ones have
you?"

Saturday thought. It was difficult to efface the image of Joan
Benbow and substitute for it a brief procession of maids. "You
mean Nelly Bly," he said at last. "She came here from an agency,
in the ordinary way, a week or ten days ago. She's a pretty girl,
isn't she?"

"Yes," said Quentin drily. "Tell me about Joan."

"No," said Saturday. "But you'll meet her. How long are you
staying?"

"Two or three days if there's a corner for me to sleep in."

"I'll have to get another bed put in my room for you. We're
full up. I've done well out of your suggestion, Quentin."

"My mother is delighted. I heard from her yesterday."

"And I sold another hundred copies of *February Fill-dyke* up to the end of March this year. People bought them out of vulgar curiosity, I suppose, but perhaps they read them."

"Losing both vulgarity and curiosity in the process. . . . Isn't Nelly Bly a ridiculous name for a girl like that?"

"There's another named Veronica Stout."

"And a hill called Popocatapetl. I should like some beer."

"Come down to the bowling-green then. It's too fine to stay indoors."

They went down the stone staircase that led into the central courtyard—pink roses assailed the galleries and in enormous wooden pots sturdy shrubs grew, thickset and glossy-green; two walls were in shadow, warm, blue-veined shadow, and an old red roof in the sun looked as though it were on fire—and through a narrow doorway to the back of the inn where the bowling-green lay smooth and calm, dappled at one side under a high awning of leaves. Beyond the green, through old and lofty-spreading trees, shone the pale brick-colour of tennis courts.

Professor Benbow and Mr. van Buren were playing bowls, two massive figures in white who stooped and got up again with stately labour, slowly approaching the earth to kneel so heavily on it, slowlier rising under the burden of their ponderous years.

"A hit, a palpable hit," said the professor as his last wood rolled shrewdly to the jack.

"It's a game that I've never given much attention to," remarked Mr. van Buren, "but I'm willing to admit its attractions. Not that it has the snap and glitter of golf of course."

"Golf? Golf was a respectable game when only men of our age, or approaching it, played. Now when it's fallen into the hands of professional footballers, androgynous pot-hunters, and American welter-weights, why, I have given it up until someone presents me with a course of my own."

"Those are hard words for a game that's highly thought of, professor. A game that's done more than anything in the American constitution to bring my country into the comity of civilized nations. All I've got against it is that it takes you so darned far away from the club house."

Saturday introduced Quentin to the professor and van Buren.

The latter immediately said, "Why, I've met your mother, Mr. Cotton. I heard her in Boston when she was lecturing on "Woman's Place in the World To-day." It was a remarkably fine lecture, and the place she assigned to woman was as elevated as her general sentiments."

The lines on Mr. van Buren's expressive face deepened to an equivocal significance, and his eyes twinkled as he continued to shake Quentin's hand.

Beyond the trees, so that their voices came faint but clearly, were people playing tennis.

"Who are they?" asked the professor.

"Miss Benbow, Colonel Waterhouse, Jean Forbes and Telfer."

"We're a strenuous people. We write revues, do daring and ingenious gymnastics on quite un-parallel critical bars, explore Central Asia and take the trouble to say what we think about it, and work as hard as gladiators for relaxation. Joan is the one idler there. I'm inclined to like the human race . . . with the trees between us."

"It's a pity they specialize," Saturday suggested. "Now, if Telfer would go to Central Asia for a change—"

"You mean that he doesn't like your poetry?"

"He compared one of my poems to an Academy painting. He went so far as to shout 'Leighton' at it."

"I'm glad," said the professor. "It's time that acrimony and bad taste came back to enliven our criticism. I could even wish that he had called some other verses Landseer. Robust vilification is the proper meat for poets—"

He was interrupted by a hesitating cough at his elbow.

"I saw you sitting here, professor, and I thought that I would take the opportunity to let you know what a ridiculous mistake I made last night."

Mr. Wesson smiled benignly down through his curious eyeglasses. His face under the mid-day sun had the texture almost of wash-leather and was nearly featureless (but for such necessary adjuncts as nose, eyes, mouth and so on) except for two things: the look of gentle benignity and heavily wrinkled, unusually obvious upper eyelids. A brown suit hung loosely on him and he carried a book in one hand.

"Oh! What was that?" With a sudden boom in his voice Professor Benbow sat up and stared at Mr. Wesson, who smiled more kindly than ever.

"I told you that I had bought some letters written to Garrick by different people. What I meant of course—it was stupid of me—was letters written by him. I saw you were puzzled when I told you about them, and just before I went to sleep—while I was sipping my milk, as a matter of fact—I remembered the unthinking error which I had made. There's quite a difference, isn't there?"

"There is," said the professor gravely. "But I'm afraid that we all make mistakes sometimes."

"Yes," replied Mr. Wesson mildly, "I think you made one too."

"Eh?"

"You spoke of the first edition of Donne's Poems as appearing in 1683. You meant 1633, didn't you? I remembered that also while I was drinking my milk, and I almost came down to tell you about it."

"*Mea maxima culpa,*" said the professor. "My wits, as well as my body, must be on holiday. You do well to rebuke me."

"Just a slip of the tongue, professor, like my own silly mistake about the letters. But I thought I would tell you."

Mr. Wesson smiled all round, an excusive, propitiating smile that seemed gently to bow him out of their circle. He turned to go, but after taking a few steps halted, came back, and showed to Professor Benbow the book which he carried.

"A first edition of Herrick's *Hesperides*," he said. "A pretty writer, don't you think? I bought it at Sotheby's last week." And without waiting for a reply walked smoothly away.

"That sounded to me like a smack on the face," said van Buren thoughtfully.

"It was," said the professor, "and after I had been knocked down first."

Quentin looked puzzled—though he had been watching the distant game of tennis rather than listening to such dull talk

for a fine day—and the professor explained, "I have been pun-
ished for trying to be clever with a fool—for I still think the
man's a fool," he added, as though it were an ultimatum, to
van Buren.

Mr. van Buren grunted.

CHAPTER IV

Quentin Cotton, waiting to buy stamps at the Downish Post
Office, saw an attractive young woman who had already
bought one. Only one. He had an aunt who bought stamps one
at a time; or three; or seven; once, while he was with her, she
had bought eleven, having newly written eleven letters. Did all
women deal on such strictly retail terms with the post office?
This one in front of him, or half in front and half beside him,
was charming so far as he could see. Her chin could scarcely
be bettered, at least from that angle. And the tip of her tongue
as it came out to moisten the little brown stamp was incredibly
delightful. He felt sure that it was a witty, purposive tongue,
a strong and yet delicate tongue that went swiftly about its
business or lay mockingly in an equally alluring cheek. Idly,
scarcely realizing what he did, his eyes followed the descent of
the stamp—between a finger and thumb that were pleasant to
look at and yet purposive too—to a long envelope addressed
in the round assured hand of the confirmed letter-writer; a
gossiping, sprightly hand that promised the happiest of indis-
cretions; and the inscription, so far as he could read—

"Well," said a cool voice, "have you enjoyed that instalment?"

Quentin was deservedly put out of countenance and replied
foolishly, "Oh, it's you, is it?"

She had spoken at first without looking round, and recognizing Quentin caught a little, but only a little, of his embarrassment. "I could say the same with equal truth," she
murmured.

"I came to buy some stamps," he explained.

"But being fond of reading—"

"Only stories with a happy ending. I hate those Russians."

"My first husband was a Cossack," she replied in a tone of definite rebuke. And walked composedly out of the post office.

That subordinate part of the civilized mind which is trained to the routine of daily life dictated to Quentin (and to the post office clerk) his original mission, and guided his fingers in sticking the stamps on the conventional right-hand-upper-corners of the several envelopes which he carried. But Quentin's higher thought centres, or at any rate those centres engaged in accepting, registering, and passing immediate judgment on incoming emotions and apprehensions, were thrown out of gear by something akin to atmospheric disturbances in the physical world. So charming a girl, and married. Young, and married to a Cossack. *A Cossack.* He had never known a Cossack personally. He had only read about them and seen them, or imitations of them, dancing in a singularly robust and agile manner; throwing knives and doing tricks with ropes—no, those were cowboys; but Cossacks also rode, generally under the belly of their horses rather than on the saddle, or if they used a saddle it was to stand on it; and they were fond of stooping just as their horses broke into a rousing gallop to pick handkerchiefs off the ground. . . .

Quentin stood on the pavement. They might be charming fellows, of course. Great, noisy children, now laughing fullheartedly, now piteously seeking comfort and dimly knowing in their wise Slav hearts—were they Slavs?—that no one on earth could comfort them. Children of the steppes who would never grow up. But they grew beards, damn them. Great sprouting bristle-patches of beards. . . .

And she had said *first* husband. Good God, how many had she had? And starting with a Russian what country had she gone to next? German waiters, Jewish tailors, French chefs, gondolieri, Swiss guides . . . but she might have been joking; though one doesn't usually make jokes of that kind in a post office. She had looked so virginal, especially in that green and white uniform. Many women of course looked more virginal after they were married than they did before—just to make it

more difficult. . . . But Saturday had said her name was Nelly
Bly, and Quentin was damned if Bly was a Russian name.

"I beg your pardon," he said to a woman who was pushing
a perambulator against him, and got into his car. He drove
slowly along and saw Nelly Bly walking a little way in front of
him. He remembered that he had not long ago boasted to Saturday of being democratic, and decided that he could be cosmopolitan as well. Any Englishman, indeed, who sympathized
with the plebs of his own country had gone half-way to thinking kindly of foreigners. He stopped a yard in front of her and
leaning out said, "I'm going to Shelton and back. Would you
care to come with me?"

"Thank you," she answered, "it's kind of you to invite me."

There seemed to be a new quietness about her; the mantle of
her widowhood, perhaps—if she was a widow.

"Bly isn't a Russian name, is it?" Quentin asked.

"I took my maiden name again after Boris—that is, after I
left my husband."

"Oh," said Quentin.

They exchanged a few cheerless but amiable remarks as they
passed the celebrated ruins of the Roman Baths and drove
through the long poplar avenue that goes all the way to Little
Needham. Quentin felt his mind uncomfortably dull beneath
its weight of curiosity, and Nelly Bly stared straight in front,
looking even lovelier than Quentin had first thought in her
grave serenity.

"You said your first husband was a Cossack," he ventured.

"Yes," she answered softly. Then, after a moment or two's
thought, added, "I might have said my only husband—"

Quentin's spirits rose considerably.

"—because I gave Boris all I had, youth, faith, everything,
and after him no one really counted."

Quentin felt depressed, and for some time drove at a beg-
garly fifteen miles an hour.

"You won't say anything of this to Mr. Keith, will you?" she
asked in a little while. "I have nothing to be ashamed of but he
might not understand so fully as you do, and I have my living
to make now. And that isn't easy, for a French convent—I was

educated in a convent, Mr. Cotton—doesn't contemplate the immediate future; at least not my kind of future."

Quentin pressed his foot hard on the accelerator and their speed increased with a leap and a swoop forward—the gale sang valiantly and the sun dashed itself to pieces on the windscreen—to fifty-five miles an hour. She had appealed to his chivalry, and Quentin's chivalry, as that of so many unromantic Englishmen, lay like a glacier ready for the warm fingers of Spring to release it. Chivalry vaunteth not itself, is not puffed up, doth not behave itself unseemly; for indeed it is so seldom taken off the ice. But once it is in the sun it passeth all understanding, for it is content to act without understanding.

"You can trust me," said Quentin, and overtook magnificently a family Daimler that almost filled the narrow road. The world was beneath him. He saw the white road like a tape running round the enormous sphere of the earth that careered hugely through cosmos, and he, Quentin, trod the earth as a superb acrobat lonely on a gigantic ball, for he felt both chivalrous and sophisticated—two proud things—in that he could count as nothing the dubious way-faring of a girl lost in a forest of men.

"Perhaps I ought to," she answered a little strangely.

"I knew at once, of course, that you weren't an ordinary maid."

"I have read *A Nettle Against May*. I got it out of a Free Library."

"Did you like it?"

"Some books exhaust you; others nourish you."

"First novels are generally indigestible, like a soul-and-kidney pie that has been baking ever since adolescence."

"Yours wasn't because it omitted the pie altogether and went straight from cocktail to savoury."

"Then it left you hungry for more?"

"But not necessarily from the same shop."

"My next one is going to be robust."

"Not too robust for a Free Library, I hope. Because I can't afford to buy novels."

The reminder of her precarious social position fell like a

cloud on Quentin's spirit, and Nelly Bly tactfully changed her direction. She changed it indeed more than once, for she talked as a hound runs, by scent; though the fox that she followed changed into a bird and a water-beast and a dining-room table at will. Some of the most entertaining talkers are like that, and as they seldom kill, so they are seldom shocked by the sight of reality. Nelly Bly began her chase by saying that Mr. Sigismund Telfer apparently wore a hair-net in bed, for she had seen one in his room and Mrs. Telfer's hair was quite obviously too short to need it. The lure of such personal gossip grew strong and both she and Quentin showed their teeth happily; but by-and-by it led, through unseen country, to some mention of music, and Nelly's confession that she liked negro spirituals best when one felt that if the singer went sharp by a hair's breadth he would be in hysterics; and thence over other lightly sown fields and a fence or two of argument to a beaten track on which she remarked, "Well, I'm glad that I'm not in love at present. Love makes a woman dull."

"Do you mean sleepy?" Quentin asked.

"No, silent. She's frightened of saying something that might shock her lover, or anticipated lover. Men in love are sometimes horrified by things that a woman never notices. So the girl in love grows dull in self-defence."

"Or it may be protective mimicry. So many men are as dull as women."

"And then the poor girl's compromised as well as bored."

"Compromised?"

"A clever girl can have only one reason for going about with a stupid man."

"Wit, then, has supplanted the duenna."

"It always did," said Nelly Bly.

Quentin sighed. He felt that she was getting the better of the rallies and he wished that he could remember some of the excellent things he had said in *A Nettle Against May*. There was spirited stuff in his mind when he wrote that. Perhaps a memory of Congreve or Vanbrugh had sometimes helped out invention; but then the gleaner has always shared with the sower. Anyway it wasn't likely that she, brought up in a convent, would be familiar with Restoration epigrams . . . if he could only think of one. But, like stammerers trying to pronounce "sforzando," he utterly failed; both memory and invention stuck.

"Well?" she said, breaking the unusual silence.

"I'm trying to compromise you by an appearance of stupidity," said Quentin with an effort.

They bumped over the stony streets of Shelton. Nelly refused tea. She was an employee on parole, she said, and it was time to turn. Quentin found matter to speak of on the return journey, for he talked about himself. And Nelly Bly listened to him.

CHAPTER V

Between half-past six and half-past seven—when they went to bathe and change out of light clothes into dark clothes, or from light to bright, according to their sex—Professor Benbow talked with Jean Forbes and Mr. van Buren with her mother, Tommy Mandeville; Saturday talked with Joan; Sir Philip Betts, the racing motorist, talked with Jacquetta Telfer; Sigismund Telfer talked with Diana Waterhouse; Colonel Waterhouse talked with Angela Scrabster while Mrs. Waterhouse listened to them; Lady Wesson sat alone, apparently reading, and Lady Porlet, somewhat surprisingly, talked with Holly the barman.

There were other people staying at "The Pelican" they, according to their minds and inclinations, found yet others with whom they talked.

At first Jean Forbes and Professor Benbow talked about Jean Forbes; then they talked about Professor Benbow.

"I did six months in the chorus of *Red Cabbage*," said Jean Forbes, "and I'll never put a foot on the stage again. I went away and hid myself in the Highlands afterwards. I got so tired of bodies. All the bodies were made in the same way. Has that ever struck you?"

"The discovery has struck—'struck' is the word—every wise man from Solomon onward," replied the professor, "though there are still many people who think that mass production is a modern idea."

"But it's funny, don't you think? There are so many different kinds of flowers. But we were all alike—and showing everybody that we were all alike as though it was something to be proud of—and we dressed alike, and sang the same things every night, and did the same steps together, and came on together and ran off together—I nearly went mad. And then mother and I wrote *Peace in Our Time* and all the critics said the same things about it."

While they discussed and confided so they heard, in snatches, Sir Philip Betts and Jacquetta Telfer talking of fear and their relations with it.

"Driving at two hundred miles an hour is a sufficient test of courage, I should think."

"Not so searching as sailing a small boat across a large sea."

"The sea is a rational friendly thing," she said. "It's solid enough to support you and mobile enough to offer you a choice of direction when it begins to get up on end. Even the wind you can learn to know, if you're not a fool. But people in a crowd are never rational and you can never tell what they will do. I'm frightened of crowds."

"And I'm frightened of the sea," said Betts.

"I should like to write a revue," said the professor. "Do you think that London would be amused by a chorus of German pedants and jokes about textual criticism? I suppose not. And yet that is what I would inevitably fall into. Though I'm sick of scholarship and the graveyard way we go to work explaining what Shakespeare meant in places where all he meant, probably, was a billiard-room joke."

"Perhaps revues ought to be more serious. Fewer legs and more heads, I mean. Will you collaborate in our next one?"

They heard Betts's voice again, though it was pitched in an unfamiliar tone. "I was in a motorboat at Zeebrugge," he said. "We got hit and it sank under us. I nearly drowned. Pure funk, because I swim rather well."

"And I went into hysterics in a crowd in one of the Tubes during an air raid," Jacquetta answered, with an uneasy laugh.

Mr. Wesson, sitting in a corner, read a book, a Brobdingnagian book a foot broad and a foot-and-a-half tall, which he held prominently before him in an uncomfortable position.

Mr. van Buren had discovered that he knew Mrs. Mandeville's first husband, Jean Forbes's father.

"Why, I met him two years ago in New York, in one of our business clubs. He'd been lecturing on Greco-Buddhist monuments at Taxila, in Northern India, and we invited him to have luncheon with us the following day. That was one of the most informative lectures I have ever heard. Scholarly and yet alive. I remember him perfectly. It was two years ago last February."

"It's five years, I think, since I saw him."

"Well, now, I know him better than you do," and van Buren chuckled wickedly.

"It must be such fun making a revue," said the professor.

"It's damned hard work," said Jean Forbes.

Diana Waterhouse, looking puzzled but defiant, proclaimed in a shrill young voice, "but I *like* Tennyson, Mr. Telfer. He makes such beautiful sounds. Like 'The mellow ousel fluting in the elm.'"

"Fluting in my back-garden!" roared Telfer in a sudden passion, and stamped out of the room.

"Come and sit beside me, dear," said Mrs. Waterhouse, and Diana, disconsolately flopping into a chair, answered, "I suppose he's beastly clever, but I know what I like just as well as anybody else."

"Of course you do," agreed Mrs. Waterhouse. "But be quiet now. Your father's talking."

Colonel Waterhouse bit his lip. "A Turanian type," he repeated.

"Did you see their women?" Angela Scrabster asked. "Even I found it difficult to get sitters among the real aristocrats. There are some left in China, you know. The thousand—ancestors, exquisitely painted, perfectly artificial, utterly composed, human-flower ones. I got two or three. But I was lucky."

"So was I," said the colonel, looking knowing and reminiscent.

"When was that?" asked his wife. "Do tell us about it."

"It wouldn't interest you," replied the colonel.

"Nothing can come of criticism," said Professor Benbow. "The first critic was the eunuch." And immediately he was annoyed with himself for saying that, for though he deprecated a mealy mouth in others he himself habitually refrained from discussing events connected with sex—even events so remotely connected as a eunuch—in the presence of young women.

Mr. Wesson turned a page of the large-paper folio of Matthew Prior's *Poems on Several Occasions*, and glanced round to see who noticed him.

And meanwhile, in the reconstructed buttery, Lady Porlet talked with Holly the barman.

It was one of Lady Porlet's frailties that she could never remember her way about a strange house, and coming in from the bowling-green, where she had been dozing in a deck-chair, she took the wrong turning and found herself in a room which she had not seen before. A curiously furnished room, but one which struck her unfamiliar eyes as being strangely attractive. Something like an immense sideboard was the principal piece of furniture in it; a sideboard big enough to hold a man, scores of glasses, and ever so many quaintly shaped, multi-coloured bottles which were reflected dimly and grotesquely in polished wood, brightly and insistently in a background of mirror-glass.

"Dear me," said Lady Porlet.

The man in the sideboard looked up; his attention had been fixed on two glasses which stood on the bar in front of him, one containing a light blue, the other a dark blue liquid.

"Yes, madam," he said a little absently.

"What a prettily furnished room," said Lady Porlet, and looked about her with a vague smile.

"This is the American Bar," Holly answered stolidly.

"Really," said Lady Porlet. "My nephew of course is a great traveller, but I know very little about foreign countries myself. Such curious chairs!"

With some difficulty she balanced herself on one of the tall stools in front of the bar and tentatively, as if for feeling for stirrups, set her feet on a convenient brass rail.

"So welcome a change from those relaxing bath-chairs beside the bowling green. Deck-chairs, I mean, though they're both bad for your spine. This is quite bracing. When I was a girl we all sat with straight backs."

"Yes, madam," said Holly. He stood as far away as he could and looked at Lady Porlet with some suspicion. His success with the blue cocktails had undermined his customary discretion and he had been tasting, first light blue, then dark blue, from early morning. All day the wonder of the artist had flooded his soul. He had invented, and the invention was greater than he. Like a poet whose tortured wit suddenly, inexplicably flowers; like a gardener when a crocus thrusts unheralded its golden spear above the snow; like a child who finds a sea-cave full of magic green—like everyone who has discovered somehow that life is more than living, Holly was slightly dazzled. He wanted to explain his feeling to himself and he could not. Only words could do that—perhaps not even words—and Holly, in spite of his cigarette pictures, knew so few words that would translate rapture. The cloudy matrix of a line like "Oh, she doth teach the torches to burn bright!" was in his brain. Perhaps another cocktail would clear away the fog and show his meaning crystal-clear. The lively smoothness of the one called Cambridge, the nobler vivacity of that named Oxford, flowed through his veins and shot into his mind. Then he would look out of the window at sunny trees and deep emerald grass and feel—though he did not make this clear to himself—that he wanted to write "Melodious birds sing madrigals" with a diamond on the glass. . . .

But this mood was insecurely poised; he was easily upset and readily became suspicious. Earlier in the day he had been questioned, too closely he thought, about his secret formula, and the incident had left a legacy of general distrust. Moreover he had a feeling—again it was too hazy to put into words, for he had drunk a lot of cocktails since morning—that there was something strange about Lady Porlet. Never before had he seen anyone quite like her in his bar. She was out of place, and what is out of place is frightening if you think of it in a certain way. He was startled and yet curious, as an Esquimaux family might

be who saw an ant-eater come into their igloo. And he backed
to the farthest wall.

"How very pretty," said Lady Porlet, and picked up one of
the cocktails. She held it to the light and a breath of its fra-
grance blew into her nostrils.

"Are they for drinking?" she asked.

"Of course they are," replied Holly indignantly.

"I thought perhaps they were like those bottles which one
used to see in chemists' shops, that, although they made such a
pleasant impression, were not really palatable." Lady Porlet
tasted her cocktail.

"Dear me," she said, "it reminds me of the elderberry wine
which an old housekeeper of mine used to make. She died from
heart-failure while she was looking at some pictures of King
Edward's coronation."

"That was the ninth of August, 1902," said Holly.

"So it was," Lady Porlet confirmed, and finished her cocktail. "You seem to be a well-read man," she said.

"Ah!" said Holly. His suspicions of Lady Porlet had disappeared and he burned with a dark flame of pride. He wanted to
show off. He knew a lot about English constitutional history,
and what is the use of knowledge unless you can display it? He
began: "William the Conqueror, 1066—he was crowned on
Christmas Day—to the 9th September, 1087. William Rufus,
or William the Second, 1087 to 1100. . . ."

He frowned and taxed his memory.

"William the Third," prompted Lady Porlet kindly.

"No ma'am," said Holly loudly. "He wasn't born. He wasn't
born for hundreds and hundreds of years."

"How very strange," said Lady Porlet.

Holly reached down into some recess behind the bar and
brought from it a thick album on to whose dark green pages
were pasted, obverse and reverse side by side, an immense
number of cigarette pictures. He rapidly turned the leaves, giving a tantalizing glimpse of foreign flags, wild animals, household devices, famous footballers, and the English kings, until
he came to what he wanted.

"There you are, ma'am," he proclaimed. "1689 to 1702,

though rightly speaking he wasn't William the Third so much as William and Mary."

"What a good idea," said Lady Porlet, and read the account, necessarily brief, of William the Dutchman and his charitable, unhappy wife.

"And where do you get all these pictures?" she asked.

"There's one in every packet of cigarettes that you buy, ma'am."

"I must ask my husband what he does with those out of his cigar-boxes."

Holly looked doubtful. He took away the empty glass and Lady Porlet, curiously examining a portrait gallery of celebrated criminals, picked up the remaining full one.

"I must get the recipe for this," she said, delicately sipping.

"No ma'am," said Holly, defiant in a moment. "It's a secret process and I won't part with it. There's been others before you trying to get it and I said no to her as I say no to you. The red-haired hussy! Coming in here as bold as brass and putting her elbows on the bar and trying to seduce me like—like Cleopatra did to Antony."

"She reigned in Egypt in the century before Christ and is said to have been an expert poisoner, testing her decoctions on her household slaves," said Lady Porlet, who happened to have turned the page to Notorious Women, a series of fifty. "You were quite right, of course, in your refusal. I have scant patience with girls of to-day. And now I must go."

She got down from her stool gravely and stood for a moment thinking. "My face feels quite warm. I believe I got sunburnt sitting beside the bowling-green this afternoon."

At the door she hesitated for a moment, and then turning asked, "I wonder if I might borrow that interesting album of yours to look at this evening? I tried to find something amusing in the library, but books are so long, and they all had such meaningless titles."

"Why, certainly, ma'am," said Holly. "I'm glad you like them. They've done a lot for me, those pictures, and I wouldn't lend them to anyone who asked. But you seem to appreciate them as much as I do myself."

He held the album across the bar, and Lady Porlet took it with a smile which, for all her stupidity, was entirely charming. She left the buttery humming a little tune to herself.

CHAPTER VI

Out of these several circumstances it came about that Quentin Cotton was not alone in a feeling of embarrassment when he came down to dinner. It was, he told himself, entirely foolish and quite wrong to be embarrassed by the recollection of his afternoon with Nelly Bly. Nothing had happened to incur the censure of even the most complex-ridden moralist. He had stopped his car two hundred yards from "The Pelican." Nelly Bly had descended, calm and decorous. He, too, had got out, taken off his hat, hoped that he might see her again, watched her walk down the street. Everything to a spectator was calm and proper. And yet Nelly Bly was a maid in his friend's pub— or his mother's pub, it really didn't matter—and he had stopped his car two hundred yards from its door. At Nelly Bly's request, naturally. She was a charming girl—or woman; a charming woman with pleasant manners and an interesting history; a woman—no, a girl, damn it, a girl down on her luck and for want of any specialized ability a maid in his mother's pub. Or Saturday's pub. There was no reason for him to be embarrassed because he had been democratic—and cosmopolitan, of course—and yet when he met Saturday and some of his fellow-guests he did feel self-conscious; as any well brought-up young Englishman would who had lately been cosmopolitan and democratic.

But he was not alone in his self-consciousness. Professor Benbow, under the harsh chastisement of shaving, remembered that in spite of one of his favourite self-denying ordinances he had spoken about sex to Miss Forbes; or at any rate on the principle of *lucus a non lucendo* he had reminded her of sex, to which he was well aware young women's thoughts were already too warmly attached. And the professor was annoyed with himself.

Sir Philip Betts, in the revealing warmth of his bath, and Jacquetta Telfer in hers, petulantly said to themselves, "Now, why the devil did I tell him—or her—that I once lost my head through fear of drowning—or of being crushed to death in a Tube—when I meant to forget it myself, and certainly never intended to speak of it to an almost utter stranger?" They were irate at their frailty. And Colonel Waterhouse remembered that, through wanting to talk about himself to Angela Scrabster, he had wakened an alert little suspicion in his wife's brain. And Sigismund Telfer cursed himself for having lost his temper, which he was prone to do and which he had sworn a thousand times not to do; though Tennyson and the pre-Raphaelites, he felt privately, were enough to rouse indignation in any man. And Diana Waterhouse was angry and sad because she had wanted to let Sigismund Telfer, whom she admired, know that she too had fine feelings for literature; an ambition in which, she realized, she had signally failed. And Mr. Æsop Wesson bit his lip because even with a work so heavy to hold—it weighed nine or ten pounds—as Matthew Prior's *Poems on Several Occasions*, he had not noticeably imprinted himself on the general consciousness as an ardent book-collector.

These little scratches and sorenesses, slight though they were, made a lot of fellow-sufferers for Quentin, and so during dinner there was more than the usual amount of vivacity and conscious gaiety. For as more than half the visitors under "The Pelican" had shown to their neighbours some tiny chink in their everyday armour of composure, so more than half of them determined to prove themselves full of a most happy assurance. And the others responded readily enough. Lady Porlet indeed— who was quite unconscious of any lapse, and looking forward to an unusually pleasant evening with Holly's cigarette-picture album—repeated a favourite anecdote of her father's which evoked more laughter than she had expected, for she was the only one who did not see the point of it. And later in the evening Mrs. Mandeville was persuaded to a piano, where she played many things in many manners. And her daughter sang. Jean Forbes's voice had that peculiar quality of huskiness which is to some people more attractive than the perfect clarity of bell

metal or a Wagner soprano. By-and-by other people sang, some
of them badly, but all with spirit.

Saturday, moving among his guests, saw all this, and realized the astonishing thing that was happening. In the warmth
of "The Pelican" the cold rind of individual reserve was slowly
thawing. English people were becoming friendly, simple and
genial, with other English people whom they had known no
more than a day, or two days, or three days. Somehow or other
the social temperature had reached melting-point. And Saturday was filled with new confidence in a scheme which he had
secretly entertained for a long time. But he wanted quietness in
which to consider it.

Joan Benbow looked up perhaps a little reproachfully as he
passed her, but when she saw the expression on his face re-
proach left her mind and she understood. Or thought she understood. "He is going to write poetry," she said to herself and
felt, what she had so often felt as a child, that the purpose of
God's creatures was unnecessarily obscure.

Saturday shut the door of his sitting-room, took a book
from his shelves, and began to read. It was not a poetry-book.

"To bake the best marrow-bone pie, after you have mixt the
crusts of the best sort of pastes, and raised the coffin in such
manner as you please," he read. He went deeper into it and
found "a layer of candied Eringo-root mixt very thicke with
the slices of dates," which was covered with "marrow, currants, great raisins, sugar, cynamon, and dates, with a few
damaske prunes." Into that coffin—a dozen other things were
richly buried there—white wine, rose-water and cinnamon
must be poured "as long as it will receive it."

"That might do," said Saturday thoughtfully, and slowly
turned the yellowish pages, considering in their turn an oyster-
pie, sauce for a green goose, carbonadoes, a warden pie, a Flo-
rentine, Ipocras, Jumbals, Leach Lumbard, marchpane, suckets
and kickshawses.

He took a sheet of paper and began to sketch out a menu.

Some of these dishes he had already tried. Once he had said
to Lady Mercy, "We're getting broader-minded but narrower-
stomached. We read Chinese poetry side by side with Ameri-

can poetry, consider Hellenism and Industrialism in the same breath, appreciate Bach and negro spirituals, divide our enthusiasm between racehorses and aeroplanes—"

"But?" suggested Lady Mercy.

"But," repeated Saturday, "as our minds grow more receptive our stomachs grow less. Our dinner tables are an insult to history. The Elizabethans were magnificent eaters. We're not. Their menus were triumphs of imagination. We count our calories before they're cooked."

"I give you *carte* blanche, Mr. Keith," Lady Mercy replied. "But use your discretion. Remember that the gastric juices of a Rowing Blue might easily overcome what would oppress a tired millionaire. And women no longer eat. Appetites went out with contours and crinolines."

"Americans are fond of food."

"Ah! but they retain the dear childhood notion that eating too much is part of the ritual of a holiday. Try your Elizabethan dishes on them by all means. They may suffer, but they are idealists, and they will not complain if you tell them that Sir Philip Sidney also suffered from heartburn, and Sir Walter Raleigh was troubled by griping pains after food similar to theirs. But our own countrymen, Mr. Keith, are unimaginative. Do not tax their digestions too rashly."

Most of Saturday's experiments had succeeded, for he had found an unexpected ally in his cook, Ignatius O'Higgins, sometime a petty officer in His Majesty's Navy, a devout Catholic with the spacious and imperturbable faith of his creed, and a natural genius whose soul had too long been shackled by the *res angusta* of an ordinary kitchen. When Saturday encouraged him to use wine instead of water for stewing apples in, his mind put forth new strength and he cooked as if for gods. He conjured magnificently with unimpressive eggs, wrought miracles with beef, and preserved as if in a limbeck the savour of Highland scenery in a grouse. "Ah!" he would say, slipping his knife into a duckling, "Michael Angelo never carved anything as good as this!" And if Saturday took him an old recipe beginning in some such way as "To make Jumbals more fine and curious than the former," Ignatius O'Higgins would go to it

like a scholar to a palimpsest or a girl to a letter from her lover
overseas.

But only in single dishes had Saturday so far ventured to re-
introduce the stronger flavours, the whimsical mixtures, and
the more imaginative juxtapositions of ancient culinary methods. Now he meditated a bolder thing, a dinner that from start
to finish should be Elizabethan in temper, quality, and, so far
as modern appetites were able, in quantity. There were two reasons for this.

The first was that his guests, for the only time in his land-
lordship, were becoming a homogeneous household. They were
mixing. They might be expected to respond together to the
suggestion he proposed to make. And the second reason was
that in two days' time would fall the most important anniversary in the history of "The Pelican": the anniversary of the day
on which Queen Elizabeth and the Earl of Leicester, with much
shouting of grooms, stamping of horses, perspiration and
oaths—"God's death," said the queen, "is a queen's leg different to all other legs that you gape so?"—rode into its courtyard. The earl's boot, in a glass case, still stood in the hall to
prove the truth of the story and give scandal a leg to stand on;
for the boot had been found in the queen's room, it was said,
and the earl had ridden away in his stockings swearing, like an
honest knight, that it was no boot of his and he had never seen
it before.

Saturday, then, struggled to compose a menu that would
honour "The Pelican" and please his guests. He worked on it
as if it had been a sonnet, polishing, cutting, dove-tailing,
striving for significance in every line. . . .

And downstairs Joan Benbow thought perhaps he was chis-
elling imagination into a real pen-and-ink sonnet, and wondered why there was so little love poetry written nowadays, and
concluded sadly that as men were no longer simple enough in
their faith to write a "Paradise Lost," so even their love was too
insecure to write anyhow but lightly of it. . . .

Saturday considered "an excellent sauce for a roast capon,"
and decided that a "cupful of claret-wine, the juyce of an orange, and three or four slices of a lemon pill," would flavour it
pleasantly. . . .

Joan tried to remember what they had been saying to each other earlier in the evening. They must have said quite a lot in three-quarters of an hour, but she could recollect nothing in particular except an arrangement to play golf the following afternoon. Now this was funny; Jean Forbes was singing a song out of her revue, a Cockney song that went:

> "And 'e said to me
> 'Well, you might 'a come earlier
> You would of for Fred, or even for Ted,
> Oh, I wish I was dead!'—
> Poor little me, tryin' to keep three,
> An' as 'e got surly and surlier,
> O' course I grew girly and girlier. . . ."

Some people apparently could remember everything that they and their—everything they and other people said, word for word, emotion for emotion. But what she said to Saturday and what Saturday said to her had vanished entirely. She concluded that no definite utterance had been made. Neither had said "Liar!" or "I love you," or "Never speak to me again," or "I hate the way you walk." They had spoken inconsequential things that slipped unobtrusively into a pleasant little stream of talk; an idle-running little stream that turned no windmills nor wore tenaciously at solid rock. They had, of course, agreed to play golf together the following afternoon. . . .

Saturday read his completed menu with satisfaction. "Rich, not gaudy," he said, "no dormice or camels' heels, but honest fruit and meat; sufficiently elaborate to impress, without reminding you of Heliogabalus."

He leaned back, filled a pipe, and contemplated life. "*Tellus Will Proceed*" lay on a table, half neatly typed, half in frantic manuscript, all held tightly in a black leather portfolio that clipped the sheets together with an air of purpose. He might, perhaps, type a little more. But there was no hurry. He thought instead of Joan Benbow. How very pleasant was such a position as his, where you met people without having actively to seek their acquaintance. Such delightful people. Joan, when she talked, had the most engaging trick of suddenly looking up so that you became instantly aware, without warning, of two clear wide-open eyes, eager and alight; it was like pulling up the blinds with a jerk on a summer morning, and seeing the earth below so full of translucent shimmering delight that you wanted to dive into it. She was—it was idle to deny it—quite unlike any other girl he had ever known; quite unlike; how exactly it was difficult to say—unless by the measure of her superiority. She was more . . . well, he was more completely attracted by her than he had been by Mrs. Travers, for instance (whose husband had got lost somewhere at the back of Brazil and who didn't know whether she was a widow or not) or by the Littlejohn girl (whose father wrote books about sociology and was the only man in England who still believed in Bentham). Not that Joan was so glitteringly handsome as Mrs. Travers—Saturday conceded that and was pleased to think that he could be level-headed in such a matter—nor had she the sleek incongruously Puritan allure of Priscilla Littlejohn. She was—oh, it was difficult to analyse anyone so completely satisfactory. He was playing golf with her tomorrow. . . .

Joan, talking to Mrs. Waterhouse, wondered at the back of her mind what she should wear when she played golf with Saturday. She made pictures of herself dressed in various syntheses of cream, grey, fawn, tan, copper, jade, and what-not; posed against a background of green turf with a little red flag at her elbow; or a fringe of trees; or a large sandy bunker . . . a good colour scheme might turn a golfing catastrophe into an artistic triumph. "No, Mrs. Waterhouse," she said, "I've never been to Bournemouth."

"We met such interesting people there," said Mrs. Waterhouse. "A Mrs. Silberstein and her sister. It was they who recommended us to come here. They simply raved about 'The Pelican,' and about Mr. Keith in particular, though of course they agreed with me that it was just a little bit dangerous— 'dangerous' was the word Mrs. Silberstein used—for such a young and attractive man to be in a position like this. So many *opportunities* as Mrs.—now what was her name? Mr. Silberstein's sister, I mean. Oh, Mrs. Macpherson, of course. There were so many *opportunities*, she said."

"I suppose so," Joan replied vaguely, and wondered what sort of opportunities Mrs. Macpherson meant. Opportunities to become Poet Laureate, or a Member of Parliament, or a director of Cotton's Breweries?

Mrs. Waterhouse purred. "There was quite a scandal, Mrs. Silberstein said, about the attentions which he paid to Mrs.— tut, tut! Her husband went up the Amazon to go somewhere or other, and never came back. A rather flashy-looking woman, I believe. It was probably her fault, they thought; as a matter of fact they agreed that she had deliberately laid herself out to captivate him, and if I hadn't been able to tell them about—Diana! what was the name of the girl you were at school with who came here and went about so much with Mr. Keith? Her father wrote books; political books. I never read any of them myself— Littlejohn, of course. Priscilla Littlejohn. Well, when Mrs. Silberstein and her sister were inclined to defend Mr. Keith in his *affaire* with Mrs.—*tch*! quite a common name too—I was fortunately able to tell them about Priscilla, who was quite young, and we came to the conclusion that perhaps Mr. Keith was as much to blame himself. Neither became public scandals, of course; just little house scandals."

"And probably quite untrue," said Joan coldly.

"People do exaggerate, don't they? Diana always said that the Littlejohn girl was an habitual liar. She is one of those prim, secret-looking girls. And as to Mrs.—you know who I mean; Mrs. Travers, of course, that was it—as for her, neither Mrs. Silberstein nor myself could condemn Mr. Keith. Indeed, Mrs. Macpherson, who was one of the most cynical women I have ever met, but quite pleasant about it, said that that sort of thing was the best advertisement 'The Pelican' could have. Dear me, do you think Miss Forbes is going to sing again?"

"I hope so," said Joan. She felt foolish and uncomfortable; a little blank or deflated, as pricked foolishness does make one feel. Perhaps she should have stood up and said, "I am not interested in scandal, Mrs. Waterhouse," and walked away. But of course she was interested. And one couldn't give public expression to a purely private emotion. An emotion, too, built on such a humorous little basis as pretending to be excited about playing golf with Saturday Keith. But when you are unhappy it is the unhappiness that matters, not the cause of it. Damn, damn, damn, she said voicelessly; a sniffing damn; a trinity of damns; three damns divisible but not divided, one for Mrs. Waterhouse, one for herself, and one for Saturday.

Jean Forbes was singing another of the songs which her revue had made popular, a song which suited her husky voice and her expression—the description was Angela Scrabster's— of "an excommunicated nun who had walked the streets and discovered that life was a good joke if you were fond of that sort of thing." Part of the chorus ran:

> "Peace in our time, but no time to be bored,
>   Peace to be strenuous,
>   Lesbian, horsey,
>   Yet look ingenuous.
>   Though a divorcée,
>   Peace in our time, O Lord!"

Joan laughed. Nearly everybody laughed and felt they belonged to an amusing generation. Joan was scornful of her own silliness. To think that she had thought of Saturday as living his life in Victorian innocence!

The time changed. Jean Forbes's voice grew a little harder— mere whimsicality, people felt—as she began the next verse:

> "We are the nephews and nieces of War,
>   As wise as our uncles were bold—
>   Too wise to go out in the cold,
>   Too witty and wise to complain and feel sore
>   That all the best fruit has been handled before
>   And all the good stories been told."

It might be a little bit disappointing till you got used to it, Joan suspected, but she told herself that undoubtedly the best way to enjoy life was to be bright and hard; not to cherish silly ideals; to be sceptical of other people and not think too highly of oneself.

"I'm playing golf with Mr. Keith to-morrow," she told Mrs. Waterhouse.

"Ah!" said Mrs. Waterhouse with a knowing smile.

"He's so amusing, don't you think?" she said coolly; and privately thought, "I don't remember him making *many* jokes."

Professor Benbow, when the song was over, said to Mr. van Buren, "We're developing a tendency to be unkind to ourselves. I think it's a healthy sign."

"I've touched my toes twenty times every morning for the last twelve years," said van Buren, "but I don't like the look of them any better. . . ."

Saturday in his room, tapped steadily at letters which fell into orderly lines. Some very splendid lines, he thought, and some that bit like acid into the soft substance of our times. The latter pleased him even better than the proud sonorous ones.

CHAPTER VII

Ignatius O'Higgins said "Shoo!" and with a long-handled spoon hit at the blue fly which buzzed exasperatingly over a sirloin of beef. He missed it. "Buzz!" said the fly, and circled viciously round his head. Again O'Higgins hit—"Swung from his brand a windy buffet out," as Tennyson would have said—and the fly sped singing harshly to the bare wall high out of reach.

"Drive him out," commanded O'Higgins, and a little kitchen-maid, climbing on a chair, made frantic dabs with a cloth.

"Zzzz," said the fly contemptuously, and sailed like a raiding Fokker round the harassed kitchen.

"Now," said O'Higgins.

The fly was in front of him, the kitchen-maid on his left hand, a kitchen-boy on his right. With dish-clout, spoon, and bread-knife they slashed in the air and the fly, yielding to numbers, fled swiftly to the open window.

They had defeated it just in time, for as the fly went out the door opened and Saturday came in on his morning rounds. Ignatius O'Higgins looked about him. His kitchen was ready for inspection.

"Dismiss!" he said to the kitchen-maid and the kitchen-boy. "Good morning, sir!" He saluted Keith Navy-fashion, hand flat and palm down, index finger to the edge of his white cap.

"Good morning, O'Higgins. I've got a difficult job for you," replied Saturday.

Ignatius leaned forward eagerly, contracting his mouth and sucking in his lips with respectful anticipation. His eyes gleamed and his face, red except where he shaved and there it was navy-blue, shone like an east window when the sun catches a lozenge of gules and the shoulder of a saint's blue cloak. His enormous body in its white clothes dominated the room. Steel glittered, cooking-pots caught the light, frying-pans hung in comely order, enamel shone like snow—hummock and berg and floe, snow-white and ice-hard—and a red nest of flames, snoring in a gentle draught, was sunk in solid black iron. Ignatius O'Higgins, sometime a petty officer in His Majesty's Navy, was accustomed to think of his kitchen as the heart and brain, the conning-tower, of "The Downy Pelican."

Saturday showed him the Elizabethan menu, explaining this and glossing that, here suggesting a sauce, there reciting a recipe. O'Higgins followed him almost breathlessly.

"Damn my eyes, sir," he said at last, slowly and reverently, "it's a poem, Mr. Keith. A node. That's what it is, sir. A node to the stomach, and I wouldn't swop it for the Lord Mayor's banquet. But, if I may make a suggestion—"

He made half-a-dozen, technical details of supply, matters of culinary convention, professional addenda to Keith's gifted amateurism. They debated a sauce, considered a gravy, settled a salad. "Get to hell out of this, you accidental offspring of a Marine sentry," said O'Higgins abstractedly when the kitchen-boy made an inopportune entrance. "Now this marrow-bone pie, sir. . . ."

Plans were at last completed, battle-orders arranged, and Saturday left O'Higgins with a feeling of confidence. He had spoken to the professor, to van Buren, and to half-a-dozen more. They were all enthusiastic and would be his apostles if necessary. He had put up a notice that the ordinary service, except for grills and such-like simplicities—there was only one vegetarian in "The Pelican"—would be suspended on Saturday night. A polite air of excitement attended on the news. Lady Porlet had offered him a recipe for elderberry wine and was grieved when he reminded her that there was scarcely time to make it. "Then rose-water?" she suggested. "My grandmother's recipe."

"I should like to have that very much indeed," said Keith tactfully.

"I must see if I can remember it," said Lady Porlet, and went away nodding brightly. She felt that she was coming into her own among these tiresomely active, inventive people. She found a chair beside the bowling-green and, closing her eyes, repeated happily: "Queen Anne came to the throne in 1702 and died in 1714. She had fifteen children, most of which were born dead. George the First. 1702 to 1727. George the Second, 1727 to 1760, George the Third, or Farmer George; in his reign the continent of America was discovered. He was a devoted husband and was widely known as The Father of his Family. Then there was either George the Fourth or William the Fourth. I can *never* remember. Though I suppose it didn't matter much to anyone except Queen Victoria. The Diamond Jubilee. . . ."

Lady Porlet let her fancy wander a little. A thrush, hopping cheerfully on the lawn, took her out of her reverie.

"The Cornish Chough," she murmured. "A corvoid bird with black plumage and red legs. Formerly a denizen of the precipitous cliffs of the south coast of England, of Wales, and of the west coast of Ireland, but it is now greatly reduced in numbers."

Her natural history reminiscences were interrupted by a pink and white duster which, escaping from an upper window, fell into the clutches of the breeze and was softly carried to her lap where it lay like a decorous napkin.

"Dear me," said Lady Porlet, and looked up.

Two heads projected from a window, one that of a pretty

red-haired maid, the other—Lady Porlet was sure of it—that of Mr. Keith's friend, young Mr. Cotton. The latter, meeting for an instant the startled eyes of Lady Porlet, quickly withdrew. The maid spoke in a clear, pleasant voice.

"I'm so sorry," she said, "I'll come down and get it."

In a minute she appeared. "It blew out of my fingers," she explained: and held out her hand for the duster which Lady Porlet was examining closely.

"What a very good duster," remarked Lady Porlet. "I wonder where Mr. Keith bought it."

"I think the housekeeper buys them," said Nelly Bly.

"My housekeeper simply won't buy dusters." She looked at it enviously, and gave it up with a sigh.

"Oh," said Lady Porlet suddenly as Nelly Bly turned to go, "was that Mr. Cotton who looked out of the window?"

"Yes. It was his room that it fell from. At least his and Mr. Keith's. They share a room in fact." Nelly Bly spoke rapidly and smiled with the air of one giving an unnecessarily full explanation out of mere politeness. "Good-bye," she said.

"Good-bye," replied Lady Porlet mechanically, and vaguely suspected that she had somehow been cheated of the pertinent facts. Her mind slipped back to the Cornish Chough. "They pair in early Spring and line their nest with pink and white dusters—what nonsense!" she exclaimed indignantly, and sat up very straight and severe.

"Well, you're a fool, aren't you?" said Nelly Bly to Quentin Cotton.

"What did she say?" asked Quentin.

"Nothing much. I told her you slept with Mr. Keith and she seemed to take that as a sign of virtue."

"What a corrupt old woman; she ought to be ashamed of herself."

"You ought to be ashamed of yourself."

"For trying to take advantage of an innocent red-haired girl in his friend's bedroom? In fact for taking advantage." And Quentin, suddenly darting forward, kissed Nelly Bly on her cheek, a corner of her mouth, and an inconsequent segment of her nose.

"That was only a sighting shot," he explained, and prepared to consolidate his position.

During the early part of the previous night he had slept badly, dozing, waking to stare into the darkness and fretfully endeavour to rationalize his relations with Nelly. The attraction of pure-minded chivalry had begun to wane. A Cossack's relict, it somehow seemed, was not so likely to appreciate Arthurian detachment as an unsophisticated orphan would be. Of course she had appealed for it. But then women—nice women—always said, "I'd just as soon have Graves" when they really wanted champagne. She would probably prefer something more exciting than still chivalry. A sparkling chivalry? It was difficult to think of the behaviour appropriate to a mood of sparkling chivalry. When did the knight cease to be a knight and become a cavalier? Quentin wondered. A sophisticated cavalier might follow a temperamental Cossack very acceptably. "Out upon it, I have loved three whole days together!" said the cavalier. "Sonia Soniabitch," said the Cossack, and wept hopelessly. Then he went away to live with Ileana. Nelly Bly would probably appreciate someone who gave his reasons and didn't cry. And to be a cavalier was certainly the more practical thing. He could retain the social graces of the knight and yet have the material pleasures accruing to one of Nature's Cossacks. Quentin sat up in bed and repeated:

"Some bays, perchance, or myrtle bough
  For difference crowns the brow
    Of those kind souls that were
    The noble martyrs here.
  And if that be the only odds,
  (As who can tell?) ye kinder gods,
    Give me the woman here."

Then he fell asleep. Now holding a very stiff and unfriendly Nelly Bly in his arms, he was ready to be the laughing, careless—yet accomplished and gracious—cavalier lover.

Nelly, when he kissed her and grappled, flushed stormy-red and her eyes sparkled frostily. Anyone but a cavalier would have been frightened and let go. But Quentin had the reward of those who follow Suckling. For Nelly, suddenly relaxing, pressed forward, flung her arms round his neck, and clung to him. This was a little unexpected, but Quentin concealed his surprise.

"You have the most beautiful back in the world," he said, peeping darkly down her spine as her dress lifted away from it. He kissed the upper border of her left trapezius muscle.

"Quentin," she whispered. "Quentin. Oh, you have made things so much easier for me. Now I can trust you perfectly and tell you everything."

She kept her face hidden from him but her body trembled as if with an emotion that might be near to sobs. The clear-cut outline of the cavalier began to fade in Quentin's mind beneath an insidious tide of sentiment. She was amazingly desirable; but she seemed smaller than he had thought; and he was beginning to feel protective again. Over her shoulder he caught sight of himself in a mirror. He really did look like Lely's portrait of Wycherley (except for the hair); couldn't he do it justice? With an effort he sent his right hand off pilgrim to Cythera.

Nelly Bly pushed him back and looked at him searchingly, deeply. He found a strangely spiritual quality in her eyes and in her firm and delicate mouth which abashed the cavalier.

"I *can* trust you?" she asked gravely.

"Of course," Quentin said.

"You want to hear? And you will help me?"

He seemed to see the shadow of that damned Cossack in her eyes, but again he said "Of course."

"Without reward?"

Quentin looked uncomfortable. He was fundamentally honest and he hesitated to assert an altruism which he did not entirely feel.

"I may declare a bonus," she said demurely. "No, not now. Someone may come at any moment. Besides, you haven't heard my story yet."

"Then tell me."

"Not here. Will you meet me at eleven o'clock under the trees beside the tennis courts?"

"I will," said Quentin eagerly. Here was mystery and romance, a hundred times better than cold-blooded cavaliering.

With a smile that was radiant kindness, beauty and kindness under a nimbus of red-gold hair, Nelly Bly repeated, "To-night, then," and left him swiftly alone.

Quentin, having read *The Times* for half-an-hour, found that there was nothing in it and decided to have a drink. He discovered Holly alone in the converted buttery staring out of the narrow window that gave a narrow glimpse of the bowling-green, a tree or two, and Lady Porlet. Holly turned round. His eyes were dark and brooding. His thin face was pale. He had the appearance of one persecuted.

"Hullo, Holly. You're looking a bit under the weather this morning," Quentin said to him.

"I have my anxieties, Mr. Cotton," Holly answered in a far-away voice. He jumped, as the door which Quentin had left open suddenly closed with a bang.

"I'd like one of your new cocktails—the light one."

"Very well, sir."

Mournfully Holly prepared it. Quentin sipped it thoughtfully. The silence in the little room grew oppressive. It seemed to contract and draw in the walls. A yellow cat leapt from nowhere on to the outer window-ledge and stared into the buttery. Holly looked at it with a kind of horror. He dabbed his moist forehead with a handkerchief.

"I think I'll have one myself, sir," he said.

"By all means," said Quentin affably. "Have it with me."

"That's Lady Porlet, isn't it?" Holly pointed through the window.

"It is."

Holly considered awhile. Then, "I suppose she's all right, sir?" he asked doubtfully. "I mean trustworthy. She's not one of those fly-by-nights without respect for truth or property or a man's feelings, is she?"

"I should say that she was perfectly trustworthy, Holly." Quentin thought of Lady Porlet smiling placidly, taking a simple pleasure in her food, puzzled by her neighbours but pleased to have neighbours; Lady Porlet in her expensive old-fashioned clothes, silk and a gold locket; inclined to think—or to feel, for she abstained from conscious cerebration—that all the pother and fuss and activity in the world were like nursery noises when the nurse has her afternoon out; Lady Porlet, whom even strangers called "poor dear Lady Porlet," was decidedly not a fly-by-night. Holly must be going off his head.

"What are you worried about?" said Quentin in a kindly voice.

"I'm not exactly worried, sir. Not if she's trustworthy, so to speak. But I lent her a book yesterday which I'm not accustomed to lend to people. It's never been out of my hands before, and you know what it is, sir, when something like that's at stake. You're apt to fret, sir, aren't you? And then there's this matter of the cocktails. They come up to me and say, 'What's in 'em, Holly? How d'you keep 'em blue?' they say. 'Come on, tell us your recipe, Holly!' It's a responsibility you wouldn't believe, sir, unless you had it. I'm the repository of one of 'The Pelican's' dearest secrets. I'm a safe, that's what I am, and they're trying to pick me."

"Surely Lady Porlet isn't trying to get your secret, is she?" Quentin was amused and yet impressed by the evident anxiety which Holly felt. He really looked like a man with a secret, Quentin thought. Or a political minority man in hiding; a fugitive; like a Russian, perhaps, in fear of the Red Terror.

"She did ask me how I made 'em," said Holly slowly. "But I said, 'No ma'am, not to the Queen of England would I tell what's a secret between me and Mr. Keith.' And then the gentlemen come in and say, 'Why, Holly, you're quite an inventor! How did you do it?' Of course I'm an inventor! Don't I know that as well as them? But an inventor doesn't tell his secrets to anyone who asks him, does he? Edison didn't, and Mrs. Curie didn't, and Mr. van Buren doesn't—he's an inventor too, they say."

Holly wiped his damp forehead and shook two more cocktails.

"Like wildflowers, aren't they?" he said. "Don't they smell like the Spring? I'll tell you this, Mr. Cotton, I was so frightened I'd forget the ingredients myself—like Ruskin, sir, with his forgetting to say 'Open, Sesame,'—that I had to write them down. All the exact proportions and that. Of course it adds to the risk. But we mortals, we suck in danger with our mother's milk, so where's the odds?"

Holly took a sheet of much-folded notepaper from his waistcoat pocket, read it, considered a moment or two, and then locked it away in a drawer beneath the bar.

"Sometimes I keep it in one place, sometimes in another," he explained, "according as I'm in a mood to think about pickpockets or safebreakers. And now what'll I do with the key of the drawer?"

"Well, I'm not surprised that people want to see your recipe," said Quentin.

"Ah, they all want to. Her, out there, and the gentlemen, and the Boots comes in and says, 'Give you ten bob for the missing word, Holly.' Ten bob! And he's not the worst. Nor the gentlemen isn't. It's that red-haired Cleopatrer, Ninong de Lengclose, Madame Pompadore. In she comes and leans across the bar and looks into my face, seductive like, and 'Be a sport,' she says. 'Tell me the truth,' she says. 'Spill the beans, Holly old man!' Her with her red hair and her baby eyes! Do you know what I said to her?"

"Said to whom? Who's been trying to lead you astray like this?"

"You may well say 'lead me astray,' sir. But I wasn't having any. I stood up and I looked her in her eyes—green as French beans they are. Twice she's been at me, Mr. Cotton. But I didn't yield, no not an inch. And do you know what I said to her? 'No, Messaliner!' That's what I said to her. 'Messaliner!'"

"But who is she, Holly? I should like to see her."

"Oh, you wouldn't know her, sir. She's got red hair."

"That, surely, isn't a serious barrier—"

Colonel Waterhouse and Sir Philip Betts came in and Quentin's curiosity remained unsatisfied. Holly made no more revelations. But as Quentin finished his drink he whispered hoarsely, "She's a holy terror, sir," and nodded with much significance.

CHAPTER VIII

Nature, the thief, had crept once again into the province of art. She does it so often, as if a dancing trollop who had posed for Degas should pose for herself as a bunch of luminous frills; as if an orchard should crowd into delicate sunlight and smile "This is just like Monet"; as if a priest should starve, rack himself, get jaundice, squint round a corner, dress in yellow satin, and put a label across his belly, "After El Greco." Nature has no conscience. You may walk at night by a river-bank towards a dim-seen bridge; shadows converge to a distant point, broken a little by streaks of grey; but a dull, lop-sided mass hangs dismally on your right hand; and then suddenly a cottage window is lighted up, the mass is broken, and harmonious composition is detestably revealed. Or you climb a hill that looks from the bottom nothing but a pointed hill, and half-way up a fir tree creeps into the sky. The sides of the hill point upwards, the spear-blade fir tree soars, and finally the clouds split significantly to repeat the climbing lines of the hill and, dismayed, you see in front of you not Nature but a patterned, pyramidal thing that only wants a gold frame to take it to the Academy. Even sheep abhor an artistic vacuum and file instinctively to that corner of a field where an artist would have them. And geese flying across the moon fly as a Chinese painter has taught them. There is nothing natural in Nature. She in her own way paints, powders, hangs a jewel in her ear, and puts a rose between her sophisticated lips.

She had just done it again.

Joan Benbow, driving ambitiously, had watched her ball land, leap forward in a series of diminishing arcs, and come to rest in Hibbett's Hole. (Hibbett was a Victorian golfer, one of John Company's colonels, who died in harness, his enlarged spleen bursting almost simultaneously with a good niblick in the bunker now called after him.) And now Joan was the centre of one of Nature's artistic supplements.

The opposing edge of the bunker rose in a steep crescent, sand lipped with green turf. To her left were two smallish, slender trees, the inner one taller than the outer. Beyond the bunker grew an oak whose leafy branches showed like a crown above the centre of the crescent. To the right and farther away a poplar gracefully soared. Behind the trees was blue sky. A white diagonal slant of cloud pointed upwards, towards the poplar, and roughly in the direction of the seventh green. Between Joan and Saturday—he stood behind and to her right—a rising slope repeated the left-hand side of the crescent, while the far slant of cloud, resting like an inclined plane on the two smaller trees and the top of the oak, held his eyes to the obtuse-angled triangle of which it was the longest side. A tilted triangle, Joan its focus of interest, lines that pointed to the open apex, and Joan also intent on that direction since it was there that the seventh green lay.

Once, twice, and again she swung with savage grace. Her ball sank deeper, moved a sluggish inch, leapt like a trout into the air and returned to its snug hole. Saturday felt that he could stand and watch her all day trying to get out of this magnificent picture. Her club traced lines of transient beauty in the air. Those graceful arcs—if they had not been blocked by the dense and impenetrable sand—would have released their shafts of energy in the precise direction of the apex of the triangle. Statically and dynamically the picture was right.

"Try again," he encouraged. "There's very fine sand in that bunker. The Romans thought a lot of it when they were building round about here."

"The Romans didn't play golf," said Joan shortly. The colours were good too, though he had thought Joan's dress a little bright at first; a kind of silk jersey with a skirt of the same stuff, a yellow jersey scored with a multitude of thin, short, broken, parallel red lines very close to each other, like basket-work, so that the whole impression was that of a splendid orange. Light grew to her as the lines of the picture sprang away. Green trees and turf, blue sky, the white slant of cloud, and on the foreground of convenient sand a glittering orange Joan.

"Splendid!" he said, as she hit her ball to the hard face of the bunker, from where it returned to its original position.

"Your hole," said Joan, and stooped to pick up.

"No, don't go," Saturday pleaded.

"Why not?"

"You'll spoil the picture. You're just right where you are."

"In a bunker? That isn't a compliment to my golf."

"There's more in golf than hitting a good ball. That sort of golf is only the reflection of one narrow facet of essential golfishness. Behind golf there is a wonderful abstraction, Golf, which shows itself in gulleys, gulches, wild flowers in the rough, lost balls forgotten and dying in impenetrable jungle, rain, wind, cirrus clouds and cumuli, Constable landscapes, orange ladies in sandy bunkers, a significant tree, the lyrical prose of a *Times* golfing correspondent, all the history of St. Andrews, turf growing into a magic carpet, craning spectators and intrusive worm-casts, the worms themselves—there's a constant underground pilgrimage from the subterrene desert of a fairway to the rich Mecca of the greens—and think of hickory forests growing to their conscious destiny in the shaft of a club, or iron-ore bursting the rock in its eagerness to be smelted and forged into a trim putter. And many other things."

"It's a good thing the course is almost empty today."

Joan sat down on the green slope beside Saturday and examined a cruel scar on her ball.

Neither of them spoke. Saturday's freshet of talk mysteriously died as Joan came within touching distance. Joan, with her head bent, looked at her wounded ball. Saturday filled his pipe and lit it. White clouds sailed slowly over a calm sky. The trees stood still. There was no one in sight.

"By the way," said Saturday, and Joan at the same moment said, "Do you think—"

"Yes?" they said together, each waiting for the other.

"Your honour," said Keith.

"I wasn't going to say anything in particular."

"I wasn't either. Thoughts that do lie."

"Too deep for tears?"

"No, just thoughts that do lie. They lied when they made me feel I was going to say something."

"And mine were too small to speak for themselves."

"Then speak for them."

"They've gone to bed again. They just woke up because everything was so quiet, and thought they would like to come downstairs. But they were really much too young."

"It's a pity not to encourage them."

"But we're supposed to be playing golf, aren't we?"

"I've already told you that golf includes so many things."

"But you must use your clubs occasionally."

"Yes, I suppose so. It's very quiet, isn't it?"

"Come on." Joan got to her feet, walked resolutely for five yards, stopped and turned. Saturday had also risen. They walked to the next tee.

The fairway ran for four hundred yards along a belt of woodland. Saturday drove and watched his ball rise on a long straight slant; then in mid-flight an impish bias took it curling ever so prettily, smoothly and leisurely it seemed, towards the wood. It curved still more, and drooped, and fell with a tiny crash among the trees. It was a perfect slice.

"Bad luck," said Joan.

She teed her ball, looked towards the distant flag, swung strongly, and hit. Her driving was generally accurate. From the tee and other fair places she played well. Only in difficulties did she grow savage and unskilful. But this time, by carelessness, by freak of fortune, by some magnetic tremor, by the sudden perversity of a well-behaved driver, who knows?—she took a line grossly divergent from the main axis of the hole and her ball flew straight for the point to which Saturday's boomerang shot had returned.

"Too bad," said Saturday.

They plunged into the wood together.

"We'll never find them," said Joan.

They searched, not arduously, here and there; prodding and poking beneath a fallen branch, gently laying back a flower or two, slashing reasonably at a nettle. The leaf-reflected light was pleasant and cooler than the unmitigated sunlight of the fairway; as if they had stepped off a pearling schooner and gently dropped into a clear green lagoon where stones looked different and weeds grew splendidly and tall. And then, when they least expected them, there were the pearls, one with a little red spot, the other with a black, lying close to each other beside an uprooted tree.

"How funny to find them together like that," said Joan.

Saturday carefully hung his clubs on a projecting branch, put his hands in his pockets, and considered the balls that lay side by side. Then he said slowly, "I wonder if you would care to marry me?"

"Yes," answered Joan, "—no, I mean *no*. I'm sure I wouldn't. That is—. Why do you ask me?"

"For the ordinary reason, I suppose," said Saturday.

"I don't think that's very nice of you."

"It used to be considered a compliment."

Joan felt a nervous impulse to laugh and an impulse, almost equally strong, to be entirely serious and throw her arms round Saturday's neck. But this, she decided, would be both stupid and forward. She also felt an elemental desire to run away and an equally elemental desire to stay where she was. She thought how pleasant and simple it would be if she could faint; but she had never felt less like fainting in her life. Allowing for certain obvious discrepancies her emotions were not unlike those she generally experienced during the third act of a drama by Mr. Edgar Wallace. So, playing for time, half hoping for the curtain and half dreading it, she sat on the trunk of the conveniently fallen tree and said, "I hardly know you yet."

"But think what a chance to get acquainted I am offering you," said Saturday, brightening a little.

"It's rather like going inside the cage to get a good view of the lions."

"Joan," said Saturday, pleading. Before she could move, if she had made up her mind to move, he was beside her and had taken her hands. Like an advancing billow, as Meredith puts it, the gulf of a caress hove in view.

"No," said Joan, struggling. "I'm not going to kiss you. I'm not going to. I haven't had time to think. And besides, it's so early. It isn't four o'clock. . . ."

She flushed and began to giggle. Saturday looked at her with some astonishment, and also laughed. He saw a kind of inspired foolishness in her last remark. Joan, laughing helplessly and very embarrassed, tried to get up, but Saturday held her.

"Do you start at four o'clock?" he asked.

"No," she snapped, "I don't start at all."

"Then let me—"

She pushed him away and said in a tone of remarkable decision, "I'm not going to marry you. I haven't the faintest intention of marrying you. I shall never marry you. Is that perfectly clear?"

"But even if you don't marry me. . . ." Again the billow heaved aloft.

"I suppose you're not used to opposition?"

The billow sank dejectedly without engulfing anything at all, and Saturday asked, "What do you mean?"

"It's fairly obvious, isn't it?"

"I don't think this is an occasion for quarrelling."

Joan was uncertain whether Saturday was offended or not. Saturday was not very sure himself. He had an idea that something unpleasant was on the horizon and he thought it might be as well to play for safety, though Joan's proximity was an increasing temptation to go straight ahead and risk the storm.

Joan stripped a piece of bark off the tree-trunk and tried to polish her nails with the smooth inner surface. "I saw all three Boat Races that you rowed in," she said.

"Enjoy them?"

"I might have enjoyed them more."

Saturday looked cheerful.

"There's always such a crowd. I'm not very fond of crowds. Are you?"

"Yes," said Saturday glumly.

Joan laughed, and reaching forward pulled off the horn-rimmed spectacles he wore.

"Here, what are you doing?" Saturday protested.

"You looked so silly, sulking behind these things. You looked like your photograph in the *Daily Day* the morning after the race. Dying in the last ditch. Though you couldn't row in a ditch, could you? You look quite nice now. You're like a portrait I've seen somewhere. I can't remember where."

"I wish you wouldn't be stupid. Do give me my spectacles. I can't see you without them. And I'm not a bit like any picture anywhere."

"You are. It's in the British Museum."

"A mummy, I suppose, or an Aztec, or a Solomon Islander. I don't think you're being funny at all."

"I was thinking of a very handsome portrait; Goya's drawing of Wellington, when Wellington was a young man. You haven't so much nose, of course, but you've got his ingenuous arched eyebrows and rather surprised eyes, and his indignant chin—"

"Do be quiet and give me back my spectacles."

Joan leapt up, still holding his glasses. Saturday's pursuit was delayed by tripping over one branch and running his head into another.

"And your hair is just like his. He looks as though he had been in prison not long before," Joan mocked. But her mocking was her undoing, for she halted to complete her sentence, and Saturday's hand, which was unnecessarily large, shot out and caught her.

"Now," he said, and first adjusting his spectacles, kissed her soundly.

"Let me go," she gasped.

"Then will you marry me?"

"No!"

"But why?"

"For a dozen reasons. And one of them is Mrs. Travers and another is Priscilla Littlejohn."

"Good God," said Saturday, and limply loosed his hold. "Who the hell—. I'm sorry. Who the devil told you about them?"

"Then it is true? I thought perhaps, when Mrs. Waterhouse mentioned them—"

"That old trout."

"I like her. I think she's a dear. Anyway she seems to speak the truth!"

"What does it matter even if she does?"

"It matters a lot, as you've asked me to marry you."

"But it doesn't matter a jot, since you've refused to." Saturday stuck his hands in his pockets and smiled triumphantly down at Joan. Joan turned red and pale again, her eyes sparkled, her mouth half-opened and shut again, and she mastered her inclination to say "You utter pig!"

Instead she remarked coldly, "Of course if you're content to accept my refusal, so much the better. Shall we go now?"

Saturday frowned. His momentary triumph turned into disaster. Then, like a guerilla general, he decided to ignore the repulse.

"Not yet," he answered. "I want to know when you're going to marry me."

"Mrs. Travers might forbid the banns."

"Confound Mrs. Travers."

"Then Priscilla Littlejohn might."

"Oh, damn it, Joan, won't you believe me when I say that neither of them matters one jot or tittle or scrap or penn'orth of dried corn?"

"Then why did you make love to them? For the same reason you make love to me? Is it a habit of yours to ask people to marry you?"

"Good Lord, I never asked them—her—any of them to marry me!"

"But you should have asked them—her—all of them, probably."

"But I didn't."

"Does that make any difference?"

"It makes all the difference in the world. I never dreamt of marrying them, any of them, and I've never dreamt of doing anything else but marry you."

"You've only know me for two days," Joan said. "Anyone can dream for two days."

Saturday looked at her unhappily. Joan considered the mess she had made on her finger-nails with the piece of bark.

"Look at my nails," she said. "Aren't they dreadful? All green."

Saturday took her hands.

"But they do matter," Joan repeated. "Mrs. Travers and all those other women."

"How do they matter? Be honest and tell me how they matter."

"I don't quite know," Joan admitted weakly. "But I'm not going to let you kiss me again," she added as Saturday once more began to look triumphant, "and I may never let you."

"Not even when we're married?"

"You won't want to then."

"So we are going to be married?"

"Certainly not, if you'll never want to kiss me afterwards."

"But I didn't say—"

"You did. Or at any rate you tacitly admitted it."

Keith sat down and took his head between his hands "It's going round and round," he said.

"That serves you right for losing it so often." Joan caught up her clubs, and before Saturday could stop her walked out of the wood to the sunny fairway.

Saturday retrieved the two balls which lay forgotten and followed her. He threw the balls on to the grass, and when Joan had hit hers straight and true with a brassie, he followed with an iron, so that again they lay together. Then he said amicably, "I shall speak to your father to-night."

Joan made no answer, mis-hit her next shot abominably, and began to cry.

"Oh, damn," said Saturday, dropping everything and hugging her unhandily, clubs and all. "Joan," he added miserably, "oh, hell, don't cry, Joan. Damn it, I'm sorry, dear, I didn't mean to swear. Joan! I'm a clumsy brute but I do love you."

"I'm not crying," said Joan, sniffing against the breast of his coat. "I—I—inff!—I'm not crying really."

"Of course you're not," Saturday confirmed, kissing what he could reach.

"And father won't know what on earth to say."

"Of course he won't."

"And, and—inff!—I believe there's someone behind us!"

A stentorian shout of "Fore!" a brazen voice expelled from titanic lungs through the throat, it seemed, of a sergeant-major, made them spring apart, Joan to dab her eyes, Saturday to glare defiantly at the approaching golfers.

They played the next two holes at a feverish pace, conscious of a too-knowing audience pressing towards them, and at the tenth decided that it was time to return to "The Pelican."

CHAPTER IX

Mr. van Buren looked round his sitting-room with a vague feeling of apprehension. He walked heavily to the writing-table—a solid unimaginative piece of furniture—and tried one of its six drawers. It was locked. Van Buren took a bunch of keys out of his pocket, unlocked it, and looked thoughtfully at the black leather portfolio which lay inside. He lifted the portfolio and examined it: pages of close-written notes, pages of formulae, neatly drawn diagrams. It seemed intact. He put it back in the drawer and looked round the room.

It was a small room, furnished with a couple of leather-covered arm-chairs, a little table in front of the fire-place, a book-case along one wall of which half the shelves were empty and the other half full of bound volumes of *Punch, The Gentleman's Magazine, Bell's Life, Jorrockses,* and so on; and at the window a massive desk or writing-table with three drawers at either side of the space left for the writer's legs. A picture or two, a bowl of flowers, looped-up dull yellow curtains, some magazines on the table, a brass pen-tray and a few letters on the desk. Mr. van Buren looked from one to the other and felt uneasy that someone had been in the room since he left it.

There was no apparent disorder. No robustious burglar had scattered his belongings like a whirlwind. But a dog knows when another dog has been in its kennel, and Mr. van Buren had a nose. He sniffed the tainted air.

"It wasn't a maid," he said to himself, "for a maid leaves a room looking as though it hadn't been lived in for a month. Someone has been looking at those letters. They're not lying naturally, and they're not stacked up as a maid would have left them. The drawer, now. . . ."

He felt the undercut finger-hold on the important drawer. It moved a little as he pulled it. The drawer was loose and slid, though locked, in and out perhaps a quarter of an inch. It was an old lock. He remembered that he had pushed it in with a little jerk before unlocking it a moment ago. It looked as though someone had tried it, pulled it to see if it was fastened. He him-

self, the last time he locked it, had probably pushed it home.
Probably, he thought; but he could not be certain.

He examined the other drawers. Most of them were empty.
None was locked. One or two contained unimportant letters, a
file of business press-cuttings, some company prospectuses. It
was difficult to say if they had been tampered with.

Perhaps I'm getting fidgety, he thought. I ought to get rid of
these papers. But I can't very well till next week when Hayward comes back. He's got to see them first. Hell, they're all
right here. This is as safe a place as there is in England, and all
England's pretty safe.

He looked out of the window that opened on to the bowling-
green he had just left. Elms untouched by age and green turf
nourished by it. Tennis-courts. And a glimpse of farm-house
roofs in the distance. Cattle and a man walking slowly through
a field.

Old van Buren scratched his leathery wrinkled cheek and
muttered, "Safe! It's dreaming-safe. It hasn't woken up yet.
And I've carried a gun in a he-country and felt pretty good.
Packed a gun wherever tailors put pockets or men could think
of. Safe? Good God, I must be getting old."

He went down to dinner comfortably enough, having assured himself that there was no cause for alarm, and after dinner settled himself beside Professor Benbow in a corner of the
smoking-room. Wesson sat a little distance away, still behind
his enormous folio. Wesson had talked old books to Sir Philip
Betts, who hated reading; to Jean Forbes, who disliked Wesson; to Sigismund Telfer, who believed only in new books; to
Jacquetta Telfer, who preferred maps; to Colonel Waterhouse,
who wasn't interested; and to Lady Porlet, who thought it a sin
and a shame to pay hundreds of pounds for dusty volumes that
nobody read when the ceilings of the London hospitals were
all falling down on top of poor patients with cancer and tumours of one kind or another—perfectly enormous tumours;
her cook's sister-in-law had had one and a piece of the ceiling
had fallen and hit her exactly on the place out of which the
surgeons had just removed it—all because they couldn't afford
to plaster them properly.

Mr. Wesson was widely regarded as a bore then, and his facile remarks on first editions were earnestly avoided. But he seemed happy enough behind his Prior. Or he might have been sleeping.

Van Buren and the professor, with sixty years, sixteen stones, and a liberal habit of mind in common, had become sound friends.

Old Benbow talked about books and men and submarines; old van Buren talked of everything between the Missouri and the Shatt-el-Arab, going either way. For years he had been interested in oil. Half-a-dozen of his inventions had expedited its passage from holes in the ground to the petrol pumps which give motorists their idea of scenery. He had known mining camps in his youth, and old Benbow groaned when he spoke of brazen days in the sun and wilder nights lit fantastically by pistol-flashes.

"And I have given my nights and days to books!" he said. "Gone whoring after strange women on paper and fought rogues in buckram."

"Well," said van Burem, "so long as they were good books I don't see what you have to regret. A good book's better than a desert to work in and gunplay is no more manly than writing a life of Shakespeare. Not to mention Wordsworth. I'll say it takes a real man to read Wordsworth and keep awake. There was a boy in Arizona once who tamed a whole camp by reading Peter Bell to them. They were tough, too. But one night he got his book and he just read, and read, and read. Nothing could stop him. He just went on, and strong men were crying before he'd half finished. Crying for him to stop. They shot up the ground about his feet, but nobody liked to shoot right at him when he only had a book in his hand. And he just read on. There was no spunk left in the whole camp when he'd finished, and after that there wasn't a soul who wouldn't rather see a two-gun man-killer ride into camp, than that boy pulling his Wordsworth."

"You're a Job's comforter, van Buren."

"I wonder if there was oil in Job's country? When he says 'My days are swifter than a weaver's shuttle and are spent without hope,' he sounds mighty like a prospector who's coming to the end of his coffee and beans."

"He also says 'They grope in the dark without light,' which is a direct incentive to go on prospecting. Is your new discovery going to dispossess the oil fields?"

"It may set your dying coal-mines to more economic work," said van Buren. "Have you ever heard of the hydrogenation of coal?"

"Never," answered Professor Benbow. "To my knowledge it hasn't once been mentioned by the whole body of critics."

"Well, that's what I'm going to do if I can persuade some of your fool coal-owners to see farther than their noses—and there's nothing like flashing the promise of a few million dollars in the air to make a man look up. You know Hayward?"

"I have heard of him."

"I'm seeing him next week. He knows that coal is carbon—or he ought to—and when you hydrogenate carbon it liquefies, and the liquid is a kind of artificial petroleum. Then you fractionate your petroleum and you get gasoline. It's not altogether a new idea, but the way I propose to do it is new. I mean to hydrogenate the coal without mining it. I've worked out the costs of production, checked them and proved them, and my gasoline won't cost—"

Van Buren looked round. The large-paper folio of Prior's *Poems on Several Occasions* had descended an inch or two, and over the top of it Mr. Wesson's curious eyes stared fixedly through his curious eyeglasses.

"You interested?" asked van Buren.

"I beg your pardon?" said Mr. Wesson. "I'm afraid my attention wandered for a moment. I was considering a passage here which seems a little obscure. Apparently the reference—"

"I thought you were considering my little lecture on oil."

"On *oil*? No, I know nothing about oil."

Van Buren growled and drank his whisky.

"Have another," said the professor, and rang a bell.

Van Buren continued to grumble and the professor said consolingly, "When I was a young man I used to make tremendous literary discoveries. They were of two kinds. I either found that my theories were already common knowledge, or that for some reason which I had completely overlooked they were quite untenable. In the latter class there is one whose memory I cherish. It was that Bacon cribbed his Essays from a notebook of Shakespeare's which he had picked up in a tavern."

Mr. Wesson closed his book and stood up. With an ingenuous smile he said to van Buren, "I've just remembered that I do know something about oil. A barber once gave me the prescription for an oil shampoo—I was getting a little bald on the crown—and it did my hair a lot of good. But perhaps it wasn't olive oil that you were talking about?"

"It wasn't," said van Buren gruffly.

"Then my little bit of information has been wasted," said Mr. Wesson sadly. He left the room with his heavy book under his left arm and stooping a little to that side.

"Sheer impudence?" asked van Buren.

"I think so," answered the professor. "Come and sit down," he called to Saturday and Quentin, who stood for a moment at the open door. "Come and talk to us. We're getting quarrelsome."

"What shall we talk about?" asked Quentin. "The most momentous things have been happening to-day."

"Keep off it," said Saturday in a fierce aside.

"Of anything you please except modern art," replied the professor.

"But that's just what I want to tell you about," said Quentin. "Have you heard of the scandal at the Milieu Galleries? There was a sculpture exhibition there last week and quite the best thing was a nude by that new fellow, Laparotumi. A nice fat girl sitting with one leg tucked under her looking stonily at a flower which Laparotumi had forgotten to finish. A very fat girl. Significant fat, you know, in rolls and unseemly bulges. Pneumatic cheeks and no forehead. A girl, in fact, with no personal appeal except to a masseur. And so naked. Well, on the opening day there were swarms of people clustered round it, all staring with utter horror at the label, which said, 'Portrait of the Artist's Mother.' And now everybody calls Laparotumi Oedipus, and he has sent a challenge to Réné Calcule, who is known to have been jealous because his nude—he had one too, of course—wasn't nearly as nude and not half so fat as Laparotumi's. Laparotumi thinks that it was Réné who stuck on the 'Mother' label," Quentin explained.

"That's worth a drink, Mr. Cotton." Van Buren rang the bell.

"It's curious," said the professor, "I never see a fat woman nowadays except in modern pictures and modern sculpture."

"That's how art balances life."

"The last revue I saw," said van Buren, "had a chorus that looked like alimony on a cold night."

"Have you seen *The Ghoul*? There's a fat woman in it who goes mad in a lonely house at midnight because she hears noises in the chimney."

"Frightening?"

"Positively diuretic."

"Do we really hate ourselves?" asked the professor. "Our most popular dramatists are those who frighten us most effectively. Our wealthiest novelists prove that we are Babbitts or perverts. Our most highly praised artists caricature us. Our almost-best living poet (no one can touch Bridges) is Housman. Our favourite doctors starve us. And we flatter the philosophers who condemn life to a geological prospect of unrelieved futility."

"That's a dismal catalogue, professor," said van Buren.

"It isn't so bad as it sounds," said Keith. "'The Spartans on the sea-wet rock sat down and combed their hair.'"

"It's better than ever it was before," added Quentin. "We face facts nowadays, however unpleasant they are. We accept lead as lead, death as real and inevitable, and don't waste our time looking for the Philosopher's Stone."

"Voronoff has found it," said the professor. "In a monkey."

Saturday moved uncomfortably. The conversation, he thought, was one that might go on indefinitely. It didn't seem the kind of conversation that started with an end in view and finished in an orderly manner when it reached that end. Van Buren looked as though he were going to tell a story. And stories were as prolific as rabbits. Saturday wanted to talk privately to the professor. He wanted the professor to be in a solemn and yet kindly mood when he talked to him. A wise, benevolent mood. And now van Buren was telling a story. A story about Mexico. But the point would be equally apparent in Manchester. And the professor, his face like a blacksmith's forge, ruddy and good to look at, was laughing with indecorous joy. It wasn't the atmosphere in which to discuss a virgin sought in marriage.

Another story. And the professor's laughter like a westerly gale. Quentin talking about romance—how had he dragged it in?—as the product of adventurous realism in literature. Conrad. And the new German school.

"Think of Russia," said Quentin. "There have been wilder adventures in Russia during the last twelve years than anything since Troy. Treat them realistically, say what people actually did and felt, manage your story so as to give form to the events and relate them with proper regard for a climax—use art, that is—and you'll get something with all the glamour that the romantic reader wants, and yet preserve the truth that more exacting critics demand. I've burnt the first chapters of my new novel and I'm going to try something different."

"You don't look very interested," Professor Benbow said to Saturday.

"There's something I want to discuss with you; something important."

"Your new poem?" asked the professor suspiciously.

"No, nothing like that."

"This dinner to-morrow night?"

"Not that either. It's a personal matter."

"God save us. Let me finish my drink first."

"Don't hurry," Quentin interjected. "Mr. van Buren and I are going to play bridge with Jean Forbes and her mother. I'll see you later, Saturday."

"Well?" said the professor when they were alone.

"I asked Joan to marry me to-day," said Saturday.

"The devil you did! I saw a dewy look in your eye when you started out this afternoon. Well, I hope she refused you?"

"As a matter of fact she didn't," said Saturday coldly.

"Then the girl's a fool. No, I didn't mean that. Sit down,

Keith, sit down. I'm getting old and you mustn't pay too much attention to what old men say. I've got nothing against you as a man. To be frank about it, I think you're a very good fellow. But as a poet I don't rate you very high, and as a son-in-law I fancy you still less."

"If you insist on having a major poet for a son-in-law, Joan's chances of getting married aren't worth much."

"You don't see my point. If a man of whom I think highly sets out to be a doctor, a soldier, or an architect, I expect him to become a good doctor or a good soldier or a good architect. Well, you set out to be a poet. You have written some good lines, even a good poem or two, but are you a good poet? Have you succeeded in your chosen line sufficiently to make me think favourably of you as a prospective son-in-law?"

"At present I am a publican rather than a poet, and whatever the value of my poetry may be, my pub-keeping has been fairly successful. Lady Mercy Cotton is pleased. I have a good salary—"

"Now wait a minute, Keith. I told you a moment ago that I was getting old. Let me tell you some other unpleasant things about myself. I am a snob, as most of us are. I am a hypocrite, as more of us are. And I am at times a liar—as we all are. I like to pose as a Philistine. I like to pooh-pooh my gods. But what I am saying now is neither hypocrisy nor lying. I have spent the greater part of my life trying to impress young men with the value, the interest, the almost incredible beauty of English literature. Sometimes I speak hard things about my profession. I sin my mercies, as the Scots say, and get a lot of enjoyment out of miscalling my trade. But the fact remains that I teach, or try to teach, the matter and methods of literature because I whole-heartedly believe in them and admire them. A professor on holiday may say a publican is a better creature than a poet, but holidays are the smaller part of the year. I like a good publican in theory or impersonally, but to be a successful publican—I admitted that I was a snob—is not in my opinion the best qualification for a candidature such as yours."

Saturday stared angrily at the professor, and the professor, solid and red and serious stared back at him. There was a patch of crimson, the size of a shilling, on Saturday's cheekbones.

His chin stuck out and his eyes, behind their spectacles, were stormy.

He said shortly: "My profession is my own choice, and if Joan doesn't object to it I don't see why you should."

"Joan can't see your profession through you. You stand in its light. But I'm not Joan, and my liking for you—I admit that I like you; you rowed three excellent races, though luck was dead against you—my liking for you doesn't dazzle me. You're a publican and I'm a snob, and there's the ineluctable antipathy. Now if you were a better poet than a publican—if the pub were only an amusing pendant to your poetry, a humorous recognition that even poets must live—my objections would vanish. But at present you're a publican who writes verses in his spare time."

"And Joan is her own mistress."

"In theory. In fact she is my youngest child."

"So you propose to use round-the-corner tyranny? You mean to exploit her natural affection for you as a barrier to her growing affection for me?"

"You can add selfishness to my other faults if you like."

"By God, I do!"

"Come, come. You must admit that I have a very direct interest in this matter. As I have said, if your poetry—"

"You know nothing about my poetry. You pat me on the head and laugh at it. You haven't seen—you haven't asked to see—my new poem. You don't know what it's like. But I do. And I know that it's good. It's damned good!"

"If the opinion of competent critics and the judgment of ordinary readers prove to be the same as your own—"

"*Vox populi vox dei!*"

"A very fair statement when it comes to poetry. The poets most generally accredited great are most often the greatest in actual fact. You can find exceptions, of course. But if England says with no uncertain voice that your new poem is a great poem, I shall not contradict her. If a man can say something that stirs the mind of a country the odds are, I think, that he is a poet. So there is your chance. What, by the way, do your publishers say of the book?"

"They haven't seen it yet."

"Oh! So your opinion is entirely an individual one?"

"Yes."

"Well, Keith, suppose we postpone this discussion for a few months till your book is published, and then we can resume it on the lines I have indicated. After all, you have known Joan for only two days. Your own views, as well as hers, may change."

Saturday laughed shortly. "I know my own mind," he said. "There aren't many things in life you can be sure of, but this is one. I love her."

"I too," said the professor gently.

Saturday stared moodily at the table and said nothing.

"Shall we declare an armistice then, or a moratorium? I don't wish to quarrel with my host."

"And I don't want to be condemned to an infinity of doubt."

"Is a few months infinity?"

"And meanwhile?"

"Meanwhile I shall say nothing to Joan unless she asks me, and then I will repeat what I have already told you. I trust you not to do anything rash or stupid or dishonourable, such as persuading her to run away, which she might afterwards regret. Law and order are the greatest comforts of civilization."

"It isn't an altogether satisfactory arrangement."

"There is nothing wrong with it from your point of view, if you have faith in your new poem. It is I who am making concessions, I who am gambling. And now let us have a drink together before joining the others."

"I'm afraid I was rather rude to you at one point," said Saturday slowly.

"A good fault in some circumstances; I say that to excuse myself. Whisky and soda, waiter. Large ones."

CHAPTER X

It was one minute past eleven. Quentin hurried soft-footed over the lawn towards the dark rampart of trees. They loomed above him, inky boles and a black lattice of leaves and branches. A gibbous moon sat unsteadily on the topmost branch of all.

He was late. The rubber had dragged its slow length along until Quentin, in desperation, despatched it with the ruthless sacrifice of two good tricks. "Imbecile!" his partner hissed. "*Quem deus vult perdere prius dementat*," Quentin replied with a hollow laugh, and left the room looking, he hoped, like the fore-shadow of a baccarat suicide. Eleven had struck. His expression changed to that of the adventurer. He raced along the corridor, down a broad flight of stairs, round the corner, through a creaking door, on to the bowling-green and over the dewy grass to the trees under which Nelly Bly was waiting.

She wasn't there. Quentin stalked from tree to tree, peering round the trunk of one, looking forward to another. No one was there. He frowned—a wasted frown—and leaned against the nearest elm hands in pockets, prepared to wait. Punctuality, he felt, was the prerequisite of plotters. But women will keep their dressmakers waiting . . . in any case there was no plot about it . . . she was going to tell him about herself and her Cossack; and all her difficulties . . . and he was going to help her with wise words, comfort her with the assurance that she had a trusty friend . . . a friend who was something between an elder brother and a light-hearted cavalier . . . and incidentally a novelist who was about to explore a new field of romantic realism . . . his next novel (when he had decided what to write about) might be dedicated to N.B., A Victim of Russian Circumstance.

Quentin started. A hand as soft as moth-wings lay on his sleeve.

"You're late," he said.

"And you are dreaming. Is this how you keep watch? I walked right up to you before you saw me."

"I thought you were a moonbeam," said Quentin pleasantly. Nelly Bly wore a long white coat of the kind that tennis-

players wear, and in the moonlight she looked even more alluring than in her apple-green costume of the daytime. Her
hair was like amber exquisitely touched with bronze in that
candid opalescence, and her eyes—

"Malachite in argentine," said Quentin. "Beryls in a frosted
mist. Green river-secrets. Do you think I am going mad?"

"No. You're talking about my eyes, aren't you?"

"But how did you know?"

"Do you think no one else has ever noticed them?"

"You torture me," he said.

Moon-shadows dappled the world and Quentin forgot the
explicit purpose of their tryst. Men have such a multitude of
purposes and Nature, more resolute than an English sailor,
more cynical than a French wit, has only one. And Nature, like
an advertising expert, seeks to effect her solitary purpose by
the mediation of beauty.

"No," said Nelly, gently pushing him away. "We came here
to talk. You promised to listen to me so that you could learn
how to help me."

"In any way I can."

"It's so complicated a story. Some of it you will never understand. To think that it should come here, to little Downish, a
story that began in Irkutsk!"

"Irkutsk?" asked Quentin.

"Irkutsk," replied Nelly gravely.

"There's a seat behind this tree," said Quentin.

The wooden seat with its back to the trees, on which visitors
sometimes sat to watch other visitors play tennis, sparkled with
dew. Quentin mopped it as well as he could with his handkerchief and they sat down with six inches of half-dried boards
between them.

"In Irkutsk," said Nelly slowly. "A foggy evening when
the town was lost in a sea of impenetrable vapour. The lamps
were drowned in it. Men moved through it like shadows.
And the shouting of drosky-drivers, the jingle of harness,
seemed strangely muffled. Boris was there on a mission for the
Komintern."

"Boris?"

"My husband."

careering through the fog, the mad clatter of hooves, the thunder of wheels and the heavy drag of his body behind. A savage mujik thrashing his horses, rejoicing over his luck, eager to find what wealth he had got. And because the Komintern was in bad odour poor Boris was suspected of the murder. Word was brought to him secretly that the G.P.U. was going to arrest him, and he fled just in time."

"But of course he hadn't done it really?"

"Do you think I would marry a garrotter? Boris was as innocent as you are. But because the Cheka is all-powerful he had to flee, and naturally he tried to come to me."

"And where were you?"

"In Batum. It was May, and Batum used to be one of the favourite summer resorts on the Black Sea. We were going to have a holiday there as soon as his work in Irkutsk was done. Imagine my horror when one day a message was brought to me that Boris was a fugitive! He had got as far as Novorossisk, but it was not safe for him to come any further. 'Wait,' he said, 'wait till this shadow has passed and I will come to you, and we will have a new, a sweeter honeymoon between the mountains and the sea.'"

"Did you?" asked Quentin jealously.

"No," said Nelly sadly. "He never came. Day after day I walked to the pier and looked out at the blue sea, the white snow-mountains to the north, waiting for the ship that would bring Boris to me from Novorossisk. The narrow harbour; the old men sitting at little tables on the quay, drinking their coffee; the long shingly beach where loafers slept in the sun; and always that white mountain barrier to the north. They became hatefully familiar as day after day I waited there alone. And then one morning something happened that almost made me regret those days of waiting; something that robbed me of the hope I had lived on. A policeman came up to me, tapped me on the shoulder, and said, 'Come with me.' I was helpless. He was a tall man in a green cap and he carried a revolver. I went with him."

"The brute," said Quentin sympathetically. He edged a little nearer and put his arm round Nelly's shoulders. She seemed grateful for the support.

"Oh, the Cossack. And the other word?"

"The Komintern is the Communist International. Bor worked for it. He was an idealist and one of its most truste servants."

"I see," said Quentin doubtfully.

"Boris was there and so was Sakhalin, the Commissar for Internal Development. There had been a full meeting of the Zik in the Kremlin, and the chief of the G.P.U. in Irkutsk—"

"Just a minute," said Quentin. "I want to be quite clear about this. You say there was a Zik in the Kremlin. Is that serious?"

"People never understand Russia. The Zik is the Central Executive Committee, and the G.P.U. is the Political Department. It used to be known as the Cheka, or the Terror, but when things became more settled they called it the Political Department."

"Of course," said Quentin.

"Well, the chief of the G.P.U. in Irkutsk submitted a report which was considered sufficiently serious for Sakhalin to go in person and investigate. The G.P.U. was at odds with the local branch of the Komintern."

"That was rather rough on Boris, wasn't it?"

"Boris did his duty as a Russian should. When Sakhalin came he avoided him. But nevertheless suspicion fell on him when Sakhalin was murdered."

"In the fog?"

"In the fog. The drosky-drivers of Irkutsk are notorious. They are garrotters by birth and education. When the fog comes they drive up and down looking for a likely victim. They see someone who appears richer than his fellow men—a prosperous citizen, as prosperity goes in Russia, seen in the dim glow of a lamp— and like a flash a noose is thrown over his neck, the drosky-driver whips up his horses— standing up, shouting to them, lashing them furiously with his whip—and races through the almost empty streets with the body dragging behind. Once outside the town the drosky is halted, the driver gets down, rifles the body, strips it, and flings it in a ditch."

"And goes back to look for more?" suggested Quentin, horror-struck.

"That was how Sakhalin was murdered. Think of it: a drosky

"He took me to Nitchevon, the head of the Cheka in Batum. Nitchevon said, 'Your husband is a traitor to the Soviet. He has been arrested and is in prison in Novorossisk.' I fainted. When I recovered consciousness, Nitchevon was bending over me. A fat man with eyes like stone and a big round head shaved all over. 'They will probably shoot him,' he said, and I was on the point of fainting again when Nitchevon added, 'Unless you like to save his life.' I looked at him with horror dawning in my eyes."

Quentin held her a little closer. The moon was peaceful. The moon was an old ship sailing on calm seas. The ground it lighted with its great stern-lantern of silver was England, a peaceful land. A piano, played somewhere in "The Pelican," was like an urbane dream of music. To all this accompaniment of peace Nelly sang an air of danger. A Russian song to a Purcell setting. Quentin heard his heart beating.

"What Nitchevon had to propose was this: that I should serve the Soviet in the outer ranks of the G.P.U., and by my service purchase Boris's freedom. They were not sure of his guilt. They did not want to stir up the Komintern unnecessarily by executing one of its most trusted members, and so this chance of freedom was offered him—or offered me. The G.P.U. is quick to see its chances, and someone was wanted who spoke French and English, someone who—a woman, in short—and I was in their power. I consented. What sort of a wife would I have been had I refused? They sent me to Constantinople first."

"What did you do there?"

"Watched people, spoke to people, listened to them. American engineers working on manganese concessions in the Caucasus, Americans who were interested in the oil wells at Baku, Americans who wanted to build railways for the Soviet. Then I was sent to Paris, because there are more Americans there, though not all of them are interested in Russia."

"What did you talk about to them?"

Nelly Bly turned to him, smiling in the moonlight, and said: "The Soviet was interested in what the concessionaires told, in their unguarded moments, of the things they had seen in Russia; in their opinions of Russian problems; in their private admissions of the profit they were likely to make out of their oil and mining rights. And I was working for Boris."

Quentin was restless. "It must have been dreadful," he said.

"Some of the Americans were very nice."

"But, Nelly, you don't mean to say that you enjoyed it?"

"I was working for Boris, Quentin."

Quentin was inclined to be rude about Boris, a maladroit Cossack who got himself arrested because there had been a fog in Irkutsk, and left a beautiful girl to work miserably to release him from the prison which was obviously the best place for him. Damn Boris. He stood up and looked gloomily at the ghostly tennis-courts.

"What are you doing here?" he asked.

"Still working for Boris," said Nelly with a pathetic smile.

"Why? Do you still love him?"

"I don't know. I don't think that I do. He's probably changed in prison. But surely that is all the more reason why I should work for him. It means that my labour is pure and selfless."

"You are an angel," said Quentin, suddenly kneeling in front of her.

"The grass is wet. Sit down again and let me tell you why I am here. Do you know Mr. van Buren?"

"Yes, a little. What has he got to do with it?"

"He has discovered something that may have the most important effect on the oil fields. What it is we don't know. It may only be a new drill, but we think it is something much more important. My chief in the G.P.U. says that he must know. Van Buren's company has interests in the Baku field. It may be necessary to take those interests away from him. It may even be to the advantage of the Russian oil fields that van Buren's discovery should never be used. I must find out what it is."

"You don't mean that van Buren is in danger, do you?"

"Lenin once said, 'Be always on guard, because you are always surrounded by enemies.' His life is in no danger—yet. It will be in no danger if I can find out what his discovery is."

"This is terrible," said Quentin. "He's the most likeable old man. He tells funny stories. You simply can't make plots against him. Oh, damn the G.P.U.! Can't you escape from them, slip

away and say nothing? You're in England now. You're safe
here. Everybody is safe in England."

"And leave Boris in prison?"

Quentin groaned. "How did you know van Buren was coming here?" he asked.

"He made his plans in New York and cabled for rooms. Another cable went to Moscow three minutes later. I was warned
for duty. My name was entered on a servants' registry in London and I came here a week before van Buren."

"But why did you come as a maid? Why not as an ad—why
not as an ordinary person?"

"I have been called an adventuress in Paris. In Downish
they would shout it. But as a maid I am unsuspected."

Quentin was exceedingly unhappy. Here was action, such as
he demanded for his contemplated novel. Here was drama. And
he did not like it. Strange forces of intrigue were thrusting
darkly into peace, destroying peace, devouring peace to satisfy
the ravening hunger of drama. Here was adventure. And he was
going to be asked, unless he was vastly mistaken, to share it
with Nelly Bly. Beautiful as she was he wished that he had
never seen her. Did all adventure look so mean and nasty from
the inside? Was action a good thing, when action must mar serenity?

"I'm not going to steal van Buren's pocket-book if that's
what you're considering," he said.

Nelly laughed. "Of course not," she said. "That must not be
disturbed. Nothing must be done to make him suspicious. But
you know him and you can talk to him. You can ask him about
his discovery. You are clever and well-known. He won't suspect
you. And when you have found out what it is you can tell me."

"That's the dirtiest piece of work I have ever been asked
to do."

"Quentin! It's the kind of thing I have done for the last year.
The thing that I have had to do. It's easy to be scornful of dirt
when you are not compelled to work."

"But I'm not concerned about Boris."

"I thought you were a little concerned about me."

Malachite in argentine, beryls in the milky way of the

moon. . . . What were the ethics of the moon? Insubstantial
things, lunar myths, the shadow of a leaf. Quentin was lost and
bent his head to the Scylla and Charybdis of her breast. "Besides," she whispered, "once his secret is known he won't be
bothered any more."

"You only want me to talk to him?"

"And then to me."

Solemn and melodious the great bell of St. Saviour's beat
twelve. Twelve for midnight, twelve for the twelve apostles,
twelve for ghosts to come out and Cinderellas go home.

"You will?" Nelly asked.

"Must you go?" said Quentin.

Like a moonbeam, he thought, as she sped over the dewy
grass. My God, he thought again, I'll call myself a fool to-
morrow. . . .

In his room, Saturday stacked neatly his typewritten sheets
and clipped them into their black leather portfolio.

"And that's that," he said aloud.

Then he considered the untidy heap of manuscript. Sheets
of paper, all sizes, written on, drawn on, blotted. When inspiration failed he would draw little geometrical patterns on the
margin, or fantastic heads, gargoyles and Julius Cæsar and
charwomen. An undignified habit. Some of his couplets were
written vertically on unoccupied edges, because correction and
re-correction had left no room for them in their proper place.
Arrows indicated their true position. Only the typewriter
had produced order out of the chaos in which his poem was
conceived.

I had better burn all this, he decided.

He picked up the mass of paper and stuffed it into the empty
grate. A line caught his eye, boldly written on an otherwise
empty page. "Ship *Tellus* will Proceed to Apogee for Orders."
He struck a match. Whatever people say about it, he thought,
there's a devil of a lot of work in it. His eyes and ears had been
active, his brain had been strenuously taught and strenuously
set to labour, blood had been pumped into his brain to feed it,
food packed into his belly to make the blood, cattle killed and

crops gathered to supply the foods, seeds had been sown and farmers got up at dawn to grow the crops and tend the cattle, invaders held off and soldiers drilled to keep safe the farmers, Romans, Danes and Normans bred into our native bone to make the soldiers—"Hell!" he exclaimed as the match burnt his finger.

And there was a consequence of all this breeding, fighting, growing and learning: a mass of scrabbled lines on crumpled paper. Lines which set in order told a story of the ship *Tellus* . . . how it started in wind and rain from an estuary beyond the stars . . . of the mad captain who called himself God, and carried a full press of sail through inter-planetary tempest, and drove headlong in the night . . . of the ship itself, little younger than Time, sun-scarred, foul-bottomed, groaning as it lifted to the sea . . . of the rats in the hold who made love, talked politics, discussed art, stole the grain and ore and silken fineries of which the hold was full . . . rats curiously like human beings, commonplace rats and rats who thought poetry was important and rats who made corners in the stolen grain . . . while the ship drove on, sometimes in calm seas, oftener in storm . . . rats who pretended to know all about morality, decadent rats, and rats who had large families almost without noticing it . . . rats who made houses and other rats who made war and knocked them down . . . but the mad captain, who laughed at the storm and shouted enormous jests to the bigger stars didn't worry much about the rats, because he was going to Apogee for orders, and he was a sailor first, not a rodentitarian. It was a good story, if he had told it well, for to all the frantic busyness of the rats, their strenuous self-importance and the noise of their theories, the sound of the sea was a burden, and every now and then their love-making and money-making were stilled by the wrath or the laughter of the captain who called himself God; laughter that they did not understand, wrath whose beginning they could not comprehend, and the footsteps of a commander who walked alone because he, and he alone, knew where his ship was going. Even the wisest rats, who saw clearly the folly and vice of ordinary rats and took pleasure in pointing them out, had no knowledge of their destination, could not think what hands had loaded the ship so richly, nor could suggest to what people the wheat and the silk were being carried.

"I think it's good," said Saturday for the hundredth time, and struck another match.

The flame spread, the papers crackled, untwisted themselves, turned black as the flame passed over them, and crumpled into tiny flakes. Saturday poked them with his fingers, and as he did so, a line or two shone brightly in the quick fire. "The corposants burnt blue on every mast," he read. Here a couplet came to light:

> "'God save the Queen' a faithful people said,
>   When Henry took Nan Bullen to his bed."

It was a pessimistic, humorous, historically-minded rat who had said that. And a reactionary-militaristic-Malthusian crony of his was responsible for

> "I've got no patience with these theories
>   That Fingal's dog was sorry for his fleas"—

another couplet to which the flames gave prominence before they consumed it. "The blackbird of a flute among the strings"— that was part of a musical, sentimental rat's conversation; and here was a line even more obviously poetical: "On Popocatapetl bright with flowers." How did that come in? Saturday couldn't remember the passage in which, perhaps, it had been carefully inlaid. Here, too, momentarily lurid, was vulgar commonsensical, unsympathetic old grandpa rat:

> "'You're right,' said grandpa rat, 'that love is blind
>   When it seeks inspiration from behind.'"

The papers crackled. They were nearly all burnt. A last line shone briefly—"A silver lane that led through cloudy steppes"— and nothing remained but ashes which curled and uncurled themselves as though the ink had given them life and they felt their death-pangs.

Saturday walked up and down. Legible and whole, his poem was safe in its portfolio and he thought of other things against a background of excited satisfaction. It was finished, done, ready like a prophet prepared for speech, waiting only for the last darkness to go and the sun to rise. Like Byron he might wake and find himself famous. Against that golden screen of optimistic suspense he thought of Joan; Joan all alone, though the cautious shadow of her father reached her feet. Only for a minute had he spoken to her after his interview with the professor. No particular chance for conversation had offered itself and Saturday was too tired of inconclusive argument to make an opportunity for explanation which could not be any more satisfactory than the argument had been.

"All clear?" she had asked him.

"Not quite," he had answered. "There's a little fog in the channel, but it won't last long."

"You mean that father wasn't pleased?"

"He didn't show any particular joy."

"I'll speak to him in the morning," Joan had said with an air of determination. And then Mrs. Waterhouse had borne down on them with a vulpine smile, and Saturday had escaped.

It was humiliating, he thought, that a poet who had the power of life and death on paper should have so little control of actual issues. On paper he could make men—or rats—after his own image, put masterful words in their mouths, make lesser men bow to them, and women fall in their path like ripe fruit. He could, when he was tired of them, kill them or forget them or drive them mad. He could explain their actions, make them do logical things, or laugh at them for cutting silly capers. He could give to Cæsar what he chose and to God as much as he cared. But in life itself he was as powerless as other men. He was subject to the same loves and fears and indignations, and acted as foolishly as people who were not poets. Perhaps even more foolishly, though that was unlikely for an obvious reason. Even his intellect, under the stress of a common-place emotion, was reduced to a common stature.

I suppose other people have made the same discovery, he admitted, but none the less it is humiliating. I may be a little different from other men, however, for circumstances alter cases, and as Joan is obviously more beautiful and better in every way than all other girls, so in my case there is a better reason for humiliation.

And comforted by this reflection he went to bed.

CHAPTER XI

Downish High Street was cool and clear in the morning, as if it had been washed with liquid air. The sky was blue except for a few indignant-looking sleepy clouds that the dawn had caught napping, and already the sun had warmed the air and was bringing out the colour in the old red roofs, the green trees in the street, and the fat gold letters over shop doors that spelt the chemist's name and the butcher's and the baker's and other well-contented names. Shopkeepers were polishing their glass and preparing tubs of potatoes, baskets of carrots and sheaves of rhubarb for the day's display. Early citizens came to their doors, looked up and down the street with satisfaction, and turned again as they sniffed the breakfast bacon. "Ah!" said Mr. Lamb the butcher, smacking a sirloin familiarly, "it's good to be alive on a day like this." And "Betsy!" shouted Mr. Trig of the Red Lion, "fill my mug for me, Betsy. It flatters humanity, does such a morning."

"Fifty-four to-day," said little Miss Tibbs of the millinery shop, "and I feel like a girl of eighteen."

Pedalling desperately over the worn stones, ringing his bell for jubilation (for there was no other traffic in sight) and whistling to spend benevolently his surplus breath, came John Jellicoe Judd, the newsagent's boy, on a red bicycle. He had been to the station to meet the London train. A stack of papers filled the fore-carrier and another stack the after-carrier of his bicycle. All the world's news was in his care: what this admiral had rashly spoken and that politician more rashly done, all the blood spilt overnight between Chicago and Cabul, a few obscure births and an illustrious death or two, the toilet secrets of three rival actresses, the marital infelicities of a jockey, and an interim report of the League of Nations; news of the world, a harvest of rumour and the busy gleaning of sharp-scissored sub-editors; all balanced on a red bicycle.

John Jellicoe Judd (his birth, in August, 1914, had been expedited by patriotic excitement) stopped outside "The Pelican," whistled more shrilly than ever, selected a bundle of papers, threw it into the open door, and went blithely on his way.

"Young villain," amiably commented the Boots as he retrieved the bundle in which, securely tied, were several copies of *The Times*, the *Daily Telegraph*, the *Morning Post*, the *Daily Mirror*, the *Daily Sketch*, various weekly papers, and, most eagerly sought of all, the *Daily Day*. It was a *Daily Day* that the Boots extracted from the bundle, and after being amused by the sporting cartoon, visibly stirred by the racing forecast, and sucking in his breath at the alarming death-rate of insured readers, ("Though some say that it serves 'em right," he murmured) he turned to the magazine page.

"Well, now," he exclaimed in delight. "'Ere, M'ria, Bill, 'Erbert, V'ronica! Come an' look at this."

"W'y," they said, coming up rubbing their hands, tidying their hair, buttoning their waistcoats, "W'y, George, wot's the excitement, George? Been left a fortune, George? Or 'ave you been chosen as the winner of the beauty competition, George?"

"Never you mind about beauty," said George, "you read this. There's a picture, too, on the back page."

"Oooh!" they said. "Well, I declare! A piece about 'The Pelican'! 'Oo wrote it, George?"

"'Oo wrote it? A journalist, of course. 'Oo d'you think writes pieces for the papers?"

"Everybody who's got time to," said the saturnine Bill.

"Shut up, Bill," they said. "Trying to be smart on a fine morning like this! Ought to be ashamed o' yourself, Bill!"

Everybody took a copy of the *Daily Day*. It was too early for visitors to be downstairs, and they settled themselves to read in comfort the neat compact-looking article on "The Pelican."

It was entitled POET'S PUB.

It began complacently with the offer to satisfy a purely hypothetical curiosity:

"If anyone wants to know whether poets are practical or not, let him—or her—go to Downish and visit 'The Pelican.' 'The Pelican' is one of our oldest English inns, and from the time of Henry VIII (who established it by dis-establishing the monastery which previously stood there) it has had many landlords, red-faced, hearty, jovial men such as you are introduced to by Dickens. But it has never had a better landlord than Mr. Saturday Keith, the well-known Oxford Rowing Blue and poet.

"At a time when so many earnest people are asking 'What can be done with our poets?' or 'What is the future of English poetry?'—and answering these questions by gloomily shaking their head—Mr. Keith has solved the problem in his own way by taking his muse to a wayside temple of Bacchus, who is, indeed, the godfather of all the Muses.

.   .   .   .   .

"The atmosphere of 'The Pelican' has apparently been suitable for poetic contemplation, as Mr. Keith has newly completed another book which will shortly be in the hands of his publishers. The title and the nature of the contents are so far a strictly kept secret, and many people will be curious to see how far keeping a 'pub' has affected his style or choice of subject. Perhaps—who knows?—new Canterbury Tales are being born. Certainly the guests who have lately been entertained at 'The Pelican' are interesting enough to provide suitable material for such a collection."

.   .   .   .   .

"What do these lines of dots mean?" asked Veronica.

"They means one of two things," said the knowing George. "Either the journalist 'as said something which 'e shouldn't of—told a risky story or something like that—or else the printer 'asn't 'ad room to put it all in, so 'e puts a row of dots instead."

"A dam' good idea," said Bill, "the more the merrier."

"Bill!" exclaimed Maria reprovingly.

"Well, you must admit that this isn't very interesting," said Veronica. "What does 'e want to talk about Canterbury for?"

"It's better further on," said George.

"What will interest people for whom poetry has little appeal," they read, "is that a new cocktail has just been invented at 'The Pelican.' Mr. Holly, who looks after the American Bar with a skill that many visitors are eager to acknowledge, has succeeded, where so many of his confreres have failed, in mixing a blue cocktail; or to be exact two blue cocktails, one light and the other dark. They have been christened Oxford and Cambridge, and the secret of their composition is being cherished even more assiduously than the name of Mr. Keith's new volume of poems."

"Fancy 'Olly 'aving 'is name in the papers," said Herbert. "They'll 'ave 'is photograph next."

"An' fancy a man like the guv'nor writing poetry," said George. "That's what beats me. A big upstanding fellow with all 'is wits about him, an' as strong as an ox, an' as nice an' simple to talk to as any one of us. Nicer than you, Bill. An' yet 'e goes an' writes poetry."

"It's something people can't 'elp," said Maria. "Like being sea-sick. I knew a postman once—"

"Is that the *Daily Day*?" said a cool voice. "Let me see it, will you?"

Nelly Bly had come in unnoticed. She reached over Bill's shoulder and took his paper from him without a scruple on her part or resistance on his.

She glanced rapidly down the column, said "Damn!" handed the paper back, and walked out again.

"Like a bloomin' empress," said Bill.

"I've never known an empress what swore like she does," said Maria.

"I'll bet you 'aven't," said Herbert with apparent simplicity. "W'y should she say 'Damn' anyway? What's it got to do with 'er what's in the paper?"

"She's a nice girl," said George, "an educated girl. You don't know what educated people think about the newspapers. I was a waiter in a club once, and the way some of them swore and cursed at what they read would astonish you. Nearly all educated people lose their temper when they read the paper. She's a nice girl is Nelly, and I don't think any the worse of 'er for an odd damn or two."

"She's that stuck-up," said Maria. "That postman I happened to know used to say about people who were stuck up—"

"Come on," said George. "What's postmen anyway? They won't do our work for us, will they? The guv'nor'll be down in a minute."

The *Daily Days* were carefully refolded and along with the *Daily Telegraphs* and the *Daily Mirrors* laid out in their accustomed places. The morning work of "The Pelican" went on.

The article entitled Poet's Pub created a slight flutter when the residents under "The Pelican" became aware of it, but as they read and discovered that no names except Keith and Holly were mentioned, their excitement sensibly abated. Still, it was pleasant to find that their temporary abode had sufficient interest to be served up as an addition to the morning bacon and eggs of two million British subjects, and everybody except Mr. Telfer was pleased at the attention given to Saturday's new poems.

"I never read advertisements," said Mr. Telfer when it was pointed out to him.

Diana Waterhouse took the opportunity to extract from Saturday the promise of an autographed copy, while Jean Forbes and Mrs. Mandeville shook him warmly by the left and right hand respectively. Mr. van Buren offered him an introduction to an American publisher, Mr. Wesson enquired whether there would be a signed and numbered *édition de luxe*, and Professor Benbow remarked genially, "You've got the bowling Keith. Now we'll see if you can score." Joan, who was genuinely in love, went so far as to ask permission to read the poem before it went to the publishers.

Lady Porlet confided to Mrs. Waterhouse that the mere thought of poets bewildered her. "I can't think what they find to say," she said.

"Sermons in stones, you know," said Mrs. Waterhouse with a pleasant condescension, though she herself would have been at a loss to find a text in Old Red Sandstone or a thesis in a brook.

"But many of them, I'm told, are irreligious," objected Lady Porlet.

"The bishops are to blame," confided Mrs. Waterhouse. "If they don't know what to believe how can other people?"

"Ah!" said Lady Porlet happily. "Archbishop Laud (1573–1645) declared that the Communion Table was more important than the pulpit. And then there was Cardinal Newman. His influence in Oxford was supreme about the year 1839."

In a few minutes Mrs. Waterhouse was routed completely and left Lady Porlet to rehearse alone her tabloid stories of Famous Churchmen through the Ages, a well-known series of cigarette pictures.

"I must take Mr. Holly's album back to him," she decided.

Holly's mood was unenviable. The publicity given to him by the *Daily Day* had swollen his pride and at the same time increased his nervous fears. He saw himself at one moment as a great man justly recogized by all England, and at another as the quarry of every crook in the kingdom bent on wresting from him the secret of his marvellous cocktails. Now he puffed out his chest, and now reflected miserably that perhaps he had been happier while still unknown to fame.

In this state of mind the return of his cigarette picture album was some consolation, and for a few moments he thought of offering Lady Porlet the loan of another, only partially filled one. Then he realized the folly of adding to his anxieties, and wisely said nothing about it. Lady Porlet's gratitude, however, and her ready understanding of the value of his collection, were very gratifying.

But if the sun, on this pleasant Saturday morning, shone only fitfully on Holly, it showed an unclouded face to Ignatius O'Higgins. His crew were at battle stations, the kitchen of "The Pelican" was like a battleship's turret in action, and O'Higgins was happier than the singing gunner's lads on the fighting *Téméraire*. His pots and pans were moved deftly here and there, filled with this and that, lids clapped on them, slid into hot ovens. Already the proleptic savours of the Elizabethan dinner stole richly to the roof. Already steam whispered coyly in certain pots, and already great coffers of pastry gaped for an unexampled hoard of riches: beef and capons and fish and orchard-fruit and spice and fruit from the Levant. The sober edicts of cookery schools were defied, as timorous injunction was defied by Nelson, and the laws of dieticians had been set at naught. Like a smuggler's cave, a poacher's den, a gun-station of the *Téméraire*, then, "The Pelican's" kitchen was full of bustle and heat and the promise of plenty.

In the cellar Keith anxiously examined the Malmsey he had apparelled, the white Bastard and the Sack. For some time he had been experimenting with the elegant mixtures of our ancestors, and though he felt a little doubtful of their reception he was determined to offer them. Sweetness and heaviness might be urged against them, but if they had not been too heavy to clog the nimble wits nor sweet enough to make sickly the subtle flame at "The Mermaid," why should "The Pelican" be frightened of them? *"Toujours l'audace,"* said Saturday. He tasted the Malmsey. *"Encore l'audace,"* he murmured, and tasted it again. . . .

About this time Quentin was nervously trying to bring round his conversation with Mr. van Buren to the subject of oil, and Joan was warmly arguing that her father had overstepped his parental authority on the previous evening.

"If any one thing was lacking to convince me that I am in love with Saturday, it was this," she said.

"I only ask you to postpone your decision for a few months," said Professor Benbow.

"You want me to sit on the fence, and wait till the chickens are hatched, and look before I leap?"

"If you care to put it in any of those ways."

"That is, you're trying to persuade me to be cowardly and middle-aged, a safety-firster. Well, I'm not going to be. . . ."

"And since when have you been interested in petroleum?" asked van Buren.

Quentin was ill-at-ease. He had rehearsed, between saying good-night to Nelly Bly and falling asleep, a dozen moves that might open the subject of oil with van Buren, and none of them had stood the cool scrutiny of morning. He had practised before a mirror expressions so unscrupulous as to persuade himself that he felt unscrupulous; and now he felt like a bashful pickpocket. He wished that the day was long past, that van Buren was a hundred miles away, that he had never been tempted into making such a dreadful promise. He thought of leaving Downish hurriedly on a fictitious errand, but honour rooted in dishonour stood too tall for that. If he could only work up a real curiosity in petroleum wells his task might be a little easier, but they were so uninteresting that he could think of nothing connected with them that he honestly wanted to know. And then inspiration came to him.

"I'm looking for a setting for my next novel," he said. "I want to do something as realistic as a Lancashire cotton mill and yet adventurous at the same time. Something with crude action in it, but action that is of genuine significance in modern life, and I thought perhaps a setting in Mexico or the Russian oil-fields would suit me."

"Do you mean to go to Mexico or Russia to see the fields for yourself?"

"Of course, if I find it necessary," said Quentin with sudden determination. . . .

"If Keith shows himself to be a real poet my objections will disappear," said the professor. "At present he is only a publican with an amateur taste for writing verse."

"You haven't seen his new book," said Joan.

"And I don't intend to see it. I dislike reading unpublished poetry as much as I dislike seeing a newly-born baby. Neither can be handled in comfort or security."

"What do you mean to do, then?"

"Precisely nothing. I shan't make myself ridiculous or give you a chance to be romantic by forbidding the marriage. But in the meantime I withhold my sanction to it. And I know you well enough to be sure that you won't readily defy me if you think for a few minutes of your life as you have lived it till this moment."

"I think you're being incredibly mean."

"A father's first duty is common-sense, and common-sense is seldom generous. . . ."

———

"So you see," said Quentin, "if you have discovered anything that will radically affect the future of the oil-fields, I should be wasting my time by visiting them. Before I had written my novel they might be deserted, or at any rate archaic survivals."

"I don't think you need worry about that," said van Buren.

"Then your discovery isn't so very important after all?"

"It's important enough to make me chary about discussing it even with the son of my old friend Lady Mercy Cotton."

"I see," said Quentin. "I'm sorry if I have appeared too inquisitive." And he thought, "Well, I've come to a dead end. I can't go any further in that direction. . . ." He was depressed at having been beaten, but at the same time he felt relieved at having a good excuse to abandon, for the moment at any rate, his unwilling part in the conspiracy.

"What about a game of bowls?" he suggested.

"An excellent idea," said van Buren. . . .

Joan and her father returned from their walk in a cheerful mood. The professor had repeated his argument of the previous evening and Joan had been convinced.

"If you are sure that Keith's new poem will be a success," he said, "then I am not asking very much when I want you to wait until it has been declared a success. I am asking you to bet on what is, in your opinion, a certainty."

"Of course it's a certainty," said Joan. "I read some of it after breakfast."

"Then will you bet on it? Will you stake yourself on it, remembering that the race can't be started till the publisher's put the book in the paddock, and consequently that you can't pay or be paid for some time after that?"

"You're a cunning old man," said Joan.

"I am," agreed the professor.

"But I'm not frightened of you, and I'm willing to wait."

"Good," said the professor.

"Because I never dreamt of getting married before Christmas anyway."

CHAPTER XII

The Oak Room, with its Gothic timbered roof and hammer beams, was ready for feasting. The small tables which usually filled it had disappeared. Small tables do very well in their way. They suggest privacy, they enable a party to declare itself a party, they denote a family, they erect an impalpable but perceptible barrier, they are both inclusive and exclusive. But small round tables are not in the manner of an Elizabethan dinner. Instead of them a long refectory table had been set up, broad enough to support decoration and redoubtable dishes, long enough to accommodate all who wished to be present. Only two indeed of the visitors to "The Pelican" were not present: a vegetarian *pour être belle* and an atheist who did not believe in Queen Elizabeth.

Saturday dined with his guests. Between him and Professor Benbow (who, with Mrs. Mandeville, sat at the head of the table) was a large confectioner's model of a pelican, a magnificent bird in sugar icing. Its beak was open and in the crystal basin of the pendulous lower-half goldfish swam, and waterweed hung prettily over the edge. Set with the ordered profusion of England's Golden Age the table already gleamed with fruit, strawberries and cherries and plums and peaches, and sugar-plums and ginger; and jumbals and marchpane and suckets of one kind or another added variety to this happy display. These were not considered or noticed on the menu, which read simply:

Salad
Kickshawses
Stewed Pike
Roast Sucking-pig
Olive Pie
Roast Capons
Marrowbone Pie

"My difficulty," Saturday explained to Jean Forbes, "was not what to put in but what to keep out. Apparently sixteen dishes used to be considered a good number for a family feast; sixteen substantial dishes, not counting sweets and salads and fruit and so on. On a really big occasion, when a nobleman was entertaining, there was an almost endless procession. Salads, roast meats, baked meats such as venison-pasty, cold meats and game, carbonadoes, then more game, little birds like snipe and plover first, then bustards and pheasants and peacocks; then a marrowbone pie, perhaps, and some tarts; and then more cold meat; fresh-water fish followed the salads and seafish—a sturgeon if you could get one—came in with the baked meats."

"And how did they reduce?" asked Jean.

"I don't know," said Saturday, "That hadn't occurred to me."

"They perspired without shame," said the professor from the top of the table. "A moist hand used to be a social asset. It was taken to mean a kindly humour and a loving nature."

"The highlanders of Central Asia stuff themselves at times with an almost incredible quantity of food," said Colonel Waterhouse. And Angela Scrabster declared that in the Orient leanness was a sign of poverty, corpulence the indication of social position.

"When I was a child," remarked Lady Porlet, "I always over-ate myself unless I was watched."

"I *like* eating," said a lady of whom everybody thought well but whose name nobody could remember.

"How many things can you find in this salad?" asked Joan. "I've got almonds, lettuce, raisins, currants, lemon, cucumber—"

"Olives, cauliflowers, and—is it spinach?"

"It is," said Saturday, "and oil and vinegar and sugar. That's about all."

"I'm dying to find out what kickshawses are," said Mrs. Waterhouse. In a few minutes she exclaimed with some disappointment, "Why, they're only omelettes!" And in another few minutes, with evident approval, "But the most delicious omelette I have ever tasted. Tell me what is in it, Mr. Keith."

"Liver and bacon, spinach, a good lot of spice, and some ginger. The other is flavoured with walnuts and walnut buds."

"'A woman, a dog, and a walnut tree,
 The more you beat 'em the better they be!'"

said the professor. "I like your walnut omelette, Keith."

"Do you really believe in beating women?" asked Tommy Mandeville.

"Of course," said a blond young man with a loud voice who sat half-way down the table. But when everybody turned and stared at him, he blushed hotly and spoke no more.

"It's a beautiful idea," suggested Quentin, "but I think it should remain an idea. One shouldn't descend to practical exposition."

"Or consider details," added Jean Forbes. "The thought of slippers or braces quite spoils it for me."

"As pictures of harps and prize cherubim spoil the idea of heaven."

"Do you believe in heaven, Mr. Cotton?"

"Sometimes. But then I don't go to church."

"Belief in the invisible is the ruin of poetry," declared Sigismund Telfer.

"Do you read much poetry?" asked Lady Porlet.

"I have written a book about it," said Telfer coldly.

"How very strange. It all seems so unnecessary to me. It is either obvious or untrue. Is that what you said about it?"

"I always thought the pike was a common no-account sort of fish till now," said van Buren. "But I guess this is cooked different to any I've tasted before."

"You put it in a chafing dish with a bottle of Graves. Then you add cinnamon and some prunes, a bottle of cream, eggs, and finally ornament it with sliced oranges and lemons," explained Saturday.

"You're like a cook's guide," said Joan.

Saturday laughed at her little jest. He was feeling very pleased with himself and his dinner, and even in ordinary circumstances a joke made by one's *fiancée* has an intimate quality that evokes a more general and more generous response than the specific reaction to absolute humour. It is indeed almost as good as a joke made by oneself.

But by this time humour of any kind was being applauded, and many remarks that would ordinarily pass unnoticed found in the genial atmosphere of the table a lustre and a light that never actually was. Things were said which implied fun or threw the shadow of wit, and those who heard, being in the same mood as the speakers, supplied the missing word themselves and laughed as much at their own perception as at the humour of the narrator. Even Sigismund Telfer recited a limerick—the roast pig was no more than a succulent memory and the olive pie was as empty as an Egyptian tomb—a limerick that ran:

> "The celibate Bishop of Bute
> Was a rationalist by repute,
> And yet traces I find
> Of a credulous mind
> In his rabid refusal of fruit."

And Angela Scrabster told a better one that produced a moment's silence—like the calm in the hollow of a great wave—before laughter broke loudly over it.

It was notable that although many had exclaimed at the solid substance of the menu, few failed to go steadily through it. The professor and van Buren ate with enormous gusto, and here and there an unsuspected trencherman was revealed. Mr. Wesson was one of them, Quentin ate as an adventurer should who is confronted with an unknown trail, Tommy Mandeville frankly declared her enjoyment, and Mrs. Waterhouse attempted to cover her excesses by deprecating greed. The young man who had spoken in favour of wife-beating was apparently bent on growing big enough to achieve his ambition, and Lady Porlet very calmly asked for a second helping of sucking-pig. Perhaps the wine that was itself so robust nourished instead of obscuring a robuster appetite. The sherry was conventional except in so far as everybody agreed to call it sack; the malmsey and the sweet muscadine were both praised and the former was extensively drunk; but the mixture called bastard suffered from its name after the lady whose own name no one could remember said to Saturday, "Do tell me how you made your bastard, Mr. Keith."

The marrowbone pie was a rich mixture of fruit and vegetables on a foundation of marrow. It was followed, slowly and now with a certain carelessness, by the marchpane and the suckets, those unsubstantial but attractive-to-look-at sweetmeats, and by the fruit whose freshness was like a reassurance of strength.

They drank to the memory of Queen Elizabeth, the anniversary of whose visit to "The Pelican" it was, and some pleasant jokes were made about the Earl of Leicester and the boot which he had so maladroitly left in the queen's room; or perhaps—to preserve that element of doubt which is the grace of scandal—one should say the boot which had so malapertly been discovered in her room. The boot was brought out of its glass-case and set on the table beside the sugar-icing pelican.

"What became of the other one?" asked Mr. Wesson.

"It's probably in the Metropolitan Museum in New York," said Quentin.

"But this is the important one," Jean Forbes insisted. "This is the one he told his chivalrous fib about. It's as important as Sir Walter Raleigh's cloak."

"This has been an excellent dinner," said the professor at last. "A dinner that I am proud to have eaten, whatever may be its consequences. But I could not often eat such a one. Novelty is the fieriest stimulant of all."

"There is a Spanish proverb," said van Buren, "that 'after three days men grow weary of a wench, a guest, and rainy weather.'"

"My mother was Spanish," said Jacquetta dreamily. (An air of drowsy good humour had succeeded the wit.) "She used to sing a little song:

> "'I love you, will always love you,
> I have told you again and again,
> And it seems to me that you listen
> As one listens to the rain.'"

"Would you call that poetry, Mr. Telfer?" asked the professor.

"Of a kind," said Telfer. "It is simple and evocative."

"What would you give as a sample of real unquestionable poetry, then?"

"This:

> "'A white crane
> Flying,
> Flew across a black cloud.'

There is a poem perfect and complete."

"It leaves plenty of room for the margin."

"I like margins," said Quentin.

"Did you say a crane, Mr. Telfer?" asked Lady Porlet.

"I did."

"Would a stork do as well, or would that spoil the poem?"

Mrs. Mandeville rose tactfully, and the ladies left the room.

The circle having become smaller the wine passed more rapidly and the conversation grew better and better. Somebody introduced discussion of the bearded Aphrodite of Cyprus, the androgynous divinity who was the symbol of luxurious growth, and somebody else lamented the decay of faith as a death-blow to blasphemy. Saturday left them, as unobtrusively as he could, to find Joan.

"Where are you going?" asked the professor.

"I've got some work to do," he said.

"A despicable excuse," said the professor.

"And as open to suspicion as an explorer's baby," added Quentin, passing the wine.

CHAPTER XIII

Nelly Bly's room was a garret under the roof. It had a steep pointed ceiling like a Noah's ark and a little window that looked at the tree-tops. By leaning out and stretching your neck it was possible to see the farthest edge of the bowling-green and some fragments of the tennis-courts beyond. Nelly Bly leaned out and saw two people walking under the trees; Saturday and Joan, she thought, though she could not be quite sure at that distance and in the deceptive mixture of moonlight and shadow. She was not very interested anyhow.

I don't suppose they're talking about Russia, she thought, and smiled so benignly that it was a pity there was no one to see her.

She lit a cigarette and got into bed. In the moonlight that coolly flowed through the small window, the cigarette smoke drifted into quaint grey patterns. Smoky flowers grew suddenly out of straight stems and were swept away; little clouds did whirling dragon dances on the yellow banner of the moonlight; and an occasional noose of smoke drifted upwards to capture some strange creature under the roof.

And Nelly Bly still smiled. Her adventure was turning out better than she had expected. She felt a little sorry for Quentin. But if he was finding trouble it was because he had asked for trouble. And it would do him no harm. She had made a fool of him but that, in a way, was a compliment, for she would not have bothered to make so complete a fool of him had he not been sufficiently attractive to gild the process with adventitious enjoyment.

He's very good-looking, she thought, and he would be really clever if he knew a little more. I like him. But fortunately I've got a lot of self-control, and I'm too interested in my job to kick my shoes over the moon. Otherwise I might be damaged goods by now. That's the trouble of a disguise. The dyer's hand is subdued to what it works in. And as a chambermaid I feel that I ought to be seduced from time to time. As myself I would be in no danger. Poor mother would be worried if she knew. And so would Quentin if he knew what mother knows. But I am the only one who knows. I think I am rather clever.

She lay and considered things. That is, a variety of things remembered, things said, done, written, wished for or previously dreamed about, presented a succession of images in her brain. Not an orderly succession like a cinema film, but a hotch-potch of events and thoughts that would be unintelligible to anyone else, but was perfectly clear to her because her memory held all the clues. The sub-titles were already written in her consciousness. Only selected incidents appeared on the film. And the story which she reviewed so haphazardly was something like this:

She saw a girl called Helen Blyesdale whose mother had a determined mouth, a habit of serving on committees, and decided opinions about the world in general. The mother was so old-fashioned that she believed her daughters should not work; that their vocation was simply to be her daughters until God, a biological instinct, or economic favouritism called them to become the wives of suitable young men. Two of her daughters were content to accept this view. But the third had red hair, had won an essay prize at school and three guineas in a *Saturday Review* literary competition, and had ideas of her own. Not exclusively her own, for they centred on journalism as a profession for young women who had won essay prizes at school and three guineas from the *Saturday Review*. She confided in her mother, and her mother was suitably scornful. But Helen, who had been born under the colours of rebellion, took her own way and went to London, where she had a friend of her own age and, what was more to the point, a sympathetic uncle who edited a weekly review.

In eighteen months she was earning almost enough to keep herself. She had written and sold three short stories, she had recounted some social episodes, she had reviewed novels of no interest to anyone except their authors, and she had had two or three articles accepted for the women's page of the *Daily Day*. Then the friend of her own age got married and Helen discovered that she was almost alone, among all her other friends, in never having been married or never having written a book. She decided that the second choice would probably have less permanent consequences, and began to think of a subject. She inclined to low life and regretted that she knew so little about it. Then one of her friends remarked, as friends will, how hard it was to find maids; and Helen resolved to become a maid and look for a novelist's theme among the other dust. In due course she found herself at "The Pelican," where there was obviously greater likelihood of getting something to write about than in a private household.

Under a promise of secrecy she had told the editor of the women's page of the *Daily Day* what she meant to do, and that practical person had said: "You may find enough for an article or two if not a novel. Important people go to 'The Pelican' sometimes. People who have news value, I mean. You can write some gossip probably. I hear that Saturday Keith has a new volume of poems almost ready. Something about them might do for the silly season. People are always interested in a Rowing Blue."

Encouraged, in a way, by this advice Helen had written her first article and seen it promptly appear in the *Daily Day*; she was young enough to be annoyed because it had been cut in a couple of places. She had also been slightly annoyed by Holly's refusal to part with his cocktail formula, for a cocktail recipe is good news. But now larger game loomed on her horizon. A scrap of overheard conversation and some servant's talk had apprised her vaguely of Mr. van Buren's importance. She knew very little about it, but she had looked him up in *Who's Who* and she had heard enough to be fairly sure, in conjunction with the information she found there, that his business was oil and to infer, optimistically, but as it happened correctly, his discovery of some new process. (Now and again such a romantic guess will prove correct.) She decided that it would be very advantageous to her—professionally, of course—to find out something about that process. She had never read City Notes or Financial News and still less ever imagined herself writing them. But here was something which would obviously affect stocks and shares and markets and "all that kind of thing," she decided. Here was news, if she could get it. Here was a regular old-fashioned scoop. And naturally, being a woman, she had no thought of dishonesty in all this. She wasn't going to steal anything. Her motives were above suspicion. She wanted to make a scoop.

The image of Helen, in Nelly Bly's brain became obscured, at this point, by an image of Quentin. Quentin in a post office succeeded her first sight of Quentin in a corridor of "The Pelican." Quentin had very gratifyingly betrayed his interest from the beginning. And he had given her a chance for one of those swift ridiculous retorts in which she took considerable pleasure. He had slighted Russian authors and she, to embarrass him, had immediately replied, "My first husband was a Cossack." Out of that small seed grew the whole fictitious tree of her political adventures, though she could not reconstruct the exact stages of its growth. Quentin himself had done a lot to help it by his curiosity in her antecedents, which compelled her to invent something. And then the idea had occurred to her that she might make him useful, and her inclination to do so was strengthened by his regrettable behaviour in trying to take advantage of her humble station; behaviour which clearly demanded revenge. The plot had another advantage in that it gave her excuses for meeting Quentin and provoking him to further essays against her respectability. It was good fun. . . . Here was Helen, who might still have been Mrs. Blythesdale's demure domestic daughter, become the centre of a little solar system of her own. She controlled planets—Quentin was a planet—and moved humorously through a universe of absorbing interest; a universe that she had in some part made for herself, adding Irkutsk to "The Pelican" and the Cheka to George and Veronica and Bill, her fellow-servants. She had even made herself, by cutting this alert, imaginative, inquisitive, scoop-hunting Nelly Bly out of the Helen Blythesdale that her ancestors and the waters of baptism had given to the world. Of her own volition she had reproduced by budding, and that was a biological feat of considerable interest.

Oh, acting a story was much more amusing than writing one. Writing, after all, was a tedious affair. The hand moved so slowly and the brain wearied of making eternal bricks without straw. She wondered why so many people did write stories when, if they had only a scrap of initiative, it was so diverting to make them real. . . .

Quentin's horror when she told him about the drosky murder in Irkutsk. His impatience at Boris. She had almost convinced herself of Boris's reality before she finished. He looked like one of the Russian Ballet, a handsome agile man with rhetorical eyes and a lyrical mouth. Poor Boris. There was something unsatisfactory about him in spite of his many good qualities. He lacked something, as fictional Russians so often do. And yet she saw herself waiting for him in Batum as clearly as she had ever seen anything in her life. It was quite by accident, too, that she had read the article in a monthly magazine which gave her sufficient local knowledge to furnish her story with Ziks and Chekas and snowy mountains. It might be amusing really to go to Russia some day.

"Clever Helen," she murmured. "Quentin will hate me when he knows how I have fooled him. But he won't hate me for long. And it did serve him right. I wonder if he found out anything from van Buren. I must make that scoop. And I ought to find what Keith's new poems are about. . . ."

She turned her back on the moonlight, crumpled her pillow into a more comfortable shape, and was about to go to sleep, when a thought suddenly stirred her to wakefulness. She got up and went to the window. On the seat where she and Quentin had sat were two figures whom she took to be Saturday and Joan.

One does lose count of time, she thought, and since they have stayed there so long there's no reason why they should come in for the next five minutes. This is an opportunity to look for the poems, I think.

On several occasions she had—being there in the course of her duties—looked round Saturday's study to see if his new book was apparent, but it had always been carefully locked away. To-day, however, he had lent it to Joan, and Nelly had seen Joan return it to him after dinner. He took it to his room and came down again in a few seconds, impatient of delay. Perhaps he had omitted to lock it up. While people were moving about there had been no opportunity for Nelly to investigate, but now, with Saturday sufficiently far away and everybody else asleep, there was a timely chance. A few minutes would give her all the information she wanted.

She put on a dressing-gown and quietly opened her door.

CHAPTER XIV

Lights glowed dimly in the corridor of "The Pelican," making the darkness in the corners which they could not reach more profound, more solemnly black than Nature had ever intended darkness to be. All Downish was asleep and dark except for pale yellow lamps which marked its streets as the corridor lights in "The Pelican" made evident—shadow-evident, twilight-obvious—the route from room to room. The houses were castles of sleep, the rooms were caves of slumber. The night lay closely on town and tavern as if the air were saturated with sleep, or as if the sky had crept down to the earth for loneliness and wrapt it warmly in moon-and-dusky veils. Sleep lay comfortable under this friendly coverlet of the night. Sleepers breathed slowly, snuggled beneath the sheets. Even the trees were still. All the dogs were kennelled and birds were no more than lifeless feather balls. A policeman yawned in the Square. A clock struck soft and drowsily. But over the roof-trees of Downish crept lean and lonely cats whose bright green eyes were alive with all the hunger and desire that the town had thrown off when the townsfolk turned their faces to the wall and gently snored *nunc dimittis.*

Sleep, its oldest guest, had returned to "The Pelican," for the ten thousandth time. Quentin and the professor slept, George the Boots and Maria and Veronica slept, Diana Waterhouse lay in her calm white-lidded virgin sleep. Lady Porlet slept with her accustomed ease, and many visitors whose daily life was full of restless thought, now as quiet as children or shepherds, slept in their appointed place. But here and there unease went slinking open-eyed, like the cats of Downish.

Nelly Bly crept quietly to Saturday's room. . . .

Angela Scrabster woke from a dream in which a gigantic Chinese general over-strode a vast green landscape; emerald-green paddy-fields, rivers of jade, grassy hills, and pagodas smeared with verdigris. Only the Chinese general was yellow, and he was all gamboge and jaundice . . . on a pea-green, bottle-green, sea-green landscape. "A metre of green is greener than a centimetre of green," she muttered (convinced, like St. Paul, by a vision) as with a shudder she woke to find verdant lights streaking the darkness.

"Oh, damn his marrow pie and his kickshawses," she groaned in her agony.

Not far away Mr. van Buren lay and stared at his invisible ceiling. His forehead was damp and he cursed the natural greed of man which even age cannot wholly subdue. His head ached dismally, his eyeballs were too large for their sockets, and a painful war was being waged in his abdomen. He remembered— it was the curse of having many friends—what a doctor had told him about his intestines. There was, in his troubled belly, twenty-two feet of troubled gut and a tortured twisting canal six feet long. From his right arm-pit, it seemed, to his waist was a mountain of liver, a volcano in the throes of imminent erup- tion. Hostile fleets sailed upon his *succus entericus*, discharging their broadsides against his shrinking mesentery; and the *ap- pendices epiploicæ*, those tattered shreds of membrane, waved helplessly in a flatulent gale like white flags of surrender that no one would see.

He even thought of death; for he was past sixty, it was stark night, and his belly was a battlefield. Miserably he contem- plated the grave and saw cemetery gates and a field of white stalagmytes that were tombstones. His throat was dry and his brow was wet.

From these funeral visions he was roused by a sudden de- mand. The embattled hosts of dissension cried to him with one voice. Their bickering ceased, they were united and they bade him get up. As clearly as they could they urged him to rise. There was no time to lose, they said. Van Buren got up.

He switched on the light, hurried to the door, and as he opened it he heard, not far off, the elemental sound of waters, abruptly released, that sought their own level. But he did not stay to put on a dressing-gown. The corridor turned right three yards from his door. Slip-slap, slip-slap, approaching him came the sound of slippered feet, and at the corner Mr. van Buren almost collided with Mr. Wesson. But Mr. van Buren did not stay to apologize.

Mr. Wesson looked tired, as a man who has passed through a trying experience may look. But the experience was over and he was sufficiently master of himself to recognize his opportunity. Like van Buren and Miss Scrabster he had wakened in an agony of intestinal disturbance, and his agony had sent him straight (or almost straight) to the chance for which he had been waiting ever since his arrival at "The Pelican"—van Buren's rooms deserted, the lights on, the doors wide open. He heard now, some distance away, another door close decisively. He was safe for at least a few minutes. He looked into the little study or sitting-room and saw through it a glimpse of the bedroom, a dressing-table with a variety of objects upon it, the corner of a disordered bed, a chair. Mr. Wesson stepped into van Buren's sitting-room, closing the door behind him. . . .

Nelly Bly listened in the darkness of Saturday's room and heard her own heart as something louder than the slippered feet and the moving doors. Her right hand clutched a rough leather portfolio, the other rested on the electric-light switch. In the suddenly darkened unfamiliar room she felt as lost as if she had gone blind. She could scarcely remember the position of the furniture, except that some pieces stood between her and the window which was a possible though unpleasant avenue of escape. Her wish to become acquainted with low life did not include any curiosity about prisons, and she was definitely frightened at the idea of being caught in Keith's study. She had found the portfolio lying on his table and had read the title of the poem and turned a few pages when the startling sound of a door roughly opened interrupted her. She fled to the switch and snapped out the light. There were footsteps, slip-slap, slip-slap, in the corridor. Puzzling footsteps that seemed to come nearer and yet die away. She listened perplexedly, feeling no more like a good conspirator than Quentin had felt on a previous occasion.

Two minutes, three minutes passed. The darkness grew oppressive, crowding in on her from all sides as she stood still. And now there was quietness outside. There were no more footsteps. It might be safe to go now. Carefully she opened the door, and still carrying the portfolio of Saturday's poem, stepped into the corridor. There was no one to be seen. Dim wall-lights spread a gentle glow, a yellow twilight broken by grotesque blotches of shadow. She looked one way and the other, and as she turned her head she saw a door—the next door to Saturday's—slowly ever so slowly opening. With a gasp she sprang to a deep alcove of darkness.

Keith's study was between Mr. Wesson's room and Mr. van Buren's two-room suite. The other side of the corridor looked through a kind of clerestory into the central courtyard. In two places the wall thrust out over corbels into deep window-places, and in one of these Nelly hid herself. By this time she was thoroughly unhappy.

The door she had seen opening was van Buren's and as she watched, almost suffocated by nervous excitement, she saw, to her immense surprise, Mr. Wesson come out; Mr. Wesson with his white expressionless face and his curious eyeglasses. He wore a drab-green dressing-gown, and in one hand he carried a black leather portfolio. Nelly caught her breath almost audibly, for she herself held a portfolio of precisely the same kind. Mr. Wesson passed stealthily to his own room.

He had been fortunate. On van Buren's dressing-table lay a bunch of keys, and if Mr. Wesson was not an accomplished picklock or cracksman (his life had led him on more urbane paths) he could use normal keys as well as anybody else. And he knew what he wanted. It was not the first time that he had been in van Buren's rooms, but it was the first time that he had had the means of opening the drawer which he particularly desired to open. He wasted no time and in a minute or so the portfolio which contained the formulæ, the plans, the drawings and all the other particulars of a revolutionary scheme for converting coal into petrol was in his hands. Mr. Wesson was of his own volition, no thief; but if he could get what he wanted only by stealing, it was necessary to become a thief. Or so he had decided. He relocked the drawer, replaced the keys on van Buren's dressing-table, and went warily out into the corridor. There was no one in sight and thankfully he regained his own room.

Nelly Bly tried to control her excitement by breathing very deeply and regularly, and at the same time she pondered the explanation of what she had seen. It was not really difficult, but to her disturbed mind the interpretation was complicated by the curiously identical appearance of the two portfolios (she had to hold Saturday's very tightly to reassure herself that Mr. Wesson had not stolen the poem) and by the fact that Mr. Wesson had bewilderingly appeared as an unrehearsed *dramatis persona* in her own plot against the secret of the oil. Her brain, not long before, had been full of the figments of an absorbing Russian mystery, and it seemed almost as if Mr. Wesson had stepped out of the same cupboard in which Boris and the Zik had been grown. She remembered her foolish boast that it was easier and pleasanter to act stories than to write them, and she confessed to herself with the sobriety which accompanies a trite reflexion, that facts are stranger than fiction and strong enough to ruin the prettiest plot.

It was clear that Mr. Wesson was a thief, and it was distressingly apparent that this actual thief had forestalled the more squeamish rifling to which she had incited Quentin. But the journalist in her rose and comforted her. Facts were facts and, what was more important, might become news. The secret of van Buren's discovery would be interesting to only a small part of the community, but the story of a desperate thief who had followed him across the Atlantic to rob him in a romantic English inn could be turned into news which would enthral a whole country. Nelly began to feel elated, and as her self-confidence came back she sturdily decided that to summon the police (especially the rustic police of Downish) and simply indicate a thief for them to arrest would be an anti-climax to this midnight adventure. She would wait till the morning and re-capture the documents herself. She might, though it was difficult to invent immediately the precise *modus operandi*, even arrest the thief herself. But certainly she would watch him, perhaps find out something about him to give body to her story, and in the end arrange a suitable *dénouement*. She must get to her room and think it out . . . but before she could do that she ought to restore the now unimportant portfolio under her arm to Saturday's table. There was no time for poetry with an international thief in the offing.

Once again she looked this way and the other, up and down

the dimly lit corridor, and as she prepared to creep back with the sheaf of poetry she heard some distance away the elemental sound of water escaping to find its own level . . . and heard, too, more footsteps approaching. All her fears returned. She shrank back into the darkness and scarcely dared to peer out and see van Buren re-enter his room. She had never thought of van Buren. She had unconsciously assumed that he was in his bedroom sound asleep while Wesson found what he wanted in his sitting-room. She dreaded more desperately than ever the danger of being discovered or the awful shock of being pounced on without warning: for now it seemed that people were everywhere night-walking, creeping in the shadows, opening doors, coming round corners, prowling, stalking, lurking, and listening. The night was full of movement and the darkness had eyes.

Oh dear, she thought. I wish I had never left London. I daren't go into Keith's room again. There may have been someone there the whole time. Or someone will be sure to come in if I do go. I simply daren't. I'm almost frightened to move.

She gathered together what courage she could find, and still carrying the only copy of Saturday's poem which the world possessed, ran to the narrow staircase which led to her own garret, and locked the door against the disturbed and terrifying world below. . . .

Angela Scrabster's room was some distance from this scene of adventure. But Angela Scrabster walked back to her room with the same look of one who had been at war with Nature as Mr. van Buren and Mr. Wesson had worn. She had to pass the main staircase that led down into the hall. It looked like a broad shaft to bottomless night. And as she was passing it she saw, to her horror, a white face in the darkness.

Angela Scrabster, in spite of physical weakness, had a courageous spirit which intercourse with Chinese generals and the pirates of the Yang-tse-kiang had toughened, and she called stoutly, "Who are you?"

"It's me," said an unhappy voice, and Holly come into the light.

"What do you mean by prowling about at this time of night?"

"I'm not prowling," said Holly.

"Well, why aren't you in bed?"

"Somebody's stolen it," said Holly.

"Stolen your bed?"

"My recipe. The recipe for the cocktails. It's gone. It was in the drawer, and it isn't there now. I had a dream that it had been stolen, and I got up to look for it, and the drawer's empty. And then I heard noises upstairs, and I thought perhaps it was the thief."

"Don't be ridiculous. You'll find your recipe in the morning. You've probably mislaid it. And now go back to your bed." Angela Scrabster spoke in the masterful tone which she was accustomed to use when dealing with servants or the natives of a foreign country, and Holly listened sulkily.

"It's all very well for you," he said. "You don't know the number of times they've tried to get it from me. My life's been a misery for the last few days. They're after it day and night. 'Come on, Holly,' they say. 'Let's have a look at it, Holly.' But I never thought they'd manage to get it. I've held 'em off—"

"I don't know who 'they' are and I can't stand here any longer. I advise you to go to bed." Angela Scrabster walked determinedly to her room.

Holly sat on the stairs and muttered to the darkness. "It's gone," he said. "The only thing I ever did in my life worth talking about, except getting bayoneted by a Prussian Guard. And then the bloody newspapers said that he was only a bloody Saxon. But they were wrong. I ought to know if anybody knows. Getting bayoneted and inventing a blue cocktail. That's all I've ever done to be proud of. And neither's done me any good."

Tears trickled coldly down Holly's nose, and he sniffed miserably. But his head began to nod, for he was very tired and not quite sober. He got to his feet, recognizing the advance of sleep, and stumbled downstairs. . . .

Under the elms between the bowling-green and the tennis-court, Joan turned to Saturday and said, "It's so late, my dear. We must go in."

The moon had travelled through space and the shadows crept lazily out on the grass. But neither Saturday nor Joan had been thinking about time, nor even of the moon, and certainly not of the shadows.

"I suppose we must," said Saturday.

They stood up and looked at the dark bulk of "The Pelican," the shadowy house with moon-glint in its windows.

"How utterly peaceful it is," said Joan. "It looks as though nothing could ever happen there except the coming of night and the coming of morning, and then night again, all through the centuries. Think of them all quietly sleeping in there. Everybody and everything sound asleep except ourselves and the moon."

"It's the most peaceful place in England," Saturday agreed.

CHAPTER XV

On Sunday morning there was a certain air of fatigue about "The Pelican." The English Sunday is normally a languid day on which even the sun frequently rises a little later than its advertised time. Nor, once they and the sun are up, do the English rush feverishly into motor-cars as the Americans do; nor do they paint themselves, dress extravagantly, and smack their lips in the anticipation of eating *en masse* at a too noisy restaurant; nor do they invade theatres, or abandon themselves to the epileptic intoxication of dancing; nor do they murder peace in any other of the glittering pastimes which profane and foolish people imagine to be enjoyment. On the contrary the English Sunday is a haven of peace; a full haven, perhaps, with its cargoes of bacon and eggs and marmalade and roast beef and potatoes and cauliflower and apple-pudding and plum-cake and so on; but still a haven. On Sunday England borrows the wisdom of the East and meditates; that is to say both mind and body become idle, spirit and flesh yawn together, and though it is written that Allah hateth him who yawns, yet God undoubtedly recognizes the yawner as one of his own Englishmen, such a one as he would choose for his highest enterprises. On Sunday John Bull becomes as placid as Buddha and looks (if you will sometimes substitute an umbrella for the lotos) not unlike Gautama in his well-fed solid security. On Sunday England is idle as a South Sea island; idler, perhaps, for we gather no hibiscus, spear no fish, nor laugh loud enough to attract a neighbour's notice.

The most godlike thing in England is its Sabbath calm, for in what other way do we surely ape divinity as in our seventh day lassitude? God took his ease, and so do we. Can you imagine God—at any rate such a God as made England, and that alone is a fair title even for Heaven—can you imagine God dancing on a Sunday afternoon as Siva of the Hindus dances? Can you imagine him joining a queue (the Milky Way) to see the Dioscuri, the Pleiades, Antares and the Snake, Arcturus and his precocious juvenile, or any other sidereal box-office attraction? God took his ease, and so does England. True, it may be necessary to relate some invasions of that ease; but they will not be related with any expression of approval. Six steps and a platform is the proper conception of a week, the ultimate step of Saturday night being steeper than the others. And on its platform the weary "Pelican" now rested.

Some of those who had dined so well on the previous evening looked pale. It was a spiritual pallor perhaps, for several decided to go to church. Most of them lounged, however, or moved slowly from chair to bookcase or on to the pleasant lawn and into the grateful shade of the elms. They moved with an easy dignity and grace, not very intent on their going, but rather as well-fed carp, in an aquarium tank who know that one place is very nearly as good as another. An aristocratic assumption—which is shared by aquarium carp—that no one would disturb them wherever they might go lent this dignity and ease to "The Pelican's" visitors; an aristocratic realization that, though the world might stare, the world did not matter, for it lay outside the tank and was forbidden by law to carry walking-sticks. But the assumption was false, and the carp deluded, for the world was going to invade their tank.

The first arrival from the outer lands was Lady Mercy Cotton, who came like a foreign disturbance indeed, driven by a chauffeur in maroon-coloured uniform in a maroon-coloured Isotta-Fraschini limousine. It was her custom to visit unexpectedly the different pubs which she owned; not, as she was careful to explain, to spy out irregularity or incompetence, for she recognized from afar competence wherever profits were made and incompetence where they were not. She visited her pubs because she was interested in them and liked to look at them, and she visited them without warning because she was a busy woman who seldom could predict a free day for herself.

"Well, Mr. Keith," she said, "and how are you getting on? I know you're getting on very well of course. I met Roger Baintry and Mrs. Anstruther and the man who makes biscuits—Brackley, isn't it? Yes, Brackley's Bran Biscuits. A dreadful idea. I always thought bran was something you make a mash of and gave to horses, but people will eat anything nowadays that's sufficiently unpalatable and properly advertised with pictures of fat children and a doctor's certificate. He makes a lot of money, I'm told. Brackley, I mean. And he and Mrs. Anstruther and Roger all insisted how much they had enjoyed themselves here. So have other people. And 'The Pelican's' making money, which is the most satisfactory proof of all. I'm heartily indebted to Quentin for the first time in my life—he's here, isn't he? he said he was coming—for introducing you to me. Who is that pretty girl over there?"

"That's Miss Benbow. Professor Benbow's daughter. They're both here."

"I'm glad to be reassured," said Lady Mercy. "I have an old woman's distrust of pretty girls who are alone in the world. How is your cook suiting you? the man you told me was a genius, and who had been in the Navy. I think everybody in the Navy is either a hero or a genius. I could never get into a hammock or understand navigation and all those electrical devices for bringing a shell out of the bowels of the ship and putting it straight into the gun. And they have to remember a hundred things like that when ordinary mortals would be too sea-sick to call for a steward. I believe in having the biggest Navy we can afford, just as an excuse to breed more sailors. I like them. Your man's name is O'Higgins, isn't it?"

"O'Higgins is splendid. If 'The Pelican' is a success it's he whom you have to thank far more than me."

"That's very nice and modest of you. Modesty is a rare virtue nowadays. Montaigne would be hard put to it to-day to find one of his favourite kind of lovers, young men with something of the shy boy in them when they—why there's Quentin."

"How are you, mother?" Quentin asked. "It's nearly a month since I've seen you."

"I was talking to your father about you yesterday. He said that you ought to get married. And I have implicit faith in your father when he talks about important commonplace matters."

"I think it's a good idea myself," said Quentin.

"I am glad to hear it. Young women are frequently so ambitious that they drive an idle husband to work, and though I am far from advocating—as some people do—indiscriminate work, work for works sake, I still think that serious occupation of some kind would be good for you. It would give you something to write about. And there are so many pretty girls that marriage is really no hardship. Miss Benbow, for example—"

"You mustn't talk about her in that light way, mother. Not while Saturday's here."

Lady Mercy turned to Saturday and her mobile eyebrows rose alarmingly.

"Have you been combining business with pleasure, Mr. Keith?" she asked.

Saturday looked uncomfortable, and said a little stiffly, "I have asked Joan Benbow to marry me."

"And if she is as sensible as she is pretty, she will," declared Lady Mercy. "But she mustn't take you away from 'The Pelican.' Let us go and talk to her."

Lady Mercy was in very good humour, and as she had momentarily exhausted her surplus of energy her conversation with Joan was less one-sided than that with Saturday. Joan, who had surfeited rather on moonlight than on marrow pie the previous evening, looked more fresh and vigorous than the majority of "The Pelican's" guests; which is gratifying to the dietician but disappointing to moralists. She and Lady Mercy rapidly established an harmonious understanding, and Quentin and Saturday found that they were not expected to contribute much to the colloquy.

The most active brain in "The Pelican" was Mr. Wesson's. Mr. Wesson had obtained what he wanted and was considerably embarrassed by it. He had hoped to acquire sufficient information about van Buren's discovery under the protective disguise of a harmless book-collector; and he had hoped to get away with that information still under the protection of the disguise. But circumstances had driven him to plain burglary. He had seen his time grow short, for van Buren would be leaving "The Pelican" in a day or two, and on more than one occasion he had been prevented in an attempt to examine the documents. He was, of course, unused to such work, and only filial exigence and a disillusioned *clientèle* had driven him to this robuster exploit. And now he was saddled with a black leather portfolio and a sheaf of papers which would convict him with unpleasant certainty as a common thief. Immediate escape was of necessity his next step. He might make a copy of van Buren's papers—though it would take him hours to do that—but he realized the extreme improbability of being able to return the portfolio before its removal had been discovered. He had no skill in opening locked doors and drawers, and he had to wait, to steal the documents, for an opportunity which was a pure gift of fortune. And fortune does not make gifts of that kind in quick succession. Therefore, since he could not return the portfolio, he had to escape with it. Nor was there time to lose.

Mr. Wesson knew all about the sailings of Atlantic liners. It was unfortunate that none of them happened to be leaving Southampton the following day. Nor was there one from Liverpool. But the *Turbania* would sail from Glasgow at two o'clock on Monday afternoon. Mr. Wesson decided to become a passenger on the *Turbania*. At that time of the year there was not a multitude of West-bound travellers, and he felt sure of being able to get a berth. He had two spare passports in different names and with different photographs. They had cost him a lot of money, but it was worth going to some expense to be able to change one's personality at will. He had only to clip his eyebrows, part his hair on the other side, alter the shape of his mouth (which he could do very well) and throw away his glasses to become Edward P. Huttar, a druggist of Indianapolis.

He thought it better to sacrifice his luggage and leave "The Pelican" unobserved. In that way his absence would be unnoticed till the following morning (van Buren would probably not discover the disappearance of his papers till then, or even later), by which time Mr. Wesson would have vanished . . . only in Glasgow a certain Edward Huttar would be enquiring in a strong Middle-Western accent whether he could make a last-minute reservation on the *Turbania*.

Mr. Wesson consulted a local time-table and found that there was a train leaving Downish at 1.55 p.m. which by devious paths would take him to Crewe, from where he could get without further trouble a connection to Glasgow. He packed an attaché case with a few shirts, a suit of pyjamas, some toilet trivia, and the embarrassing portfolio, and prepared himself to wait with fortitude till 1.55.

Meanwhile, Lady Mercy's party had grown. Several people, anxious to meet her, had persuaded either Quentin or Saturday—standing semi-connected on the fringe of her dialogue with Joan—to introduce them, and Lady Mercy liked meeting people though she had no inflated ideas about the importance or attractiveness of humanity in general. Professor Benbow had been summoned to the group by his daughter; Mr. van Buren had been eager to renew his friendship (a friendship of one meeting; but American hearts are warm) with Lady Mercy; Mrs. Waterhouse considered that it was due to her as the wife of a distinguished explorer and author to be introduced, and regretted having sent Diana to church; Sigismund Telfer was interested in people who had more money than they spent, for he contemplated a new literary review—a pity that Jacquetta, who had a bluff engaging manner, had also gone to church. So had Lady Porlet and one or two more. But the majority of those who had felt no inclination to worship God went to Lady Mercy, and the lounge of "The Pelican" was like a morning salon.

The conversation, however, was not literary. Lady Mercy heard an enthusiastic account of the Elizabethan dinner from those whose digestions had not been seriously disturbed and a more qualified appreciation from the sufferers—a story such as survivors of a shipwreck might tell, who have had time to notice the glory of the sunset as their vessel sank beneath the purple waves. And from gastronomy the talk turned to crime, that specific luxury of civilization. A jewel-thief had recently robbed an actress in a London hotel.

"It's a case of supply and demand," said Lady Mercy. "And where the supply is well advertised the demand becomes brisker. But luckily the market is localized. I've never had a thief in any of my pubs. They're all a fair distance from London and the modern thief dosen't like to travel far from his base."

"Murderers frequently live in the country," said Mrs. Waterhouse impressively.

"So do their victims," added Quentin; and Mrs. Waterhouse looked puzzled, as though her concept of cause and effect had been complicated.

"I once travelled in the Blue Train with a man who had served fourteen years imprisonment for robbing a bank and hitting the caretaker on the head with a gold watch; one of those very large and heavy gold watches—he showed it to me, a little proudly, I think, though he had given up burglary—that swung on the most massive chain I have ever seen. A dreadful weapon. It almost killed the poor man and broke the mainspring of the watch. Have you ever been at a highland gathering where people throw the hammer? The assault on the caretaker must have been just like that."

"But how could you bring yourself to talk to a burglar?" said an ash-blond lady of thirty-five with wiry neck muscles and jade earrings. "I should have fainted, I know. My nerves instantly tell me if there is anything foreign in the atmosphere. If I were to go into a house where there was a criminal of any kind, every nerve in my body would jangle like a fire-alarm. I react intensely to everything."

"Lend me your car for an hour," said Joan to Quentin in an aside. "I feel a *besoin de m'en aller.*"

"Certainly," said Quentin, "but it's getting near lunch time."

"I'm not hungry."

"A bad sign. You're probably sickening for something. Shall I come with you?"

"No I want to be alone."

Quentin had left his car in a small alley called Pelican Lane a few yards from the inn. Lady Mercy's moroon-coloured Isotta-Fraschini was also there, for one of the few disadvantages of "The Pelican" was that its garage was more than a hundred yards away, the old stables of its coaching days having been pulled down.

Quentin watched Joan drive away to feed her fancy in solitude for an hour. Saturday was busy with some detail or other of administration. Quentin strolled moodily along the almost deserted Sunday street, wondering what he could do to discharge his promise to Nelly. Because of his failure with van Buren he had avoided her since the evening painted so notably with her Russian pigments. He had sat closely with van Buren, walked with him, talked with him, but the old man had never again mentioned oil. And all the time Quentin's mind had been burdened by the secret of Nelly's disclosures, a secret which inflamed his imagination and made him impatient of other subjects, eager only to discuss and re-discuss the topic which he could not even mention. It had required a Spartan discipline to keep silent about it, and Quentin was feeling a little tired as even the Spartans themselves must occasionally have felt. Moreover he was at a loss and did not know what to do except look for Nelly and admit his incompetence. It was a cheerless prospect.

In these several ways Joan, Saturday and Quentin missed an amusing story of the uplands of Asia, told by Colonel Waterhouse.

"It was the only table in the countryside," he explained, "and as I was to be entertained a table was clearly necessary, so my host sent his servant for the solitary exhibit. They tied it on the back of a horse and the horse took fright and ran away, for it was the first time that it had ever been ridden by a table. . . ."

———

Saturday, having finished his work, looked idly out at Downish High Street. Little Miss Tibbs of the millinery shop was going home from church under the protection of a lilac sunshade, and as she passed a shop with green shutters—the street was suffused with light—it struck Saturday that there was something in Telfer's sino-colourist theories of poetry. . . . It required an imaginative observation to see and be impressed by a crane flying across a black cloud. The observation was specific, but the weakness of Telfer's poem was that the accompanying imagination was unspecific, a general emotional background to imagination rather than definite vision. In the same way little Miss Tibbs with her lilac sunshade and the green shutters and the sunny street could be made into a poem which tickled the brain without telling it anything. . . .

> Little Miss Tibb's lilac parasol
> On a sunny Sunday morning
> Bobbed by a shop with green shutters. . . .

I must ask Telfer about that, he decided. And then another thought struck him: had he locked up his own poem when Joan returned it? He couldn't remember having seen it since then, nor did he remember having put it away. He was on the point of going to reassure himself when like a trumpet a motor-horn sounded and a vast blue charabanc slid into the oval of light made by the open door of "The Pelican." A superb monster on fat white tyres, its sleek polished sides a gorgeous blue variegated with a gold name in bold running script. A charabanc as powerful as a tank—but no more like a tank than a Bond Street exquisite is like the Piltdown Man— and impressive as an Ambassador's limousine—and yet more like a bus than a limousine, for thirty travellers (which is more than follow even the least important of ambassadors) looked at "The Pelican" from its superb upholstery, A Cleopatra's barge of a charabanc; and its name was the "Blue Bird."

A brisk young man with a badge in his buttonhole got down and walked confidently into "The Pelican."

CHAPTER XVI

The Giggleswade Literary Society was a cut above the Giggleswade Dramatic Association and definitely superior to the
Giggleswade Debating Club. Once upon a time the Literary Society and the Dramatic Association had been one flesh, and if
Miss Horsfall-Hughes had never heard of Pirandello they might
so have continued. But in 1926 when the annual discussion
arose as to whether they should produce the *Gondoliers* or the
Mikado for Christmas, Miss Horsfall-Hughes tried to make
hay out of dissension by suggesting a ridiculous play about several characters who were in search of an author. "Several credi-
tors, I suppose you mean," interjected young Mr. Saunders, who
hoped to be Nanki-poo. Whereupon Miss Horsfall-Hughes lost
her temper—having just discovered Pirandello she felt obliged
to defend him—and accused the Society of hyprocrisy, blatancy,
cheapness, nastiness, little-mindedness, lack of originality, Vic-
torianism, brains like rocking-chairs, blindness, aspidistras,
and general illiteracy. A number of people applauded her, and
following her from the Church Hall, in which the meetings of
the Society took place, declared themselves divorced from it for
ever. Immediately, under a lamp-post, a new society was formed
with Miss Horsfall-Hughes as its first president, everyone of
whose members pretended to be familiar with the works of
Joyce, Proust, Stendhal, Virginia Woolf and Mr. Eliot. And
what was left of the old society made the very happy choice of
Iolanthe for their Christmas production.

The seceders included in their summer programme a series
of visits to places of literary interest—"neighbourhoods still
peopled with the ghosts of the pioneers; of the rude craftsmen
of letters, of the strong sowers of the sixteenth, seventeenth and
eighteenth centuries," as Miss Horsfall-Hughes strikingly expressed it—and they chose to travel by charabanc because of
the opportunities afforded by such vehicles for informal discussion (if one's voice is sufficiently robust), because their new
society was of precisely such a size as would comfortably fill a
charabanc, and because of the uncertainty of Sunday train-
services; Sunday being their favourite day for excursions as

Sabbath quiet was one of their favourite jibes at England. It is hardly necessary to say that the present pilgrimage to Downish had not been inspired by Saturday's poetry. There had been poets in "The Pelican" before Saturday, worse poets by far, and the ghosts of Fabian Metcalf, Philip Goode, and Martin Stout were presently to be disturbed—those three poor poets of the seventeenth century who wrote in the manner (they thought) of Abraham Cowley and sometimes even in the manner of Donne; and who wrote so badly that scarce a scholar had disturbed them, never an editor edited them, nor a commentator commented on them (though in their day a landlord of "The Pelican" listened reverently to their sick-room conceits, their limping camel-like metaphors, and rarely charged them for what they drank). Happy poets, who were contented in their lives and in their deaths were not derided, being already forgotten. But their obscurity, which so long had left their ghosts in peace, had now betrayed them and brought the Giggleswaders to posture about their tombs.

Mr. Sidgwick, the energetic secretary of the Literary Society, explained to Saturday why he had forgotten to warn him of their arrival and order a modest but satisfying lunch for thirty people.

"In Giggleswade, of course, everyone knows our plans as well as we do ourselves," he said. "The *Weekly Gazette* always gives us a lot of space and we're such a general topic of conversation that it's sometimes difficult to remember that other places—Downish, for example—aren't equally *au fait* with our movements. But I suppose you can give us lunch all right? An establishment like this—"

"Naturally," Saturday answered, and mentioned the price of lunch at "The Pelican"; a price intended to make charabanc parties wince and drive on. Mr. Sidgwick whistled protestingly. But by this time the charabanc had emptied, and Miss Horsfall-Hughes bore down on them.

"Mr. Keith, I presume?" she said. "How interesting to meet you. And still more interesting to think that Fabian Metcalf once stood here. Mr. Sidgwick has told you we want lunch, I suppose?"

"Eight-and-six a head," whispered Mr. Sidgwick.

"Grossly excessive, of course, but one expects that. When will it be ready, Mr. Keith?"

"In half-an-hour," said Saturday. "The church where Metcalf is buried is only five minutes' walk from here."

The pilgrimage moved off in the direction he indicated, an untidy procession in which the men were outnumbered three to one and the spinsters had a clear majority of nine over the bachelors. Saturday rapidly gave instructions for their entertainment, a task which was made easier by O'Higgins's report that some dishes remained untouched from the previous night's dinner. It was a triumph calmly to be able to accept such an incursion, to cater for thirty unexpected visitors, and he was glad that Lady Mercy was there to see how he handled an emergency. She and everybody else living in "The Pelican" had heard the arrival of the "Blue Bird," and some were a little upset at the contiguity of wayfarers so crude as to go anywhere in a charabanc. . . .

All morning Nelly Bly had been looking for an opportunity to replace the embarrassing portfolio containing "*Tellus* Will Proceed," and all morning, it seemed, there had been a continuous procession past Saturday's door. Twice she had come down the tortuous staircase from her room with the fat leather envelope under her apron, and twice she had fled upstairs again to hide it beneath her mattress. She was puzzled, too, by the behaviour of Mr. Wesson, who had stayed in his room since breakfast. She had looked through the keyhole and found that, in spite of all that has been written about them, keyholes afford a very poor view. She could see nothing but a portion of the trousers which Mr. Wesson was wearing, and in them she rapidly exhausted her interest. . . .

Mr. Wesson had looked at his watch every five minutes since packing his attaché case. Sometimes he sat down and tried to read, sometimes he paced his carpet. Neither activity helped time onward in its measured round. Twice Mr. Wesson held the watch to his ear, suspecting it had stopped; but its remorseless, unhurried ticking disproved his hope. He heard the swollen note of a motor-horn, and looked at his watch again. It was one o'clock. He could not face his fellow-guests at lunch. He decided to walk to the station, put his attaché case in the left-luggage room, and go for a stroll till train-time. Mr. Wesson put on his hat, picked up the attaché case, and softly opened the door. For a moment he held it ajar.

Across the narrow opening, soft-footed, stole Nelly Bly. Mr. Wesson was about to close his door again and wait, when he saw to his amazement that she carried what appeared to be van Buren's black leather portfolio. Two hours before he had put that portfolio in his attaché case. And there it was in Nelly Bly's hand. Tortured by two hours of waiting, Mr. Wesson's nerve snapped like one fiddle-string and his common-sense like another. He heard them, quite clearly, snap in his head.

"Here!" he said hoarsely, and stepped into the corridor. "What are you doing with that ring-book?"

Nelly turned and vainly tried to hide the portfolio behind her. Mr. Wesson had startled her as badly as she had startled him.

"That's none of your business," she said with a gasp.

"Give it to me," said Mr. Wesson.

"I shall do nothing of the sort."

Mr. Wesson took a step towards her. His face, normally so expressionless, looked suddenly hard and dangerous. Nelly handed him the portfolio.

Mr. Wesson took it, stared at her for a moment and opened it.

"Holy Christ!" he said.

"If you're going to say your prayers," Nelly began.

Enlightenment suddenly came to Mr. Wesson. Double enlightenment.

"You stole this," he said.

"What if I did?"

"I ought to give you in charge."

"But you won't."

"Why do you think that?"

"Because you have stolen the other one." A foolish dramatic instinct compelled Nelly to say this. It came pat to her tongue as she knew it would have come pat to the tongue of a young woman in a similar situation on the popular stage. But no sooner had she said it than she regretted her rashness, for Mr. Wesson's expression, which had relaxed, became dangerous again and loomed like the close-up photograph of a villain in the cinema.

"I don't understand you," said Mr. Wesson mendaciously. "You have stolen this"—he opened the portfolio again—"this poetry, which by the name on it is the property of Mr. Keith, and my duty is to give you in charge."

"Mr. Keith lent it to me."

Mr. Wesson laughed unpleasantly.

"There's someone coming," said Nelly quickly, losing her head at the idea of being caught with Keith's poem.

Mr. Wesson pushed her, scarcely protesting, into his room and locked the door. Footsteps went past and Mr. Wesson looked at his watch.

"If I let you go without telling Mr. Keith about this," he said, and paused. "What did you mean by saying that I had stolen 'the other one'?" he concluded.

"Do you want to make a bargain?" Nelly suggested.

"Yes," Mr. Wesson agreed.

"You are trying to escape?"

"I am leaving 'The Pelican.'"

"Then tell me why you stole van Buren's papers and I'll do nothing to hinder you."

"That is very kind of you," said Mr. Wesson suavely. "But who told you that I had stolen any papers?"

"I saw you take them, and you practically confessed it yourself by mistaking this portfolio for van Buren's."

"So I did," said Mr. Wesson. "You're a very clever young lady."

Nelly was inclined to agree with him, for though she could not imagine how the affair was going to end it appeared that she had the upper hand.

"And you know too much for my comfort and far too much for your own," he continued. "Sit down there, will you?" He pointed to a plain bedroom chair.

"Why?" demanded Nelly.

"Because I tell you to," said Mr. Wesson, and picked up a small bottle which stood on his dressing-table.

"What's that?" asked Nelly.

"Vitriol," replied Mr. Wesson smoothly.

Nelly sat down quickly. Her face was white and she felt a sudden terror which made her fingers limp, her tongue dry, and her knees tremble. All thought of her own cleverness vanished, and the situation became void of any meaning except the threat of scorching acid.

Mr. Wesson took out the cork and set the bottle within easy reach on the dressing-table. He then pulled half-a-dozen ties and a few handkerchiefs from a drawer.

"Please sit quite still," he said.

Nelly obeyed so far as her trembling knees would let her, and Mr. Wesson tied her securely to the chair with his neckties, some of which were too gaudy for English taste. Carefully he tested the ligatures, and one, he discovered, was a little loose. A pamphlet with the picture of a ship on it lay on his table, and Mr. Wesson doubled and re-doubled it into a wedge which he forced beneath the slack necktie and the chair-leg, so that this fastening became as tight as the others.

"I shall have to gag you, of course," he continued. "Open your mouth."

"No!" said Nelly desperately.

Mr. Wesson's hand went out to the bottle on the dressing-table, and Nelly's mouth opened wide. Mr. Wesson made a ball of a linen handkerchief and thrust it in, but seeing her shudder he removed it and substituted a silk one. Then he tied in the gag with another handkerchief.

"I'm sorry to have to do this," he said, "it's the first time in my life that I have ever insulted a woman. But necessity knows no law. You'll have to wait here till the morning, when I suppose they'll find you. Though no one will become suspicious till about mid-day, nor curious enough about my non-appearance to force the door till then. But you'll be none the worst after a rest, and by that time I shall be on my way to America. I don't know who you are or what you are, but you know too much for my liking. That's all I've got against you, and I'd like to have you believe that I'm real sorry to treat a woman like this. And now I must go."

Mr. Wesson picked up his attaché case and turned to the

door. Then he remembered the little bottle, and carefully re-
placing the cork, slipped it into his pocket. He left the room,
locked the door, and removed the key.

Nelly, of necessity, sat mute and still as a mummy.

CHAPTER XVII

The Giggleswaders returned from St. Saviour's having inspected
the tombs of Fabian Metcalf and Martin Stout. Philip Goode,
of course, was drowned in the Teem, the little river which en-
closes Downish in a sickle-like bend, and as his last poem had
dealt academically with the occasional necessity of suicide, what
was left of him had been buried in unconsecrated ground. But
Fabian Metcalf had a handsome epitaph in Latin, and Martin
Stout one of his own composition in English more difficult by
far than any Latin. The Giggleswaders, then, sat down to lunch
with an adequate topic of conversation.

Miss Horsfall-Hughes wanted to recall, for the sixth or seventh time, the process of exhaustive reading and intensive re-
search by which she had discovered the now immortal trio, but
a strong opposition party arose in Mr. and Mrs. Harringay, Miss
Beastly, and Mrs. Duluth, who had recently spent some time
abroad and were naturally anxious not only to make other people aware of the advantages of travel, but to discuss with each
other the astonishing behaviour of the French and Italians. So
that whenever Miss Horsfall-Hughes said anything about the
British Museum Mrs. Harringay countered with news from the
Rialto, and to enlightened criticism of meta-physical poetry
Miss Beastly opposed an anecdote about Mussolini.

Mrs. Harringay had met someone who knew intimately the
friend of an Italian princess who had, not long before, married
a wealthy American.

"It seems that she did most of the courting," said Mrs.
Harringay.

"Of course, being royal, she would have to," explained Miss
Beastly.

"No, it wasn't that at all. It was just that she was crazy about him. She used to send him telegrams."

"Foreigners have no restraint," said Mr. Harringay. "And what is worse, they're greedy. Neither in France nor in Italy is there any commercial conscience nowadays. I remember going into a chemist's shop in Nice to buy a corn-plaster. They were fifteen centimes each. I took one and gave the shop-assistant twenty-five centimes. He put it into the till. I asked him for the change, and he said that he hadn't got any change. So I said, 'Well, suppose you give me another plaster?' Which he did. And do you know, he absolutely insisted on my paying him the odd five centimes?"

"The Germans are still sentimental," interposed the only really pretty girl in the party.

Miss Horsfall-Hughes looked expressively at Mr. Sidgwick, murmuring, "And we are a literary society!" Mr. Sidgwick, who had the soul of one who shows people into their proper seat at a subscription concert, shrugged his shoulders and tried to look both plaintive and amused at the littleness of life.

"I met him in Venice," explained the pretty girl, "and he took me out in a gondola. He had been a musician at one time, but he was selling aluminium then. He was very sentimental. He wept because of the moonlight on the canal. And when I told him that my brother was twenty-one, he said, 'Ah, to be twenty-one!' and wept a lot more."

"I wonder if we could arrange for a Downish edition of Metcalf and his friends," said Mr. Sidgwick. "Not a complete edition, perhaps, but a selection of their works?"

"An idea that I have entertained for some time," said Miss Horsfall-Hughes.

But the Giggleswaders, having looked at two tombs and puzzled over two obscure epitaphs, were concerned with livelier matters.

"It was the war which ruined these Continental people," said Mr. Harringay with the mien of a seer and the assurance of a meteorologist.

"And the peace," added Mrs. Harringay knowingly. "President Wilson and all those foolish discussions in Versailles."

"My husband knew Wilson intimately," said Mrs. Duluth, "and thought the world of him. But he still says that he was eaten up with vanity, and because of that everybody could pull the wool over his eyes."

Miss Beastly had a tripartite reverence for Woodrow Wilson, Lenin and Benito Mussolini.

"That was because President Wilson was too good for them," she said warmly. "I mean *good* in its proper sense. He thought that everything was going to be fair and above-board, and it wasn't."

"Well, anyway, he was very vain," persisted Mrs. Duluth. "Do you remember what Clemenceau—I think it was Clemenceau—said about him? Of course he said it in French, and I don't speak French, but my husband does, naturally, and tells it so funnily. Clemenceau said, 'What does this man Wilson mean by coming over here with his Fourteen Points? Why, even the good God—*le bon Dieu*, you know—found Ten sufficient!' But you should hear it in French. It sounds so much funnier in French, as my husband tells it."

The lunch pursued its course in a warring atmosphere of literary and cosmopolitan interests, the only apparent union between the two parties being a general though unspoken decision to extract the utmost return from their eight-and-sixpences, and by the time that coffee appeared there was a general air of repletion.

A motor-car went noisily up the High Street.

"I wonder what is going on outside?" said Mrs. Harringay lazily, as she lit her second cigarette.

"There seems to be a disturbance of some kind," remarked the lady to whom no one had paid attention till then.

Everybody listened carefully. There was the sound of hurrying feet in the passage outside, and a subdued tumult of voices abruptly dominated by a man who declared, for some unknown reason, "I'm coming, too!"

"Hurry up then," replied a deeper voice.

"That sounded like Mr. Keith," said Miss Horsfall-Hughes.

Mr. Sidgwick and several other Giggleswaders got up and went to the window that gave them a view of Downish High

Street and the after part of the "Blue Bird" which, with no concern for the narrowness of the thoroughfare, had been left standing in front of "The Pelican."

"Why, it's going!" exclaimed Mr. Sidgwick.

"Motor-car thieves!" said the only pretty girl in something like ecstasy.

Half the party rushed to the window and half to the door. Those who went to the door got out in time to see Lady Mercy, Professor Benbow, Mr. van Buren and several others standing at the main entrance of "The Pelican" in the attitude of a Greek chorus when the messenger has just announced a fresh crisis; and disappearing up Downish High Street, with a feather of blue smoke behind it, the swollen cerulean stern of the "Blue Bird."

CHAPTER XVIII

Mr. Wesson arrived at the station with plenty of time to spare. The booking-office had not opened, but Mr. Wesson properly assumed that the booking-clerk knew his own business. Before the 1.55 came snorting and roaring into Downish he would bang up his little window in time to sell tickets to Glasgow (change at Dullage, Stafford and Crewe) or any other town that travellers might consider worth visiting.

Mr. Wesson walked on to the platform. It wasn't worth while putting his attaché case in the left-luggage room—the left-luggage room appeared to be closed anyhow—as the intrusion of Nelly Bly into his affairs had taken up so much time that he now had barely twenty minutes or so to wait. There was no one else on the platform and Mr. Wesson strolled up and down feeling more at ease than he had done for some days. The van Buren papers were safely hidden between his pyjamas and his shirts, he had a useful selection of passports, no one at "The Pelican" would notice his disappearance till the following day, and then no one would know where he had gone . . . that, he remembered, was not quite accurate. He had told the red-haired chambermaid that he was going to America. A foolish thing to do, but he had felt some compunction at having to tie her up, and the admission that he was going so far away as America had been in the nature of an explanation. Mr. Wesson belonged to a courteous nation, a nation reverent of its womanhood, and he realized that any man owes an explanation to a girl whom he ties to a bedroom chair under the threat of splashing her with vitriol. Perhaps on this occasion he should have suppressed his better feelings, though. But it did not matter. In less than twenty minutes he would be on the train, and by Monday morning he would have disappeared entirely; while in the unremarkable grey suit which Mr. Wesson was wearing, Mr. Edward P. Huttar of Indianapolis would be booking an Atlantic passage in Glasgow.

His spirits rose, and as he walked light-heartedly to the south end of the platform Mr. Wesson whistled a little tune. They were pleasant places, these English country stations, with their clean white platforms, and beyond the platforms flower-beds which the station-master assiduously tended in his spare time. Even the advertisements were in harmony with the semi-rural scene; they humanized it, these bright injunctions to buy Oxo and Bovril and Swan Vestas. And the rails, steely straight ribbons shining so fiercely, were indescribably attractive.

Mr. Wesson walked northwards again. He was still the only prospective passenger on his own side of the station, but on the opposite platform a man sat reading. A comfortable-looking man who had discarded his coat and sat very contentedly in his shirt-sleeves, smoking his pipe and reading his Sunday newspaper. It was curious, thought Mr. Wesson, that no one else was travelling, though he knew very well that the better kind of English people rarely leave their homes on a Sunday.

It occurred to him that he could pleasantly spend a few minutes in talking to the comfortable-looking man opposite, and with a ready introduction on his tongue he crossed the foot-bridge.

"A fine day," said Mr. Wesson.

"There's nothing wrong with it," agreed the man, looking up from his paper.

"It's from that platform, isn't it"—Mr. Wesson pointed across the lines—"that the 1.55 goes to Dullage? I'm travelling farther," he explained, "but I have to change at Dullage."

"Maybe," said the man, "I've never been further than Bromley myself."

"Is Bromley on the way to Dullage?" asked Mr. Wesson.

"It is," said the man, "if you go that way."

"And when you went to Bromley, did you leave from that platform?"

"Ar!" said the man, "you've taken me up wrongly. I was living in Thorple then."

"I see," said Mr. Wesson—which was not strictly true—and walked up and down for a few minutes while the man continued to read his paper. Then he crossed the footbridge to see if the booking-clerk had arrived, and was slightly perturbed to find that there was no sign of life in the book-office, or the station-master's office, or the waiting-room, or even the left-luggage room.

Mr. Wesson re-crossed the footbridge and said to the man, who was filling his pipe, "I suppose you aren't the station-master, are you?"

"No, I'm not," said the man. "I'm a rat-catcher. Rats and weasels and stoats and moles. Vermin of all kind. Sometimes a cat, if I know someone that wants one. But chiefly rats. Though I'm pretty good with weasels."

"Do you know when the booking-office opens?" interrupted Mr. Wesson.

"'Bout nine o'clock if there happens to be an early train," said the rat-catcher.

"Nine o'clock! But it's nearly two, and there's no one in the station except ourselves."

"Ar!" said the rat-catcher, "this is Sunday, you see."

"But what difference does, that make?"

"Just you wait here for an hour or two and you'll see for yourself."

"Do you mean to say that there aren't any trains on Sunday?"

"Some of them goes through here," said the rat-catcher, "but I've never seen one stop."

"Good God in Heaven!" exclaimed Mr. Wesson.

"So they say," agreed the rat-catcher.

Mr. Wesson was stunned. The metaphor is violent (though not uncommon), but only a violent figure can illustrate the shock to which he had been subjected. He sat down and tried to compose the agitation which succeeded his first feeling of stupor.

"An automobile!" he exclaimed.

The rat-catcher looked at him curiously.

"A motor-car," Mr. Wesson explained. "Can I hire a motor-car?"

The rat-catcher shook his head. "Not on a Sunday. There is a garage in Downish, but it's closed on Sunday, and all the drivers, or both of them, I should say, 'll be at home sleeping, or digging in their gardens, or listening to their missuses, or reading the paper, same as I am. I like the station on a Sunday morning—it's a nice quiet place to have a bit of a read—but those motor-car drivers generally stays at home."

Mr. Wesson got up distractedly and crossed the bridge for the fourth time. He felt very like one of the weasels which his new friend was pretty good at catching, and as a cornered weasel will, it is asserted, leap for the throat of the hunter, so Mr. Wesson was prepared to add crime to crime in his reasonable determination—for he could not return to "The Pelican"—to get out of Downish. If he could not hire a car he was ready to steal one.

There might be a car or two in "The Pelican" garage, though to reach that he would have to pass "The Pelican" itself. And then the garage might be locked or empty, for few of the visitors had brought motor-cars with them. Mr. Wesson gloomily remembered that in England a car is not considered a necessary domestic utensil, as it is in America. In America one could pick up an automobile at any street corner. But rural England is still a vacant parking-ground.

Quentin Cotton had a Bentley, he recalled, and Holly the barman had an aged Morris-Cowley. Sir Philip Betts, the racing motorist, had been riding a bicycle to keep his weight down. . . . The sun shone out of a clear sky and Mr. Wesson felt perspiration clammily oozing under his hat. He was nearing "The Pelican." A huge blue charabanc stood in front of it. He couldn't very well steal a charabanc. It was too conspicuous for his purpose. But there was no other car in sight. Not a vehicle of any sort standing trustfully under tree or lamp-post, and Mr. Wesson knew nothing about Lady Mercy's Isotta-Fraschini which stood in the little cul-de-sac called Pelican Lane.

He braced himself to walk past the inn as though he had no interest in it, or as though he were as innocent as Lady Porlet whom he saw approaching it from the opposite direction. She would probably stop and speak to him, he thought viciously. The old busybody! And then, coming towards him, rapidly overtaking Lady Porlet, smoothly running, shining in the sun, he saw a two-seater car such as any fugitive would give his kingdom for. It was Quentin Cotton's Bentley driven by Joan Benbow, who had been far enough to feed her thoughts on loneliness.

The charabanc filled half the street in front of "The Pelican" and Joan stopped a little short of it. Mr. Wesson crossed to the opposite pavement. Joan turned in her seat and called to Lady Porlet, who was no more than a couple of yards away, "Are you going in, Lady Porlet?"

"Yes, my dear," said Lady Porlet. "I've just had lunch at the Vicarage. Such a charming man. And his wife a most sensible woman. Is there anything I can do for you?"

"Tell George or someone to bring out the key of the garage, will you, so that I can put Mr. Cotton's car in?"

"Certainly," said Lady Porlet. "How very nice for you to be able to drive all by yourself."

She smiled graciously and walked on towards "The Pelican."

Mr. Wesson had meanwhile made up his mind. Here was the car he wanted—a Bentley has the reputation of easily acquiring a speed which pedestrians consider excessive—and though he had no desire for a companion, if he didn't take both the car and its present driver it would be out of his reach in a few minutes.

Joan looked round to find Mr. Wesson getting into the seat beside her.

"Drive down to the Square," he said before she could speak.

"Why," she exclaimed, "what do you mean? Is this a joke?"

He put an attaché case which he carried on to the floor be-

tween his feet and repeated, "Drive down to the Square—
quickly!"

"Mr. Wesson!" said Joan, and stopped curiously as he took
a small bottle out of his pocket.

"What is that?" she asked.

"Vitriol," replied Mr. Wesson. He removed the cork, and as
Joan shrank away, held the bottle a few inches under her nose.
It had a pungent smell.

"Now will you drive on?" he asked.

"But why?" persisted Joan, tearful and already feeling for
the clutch.

"Because I tell you to," said Mr. Wesson.

A familiar voice interrupted them. Lady Porlet had come
back to ask, "Was it George whom you wanted, my dear?"

"*Say 'No, I don't want him now,'*" whispered Mr. Wesson,
and tilted the little bottle towards Joan. His hand concealed it
from Lady Porlet, to whom he presented an appearance of one
unconcernedly dallying.

"I don't want him now," repeated Joan in a high-pitched,
breathless kind of voice.

"*And hurry up.*"

The car shot forward, swerving past the charabanc, leaving
Lady Porlet with a look of mild surprise on her face, and in a
few seconds reached the Square.

"Now turn and go back," said Mr. Wesson, "I want to go
northwards."

Joan was sobbing tearlessly, almost frightened out of her
wits, and driving very badly. Mr. Wesson said comfortingly, "I
have no intention of hurting you if you do what I tell you to.
Now be a good girl and drive a little, straighter."

"Then put that bottle away," Joan gasped.

"You promise to drive on?"

"Yes!"

Mr. Wesson put the bottle in his pocket and they repassed
"The Pelican" at fair speed. Mr. Wesson, looking round as
they passed, saw Lady Porlet just about to go in. Evidently her
curiosity had kept her meditating on the pavement for a space
of some seconds.

They left Downish behind them, The road, between the poplars which go all the way to Little Needham, was quieter than the street, for the trees returned no echo of their passing.

"I can't drive any longer," said Joan suddenly. "I don't feel well."

"Then stop the car," said Mr. Wesson, "and I'll take your place."

"Are you going to let me out?"

"I can't" said Mr. Wesson regretfully, "not yet at any rate. Because I don't want anyone to know where I am or what I'm doing at present. I'm in a very difficult position. For the second time in an hour I have been forced to treat a lady in a way which I shall always deplore, and I'm real sorry. But courtesy must bow to circumstance. I'm going to Scotland. Do I turn left or right here?"

"Right," said Joan.

"Thank you," said Mr. Wesson.

Joan began to recover her composure. She had felt as once when swimming too far out at sea the tide pulled at her legs and the beach would come no closer; a flutter of panic weakened her, a wave leapt in her face as if to choke her, and for a moment or two her arms beat wildly; and then she set her teeth and swam strongly and never looked up to see how far away the beach was; and presently she found herself in shallow water. Now that Mr. Wesson was driving the terrible little bottle which smelt so pungently was in the pocket farther away from her.

They passed a scout of the Automobile Association.

"You should have returned that A.A. man's salute," she said.

"I'm sorry. We don't have them in the States, but I'll remember the next time."

"Why are you going to Scotland? And why are you taking me? And what are you going to do when you get there?"

"You needn't be afraid of anything so long as you sit quiet," said Mr. Wesson comfortingly. "I shan't hurt you or do anything to upset you; at least as little as possible."

"But why have you kidnapped me like this? It's no use holding me to ransom, because father hasn't got a great deal of money."

"You misjudge me," said Mr. Wesson. "I am not a kidnapper."

"Then what are you? I thought you collected old books."

Mr. Wesson shuddered. "I hate them," he said with some feeling.

Fields slid past them in a green blur that travelled at fifty-five miles an hour. Trees grew tall in front of them, loomed tremendously, passed them, and dwindled in their wake. A dog barked. A hen fluttered madly over the road, squawking hysterically. Two or three little houses went by in a red-brick haze. Green hedges lined the road. A farmyard smell swept over them. Five cows looked up, still chewing the cud, and a calf took fright in its friendly field.

Mr. Wesson began to explain.

CHAPTER XIX

Hot and dishevelled from her struggle, Nelly Bly twisted her foot out of the last of Mr. Wesson's neckties and stood up free. The door was still locked but she carried a master-key, as other maids did, and the final barrier swung urbanely back. On the point of leaving the bedroom she turned and picked up the black portfolio which held "*Tellus* Will Proceed." Mr. Wesson had contemptuously tossed it into a corner. But since it had shared her misfortune Nelly felt attached to it. She ran hastily downstairs.

She knew more about the English railway system than Mr. Wesson did, and she was almost sure that on Sunday the Down-ish train-service was non-existent. But he had spoken so calmly, with such an assumption of fact, about the 1:55 that she was going to the station to make certain. She was still determined on an individual scoop, and the scoop now depended wholly on the capture of Mr. Wesson. Naturally enough she was very excited, and when she ran through the door of "The Pelican" into the arms of Lady Porlet she was impatient at the delay.

"Dear me," said Lady Porlet, staggering a little.

"I'm sorry," said Nelly, and tried to get past her, first on one side and then on the other.

"You ought indeed to be sorry—"

"But, I'm in a hurry—"

"Like a jack-in-the-box, both you and—"

"I didn't mean to—"

"Mr. Wesson appearing from nowhere—"

"*Wesson?* When did you see him?"

"He suddenly appeared beside Miss Benbow in Mr. Cotton's car, which she was driving—"

"What the devil was he doing with her? And when?"

"He seemed to be taking her for a ride," said Lady Porlet. "About a minute ago."

"Which way did they go?"

"First of all they went down that way and then they came back. Perhaps I should say that she appeared to be taking him for a ride. She asked me to go and find George—"

"You spoke to them?"

"When I was coming back from the Vicarage. But I wish you wouldn't swear. A girl in your position can't be too careful, and it was unnecessary to say, 'What the devil,' because even if he exists, which many people doubt nowadays, though I think they have less reason for doubting his existence than their parents had, it is an unseemly expression—"

"Listen," said Nelly firmly. She had reflected for a few seconds—she seldom reflected longer—and decided what to do. She put her arm through Lady Porlet's and walked her out of "The Pelican" and up the pavement towards Pelican Lane, where she had abruptly, brilliantly remembered Lady Mercy's car was standing. "Listen," she said, and Lady Porlet was not a little ruffled at being spoken to in such a tone by a maid. "Go and tell Mr. Keith that Wesson has stolen van Buren's portfolio. A portfolio like this."—She waved Saturday's poem before Lady Porlet's startled eyes.—"Tell him that Wesson and Joan Benbow are together in Quentin Cotton's car, heading north, probably for Scotland, and that I am following them in Lady Mercy's. Do you understand?"

"No," said Lady Porlet, "I'm afraid I don't. You say Mr. Wesson has stolen something?"

"O my God," said Nelly. They had come to the little crooked lane and the dark-red opulent limousine was before them. "Tell Mr. Keith that Wesson has stolen the portfolio. Tell him that he is escaping in Quentin Cotton's car. Tell him that I think Wesson is making for Glasgow. Joan Benbow is with him—"

"I know that," said Lady Porlet with some dignity. "It was I who told you that, as a matter of fact!"

"Then tell Keith!"

Nelly could wait no longer. She got into the Isotta-Fraschini, backed it out of the cul-de-sac, shouted "There's not a second to lose!" as stern-first she passed Lady Porlet, and shot up the High Street in pursuit of the long-vanished Bentley.

"Not a second to lose!" repeated Lady Porlet with a sudden realization that something serious was happening, and ran in an old-lady-like but well-meant manner back to "The Pelican." She found Saturday in his office with Lady Mercy and Quentin.

Saturday had just discovered the loss of his poem and they were all in a state of half-ashamed consternation, unwilling to believe in theft, unable to think of a different explanation of its disappearance, when Lady Porlet appeared at the door in evident distress. She was out of breath but full of some tremendous purpose.

"There's not a second to lose!" she gasped. "He has stolen your portfolio and is going to Scotland with Joan Benbow!"

Saturday and Quentin leapt to their feet. Lady Mercy looked equally amazed, but sat still. With praiseworthy control Saturday helped Lady Porlet to a chair. "I don't understand," he said.

"She told me to say that there wasn't a second to lose," repeated Lady Porlet, "and she is following them in your car."

"My car?" asked Lady Mercy. "Who is following whom in my car?"

"A red-haired girl. One of the maids here. And Mr. Wesson and Joan Benbow are in the other car—your car, Mr. Cotton— and he has got your portfolio."

"Joan!" said Saturday. "And *Wesson*!"

"Nelly!" said Quentin.

"And who is Mr. Wesson?" Lady Mercy enquired.

"Wesson is a book-collector. Good God!" Saturday exclaimed, as an image of comprehension, tragic and magnificent, came to him, "he's stolen my manuscript—he collects first editions—the only copy I have! And Joan—"

"Tried to stop him," said Quentin.

"And she's with him now?" asked Lady Mercy.

"I saw them," said Lady Porlet. "She asked me to send George out to her with the key of the garage, and then Mr. Wesson mysteriously appeared and got into the car, and she said that she didn't want George after all, and they drove away. Then the red-haired girl came out with the portfolio—"

"*Nelly* had the portfolio?"

"You said Wesson had stolen it."

"Yes, and the red-haired girl showed it to me, though whether her name is Nelly or not I can't say. She swore twice and drove away very quickly—"

"I'm completely bewildered," said Lady Mercy.

"So am I," said Saturday, "but we've got to follow them."

"There isn't a car in the place if mine is gone, and mother's is gone—"

"You can telephone—"

"To the Downish police? That won't be much good."

By this time they were in the hall, and the sound of their excitement (for their voices had risen a little) was attracting attention. Mr. van Buren, Colonel Waterhouse, Jacquetta Telfer and some others strolled out to see what was happening.

"I'm going to take the charabanc," said Saturday resolutely. "Which way did they go?"

"Towards Scotland. That's where the girl told me they were going," said Lady Porlet, and pointed vaguely northwards.

"I'm coming too," declared Quentin.

"Hurry up then," said Saturday over his shoulder.

"What's all the excitement?" asked Mr. van Buren.

"Mr. Wesson has stolen something and is going to Scotland"— Lady Porlet had recovered her breath and was beginning to enjoy her position as messenger and incentive to action—"I was coming back from the Vicarage, after lunching with the vicar and his wife—"

But everybody pressed forward as Saturday and Quentin climbed into the charabanc. With a deep metallic purr the engine started, its note shrilly changed, the azure hull leapt forward, soft thunder-echoes rolled back from the startled High Street, a plume of blue smoke emerged from the swollen cerulean stern. The "Blue Bird" was in pursuit.

Utter silence succeeded the dying echoes of its reverberant progress. The hollow chasm of the High Street emptied its thunder and was mute. The speechless group at the door of "The Pelican" stared at the vacant thoroughfare.

Then, like a soldier in a still cathedral, Miss Horsfall-Hughes's clear voice broke the quietude. She addressed Lady Mercy who, even in a group not undistinguished, was obviously the proper person to be addressed.

"Can you tell me the meaning of this escapade?" asked Miss Horsfall-Hughes in a voice as cold and hard as ice. "Has our charabanc been stolen or merely borrowed?"

"It has been commandeered," replied Lady Mercy, "for the furtherance of justice."

"Why was I not consulted?" demanded Miss Horsfall-Hughes. "When will it be returned? We have no wish to stay here indefinitely."

"As we hired the charabanc," said Mr. Sidgwick—

"I must say," began Mrs. Duluth—

"Why was there no policeman if justice was being done?" asked Mr. Harringay.

"Where was the driver?" said someone else; and other Giggleswaders declared that it was an outrage and they were not going to submit to it and the immediate return of the charabanc was imperative.

Lady Mercy's imperturbable eyes traversed their indignant faces and they were silent.

"If you will leave everything to me," she said, "I will guarantee that you suffer no undue inconvenience. Please find your driver and send him here."

Like a ripe egg doomed by dark urging to fission the group

divided, the Giggleswaders muttering and unsatisfied on one side, the Pelicans curious but controlled on the other.

"Shall we go in?" said Lady Mercy to the latter. "I am going to call up the police. I shall be with you in a minute."

"Nothing has happened that will disturb your visit," she assured them after having telephoned. "Professor Benbow is the only one who is directly concerned."

"I am completely in the dark as to what has happened," said the professor.

"I am not too clear myself," said Lady Mercy. "What I know is this: Somebody has stolen the manuscript of Mr. Keith's new poem. Lady Porlet saw Mr. Wesson and your daughter in my son's car—"

"Joan with Wesson! It doesn't sound probable."

"I saw them myself," said Lady Porlet, "and no one could have been more surprised than I was. I had been lunching at the Vicarage, and Joan spoke to me as I was returning. She was alone then, but a minute later I saw Mr. Wesson in the car—I turned back to ask her what she had asked me to do. My memory is a little playful at times—"

"And where is Joan now?"

"That is what Mr. Keith and my son have gone to find out," said Lady Mercy.

"And the red-haired maid as well," added Lady Porlet. "It was she who told me about the portfolio, and she drove off at once in your car."

"What portfolio?" suddenly demanded Mr. van Buren.

"A portfolio containing Mr. Keith's poem, I gather."

"Yes," said Lady Porlet, "the red-haired girl showed it to me."

"But if the red-haired girl, whoever she is, had the portfolio, what had Wesson stolen?" asked the professor.

"The portfolio!" said Lady Porlet. "She told me there wasn't a minute to lose."

There was a moment of silence as they tried to reconcile the difficulties of the story.

"You say that the red-haired girl, one of the maids here, that is, told you that Wesson has stolen a portfolio, and that she herself also had a portfolio?"

"That's exactly what I have said from the beginning," said Lady Porlet.

"Then there are two portfolios?"

Mr. van Buren got up hurriedly and left the room, while in the imagination of everyone else mysterious portfolios fluttered madly like bats in a tomb.

"You must notify Scotland Yard," declared Mrs. Waterhouse.

"I shall as soon as I know precisely what to tell them," said Lady Mercy, "but the connection between Wesson and this red-haired maid is troubling me. You are sure that she had a portfolio—you actually saw it?"

"She waved it in my face," said Lady Porlet.

"She and Wesson are in league," suggested Diana Waterhouse in a voice that thrilled with excitement.

"Then why should she take Lady Porlet into her confidence?"

"To confuse the trail, of course."

"I don't quite see how."

"Neither do I," admitted Diana Waterhouse weakly.

Mr. van Buren re-entered the room. His seamed and battered face was set more grimly than any there had seen it. He spoke harshly.

"I know nothing about Keith's manuscript," he said, "but a black leather portfolio has been taken from my desk. A portfolio containing documents of considerable value in themselves and of the utmost importance to me."

"A black leather one?" asked Lady Porlet.

"Yes," said van Buren.

"I knew it," said Lady Porlet triumphantly. "She waved it in my face!"

Van Buren looked at her curiously. "I suspect Wesson," he said. "I think he followed me here from New York."

"Of course Wesson is the real cause of the trouble," said Lady Mercy.

"That's precisely what I have told you all along," said Lady Porlet.

"And both portfolios are missing."

"Two portfolios and Joan," said the professor.

Lady Mercy said gently: "She can be in no real danger. I

don't understand exactly what has happened, but she can scarcely come to harm in broad daylight. Quentin and Mr. Keith are following them. I am going to call up Scotland Yard and I am returning to London myself—I want your help in that, Sir Philip—to explain everything in what detail I can. I rang up the local police station but there was no one in except the sergeant's wife, who said that her husband had gone for a walk."

Colonel Waterhouse said: "The situation, so far as I can see, is this: there are three cars on the road, all heading north. Miss Benbow and Wesson are in the first, a red-haired girl and a portfolio—whose I don't know—in the second, and in the third one Keith and Quentin Cotton. We may take it that the first car contains the real fugitive and the last one the genuine pursuers. The purpose of the intermediate car is uncertain, but its driver is apparently friendly to us—I identify 'us' with justice—and it forms a useful connecting file."

"That is a lucid exposition," said Lady Mercy, "which I shall repeat to Scotland Yard. Mr. van Buren, you also want to speak to them, I imagine."

"I do," said van Buren, and they went out together.

Mrs. Waterhouse looked admiringly at her husband, and Lady Porlet complacently repeated her story, enlarging it with some description of the Vicarage and the vicar's wife—who was a sensible woman, it seemed, very well aware of the duties incumbent on a vicar's wife. Professor Benbow listened as long as he could, saying nothing, trying to conceal his anxiety. When he could stand no more he got up and went out.

After he had gone they talked about Joan, darkly, hopefully, each one aware of her precarious position, everyone discounting its danger; praising her looks, her disposition, remembering what they had said to her on different occasions; glancing at her friendship with Saturday. Then they spoke of the red-haired girl. Everyone had seen a red-haired chamber-maid; some (then now confessed) had suspected there was more in her than met the casual eye. A good-looking girl, the men thought. Red-haired reflected the women.

"Now I remember!" exclaimed Lady Porlet. "It was she

whom I saw in Mr. Cotton's room one day. I was sitting on the edge of the bowling-green reading a book which I had borrowed when I was startled by a duster falling on my lap, and when I glanced up there were Mr. Cotton and this girl looking at me out of a window!"

The effect of this exciting complication was interrupted by the reappearance of Lady Mercy.

"Everything is settled so far as it can be settled," she said. "I have described Quentin's car to the police and they will broadcast the information and probably have it stopped quite soon. Where is Professor Benbow? I wanted to reassure him. I said nothing about my Isotta because I thought, if the girl is as honest as she appears to be, it ought to be unimpeded. Now Sir Philip, will you drive Mr. van Buren and me to London?"

"I shall be delighted to help you in any way I can."

"That's very nice of you. I have borrowed the mayor's car. It's a good one, and he will send it along here in a few minutes. You, I know, don't waste time when you drive."

"What about the tourists?" somebody asked.

Lady Mercy smiled. "They won't trouble you. I arranged for another charabanc to come and pick them up."

Before she left for London she saw the professor and comforted him by the police assurance that Wesson would certainly be stopped before he had gone far. Then, with Mr. van Buren, she got into the Mayor of Downish's Daimler, and Sir Philip Betts drove southwards as one would expect a racing motorist to drive.

Lady Mercy's chauffeur and the driver of the charabanc, both a little better for some beer, returned from wherever they had been and the latter offered an excuse for the Giggleswaders to release their thwarted indignation. If he, they said, had sat still and steadfast in his charabanc, the charabanc would not have been stolen. The driver discussed his rights as a free citizen of the Empire, and the Giggleswaders countered with the inalienable privileges of the hiring class. This occupied their time till the substitute charabanc arrived.

The more permanent guests at "The Pelican" argued, dissected and synthesized explanations with unabated interest, and Lady Porlet was annoyed to find that her incontrovertible, though not always intelligible evidence was frequently disregarded when it upset some ingenious solution.

They were, however, unanimous on this point: that Mr. Wesson, the soi-disant collector of first editions, was a folio-sized wolf in calf's clothing.

CHAPTER XX

Professor Benbow sat miserably alone. Reason told him that Joan was in no danger; reason bade him think of England, calm and sunny, on a peaceful Sunday afternoon; reason said crime had no place in such a picture. Optimism urged him to think of the whole business as some ridiculous escapade which would come with explanatory laughter safe to harbour. Common sense declared that even a thief shrank from assault, that abduction was story-book stuff. But neither common sense nor careful reason nor the optimism which he had cherished for years could wholly comfort him. Joan was being driven, somewhere out of sight to somewhere out of his ken, by a detestable bogus collector of first editions with a suspiciously expressionless face and curious eye-glasses. And the simulacrum of a sea-dog sat powerless to help her, impotent, without an idea of what to do.

He remembered what Plato and Bacon had said in dispraise of literary men, and cursed his lifetime with books that blurred the eyes and dulled the will and thrust, like cuckoos, action out of its native heart to make room for their clumsy eggs of doubt and deliberation. He thought how Lady Mercy, faced with a difficulty, had emerged from her customary cocoon of volubility and taken charge of the situation. Unflustered, placidly dealing with the contradictory evidence of Lady Porlet, suavely accepting the presence of "The Pelican's" guests, calmly dismissing the Giggleswaders—Lady Mercy, the business woman, the controller of Cotton's Beer and half-a-dozen distinguished pubs, had stepped clearly out of Lady Mercy on holiday. He thought of van Buren accepting his loss almost in silence and immediately perceiving his proper course. He thought of Colonel Waterhouse, the old bore, whose training told when it was required and who made a map out of chaos.

Professor Benbow was unhappy because of Joan's disappearance; that unhappiness, he realized, could not be helped. He was unhappy, too, because of his own inadequacy; that, he decided, was foolish and unmanly. He ought to accept his shortcomings as a necessary complement to his undoubted talents.

"I will," he said, and went to the buttery to moisten such desert philosophy.

There were half-a-dozen servants in the buttery—George and Bill and Maria and Veronica and O'Higgins—and Holly was holding a tragic-comic audience.

They left when the professor went in. They had been talking of the recent events which had so rudely disturbed the peace of "The Pelican." Holly's face was red and white, like a clown's.

"I suppose you knew that I'd lost it, sir?" he said.

"Lost what?" asked the professor. "I want some beer, please."

"The recipe for my blue cocktails, sir. Last night—there was things happening last night that neither I nor you knows anything about—last night I had a dream, like Pharaoh, and I got up and come down here, and the recipe was gone. And then I went upstairs—or halfway upstairs, as Miss Scrabster can tell you—and I heard 'em moving. Doors opening, sir, and feet shuffling along the corridor. There was dirty work in 'The Pelican' last night, sir, and now the thieves 'ave vanished with their booty."

The professor drank his beer.

"You mean your recipe?" he asked, "Have you really lost it?"

"I mean my recipe, which I wrote down carefully—for the memory of man is only a sandy beach, sir, and nothing 'olds on sand—and put in this drawer. And now the drawer is empty."

"But you don't think that Wesson stole it, do you?"

"If he didn't steal it, why has he fled like a thief? And that red-'aired vixen's on his trail, they say, and she's not going riding for nothing. She wants the recipe too, and she knows he's got it. They told me something about a black portfolio, though none of them knew what a portfolio was when I asked them. George and Bill, I mean, and Veronica. O'Higgins said it was something a Cabinet Minister had, and when they hadn't it, it was because the Prime Minister was short of them owing to a Labour Government having been there before. But he's a sailor, and sailors 'll tell you anything. The lies that I've heard sailors tell would make a widow blush. And often do, I expect. But that's what he said. And I said 'Bulrushes!' to him. 'Bulrushes!' I said. And 'e knew the significance of it. I say that that Wesson's got my recipe."

The professor sighed and asked for some more beer. He liked Holly and was sorry for his loss, though he hardly knew whether to believe it or not. So many things had happened that another one or two seemed to make little difference.

"You say that people were moving about last night?" he asked.

"This 'Pelican' was like a mole-hill, sir, all alive with movement. I knew it boded something for today."

"Some strange eruption to our state. Was that the gross and scope of your opinion?"

"I know nothing about eruptions, sir, but I had my opinions. And there was I in the mole-hill too, as wide awake as the rest of them, looking here and there, but always too late to see anyone."

"Canst work i' the earth so fast?" murmured the professor, and was cheered a little by his brace of quotations, which made him feel more at home and reminded him of Hamlet's dilemma; who, like himself, was a man resolute by instinct but hindered by intellect. "If you'd like any more beer, sir, would you have it now? Because I'm going to follow them. I've got a motor-car myself. I've been robbed, Professor Benbow, and a man of spirit doesn't sit still and turn his other pockets out to Tom, Dick and Harry. I'm going in pursuit of my own."

"Let me come with you," said the professor. "I, too, have been robbed."

Holly stared at him. "So I heard, sir, though I didn't like to mention it. But Miss Benbow's all right. It's only shady people that shady things happen to. Nobody'll hurt her."

"Thank you, Holly. You're a good fellow."

"That's as it may be, sir. And now I'm ready if you are. I keep my motor-car in a shed at the back of Horrocks's the baker."

"As soon as I get a cap and a coat, Holly."

"And a good thick stick, sir."

Holly picked up a small suit-case, which seemed heavy; the professor got his cap, his coat, and his stick; and they left "The Pelican" together without attracting anybody's attention.

CHAPTER XXI

There were some on that Sunday afternoon who pretended that "The Downish Pelican" looked a lonely bird; like a pelican in the wilderness, a widowed pelican, or a pelican whose children have turned up their beaks at a fish diet. It may have been idle fancy, for an inn-sign does not readily change its expression. And yet inanimate things do change. Who has not seen the Gioconda turn without reason from Lilith to arch young Eve, from Eve to middle-aged stupidity? Who has not thought Venus now heavenly serene, now marmoreally blowsy? Who has not observed that the agonized posture of Laocoön might be stimulated by a man stretched in a terrible yawn of boredom? Perhaps to a seeing eye "The Pelican" did look lonely.

Its interests were scattered here and there. North and south frail filaments stretched from it, farther and farther as time went on, to people whose interest in each other was due to "The Pelican," the common origin of that interest. One thread went south-east to Lady Mercy and Mr. van Buren who, rapidly driven by Sir Philip Betts, were approaching London. Four threads ran north: a short one to the tail of an aged, high-seated Morris-Cowley in which Professor Benbow and Holly followed doggedly a dying scent; a longer one to the rocking charabanc which Saturday drove with Quentin to keep him company; a still longer one to the maroon-coloured Isotta-

Fraschini in which Nelly Bly exultantly pursued adventure; and longest of all, a long, long thread to the swift Bentley, the fugitive Wesson, and the helpless Joan.

Lady Mercy and Mr. van Buren travelled almost in silence, for Lady Mercy was wondering whether it would be wiser to advertise the events at "The Pelican" or to conceal them, and van Buren sat like a statue under rain apparently without feeling, certainly without comment. From boyhood he had met trouble with taciturnity. When they were on the outskirts of London, Lady Mercy suddenly sat up and said, "I have decided to take the newspapers into my confidence. We have nothing to be ashamed of and nothing to gain by concealment. I shall go to the office of the *Daily Day* immediately after consulting with the authorities at Scotland Yard."

Mr. van Buren made no objection. The possibility of concealing his loss had never occurred to him. To keep a crime story from the newspapers would seem to a good American more cruel than keeping its vitamins from a child.

Holly and the professor made a rather noisy journey. Ten miles out of Downish a puncture halted them, and after Holly had changed the tyre he opened his suit-case and revealed twelve bottles of beer and a packet of Abernethy biscuits. This pleased the professor greatly and made him say, "O monstrous! but one half-pennyworth of bread to this intolerable deal of sack!"

Holly was even more delighted when the allusion was explained, and after thay had drunk a bottle or two of beer he confided to the professor that he had always yearned for a literary education. Encouraged by this and enlivened by the beer and the fine fresh air, the professor began to recite certain passages from Shakespeare, to which Holly listened attentively. The Morris-Cowley, though still full of strength, had become noisy in its old age, and so the professor had to declaim in a good round voice, which indeed suited lines like:

> "As full of spirit as the month of May,
>   And gorgeous as the sun at midsummer;
>   Wanton as youthful goats, wild as young bulls."

And when he remembered Hotspur's description of the pop-injay on the battlefield, he repeated, it as though he too were between the cannon and the drums, and brought it to its conclusion—

> "and but for these vile guns
> He would himself have been a soldier"—

with such stentorian scorn and laughter that a passing motor-cyclist with a girl on the pillion looked round and shook his fist at them.

Saturday and Quentin in the charabanc were very serious. The empty hull behind them swung perilously as they rounded corners and leapt with a clumsy vigour over casual irregularities. It was fast, but it needed strong hands to hold it on the road. Their minds were too occupied to be embarrassed by the curiosity they aroused in occasional motorists and the few pedestrians in Little Needham. Where the road branched north and west they saw an A.A. man and stopped to ask if a Bentley and a dark red Isotta-Fraschini had passed recently.

"The Bentley went by a quarter of an hour ago. The driver failed to return my salute. The Isotta followed a few minutes later, driven by a lady with no hat on. They went north," he said.

He looked curiously at the empty charabanc and said, "You're Mr. Keith of 'The Pelican' at Downish, aren't you, sir? I suppose you're having a bit of fun?"

"A hell of a lot of fun," said Saturday, and drove on.

"I don't pretend to understand what all this is about," he said, "but one thing certain is that Joan has gone off with Wesson, and it must have been against her will that she went. Lady Porlet muddled her story as much as she could, but that's clear. Anyway, Joan wouldn't have gone with that damned fishy-looking book-collector unless she had been forced to. Why he forced her, or how, I can't imagine. Another fact is that I've lost my poem. The only copy of it I had. I burnt the manuscript because it was in such a mess. The red-haired girl—Nelly Bly, I suppose; she's the only maid with red hair—was primarily excited about the portfolio, which was very decent of her. It seems clear that Wesson has stolen it. He's a book collector. And yet no one but a mad book-collector would do a thing like that. Do you think his first editions had driven him mad?"

Quentin was far more puzzled than Saturday, for the adventure had burst on Saturday out of a clear sky, whereas to Quentin it had come out of an atmosphere already charged with mysterious clouds. Saturday was perplexed and angry and anxious; Joan had been abducted, his poem stolen, and there was, so far as he could see, neither rhyme nor reason in either abduction or theft. But Quentin was mystified and astounded and simmering with excitement; it seemed to him that Nelly Bly's conspiracy had come to irrational life and that the origin of this commotion was undoubtedly Russian. The Cheka had stretched a long finger and pressed a button, and now its puppets were dancing. Poems and Joan were nothing but episodic, adventitious complications; incidental additions to the principal theme which—surely it was obvious—could only be a continuation of the sequence that started in the fog at Irkutsk. Wesson was, evidently a spy, a Tsarist, an emissary of the Zik, an agent of the Komintern, or a private enemy of the egregious Boris; and Nelly was on his trail.

"Look here, Saturday," he said, "there's far more in this than you imagine. Possibly Wesson is mad, but I'm sure he isn't a book-collector. I think he's a Russian Royalist."

"I don't see the joke," replied Saturday.

"It isn't a joke. Things have been going on in 'The Pelican' for the last few days of which you know nothing."

"What kind of things?"

Quentin was between the deep sea of the present situation and the devil of a promise to Nelly Bly. He struggled for awhile, and then turned his back on Satan.

"A conspiracy," he said.

Saturday drove some distance in silence.

"Do you mean," he said at last, "that you know something about Wesson? That you expected this to happen, and never thought of warning me or of warning Joan?"

"My God, no! I never dreamt that Joan would be involved. I didn't even know that Wesson was in it. Nelly is the "only one I knew about. Nelly Bly."

"And what do you know about her?"

"Her husband is a Cossack."

Saturday shied like a nervous horse, almost went into the ditch, and decided to stop the charabanc and hold a *post-mortem* on Quentin's mind.

"Are you drunk," he asked rudely, "or as mad as I imagine Wesson to be? Or are you trying to be amusing? I've already told you that I don't see the point in imbecile remarks about Russian Royalists, and the same objection holds for Cossack husbands."

Quentin lost his temper. "Don't be more beef-witted than God made you," he said. "Do you think, because you've never seen one, that there's no such thing as a Cossack husband? There are plenty of Cossacks, aren't there? Well, how the hell do you think they came into existence if their mothers had no husbands?"

"My dear Quentin, I'm not interested in family life on the steppes. All I want to know is what the devil Russia has to do with Joan and Wesson and my poem?"

"And aren't I trying to tell you? I say that Nelly Bly's husband is a Cossack. I suppose you didn't even know that she had a husband. Well, I do know. He's in prison in Novoro—, Novoro—something or other, and she's working for the Cheka—or it may be the Zik—to help him. Though she's pretty tired of the game, I think, and never wants to see old Boris again if the truth were told!"

Saturday re-started the charabanc a little wearily. "How did you discover all this?" he asked.

"She told me. And there's no sense in your being supercilious about it. I promised her that I wouldn't tell anyone, and I've broken my promise because you're in a hole—or because Joan's in a hole, and that's your concern as much as anyone's."

"It's good of you, Quentin, and I'm sorry for being rude. But still I don't understand how Nelly Bly's Cossack husband accounts for Wesson having kidnapped Joan."

"There was a conspiracy," said Quentin, "and wherever there's a conspiracy all sorts of innocent people get caught up in it. It's well known that innocent people always suffer more than the guilty ones, and Joan's innocent enough isn't she?"

"But what about Wesson?"

"Wesson came over from America with van Buren. Therefore he was probably connected with him, or interested in him in some way; either honestly or dishonestly. And Nelly was after van Buren's oil secret!"

"*What?*"

"I knew you wouldn't understand. But my God, if you had only heard that poor girl's experiences you would realize the magnificent fight she's putting up to save a creeper like Boris—Boris is her husband. He's in prison because he quarrelled with the Cheka; or it may have been the Zik. I don't remember."

"What the devil is a Zik?"

"I've forgotten. But it's Russian, and if you offend one there's hell to pay. And van Buren's secret, I gather, was the price put on Boris's head."

"I can't readily forgive a girl in my employment who has been trying to rob one of my visitors."

"Don't you see that there are circumstances here which upset all ordinary standards? Nelly is a Russian, by marriage at any rate; living in a foreign country; fighting all alone for an unselfish cause."

"And yet judged by any normal code she is a thief in intention if not in fact."

"When a bourgeois code comes between life and death it's going to get squeezed out of shape," said Quentin.

"She seems to have handled her case well. She's a pretty girl, isn't she?"

"Pretty? She's the most beautiful girl I've ever seen."

"And her husband is in a Russian prison."

Saturday mused for awhile on the discovery of this alien focus in his apparently peaceful household. He felt like a man who has slept all afternoon in a hammock and wakes up to find a wasps' nest hanging from the bough above him; or like a barnyard fowl that has hatched out a young flamingo; or a

boy who pulls the trigger of an unloaded gun, and sees his
baby brother change suddenly as the shot goes off.

"I thought there was something unusual about her as soon
as I saw her," he said.

"I should damned well think so," said Quentin. "A blind
man could tell that she wasn't an ordinary maid. She was educated in a convent, she says."

"She didn't tell you that her father was a clergyman, did
she?"

"No, but he might very well have been. That would account
for her idealism."

Saturday thought it only fair to talk about Joan a little, and
they reached Doncaster before either of them remembered that
Wesson's connection with the Cheka-Nelly Bly-van Buren
chain had not been properly established. They discussed that,
the cognate question of why he had stolen the poem, and the
reason for Joan's abduction till they came to York. Saturday
guessed the last one correctly.

"I suppose he wanted the car, and as Joan was in it and he
couldn't get rid of her without advertising his intention, he took
both. But how far is he going to take her? Where is he going
himself?"

"Scotland, Lady Porlet said."

"Why? And what part of Scotland? Gretna Green or John
o'Groats? Glasgow or Kirriemuir?"

They stopped in York and bought a large quantity of petrol,
for the charabanc appeared to burn its own weight in an hour.
It drew wondering glances where-ever it went, for an empty
charabanc is more unnatural than an empty perambulator. Its
desolation is so vast, and somehow a little ludicrous, like an
orphaned behemoth.

They enquired at several filling-stations for a passing Bentley, but no one had seen it. And once while the gleaming "Blue
Bird" stood beside a glittering golden pump, a policeman came
up, curious, and asked, "Is that your charabanc?"

"No, thank God," said Saturday. And the answer apparently satisfied the Official conscience.

They were leaving York by a road lined with pleasant houses

when Quentin, who was driving, suddenly stopped and said, "I've got an idea. Wait here for a minute."

He got down, opened a gate, and knocked at the door of a house called "Mangaldai."

Saturday, from a commanding position in the "Blue Bird," saw a maid open the door and try almost immediately to shut it again; observed Quentin deftly prevent her; watched her listen and finally disappear; perceived a red-faced man with a white moustache come and also listen to Quentin; beheld Quentin turn and point to the charabanc, at which both of them laughed; and then they went into the house and the door was shut.

Presently Quentin reappeared, evidently pleased with himself, and as he got into the charabanc he told Saturday that their proper destination was Glasgow.

"I suppose," he said, "that once again you're puzzled by my superior knowledge. Well, when you posed the ridiculous alternative of Glasgow or Kirriemuir some time ago, my brain began to work. It invariably responds to stimuli. And talking of stimuli the old boy in that house gave me a three-finger peg of very good whisky. He's a retired planter from Assam, and he got quite friendly when I told him that you were on leave from a tea-garden in Ceylon, and at present too tight to meet strangers. I like people who have lived in the East—"

"Did he tell you to go to Glasgow?" interrupted Saturday.

"Not a bit of it. That's my own discovery. I remembered two things, two obvious things, which are always the hardest kind to remember. One was that Wesson is an American. The other, that not-infrequent ships leave Glasgow to go to America. Wesson is a fugitive. Wesson is going to Scotland. The only place in Scotland from which he can sail to America is Glasgow. Therefore he is going to Glasgow."

"I should think that Southampton or Liverpool would be likelier places for him to choose."

"That is what the ordinary man would assume." said Quentin, and dexterously kept the centrifugal tail of the charabanc on the road as he went round a corner too fast for comfort. "But I'm not easily led away by facile inference. What do you think I went to that house for? Why, to ask them if they took

The Times. And if they did, could I please see yesterday's copy if it wasn't already destroyed; for *The Times* (you probably don't know this either) is a magnificent thing for lighting fires in the morning. Well, I got it, and while my ex-planter host was squirting in the soda—damn it, they know the meaning of hospitality in the East!—I looked up the shipping lists. And what do I find, says you? R.M.S. *Turbania*, says I, sailing from Glasgow at two o'clock to-morrow afternoon. Nothing bound for America out of Southampton or Liverpool, though the *Corybantic* is leaving Liverpool for a fourteen-day cruise to Madeira and the Atlantic Islands, if you think Wesson is going on holiday. But personally I put my money on the *Turbania*."

"You may be right. If you are it certainly gives us somewhere to aim at. I was beginning to wonder what to do. At first I thought we would overtake them or strike their trail somewhere. They must have made for the North Road. But after drawing blank at York I began to get doubtful."

"I'm rather good at this kind of thing, don't you think? The last few days have wakened me up. There's more in life than we think. An adventure round every corner. I tell you, Saturday, my next novel is going to be an eye-opener. It's going to show—what there really is in life, under its appearance of peace. We're too apt to forget that there's blood and nerves and bone under the skin of life, which is all that most of us see."

"How did you explain the charabanc to your planter friend?" asked Saturday.

"That was easy. I told him, as I said before, that you too were a planter, on leave, and when I added that you'd been drinking pretty heavily he seemed quite to take it for granted that you might want to drive round in a charabanc."

The "Blue Bird" sped steadily northwards, roaring gently, the susurrus of tyres on the level road mingling with the hum of the engine and the brave noise of the wind. The countryside was changing in appearance, and the light changed with it to the golden glow of evening.

CHAPTER XXII

Mr. Wesson took off his curiously shaped eyeglasses and put them into a little leather case.

"Thank goodness I don't have to wear those any longer," he said. "I find something oddly humiliating in spectacles, though there are certain people who wear them with considerable dignity. But for me they are part of an always changing uniform."

He sighed and looked about him, at the pleasant landscape of small fields rising to a line of trees, undulating grass-land and hedges that grew under easy control; not mathematically clipped and measured hedges, nor altogether sprawling and unruly hedges; but hedges that knew their place and neither presumed on liberty nor stood too stiffly to attention. And there were farmhouses that seemed a natural part of the country, so mellow and old and happy in their lot they looked.

"A friendly comfortable land," said Mr. Wesson. "In my country they mostly build frame houses that stand on the surface and never look permanent. These houses of yours seem to grow out of the earth itself. I'll tell you a funny thing. When you see a deserted farm-house in the States, anywhere from New York to California, it's an ugly thing, a scarecrow, broken, dirty thing that you shudder at. But here a ruined house is pretty, it's a thing to write poetry about, it makes you feel tender and sorry for it. And that's a remarkable difference between my country and yours, though I can't just explain what it signifies."

Joan was beginning to think better of Mr. Wesson. At "The Pelican," in his character of a wealthy and obtrusive book-collector, he had been definitely unpleasant. He had carried about with him the circumstantial evidence of his occupation, and his conversation had consisted of extracts from Messrs. Sotheby's catalogues; often inaccurate extracts, her father said, though to Joan and most of the others accuracy and error had been undifferentiated in their capacity for boredom. Now Mr. Wesson confessed that he had been quite as bored as his audience.

She had recovered from the shock of her abduction. It is dif-

ficult for anyone who is young and perfectly healthy and, moreover, exhilarated by rapid movement in the open air, to remain
in a condition of shock for any considerable time. And though
the sinister little brown bottle of vitriol had made her shrink
back as if from a pit full of snakes—she had felt her heart almost wither with horror—yet Mr. Wesson had been so very
apologetic about it, and had so assured her that he had no intention of hurting her, that Joan had almost forgiven him. He
reminded her, during his earnest protestations, of statesmen
who like their countries to have a truculent-looking army and
navy, and yet assure the world that nothing could be more do-
mestically inclined than their cruisers, nothing more indicative
of international camaraderie, more typically *gemütlig*, than
their heavy artillery.

And Mr. Wesson had confessed that he was, in a way, a
criminal. He admitted that he had stolen some papers belong-
ing to van Buren and that in consequence he was forced to flee.
He had made this confession to show Joan that he had acted, in
forcibly borrowing Quentin's car, only under dire necessity. He
was in fact an unfortunate man, not a desperado, but one who
had been driven by sheer force of circumstance firstly to become a thief and secondly (on two occasions indeed) to insult
a lady. The latter fault weighed more heavily on him than the
former.

He had laboured his apology till Joan began to feel uncomfortable, and assured him that she did not in the least object to
abduction, and that she was ready to accept his regrets for having threatened to pour vitriol on her.

They fled smoothly northwards.

If the first instinct of man is for self-preservation, his first
weakness is over-confidence. He may be ready to run away
at one minute, but the next minute he is just as ready to stop.
No one, savage or citizen, can be steadfast in flight, for the
memory of a savage is short and so is the wind of a civilized
man. Physical weakness and mental instability too often com-
bine to give the appearance of reckless bravery.

Joan had long ceased to be nervous, and Mr. Wesson grew
careless. His surroundings all suggested security, and two

hours, three hours of flight were like two or three doors shut fast behind him. He drove more slowly, until his pace became not that of a fugitive but the easy progress of a Sunday afternoon excursionist. A few cars overtook them, who a little before had roared past all cars.

In the little mirror which gave him a glimpse of the road behind, Mr. Wesson saw a dark red limousine reflected. It was gaining on them and he drew into the side to let it pass. But the limousine, after it had come very close, dropped to the rear again. Mr. Wesson thought no more about it but continued to talk to Joan of automobile roads in the States, the necessity for chivalry, and the possibility of stopping somewhere for tea, for Joan, who had had no lunch, was getting hungry. Then, in the square of mirror, he saw the dark red limousine again, and somehow it worried him.

It was too far away for him to see the driver, and when he slowed down so did the limousine. Joan looked over her shoulder and bit her lip to restrain an exclamation of delight; for she recognised Lady Mercy's car, which Mr. Wesson had not seen before.

"Do you know whose automobile that is?" asked Mr. Wesson.

"I'm not sure," said Joan, and blushed for the puny falsehood.

Mr. Wesson resorted to a simple trick. Round a bend in the road, where the hedges hid him, he stopped short. And presently, into the square of mirror, shot the dark red limousine. At once the Bentley leapt forward, as when the starter's pistol wakes to flying life the statue of a runner, for Mr. Wesson had seen behind the glass in the twilight interior of the limousine a girl with red hair and an apple-green dress. A girl whom, not long before, he had tied to a bedroom chair. Naturally it worried him, for Nelly had no more right to appear in public than a ghost. She had been deprived of movement and the privilege of speech, and her return to active life was as inexplicable as it was inconvenient. In his startled mind Mr. Wesson reviewed every knot that he had made in his elaborate neckties, and saw again her slender ankles and pleasant wrists securely lashed to the spars of an ordinary but apparently substantial bedroom chair. He remembered her open mouth—such a sight as only a dentist customarily sees—and the silk handkerchief he had carefully thrust into it. And after binding Nelly to silence and the bedroom chair he had tied a leg of the chair to his bed so that she could not, by a series of muscular spasms, shuffle across the floor. She had no business to be at liberty and Mr. Wesson's confidence was shaken by her appearance, though he comforted himself by thinking that the Bentley had probably fleeter heels than the Italian car.

His mobile face assumed its most determined expression and the speedometer promptly indicated sixty miles an hour, the needle trembling nervously at this extreme velocity.

In ten minutes' time the limousine had been left a good distance behind, but as the road was undulating it was still, from vantage points, intermittently visible. Mr. Wesson ingeniously decided to lure Nelly on to a false trail instead of merely trying to out-distance her, and when he came to cross-roads where he was under observation from the limousine (he had reduced his speed somewhat) he turned to the left, though his proper course was northwards. He had all the confidence which an American motorist in England naturally has, and which comes from the knowledge that England is only a little island where one cannot go seriously out of one's way. There were a large number of roads in the island, a multitude of small towns, a pleasant variety of scenery, and no possibility of being stranded in the middle of a prairie, a mountain range, or a desert. So Mr. Wesson now drove rapidly westwards and had the satisfaction, every so often, of seeing the limousine following him. It was hilly country that he drove through; hilly for a small island, that is.

"Do you know where we are?" he asked Joan.

"Somewhere in Yorkshire, I suppose," she answered, for though Joan knew several capitals in Europe and the more widely advertised towns of France and Italy (together with the principal exports of Japan, Australia, and South Wales), she had only a vague notion of her own country's geography, and this rapid progression was very bewildering.

"Thank you," said Mr. Wesson, who had heard of Yorkshire and was pleased to fancy himself familiar with his surroundings.

He drove in silence for some considerable time and when there was no sign of the limousine behind—though he felt reasonably sure that it still held to this misleading trail—he took a convenient road that branched northward again.

"If we go this way we're pretty sure to reach Scotland, aren't we?" he said.

"I suppose so," said Joan, with a sigh. The pursuit of the limousine had encouraged her to think of escape, but the speed of Quentin's car and Mr. Wesson's masterly driving had disappointed her. And she was hungry.

"There's a lot of desolate, hilly country before us," she said. "The borders are very wild in parts."

"I've driven from New Mexico to Oregon," said Mr. Wesson.

"Did you stop anywhere for tea?" asked Joan.

"I'm very sorry," said Mr. Wesson. "We'll pull up at some place quite soon if you'll promise not to run away or talk to people."

"But how far are you going to take me?"

"I've been considering that, but I find it difficult to decide because there are so many towns all round here. You say the border country between England and Scotland is pretty lonely?"

"Very lonely."

"Then I'll probably leave you somewhere there. I can't drop you beside a telegraph office or a police station."

"Even if I promise not to interfere with your plans?"

"The temptation would be too strong for you," said Mr. Wesson simply.

Joan felt an impulse towards angry denial of this assertion, and indignantly said, "You wouldn't trust me?"

"You put me in a very awkward position," said Mr. Wesson.

His profile was serene and grave. Joan's anger began to weaken as the thought came to her that it really might be difficult to keep such a promise. She leaned back and faintly contemplated the prospect of being deserted on some desolate moor or hill-road in the marches of southern Scotland or northern England.

"The weather is quite warm," said Mr. Wesson, as though he read her thoughts. . . .

Nelly Bly drove fiercely up hill and down, her heart hot with the joy or anxiety of pursuit, desperately intent on catching another glimpse of the flying Bentley. She had not seen it for a long time now, but she felt confident—or almost confident—after having caught it once and followed it so closely for twenty glorious miles. Why Wesson had turned westwards off his proper road she could not understand. The evidence which he had so gratuitously left behind pointed without a doubt to Glasgow as his destination; and now he was going west—or southwest it seemed, for the afternoon sun was in her eyes—on a route absurdly divergent from the road to Scotland. And yet she must follow him wherever he might go. Up hill she went, breathlessly expecting to see her quarry far off when she reached the top. Down hill she raced, eager for the next summit which might show her a dark patch on the road, a dark patch and a little cloud of dust behind it which should be the fugitive car. Impatiently she slowed down for a corner, and as she pulled round the Isotta bumped sadly and significantly. One of the tight fat tyres had gone damnably, tearfully, hopelessly flabby and soft.

She stopped at the roadside and sat still, miserably looking ahead and seeing nothing. Her confident heart felt suddenly flat and empty like the punctured tyre. Her lower lip quivered under her teeth and the triple "damn" which she muttered to her loneliness dissolved in a triple sniff.

She got out and looked at the dismal mis-shapen tyre. A limp and ugly-looking thing, a defeated thing, a flaccid drooping thing. Jacks, she thought, and levers. Nuts to unscrew, bolts and spanners, dirty hands. Struggling and wrestling. A patent hydraulic jack, perhaps. But how did you use them? She had never changed a tyre. There had always been a man to do it. She sat down on the running-board and cupped her chin in her hands. She felt dispirited and weary.

It had been a tiring day for her. No one can unmask a villain, hold him in parley, feel the quick spring of triumph and the black ebb of defeat, endure the threat of vitriol, be tied to a bedroom chair with neckties, break loose, and then pursue the criminal for miles and hours and miles again without feeling tired when abruptly disaster comes.

The struggle to free herself from Mr. Wesson's chromatic neckties had been very severe. He had tied his knots like an expert, and her legs and arms had been as securely fastened to the struts and legs of the chair as a broken limb to a splint. Nelly had tried to wriggle and found that she could not wriggle. She had tried to twist, and could not twist. By a series of contractions and spasmodic efforts of every muscle in her body—every muscle from her throat to her toes, she thought—she had managed to move the chair an inch or two, but the necktie which tied it to the foot of the bed kept her from going farther than a few inches, even if she had had the strength to progress by what seemed principally diaphragmatic and abdominal force. And all the time she was exasperated almost beyond endurance by the gag which filled her mouth.

Her discomfort was increased (though there was no one to see her) by an embarrassment which people often suffer in a dentist's chair when the little suction-pumps which are supposed to remove excess of saliva fail to cope with the rush. Nelly's mouth began to water, and as Mr. Wesson's silk handkerchief was soon saturated she dribbled in a way which only a child could have endured. Angered by this more than by anything else, Nelly wrenched her shoulders from side to side, and was rewarded by hearing the back of the chair creak. Then she discovered that she could rock backwards and forwards, and without waiting to be frightened of bumping her head, she leaned first forwards and afterwards threw her weight violently backwards.

The chair toppled and fell. It was only an ordinary bedroom chair, not made for such rough usage, and a sharp double crack sounded cheerfully as it met the floor. The back had broken off. Nelly could wriggle now, and some snake-like writhing brought one necktie over the end of a broken spar, the coils fell loose, and Nelly's right hand was free. In a few minutes she stood up free altogether, and as she stretched herself and rubbed her wrists and ankles she noticed the screwed-up pamphlet which Wesson had used to tighten a leg-band. Curiously she picked it up and unfolded it. A picture of the *Loretania*, that proud ship, decorated its front page, and on the back page was a list of steamers with parallel columns of ports and dates. Half-way down the list was the name *Turbania* (16,600 tons) and oppo-

site it a faint, pencilled question-mark. Nelly's heart leapt up as
if at a rainbow—and indeed such a bright and obvious clue was
very like a rainbow—for the *Turbania* was to sail from Glasgow
for New York at 2 p.m. on the following day. And had not
Wesson said that by the morrow he would be on his way to
America? This was more than a clue; it was a finger-post.

How her pursuit, at its inception, had been deflected from
railway to road by the timely interposition of Lady Porlet has
already been told. And now her pursuit, after bringing her in
sight of the quarry, was halted by the magnificent Isotta going
lame.

She looked apathetically out at rolling moorland. Where
was she? Yorkshire, she surmised. It was always safe to say
Yorkshire after you had been driving northwards for a long,
long time. . . . The West Riding, possibly. Ilkley Moor, perhaps; of which she knew nothing except that there was a song
about it in dialect practically incomprehensible to anyone but
a patriotic and imaginative Yorkshireman. . . . "On Ilkla Moor
baht 'at." . . . Baht 'at, indeed, for like a new calamity it occurred to Nelly that she was not dressed for motoring. Hith-
erto she had been so single in purpose as to think nothing of
her appearance. Now she realized that a maid, in maid's uniform, was incongruous as the driver of an opulent limousine.

She took off the frilled apron and threw it into the back of the
car. Her apple-green dress was plain and non-committal, but
she could not persuade herself that it was the kind of costume
the owner of an Isotta-Fraschini would normally choose. And
then, to complete her discomfiture, she remembered that she
had no money. Not a penny. In one small pocket she carried a
small silver cigarette-case which contained three cigarettes—
Gold Flake—and three cards on which was printed with no
more distinction than the Gold Flake lettering:

HELEN BLYTHESDALE

The *Daily Day*

Whether as a casual contributor to the *Daily Day* she had
the right to put its name on her cards Nelly had never com-

pletely made up her mind, but on more than one occasion the addition had been useful; and that, she decided, was an adequate excuse for retaining it.

Three cigarettes and some evidence of a journalistic vocation, no money, a punctured tyre, and Ilkley Moor—if it was Ilkley Moor—all around. No matches even. But luckily the car had one of those ingenious contrivances which, in response to pressure, glow brightly and suffice to light a cigarette. Nelly smoked one of her Gold Flakes and decided listlessly that she had better look for some tools with which to change the wounded tyre.

Just as she threw away the end of her cigarette a small but aggressively new car came round the corner, passed her, and stopped by means of aggressively efficient brakes a few yards away. A young man got out. A young man dressed with notable care in a suit which continued the uniform colour-motif of his shirt, collar, and tie, and who wore footgear of that particoloured kind which Nelly was vulgarly accustomed to call co-respondent's shoes. He asked, very politely, if he could be of assistance.

"You can," said Nelly, smiling kindly at him. And while he took off his coat, dirtied his hands, endangered the trim fall of his trousers by stooping and squatting, and finally changed the tyre, she talked to him with such charm that he forgot the unpleasant nature of his work.

"Are you going far?" he asked her presently.

"Not very," she said. "Are you?"

"To Liverpool," said the young man. "I've been to Harrogate, I often go to Harrogate. It's an amusing place, don't you think?"

"I've never been there," said Nelly.

"Oh, you should," said the young man. "It's really a good place to go. You can play tennis there, and dance, and do all sorts of things. I go there frequently. My home's in Liverpool, you see, so it's quite handy for me."

"To dance in Harrogate?"

"Yes," said the young man. He put on his coat, sat down beside Nelly on the running-board of the Isotta, and offered her a gold-lettered, ivory-tipped, probably Egyptian cigarette.

He sat closer than was necessary, with that absurd craving for contiguity which young men so often exhibit.

"I prefer Gold Flake," said Nelly, and took one of her two which remained.

The young man held a match for her with caressive dexterity.

"You've been very kind," said Nelly. "Thank you so much."

She stood up, but the young man caught hold of her hand and said, "Do sit down again and tell me who you are. I almost think I've met you somewhere, haven't I?"

"My name is Dashenka Zogu," said Nelly.

"I beg pardon?"

"Dashenka Zogu," Nelly repeated. "My husband is an Albanian."

The young man laughed nervously, and Nelly looked at him with grave and warning eyes.

"Well, I'm glad to have helped you," he said.

"Not at all," replied Nelly, bowing slightly.

The young man retired in some confusion to his own car, and speedily drove away.

"Sometimes they're nice and sometimes they're not, but they're always useful if you know how to use them," Nelly murmured, and thought no longer about him. She considered her own problems with more spirit, however.

So this road went to Liverpool, and Liverpool, as everyone knew, was a port from which vessels might sail to New York. Wesson, when last seen, was going in this direction. Wesson, then, in spite of the obvious shipping-list finger-post, was sailing from Liverpool? Nelly had accepted the clue (in the pamphlet which had helped to keep her right ankle tied) with such over-weighted confidence that the slightest doubt was enough to upset her assurance. With the evidence of the Liverpool road before her, the shipping-list, with its blatantly pencilled mark against *Turbania*, at once took on the likeness of a red herring. Of course Wesson wouldn't leave such a thing about unless to mislead people, and equally of course her celerity in pursuit had put her on the right trail. O fortunately breaking chair and blessed, blessed promptitude!

"Helen's herself again," she confided to Ilkley Moor.

But I've got no money, she remembered. And I'm hungry, she thought. And I can't drive into Liverpool and go to a hotel—I'm *not* going to ask the police for help and give them all the credit—on a Sunday evening with no recommendation but a green cotton frock, she decided. There's a rug on the back seat, she considered, but that's not much use.

She opened the other door and lifted up the rug which lay on the back seat. With a gasp of joy she found that under it were a raincoat and a small attaché case.

"Lady Mercy's!" she whispered.

She opened the attaché case.

"Oh, my God," she said.

In it were two letters and a book entitled *The Intelligent Woman's Guide to Socialism and Capitalism*. Nothing else.

"Useless," said Nelly bitterly. "Absolutely useless. Will any intelligent woman between here and Liverpool give me a meal for this? Or her husband exchange a gallon of petrol for it? I've never said a word against Shaw till now, but for an economic reformer his books haven't much practical value when you put them to the test. If it were Edgar Wallace every house in the country would give me bed and breakfast for it."

She got into the car, sat down, and moodily considered what to do. There was no hurry now, for Atlantic liners do not leave port on a Sunday night, and she could not hope to find Wesson anywhere except on the embarkation stage. And she had no money to buy a hat, a meal, a night's lodging, or petrol; the Isotta would soon require petrol as badly as she wanted food.

She turned the leaves of *The Intelligent Woman's Guide* to see if Mr. Shaw said anything about barter, the exchange value of a limousine, or how to acquire petrol and a fillet steak on note-of-hand alone.

And as she turned a page there appeared like manna raining from the Socialist heaven a stiff new brown and white one pound note . . . for Lady Mercy had been reading the book, and to mark the place where she had wearied of instruction she had slipped in the Treasury Note; a thing she often did, being prejudiced against dog's ears and having a sufficiency of money. Nelly, of course, was unaware of this habit—though many people who borrowed Lady Mercy's books had been gratified by it—and thought for a moment that Mr. Shaw was inserting one pound notes into every copy of his manual to celebrate a new edition or to make it a really practical guide to Capitalism.

The idea faded, as such fancies will, but the Treasury Note remained indisputably real. And with its help Nelly began to re-model her plan of campaign.

CHAPTER XXIII

Joan and Mr. Wesson had a large and inexpensive semi-nursery, semi-farmhouse meal at a roadside house which advertised teas for tourists. Not that Mr. Wesson was mean; he was an American, and Americans are habitually lavish in their hospitality. But he was also a fugitive and he had a cautious disinclination to take Joan into a hotel where the crowd might interfere with his control of her. So Joan ate brown bread and ham and eggs and shiny buns and fresh butter and raspberry jam, and drank several cups of tea, and sighed for no richer flesh-pots, but smiled pleasantly at Mr. Wesson and began to like him although he was a criminal.

And as they drove away again on hill-roads and between hills that the westering sun made dark on one side and golden-clear on the other, she asked him questions about his manner of life, friendly and tactful questions, and enquired what it felt like to be a thief.

Mr. Wesson was a lonely man, a man condemned by his position in society to a solitude such as most of us fear and detest, and the pleasant circumstance of Joan's company made him communicative. He was, indeed, looking forward with some dismay to the time when he should have to sever the association so violently begun, and he was quite willing to expand, explain, and confess his unusual personality.

"Strictly speaking," he said, "I am not a thief. That is, I am not an habitual thief. I feel pretty strongly about stealing. To my mind there's something mean about the man who makes his living out of it. I've known plenty of thieves of all sorts, from pickpockets to bank-robbers, and there wasn't one of them with whom I ever felt really friendly and at home. They were narrow-minded for one thing, because they had so many grievances, and I can't make friends with a narrow-minded man. That's how I quarrelled with my father when I was a boy. He was as narrow as a knife looked at edgeways, and had more grievances than Job's neck had boils. We lived in Concord, Massachusetts."

For some time Mr. Wesson thought sentimentally of his boyhood's home.

"I've never stolen anything except when there was a good case to be made out for stealing," he continued. "Do you play poker, Miss Benbow?"

"Not for high stakes," said Joan.

"But the rules are the same whatever the stakes. You can't take anything out of the pool unless you put something in. If you don't play you can't hope for profit. The ideal of service, which is a well-thought-of ideal in my country, is based on this fact. Now life is like a big poker game, with luck for the joker, and the thief is a man who tries to take the kitty without putting in his ante, let alone betting on his cards; without using his five talents, as the Gospel has it. Therefore by Biblical precedent as well as by own observation I believe that the thief is doomed to failure. When I steal anything, Miss Benbow, it's because I have a good reason for it."

"I'm sure you have," said Joan, who was impressed by Mr. Wesson's almost religious sincerity.

"When I forged my father's name to a cheque— you'll understand how strained our relations were before I was compelled to do such a thing—it was because I needed the money to get married. It's the foolhardiest kind of thing to get married without any capital. It's just asking for trouble. Now I had given my word of honour, to her and her mother and to her elder brother as well, to marry the girl who lived next door to us. That was in Concord, Massachusetts. She was one of the sweetest girls in town and I've never regretted it, though I spent

the first year of my married life in gaol. My father—I'll say this
for him, though he was as narrow-minded as a silhouette—
came of good Pilgrim stock and believed in an eye for an eye
and rigorous imprisonment for forgery. He had no mercy."

"A year in prison!" said Joan. "How terrible. I think I
should go mad in prison. Didn't it embitter you against everything?"

"It was a blessing in disguise. It was there that I first turned
my thoughts to literature as a means of livelihood, for though
I recognized the sanity and moral value of a routine life I didn't
think I could submit to it very willingly after having lived one
under compulsion for a year. Authors and uncaptured criminals, Miss Benbow, are the only people free from routine.
Moreover, they gave us some good books to read, for it was a
well-conducted prison, and I was stimulated to do a little writing myself. I wrote a song which was sung at the annual prison
concert and a hymn which was included in the prison hymnal.
And after I was discharged I got a job on a newspaper."

"As a reporter?"

"Well, I was in the advertising department at first. But that
didn't satisfy me. I wanted to write. I felt the need to create.
My one ambition was to become an author. But it was not to
be. It became evident in a few months that the Creator had not
intended me for a dramatist, a novelist, or even a poet."

"I suppose you found it difficult to think of plots," said
Joan. "I should love to write if only I could think of something
to write about."

"My difficulty was to forget plots," said Mr. Wesson. "I have
an abnormally retentive sub-conscious memory, and whenever I
wrote I transcribed, without realizing it, something that I had
read a short while before. The result was that I wrote some
short stories which had already been written by a certain distinguished author, and when I sold them there were serious misun-
derstandings. I narrowly escaped going to prison for the second
time. The distinguished author, for whom I have the warmest
admiration, refused to prosecute. On a subsequent occasion another equally distinguished author was not so generous."

"Did you go to prison for copying—I mean transcribing,
some of his stories?"

"For six months," said Mr. Wesson, "and I have never published anything since except some verses for Christmas cards, which I am glad to say are still in regular use. But I thought of a plan for putting my talent—for it is a talent—to better employment."

By this time they had left behind them that England which is alternately garden and factory town. They had sped between green fields and through streets of red brick villas, by gently meandering rivers and past towering chimneys, now under trees, now looking at lamp-posts; and were coming at last to the hill country which gave such good battlefields to the Southern Scots and the Northern English in the days before they became liberal-minded enough to consider other nations worth picking a quarrel with. The country which had daunted the Romans lay before them, the hills which Rome had crowned with a wall to keep off the hairy-kneed, blue-painted, long-armed fighting tribes beyond. And it was growing dark, slowly but surely. The hills added to their stature. It was the time of evening when the Roman under officers visited their sentries on the Wall, saying to this one, "Well, Balbus" who according to the Latin grammar, helped to build the Wall, "got your eyes skinned to-night?" And to that one, who was a veteran, "Don't you wish you'd stayed in Spain, Shorty?" To which Shorty would reply, "It's so bloody cold, sergeant. I'll have fever to-morrow, you see if I don't." And the sergeant probably answered, "You'll be lucky if you don't get worse than fever. I heard the captain say as how those blue-arsed beggars might be coming over to-night." "Pollux!" said Shorty, "I bet they don't."

That was the time of night, rumour-time, darkening-time, when Joan and Mr. Wesson approached the Roman Wall. And it looked like rain.

But Mr. Wesson continued the story of his life and Joan continued to listen to him with the interest which his recital demanded; though it sounded to her a little unreal, as so many stories do while they lack the apparent verification of print.

"As I couldn't write without getting into trouble," said Mr. Wesson, "I decided to lecture, so I took a course in public speaking and acquired a good English accent."

"I thought you were an Englishman at first," said Joan.

"Is that so?" said Mr. Wesson, and cleared his throat. "The advantages of the spoken word over the written one are obvious," he continued. "It leaves no trace. The printed word is static, defenceless, and potential evidence against you. But the spoken word is a bird of passage, very difficult to hit. The objection to lecturing, however, is that the audience isn't interested in the words so much as in the speaker, and consequently a man of nation-wide repute who's got nothing more vital to America than sex-life in Lapland to talk about gets a hearing and suitable emoluments, when an unknown man with a genuine message is unregarded. I spoke in my own name on two occasions, and both times the results were disappointing in the extreme. The third time I spoke the hall was full, I was applauded to the echo, and the emoluments were very gratifying. Can you guess why? No? Well, all I did was to repeat my original lecture—on More Money or Matri-Mony—and have myself billed as Mr. George Moore, the famous English author."

"What fun," said Joan. "Did you dress up?"

"I made some changes in my ordinary appearance," said Mr. Wesson, "but as I had never seen Mr. Moore, or even a photograph of him, I was compelled to use my imagination, The local papers—it was in Skyburg, Minnesota, that I made my debut—said I presented a sinister and impressive figure, and my lecture was a kaleidoscope of audacious dissection. This was shortly after Mr. Moore had written *The Brook Kerith*, which was known to be daring. The book itself, however, had not reached Skyburg, and in the absence of specific information 'daring' has only one connotation. It implies, in the general consciousness, the act of unbuttoning the habiliments which have eternally shrouded the intimacies of marital and extra-marital adjustment. That was the interpretation which I assumed in my lecture, and Skyburg liked it. I delivered it eight times altogether, in small towns in Minnesota and Iowa, and I should have continued to deliver it had it not been for a woman who had made a pilgrimage to the shrines of modern literature in England and waited three days outside Mr. Moore's London residence in order to see him face to face. Which eventually she did, and retained so vivid a memory of him that she instantly penetrated my disguise—I wore a little red beard which apparently was unjustified—and denounced me to her fellow Iowans. I had to alter my plans and my appearance with the utmost celerity."

Joan leaned back and looked at Mr. Wesson driving so impassively into the darkening Cheviots, and bubbled with laughter to think of him masquerading as Mr. George Moore and delivering "daring" lectures to the Middle West of America.

"I think you're wonderful," she said.

"That's nothing," boasted Mr. Wesson. "That was only my novitiate, the prelude to my vocation. Since then I have appeared as Mr. Rudyard Kipling, the Bishop of London, George Bernard Shaw, Conan Doyle, Mr. Galsworthy, Mr. Alfred Noyes, G. K. Chesterton, Sir Oliver Lodge, Walter de la Mare, and several others. I studied photographs of these eminent men, so as not to repeat my early blunder, and I exploited to the full my mobile features and a certain talent for making-up."

Mr. Wesson stopped the car, and contorting his features in a peculiar way, said to Joan: "Imagine that my head is bald and my eyebrows very bushy. Now, who do you think I am?"

"Bernard Shaw," Joan hazarded foolishly.

"Nonsense," said Mr. Wesson. "I was Rudyard Kipling. Now I am Bernard Shaw." And he assumed the expression of a milk-fed satyr.

"Of course," said Joan, "I would recognize you anywhere."

"Naturally I require a beard to complete the resemblance, just as I needed thicker eyebrows and a shaved head to become Mr. Kipling's double. Now who is this, do you think?"

Mr. Wesson blew and puffed out his cheeks till his face was all red and swollen, and in a rarefied, high-piping voice recited:

> "'They bred like birds in English woods,
>   They rooted like the rose,
> When Alfred came to Athelney
>   To hide him from their bows.'"

"G. K. Chesterton!" said Joan.

Mr. Wesson smiled in a superior manner and restarted the car. "You see," he said, "that I have some qualifications for my self-invented profession. And I knew the country in which I practised. The small towns in the Middle Western States of America are remote from artistic reality and therefore incurably avid for it. They have the lecture habit as other people have the drug habit. They will listen to anything that is sponsored by a well-known name, just as they will drink out of any bottle that has a handsome label. They know that there are good things in the world, and they believe that most of them gravitate to America. That is why they saw nothing incongruous in Galsworthy taking Oshkosh into his confidence or opening his heart to Hicksville. Mr. G. B. Shaw says that he will never go to the United States. Say, listen: there's a score of towns between Boonville, Missouri, and Little Rock in Arkansas which think that's the best joke he ever made. Why? Because they've seen him as plain as you see me, and heard him lecture on such typical subjects as Woman and Superwoman, You Know Mrs. Warren! (For Men Only), and Marriage for Morons."

"You mean—?"

"I do," said Mr. Wesson, "and they were right good lectures which he himself would not be ashamed to deliver anywhere. I borrowed freely from his own prefaces and spiced them up with topical allusions, popular psychology, and some red-hot Revivalism. They were real smart lectures, though for domestic appeal and poignant heart-throbs—pure sentiment with a kick in every clause—I prefer my Galsworthy series."

"It's raining," said Joan. "I knew it was going to."

"So it is," said Mr. Wesson.

He switched on the head-lights, which threw into the oncoming dusk dim pearly shafts slashed with diamond-bright arrows. Raindrops pattered on the weatherproof hood, and as he could find no side-curtains to put up rain drove steadily in at Mr. Wesson, who sat on the windward side. But such slight discomfort was not enough to check his narrative. For years he had been compelled to suppress the too-human instinct for confession and boasting and self-explanation. While half mankind took the other half into its confidence, spilling its gushes and overflow of sentiment, discovery, and loneliness, Mr. Wesson had stood silent and apart in the awful solitude of a dictator or a leper, friendless from his very manner of existence, of necessity self-contained. And now he had a confidante. A girl charming to the sight and gifted with understanding. Such a girl as most men would strive to impress with the individual strangeness of their character and destiny. A girl like a white tablet that is a perpetual temptation to autobiography.

Disregarding the rain, Mr. Wesson continued his story.

When Joan asked whether his impersonations had always been successful—with the exception of the George Moore episode—he admitted that at the height of his career a catastrophic failure had daunted him.

"Partly it was due to carelessness," he said, "partly to a genuine artistic surrender to the art of Thomas Hardy. I took a holiday with my wife and daughter—an only child, Miss Benbow—and while on holiday I read all those great sages of Wessex, those epics of the untamed earth as I named them to myself, and I became convinced that out of them should be framed a message to the American people. I composed a lecture which was more of a pæan of nature than a lecture, and billed it 'The Soil is Sacred,' by the Seer of Wessex, England. It contained my best work. It had a voice of thunder and a voice of gentle streams, the mutter of clay, the tone of winter winds, and the accent of sudden Spring. It was the hell of a fine lecture, Miss Benbow. And the Rotary Club of a certain town in South Dakota was only too willing for me, *in persona* Thomas Hardy, to put it across."

Mr. Wesson drove in silence for some minutes while Joan waited dumbly for the inevitable catastrophe.

"I sent a telegram to that town in South Dakota," he continued, "to confirm the time of my arrival. When I stepped on to the platform there was a gasp from the audience. The sea of faces—for naturally the hall was full—visibly blanched. It seemed to recede. I assumed that they were impressed with my appearance. A strange muttering arose, a sibilant murmur, which quickly died away as I began to speak. Then the noise woke again, hissing and shouting, catcalls. It swelled into a storm. Things were thrown at me. The audience got up on end and rushed the platform. I was seized, my clothes pulled off me. I was ridden on a rail, Miss Benbow, through the streets of that town in South Dakota, in nothing but a torn shirt. How I escaped with my life I have never been able to figure out, except that the First National Bank happened to go on fire right at that time."

"They knew that Hardy was dead?"

"He had just died, and wireless telegraphy has narrowed the earth to the width of a mean street so that you can shout across it from window to window. Everybody knew except me. I hadn't even seen a newspaper for several days. Everybody except me who would have been the first to mourn him, for I thought more highly of Thomas Hardy than the whole darned state of South Dakota did. I meant to give that lecture far and wide."

Joan said nothing, being touched by the clownish horror of Mr. Wesson's downfall.

"It upset me more than you can think," he said. "My confidence went. I saw that people were getting too wise to fool with safety. And anyway broadcasting was spoiling the field for me. Lecture tours were a losing game. So I quit. I had made enough with the help of a little speculation to retire on. I quit, Miss Benbow. But I quit without thinking enough about my daughter."

"How old is she?"

"Eighteen. And she wants to go to Paris to study art. She says they can't teach her to draw in America—which is perfectly true—and she thinks Paris would be more stimulating. Well, I consider that any man who is a father has his responsibilities, and her mother shares my opinion. But my bank account didn't support the theory. So when a friend in New York said he was interested in van Buren's oil business, and would be willing to pay handsomely for information, I got busy and transformed myself into book-collector, which was a disguise, I reckoned, sufficient to disarm suspicion in a rattlesnake. You know the rest of the story, or as much as you want to."

"I scarcely know what to say," Joan began.

"Romaine—that's my daughter—will go to Paris now, I suppose," said Mr. Wesson.

Behind the rain great gusts of wind came swooping off the moors. With the rain in their folds they flung themselves across the road, now this way, now that, as though an invisible giant dancer were leaping in a swirl of black tempestuous rapperies on a platform of the hills. Through the holes of her ragged skirts stars flickered. *Whisssssh!* went her skirts as she whirled on one toe, *Wheee-ooo!* as she turned on the other; and water flew off them as when a man shakes a sea-drenched oilskin. The headlights, like eyes on long white stalks, peered for the road. The road was lost in the hills. The hills were half lost in darkness. The wind and the rain danced a boisterous country dance. Through the open sides of the car rain leapt desperately, wind followed with a shout.

Joan hugged herself in her corner. Mr. Wesson shook his soaking sleeve.

Joan thought with dismay of being jettisoned on this wild hill-road. Mr. Wesson began to realize that one country seems as large as another when night and rain fall together and the wind gets up to greet them.

The headlights pointed a thin silver path into Scotland. The border hills were about them, and as they climbed the broad rampart the storm grew wilder, the moss-troopers' wind hallooed.

"It may clear up," said Mr. Wesson hopefully.

"It may," said Joan dismally, knowing better.

CHAPTER XXIV

Saturday and Quentin struggled to put up the great rainproof top of their borrowed charabanc. The storm harried them as they worked, shrewdly beating their faces, getting with cold hands under their coats, spilling colder runnels of water down their arms as they toiled with the unwieldy hood.

No sooner had they unfurled the canvas from its snug casing than the wind with a whoop of joy, filled its slack belly alderman-full and tore it from their hands. They seized its flap-

ping edges, hauled it and swore at it, the wind slackened, they
drew it down. Then with a howl the wind came back, and like
a hobbledehoy in rut among farthingales, tossing and tumbling
them, blew up the hood again to explore its vast concavity.

With bleeding fingers Saturday and Quentin fought the wind
and the rowdy canvas. Save that their ship was stable it was like
stowing topsails off Cape Horn. And the wind slapped their
faces, their ties were whipped out, the rain ran down their
sleeves to tickle their armpits. "Hell!" said Quentin.

"Hell and damnation!" said Saturday. "Heave!" said Quentin. "Heave and hold!" answered Saturday. And at last, braced
and buckled trimly down, the canvas cover was in place and
under it they found a measure of shelter.

Saturday wiped the rain off his spectacles and stared, myo-
pic and grim, into the darkness. Joan's fate seemed desperate
in this *décor* of night. In daylight and fine weather her plight
had angered him and worried him. Now it enraged and frightened him. The wind struck inward and his mind was full of the
noise of the storm. Joan was somewhere in this border of wilderness. Joan and a white-faced, heavy-eyed folio-hunter. And
somewhere with them— yielding to pulp, perhaps, in seeping
rain—was the manuscript of "*Tellus* Will Proceed." His girl
and his work, both in danger of the night. He tried to forget
about the poem, because to think of it argued unwhole love.
Lost Joan, he thought, should fill his heart; as if Hamlet had
written verse and Ophelia had taken his manuscript to drown
in company with her under the water-weeds—but would not
Hamlet have given a thought to the life-blood of good lively
words washed away by the brook that filled Ophelia's mouth?

Like a spate in March wind came off the hills and the taut
canvas roof thundered beneath its charge. Anxiety for his poem
vanished, blown into shreds, and poor Joan crowded his mind.

And Quentin thought about Nelly Bly, who was also lost.
But Quentin's anxiety was tempered by respect for Nelly's re-
sourcefulness. Moreover she was not a captive, or at any rate
not a close captive, and her bondage to the Soviet was not
likely to be aggravated by a storm in the Cheviots. So Quentin
had more time to think about his own discomfort, which was

considerable. He was wet and cold and hungry, and the empty charabanc under its spread of sail was almost unmanageable. It lurched against the wheel, tried to throw its head into the wind, swung cumbrously behind the swaying silver beam of its headlights.

"Do you know where we are?" shouted Quentin.

"Of course I do," said Saturday. "This is my own country."

Wheeee-ooh! yelled the wind, and the "Blue Bird" roared down hill.

"*Your* country?"

"Calf country. . . . Keith Hall . . . over the river . . . round the hill."

"Then for God's sake let's go there . . . hungry as hell . . . soaked to the skin."

"Leave Joan . . . night like this . . . Wesson?"

"Can't find them . . . do no good . . . damned hungry."

The wind blew words away like feathers and the noise of the "Blue Bird"—engine and straining structure—swallowed whole sentences.

"They may be quite near," Saturday shouted.

"More likely a hundred miles away," roared Quentin.

"Don't like . . . give up search . . . comfort . . . Joan still out."

". . . damned hungry . . . hell . . . no bloody good."

The road ran down hill to a bridge and a river that sang in its own way the drinking-song which all rivers sing when the rain comes slanting down. On the near side of the bridge a cattle-track led straight into the water, branching V-like off the road. The banks were low and this was a convenient drinking-place for homeward-driven animals. But in the darkness the cattle-track looked as much like road as the real road, and Quentin would have steered the charabanc into the river had not Saturday gripped the wheel and violently swung it inwards. The "Blue Bird" slid uncertainly, held the road, but crashed into the right-hand ramp of the bridge. A head-light went out, like a heavy-weight boxer's eye closing suddenly under the impact of a left hook.

"There!" said Quentin triumphantly. "If it's too dark to see a bridge, how the hell are you going to find Joan?"

"Well, keep calm," said Saturday.

"Calm! I'm perfectly calm. It's you who are excited. Now do be reasonable, old man, and admit that we're doing no good and just making ourselves thoroughly uncomfortable here. How far away is Keith Hall?"

"A mile or two. By Crosier's Edge and Cawfield."

"That explains it perfectly, of course."

"We can get dry clothes and something to eat there if you like," said Saturday, "and then carry on."

Quentin re-started without further discussion. The "Blue Bird" was not damaged except for a broken head-light, a crumpled mudguard, and a splintered running-board. In a few minutes after leaving the main road, some lights showed dimly over the black slant of a hill.

"That's it," said Saturday.

They passed a squat tree-hidden lodge, drove round the bulging flank of a hill—somewhere beneath them the river sank deeply and the wind harped wildly in the birches—and came at last to a big solid house that looked an ungainly shadow-mass with an ominous tower by night; but would by day appear comfortable, safe, spacious, wise and weatherbeaten.

"Her ladyship and the laird are in the library," said the butler.

Lady Keith was a big gaunt woman with brown eyes, black eyebrows, and white hair. She had been a Matheson from about Lochalsh. Crossed with sturdy Lowland stock she had borne strong sons. Sir Colin, by grace of war the laird, walked clumsily, for he was heavy, on his artificial leg. Neither showed much surprise when Saturday and Quentin appeared all wet and tired, and not till they had bathed, changed their clothes, eaten and drunk, did Lady Keith ask why they came so late and so uncomfortably.

Saturday told the story while Quentin frankly stared round the room. It was nobly planned, pine-panelled, lighted with mellow light and red flicker from a fireplace at either end, and it had shelves on every wall designed for companies and cohorts of books in formal line. But the shelves were nearly empty. A few rows of volumes, clad in orthodox calf, stood stiffly like ancient defenders on one side; two rows or three of novels, some with their bright paper jackets still on them, were more at ease on the other. And elsewhere were a dozen badly stuffed birds: blackgame, plover, a cock grouse on a plaster rock, widgeon and pintail ducks, a couple of snipe, and a hen-harrier. On a large table were a pair of guns, a cartridge bag, and a number of cardboard targets peppered with holes. A pile of unmounted photographs lay on a stool beside Lady Keith. In front of one fireplace a Scots deerhound stretched, with a couple of West Highland terriers asleep between its stiffly out-flung legs.

"And so the villain is a book-collector," said Lady Keith when Saturday had told his adventures. "We don't like book-buyers, do we, Colin?"

"They leave room for my birds," Sir Colin answered.

"Colin had to sell the library to pay taxes on his non-existent income," Saturday explained to Quentin, "and the fellow who bought it sold it at two hundred per cent. profit three weeks after carting it away. How are the birds, mother?"

"I got these photographs of black-cock this Spring," said Lady Keith. "But you don't want to see them now, do you?"

He sat down beside her and looked at photographs—taken with skill and infinite patience—of black-cock strutting and dancing before their unimpressed harems; here was one with swollen neck, trailing his magnificent wings and curved tail-feathers on the ground, there one charging a rival, and another erect, shouting and clapping his wings against his flanks.

Saturday praised them. His mother said softly, "Tell me about Joan."

Sir Colin showed Quentin the birds he had tried to stuff. He had, perhaps, the manner of a father caught playing with his children's toys.

"I haven't the patience to get satisfactory photographs," he explained.

"I think the hen-harrier is extremely good," Quentin said.

"It isn't bad. I shot it on Crosier's Edge, a mile or so from here. But you're not really interested in birds, are you?"

Quentin considered that.

"I wasn't either till a couple of years ago. And now—oh, well, a man's got to do something. I play with birds."

He sat down with his artificial leg thrust stiffly out.

"What perfect guns!" said Quentin.

"They're old-fashioned Joe Mantons. I've been testing them. They're as good as ever. A killing circle of thirty inches at thirty yards; forty yards from choke."

In appearance Sir Colin was like his mother, with brown eyes under black brows. He had been a notable athlete till three machine-gun bullets smashed his left thigh and thirteen years had not sufficed to reconcile him to lameness. He found in the flight of birds an externalization of his desire for free movement.

Quentin did not feel at home beside this crippled giant who amused himself with stuffing snipe; and yet, in the presence of bird lovers Quentin was becoming sensitive to the charms of ornithology.

He tried to capture some bird memories of his own to talk about . . . chaffinches mobbing a—what was it they had mobbed? A rook? He couldn't remember. . . . A peewit fighting a crow. . . .

"I remember," he said, "once seeing a peewit attack a crow in the most spirited manner. . . ."

Lady Keith smiled at him.

"Another enthusiast?" she asked. "All the nicest people who come here seem to be fond of birds."

"Mother once turned a man out of the house because he admitted having shot a red-necked phale-rope," said Saturday.

"That isn't quite true," Lady Keith protested.

"Then it was a dotterel."

"She was nearly lost in a blizzard last winter," said Colin, "trying to find out whether grouse make snow-burrows."

"Well, they do," said Lady Keith. "They choose places where the heather is old and thick and wiry, so that the snow lies loosely, and they make great warrens before the surface snow has time to freeze."

"I've just remembered something that may interest you," Quentin interposed. "You've heard of the duck-billed platypus? It's nearly extinct, you know. The decadent remnant of the vanished species. And that means the individual platypus is rather a delicate creature. Well, I discovered, almost by accident, the nature of its hereditary weakness."

"What is it?" asked Saturday.

"Catarrh," said Quentin solemnly.

Lady Keith looked puzzled, Sir Colin sceptical, and Saturday derisive.

"It makes its nest of eucalyptus leaves," said Quentin. "Now everybody knows that animals and birds have their own remedies—a dog eats grass to make itself sick, for example—and as eucalyptus is a popular cure for colds it seems clear that the duck-billed platypus is subject to catarrh and knows it. Therefore it surrounds itself with an obvious remedy. To my mind it's plain that catarrh carried off millions of platypi before they discovered the use of eucalyptus."

Sir Colin and Saturday laughed coarsely while Lady Keith wondered if Quentin was trying to make fun of her. But he looked at her photographs with such genuine interest that she abandoned the idea, and when he exclaimed at the picture of a cock grouse alighting on a heather-hidden rock, "You can almost hear him talking," Lady Keith said, "You can hear him, if you want to," and took a gramophone record out of a box.

The gramophone whirred in its usual way, and then out of it a grouse spoke harshly: *Bek-ek-ek-ek-ek e-ek!*

"That's at the end of its morning flight, just before it lands."

In another minute an old gobbling voice was heard saying, it seemed, *Go-back, go-back, go-back!*

"Now it's down," said Lady Keith. "I went to a lot of trouble to make that record."

The dogs, which had wakened when the gramophone started and hearkened excitedly to the mysterious grouse noises, now sprang to the door, excited by something else, listening intently.

When it was opened they ran out, barking, past the butler.

The butler (who had been old Sir Colin's regimental sergeant-major and looked it) said, "There's a man and a lady oot-by, drookin' wet, wanting to know if you can help them, your ladyship."

"Go and see who they are, Colin," said Lady Keith. "And tell the dogs to be quiet," she added.

CHAPTER XXV

With some difficulty Mr. Wesson turned the car and went back the way he had come. It was the second time that he had taken the wrong turning. On the first occasion the road had ended abruptly without apparent reason; now it led to a tall lodge gate and private grounds.

Joan said nothing, but tried to keep her teeth from chattering. Mr. Wesson was also silent, his stream of reminiscence having been beaten back at last by the tireless rain. The wind howled dismally as he found the main road again and turned north. They climbed hill after hill and the rain leapt in beside them. He drove carefully on a long down gradient and the wind danced outrageously all about.

The road was black as earth and the lights scarcely showed its difference from the black moor on either side. The silver rain-arrows in the gleam dazzled him. Somewhere at the bottom of the hill a river sang its drinking-song, and the wind harped wildly in the birches. The road blurred before him, seeming to split in two.

Joan shouted "Left, left!" but it was too late.

The car skidded over shingle, bumped across a rock, and ran straight into the river till a boulder stopped it. Mr. Wesson sat dazed while the water lipped the top of the door and presently flowed over and all around him. The engine had stopped and the river-song was heard more clearly. The water was cold.

Mr. Wesson suddenly remembered van Buren's papers, found his attaché case, and held it above his head out of the river's reach. He sat thus for some moments, like Patience in a reservoir, thinking.

Joan struggled to open the door beside her, but found it difficult because of the pressure of the stream outside. She was laughing hysterically and at the same time her teeth were chattering with cold, so that she seemed to be pronouncing the second letter of the alphabet with incredible reiteration.

The black river swirled past them, chuckling and chanting, the outrageous wind laughed again, and the rain beat a roll on the taut roof of the car.

"Be-be-be-be-be-be-be-be," said Joan, struggling with the door.

"Please be quiet," said Mr. Wesson. "I'm thinking."

"Be quiet!" exclaimed Joan shrilly. "We'll be d-d-d-drowned if we stay here any longer, and then we'll be q-quiet enough!"

Mr. Wesson looked startled. Even in the dark it could be seen that he looked startled.

"Climb over the top if you can't open it," he said sharply, and Joan struggled out between the door and the roof, tearing her thin cloth skirt as she went.

She stood on the running board up to her knees in water, and Mr. Wesson handed her his valuable attaché case. Then he also climbed out of the car.

But he was too precipitate and instead of finding a safe position on the running-board he fell headlong into the river. He emerged a moment later, flinging his arms wide in the attitude of an earnest young swimmer, and said "Bhou! Bhou!" very loudly. He was so upset by his accident that he began to wade farther into the river.

"Come back!" Joan shouted, and Mr. Wesson turned obediently.

"I mistook my direction," he said. "Thank you for your timely warning." A piece of politeness which was entirely wasted, for the wind and the rollicking river swallowed it between them.

They struggled to the bank and found their way on to the bridge where, not long before, the "Blue Bird" had crumpled her shapely mudguards. The Bentley was just visible in the darkness. The river made a little whitish foam about it and sang more loudly against its drowned sides.

"We must get shelter somewhere," said Joan. "The first house we can find."

"You will give me your word of honour not to—"

"I'll give you anything you like if you'll take me to a big fire."

They walked on hurriedly, trudging through the mud, shivering, wet through. Mr. Wesson took off his coat and tried to wring it dry. When they came to a road that branched left he said, "I suppose we had better keep straight on."

Joan, who was too miserable to agree with anyone or any-thing, immediately said, "I'm going this way," and took the road to the left, which led to Crosier's Edge and Cawfield. Mr. Wesson followed her.

By-and-by they saw dim lights over the slant of a hill.

"Look!" said Joan, "there's a house!" And at once she struck across country in a direct line for the yellow-starred shadow which meant, with luck, dry clothes and a fire. There were trees in her way. A branch scratched her cheek as she brushed through them. There was a stone dyke to climb on which she tore her skirt again, for somehow she managed to kneel on it (and that was not easy, for it was short) and the sodden cloth parted will-ingly. Mr. Wesson followed her without a word. Only at the very doors of Keith Hall did he remember something: propriety.

"Don't you think it will appear strange," he said earnestly, "if we are seen together at this time of night? You are young and unmarried. I—well, I am not related to you in any way. It is unusual, you must admit—"

"I'm cold," said Joan.

"I suggest, if anybody enquires, that you should pretend to be my sister."

"Your aunt, if you like," said Joan.

"We've had an accident," she told the maid who opened the door.

"A serious accident," Mr. Wesson added.

The maid looked frightened, for their appearance was against them, and Joan swiftly stepped past her when she caught sight of the butler crossing the hall with a silver tray on which decanters stood.

Undaunted by his military expression—which was exacer-bated when he saw Mr. Wesson, who looked unpleasant in wet clothes—Joan explained, "We fell into the river. At least our car did. And personally I'm frightened of getting pneumonia. Will you tell— I don't know who lives here, but—"

"This young lady," Mr. Wesson began, while a pool steadily gathered round his feet—

"I shall inform her ladyship," said the butler, looking at Mr. Wesson as though he were defaulter's parade.

The deerhound and the two West Highland terriers rushed out, barking, and Sir Colin limped after them.

"I am Joan Benbow," said Joan. "This is—"

"I am her brother," said Mr. Wesson ingratiatingly.

"There's a large fire inside," Sir Colin said, "I think you had better come in at once and get warm."

He held open the door for them. The brighter light of the library made them blink for a moment.

"Joan," exclaimed Saturday springing to his feet.

"And Wesson," added Quentin.

Mr. Wesson's wits returned immediately. He recognized Saturday and his unfortunate position in the same instant and became, after some hours of comparative gentleness, once more like a cornered weasel. His face hardened and his heavy eyebrows half-hooded his expressionless eyes. He took a small bottle from his pocket and with his thumb forced out the cork.

"Stay right where you are," he said harshly. "I've got a little bottle of vitriol here, and if anyone moves an inch it goes straight into Miss Benbow's face."

He stood to one side of the door with Joan beside him and kept her back by his left arm which stretched in front of her like a barrier. In his left hand he held the attaché case.

Sir Colin was nearest him.

"Get farther back," said Mr. Wesson; and Sir Colin obeyed.

Joan stood white and still; or almost white, for the rain off her hair mixed with blood from her tree-torn cheek and ran pinkly over her chin. Her tattered skirt gaped open, rent from waist to hem, and her hat was sodden and shapeless. But Saturday looked at her longingly. Bewilderment petrified his face and wrath made it red. Like waxworks, embarrassingly realistic but unnaturally still, Lady Keith and Quentin and Sir Colin stood at gaze.

Mr. Wesson's throat moved jerkily. He was thinking desperately what to do. It was stalemate unless he could make a bargain of some kind. No one spoke. And the water dripped audibly off his clothes, falling with a tiny bell-like note on to the hard floor.

Saturday could keep quiet no longer.

"Put that bottle down," he said hoarsely, and took a step forward.

"It's she who gets it all, if you don't stay where you are," said Mr. Wesson, and raised the small brown bottle threateningly. Joan shrank against the wall.

The dogs had watched intently this strange performance, the terriers alert and questioning, the deerhound still and suspicious. Now, when Wesson threatened Joan, he leapt forward with a growl in his deep throat. The terriers followed, shrilly yelping.

Mr. Wesson saw bright eyes in a rough grey head, white teeth shining, and a glimpse of red mouth. His right hand dropped and he shot the contents of the small brown bottle into the deerhound's face.

The dog's growl turned into high-pitched ululation, he checked in mid-air, dropped to the floor, and with frantic paws rubbed at his eyes.

Mr. Wesson pushed Joan aside and darted through the door.

"You damned swine!" roared Saturday, and snatching a gun and a handful of cartridges from the table sprang after Wesson. The outer door closed with a bang. Saturday ran across the hall. A swoop of wind and rain met him as he opened the door. The terriers followed him.

In the library they stooped round the agonized deerhound.

"Don't touch him," Colin warned them, "or you'll get burnt too. Bring some wet cloths, Grant," he said as the butler, who had heard strange noises, opportunely appeared.

The dog was quieter, though he still rubbed his eyes and whined. There was a pungent smell in the air.

"Come to the fire," said Lady Keith, putting her arm round Joan's waist.

"But Saturday!" said Joan tearfully, "he'll shoot Wesson, He'll kill him!"

"I'll go after them," said Quentin.

"It's all right," Sir Colin said from where he sat on the floor beside the dog. "It's all right, you needn't worry. Saturday could never hit anything he aimed at. They're both perfectly safe."

"Colin knows best," said Lady Keith, and wiped Joan's

cheeks, and comforted her, and took off her wet hat, and rubbed her cold hands.

Quentin stepped out into the stormy darkness. He could see nothing, and the rain greeted him. But suddenly he heard a shot, made faint by the wind, and then another. He hurried in the direction from which they came.

Saturday, loading as he went, had run blindly. The transition from a lighted room to rainy night was too sudden. And the rain blurred his spectacles, so that he looked dimly through a film of water. He took them off and thought he saw more clearly.

There was a shrubbery to his left, in which Wesson might possibly be hiding. He stalked towards it with a mind too murderously inclined to think of rain or wind or common sense.

Joan with a cut on her cheek and her torn dress; rain-soaked, white and miserable; Joan who had been ill-treated by that swine Wesson; and Bran the deerhound blinded by hot acid— these pictures turbulently filled his brain, and his hands trembled slightly with the surplus of his rage. All the anger of that long day had come to a head and murder crowed cheerfully in his heart.

The terriers had disappeared. Now he heard them barking and ran towards them. Something showed darker than the leaves and Saturday fired at it, once and again. It disappeared.

"Come out of that, Wesson," he ordered.

There was no reply.

Saturday re-loaded and as he snapped-to the barrel there were footsteps on the gravel behind him. He turned and fired for the third time.

"You bloody fool!" came a frightened voice. "You awful bloody fool! You might have hit me!"

"I thought it was Wesson," growled Saturday.

"Well, it wasn't," said Quentin, "and anyway you've got no more right to shoot him than you have to shoot me. Come in and leave him alone."

"I'm going to kill him," said Saturday. "I think he's in these bushes. Will you go in and beat him out?"

"While you shoot at both of us? Not likely."

"Then stay here and keep your eyes open."

Saturday pushed half-blindly—for his spectacles were in his pocket—between enormous rhododendrons, hollies, and laurels in search of the fugitive Wesson. Leaves dark and pectinated thrust into his face. Swag-bellied, water-dripping bushes opposed a barrier that was the more effective for its Dædalian recesses. Leaves full of rain emptied their store on him. And still he thrust more deeply into the jungle. There was a smell of wet earth and laurel. Somewhere the wind shrieked *Wheee-ooo hoo-hooh!* but its voice was muffled by thick black foliage. Shrubs of a fantastic girth, incredibly guarded with branches and masked with a myriad moving leaves, surrounded him. But neither Wesson nor the dogs were there.

As Saturday fought his way out again he heard Quentin hallooing, "Go-one awa-ay!"

"Which way?" he shouted.

Quentin was excitedly marking double-time like a small boy at odds with nature from hydropathy.

"Straight down towards the lodge with the dogs at his heel," he chattered.

They ran side by side, splashing in puddles, straining to see through the dark. Quentin's momentary scruples had vanished. It is seldom that one is allowed the thrill of a man-hunt. And the night was savage.

Mr. Wesson, though hampered by his attaché case, made good time, for he had been seriously alarmed by Saturday's two shots, one of which had spattered a tree not more than a yard from him. The West Highland terriers followed more discreetly than at first, for he had managed to kick both of them.

The road stretched on obscurely, the wind whistled in the birches by the unseen river—to his right a flank of grass dropped steeply towards it—and his breath came short. Black clouds with here and there a star lit weal thronged the sky. For a few minutes he thought he had tricked the pursuit. And then he heard it behind him.

He began to run from side to side of the road, zigzag, like a merchant ship in war-time when a periscope comes sinister out of the waves.

By screwing up his eyes Saturday could see a dim shape flying before him. He shouted, and might not have fired. But when the shape started to flicker snipe-fashion over the road the temptation became irresistible. He stopped, hurriedly sighted, and pulled the trigger.

"I think I've hit him," he gasped.

Mr. Wesson staggered to a halt and put up his hands.

"I guess you win," he called, panting for breath.

Saturday and Quentin, who were also badly winded, glared at him through the darkness.

"I don't think you did," said Quentin.

"It was a good shot."

"But you missed him."

"Did that last one hit you?"

"No," said Mr. Wesson, "but it might have if I'd stayed on the other edge of the road. Do you mind if I take my hands down? I've got a pretty sore stitch in my side. That's why I had to stop."

"Where's my manuscript?" asked Saturday.

"I don't know and I don't care," groaned Mr. Wesson.

He huddled down to relieve the pain at his midriff while Quentin and Saturday watched him silently. Quentin wanted to make facetious remarks about Saturday's shooting, but decided that it would be tactless to do so in the presence of the intended victim. Saturday's inclination to manslaughter was not radical enough to suggest putting a captive to death. And so when Mr. Wesson had sufficiently recovered they walked back to the Hall, Mr. Wesson still carrying his attaché case.

In the meanwhile Joan had been bathed and wrapped warmly in pyjamas and a dressing-gown, and Bran the deerhound made uncomfortable with boracic lotion in his eyes and a bread poultice over his face.

Joan sat by the fire. Sir Colin's pyjamas which she wore were yellow silk that caught the firelight, and the dressing-gown was an elaborate affair with gold dragons on it. To Saturday she appeared infinitely desirable, and the thought of revenge on the unhappy Wesson faded almost completely from his mind. No more than a little crooked shadow was left.

"Good shooting?" Sir Colin asked.

"He missed Wesson three times," said Quentin, "but he nearly hit me."

Mr. Wesson looked depressed.

Lady Keith suggested that they should go and find more dry clothes. "And get some for Mr. Wesson," she added.

"People who throw vitriol can stay wet," growled Saturday.

A triumphant smile creased Mr. Wesson's face.

"I fooled you there," he said complacently. "Do you think I carry flasks of vitriol about with me as well as first editions? Boloney!—I beg your ladyship's pardon. That is an American vulgarism indicative of scorn or contempt. But you will admit that it was justified if you read the label on this bottle."

He took the little brown bottle, now empty, from his pocket and showed it to Lady Keith.

"Iodine?"

"Tincture of iodine," said Mr. Wesson with insufferable self-satisfaction.

"Well, of all the cheek!" Joan exclaimed.

"So that's why Bran stopped howling so quickly," said Colin; and Quentin looked at Mr. Wesson with open admiration.

For fully a minute he kept the stage. Held at bay by a bottle of iodine, the others thought. Bluffed by a tenpenny antiseptic. Cozened, bilked, gulled, gammoned and hocus-pocus'd by two fluid ounces of germicide. The just comment was silence, they felt. And little smiles of pleasure that would not be suppressed crinkled Mr. Wesson's mouth. He had filled the kitty roof-high, bluffed the four-ace-players, scared the full-house-holders, and seen faces pale behind a straight flush; while he himself carried no more than a broken straight and an empty gun. What though he had lost the game? The laugh was his.

"You've earned dry clothes," said Saturday.

Bran the deerhound, unobserved, ate his bread poultice in spite of its sick-room flavour.

By-and-by they re-appeared, all three in dressing-gowns, and Sir Colin proposed that they should decide immediately what was to be done with the prisoner.

"I shall go to bed, I think," said Lady Keith. "I am not very

fond of courts of justice. Colin knows what rooms are ready
for you when you feel sleepy. Joan, my dear, I am so very glad
that you have come scatheless out of this trying ordeal, and
I think it was extremely clever of you to find your way so
quickly to my fireside. Are you sure that you are not too tired
to stay up?"

Lady Keith said good-night; hesitated; and added, "Good-
night, Mr. Wesson. I'm glad it was only iodine."

"I'm very pleased to have met your ladyship," said Mr.
Wesson.

"Now," said Sir Colin cheerfully, "a small drink for the prisoner and very large drinks for the jury. Miss Benbow approves
our port, and everybody else, I suppose, wants whisky. Saturday, you're the worst shot in Scotland and I was never glad of
it till now. By Gad, Bran's eaten his poultice! Well, I'm—now
isn't he a fine old dog!"

Sir Colin poured drinks, threw another log on the fire, patted
Bran's head, and then sat down beside Joan and patted her
hand. He was enjoying himself. Over one half of the room the
lamps were out and the stripped shelves covered their nakedness
in shadow. The other half, amber-lighted and warm, had lost its
moiety of long and lofty proportion with relief. It drew into the
fire, hearing the wind outside. It relaxed. It became snug and
informal. Prisoner and captor stretched themselves gratefully,
having the echo of storm still in their ears and fatigue, half-
beaten, tingling under their skin. Gratified by the speedy recov-
ery of van Buren's documents—they had been recovered before
Saturday fully realized that they had been stolen—and amiably
conscious of power, the captors forbore from expressing it by
ropes, gyves, or countenances of iron. Under their dressing-
gowns they had donned an evening habit of indulgence.

Very solemnly Joan said, "If it weren't for Bran's sake I could
wish that it really had been vitriol. It's so silly to have been
frightened by iodine."

Still more solemnly Mr. Wesson replied, "Not even for you,
Miss Benbow, would I condescend to threaten a lady with genuine vitriol. I believe in certain standards of decency, and vitriol
does not occur within the boundaries which they demarcate."

"Will you explain to us your connection with the Cheka?" said Quentin, bending forward impressively.

"With the checker? I don't get you," answered Mr. Wesson.

"I mean with Russia. Have you ever been interested in the Zik?"

"I have a Christian man's sympathy for those smitten with disease, but I must admit that I never felt any particular call to send grapes to a Russian hospital."

"I didn't say the sick. I said the Zik. Are you wilfully misunderstanding me?"

"Mr. Cotton has some reason to believe that you are concerned with a Russian plot to rob Mr. van Buren," explained Saturday.

"It's the first I've heard of it," said Mr. Wesson, who seemed completely mystified. His bewilderment was shared by Joan and Sir Colin, who looked at Quentin with some suspicion.

"And you didn't steal my poem along with van Buren's papers?"

"I did not. But I saw your poem, or a work answering to that description, in the possession of a red-haired chamber-maid with whom I—well, to whom my attention was drawn."

"Nelly!" exclaimed Quentin. "Now what was your connection with her?"

"It was brief and not so secure as I imagined."

"But you know that she had my poem?"

"She certainly had."

"And where is she now?"

"I am no crystal-gazer, Mr. Keith."

"Was it she who followed us in Lady Mercy's car?" asked Joan. "Because if so we lost her somewhere in Yorkshire."

"I thought I understood what all this was about," Sir Colin said, "but I'm getting rather mixed. Who is Nelly? What has Russia to do with it? Why should anyone steal a poem?"

Their explanation, which was more involved than the Athanasian Creed but not so authoritative, dulled Sir Colin's curiosity without precisely answering his questions. He poured more drinks and the inexplicable lost significance.

"We've recovered van Buren's property," said Saturday. "Now what are we going to do with Wesson?"

"Consider me entirely at your disposal," said Mr. Wesson comfortably, and stifled a yawn.

"We do," said Quentin.

"The turret room has a strong door," Sir Colin suggested, "and the window is a long way from the ground. I propose that we lock him up there for the night."

"And take away all his clothes?"

"Take him away first," said Saturday. "I want to talk to Joan."

Reluctantly Colin got up and looked down at his brother's *fiancée* with a wistful idea that she was more interesting than a stuffed hen-harrier. He sighed, and limped to the door.

"Come on, Wesson," he said.

Quentin followed readily because of a notion, which had just occurred to him, that Wesson might be persuaded to talk more freely of his undoubted connection with Russia under the influence of the Third Degree . . . if Sir Colin would collaborate, that is.

"Joan!" said Saturday when they had gone.

"Oh, Saturday!" she replied, simply but sufficiently.

And in a little while, "I wonder if father is worrying very much about me?"

"We can telephone to Downish in the morning."

"And ask for his blessing?"

"There's not much chance of getting that. I've lost my poem and his blessing depends on it. I'm farther from you than ever, Joan."

"You've never been so near . . . and your poem will turn up somewhere even if that girl has taken it."

"My dear," said Saturday.

"My dear," she answered, Venus's birds being parrots as often to doves.

Then, reflectively, "I'm glad you didn't shoot Mr. Wesson. I think he's an interesting man."

"He's a sportsman in his own way. Do you know, he never complained about being shot at? He seemed to take it as quite an ordinary occurrence."

"Of course," said Joan. "He's an American."

CHAPTER XXVI

The storm, which had originated as an obscure depression over Iceland, gathered strength from every tide, wind and cloud between the Faroes and the Pentland Firth, exercised itself over Scotland and shaken braggart wings about Northumberland, continued to travel southwards. It met Holly and Professor Benbow in Yorkshire, slapped, buffeted, banged and blinded them, and surveyed the parching Midlands ahead of it with oceanic zest.

Holly had one of those sensitive natures which react to variable weather, giving sunlight to sunlight and cold displeasure for hail. Now he turned sullen. The beer was finished. The professor, who had recited several thousand lines of Shakespeare, felt the tiresomeness of quoting Lear to a real storm. Essentially an honest man, he could not honestly say "I tax not you, you elements, with unkindness;" for he did. To find that the beer was done had also distressed him, not so much because he wanted more as because of the obvious inference that he had in the course of a few hours already drunk six bottles; which, at his age, was probably excessive. . . . Years, years grew around him like elm-trees, coffin-wood-trees, stopping his hand from this and that, darkening the fields, narrowing his world. A Birnam Wood of coffin-trees marching irresistibly to the stout heart of Dunsinane. Age may well have deeper thoughts than youth, for they are an earnest of the deepness of the grave. The beer lay cold in his belly. . . .

But age comes quickest and most irremediable to mechanical things. The life of a sparking-plug is a fierce tropical existence of days only. No healing leucocytes rush to the aid of a cracked cylinder, nor anastomosing tributaries expand to carry the lifeblood of a choked feed-pipe. Old motor-cars grow asthmatic, systolic murmurs betray their weakened power, and carbon comes to poison them outright. And so the aged Morris staggered in its gait like an old lady in the rain, wheezing a little, anxious about her umbrella which the wind was bullying. It grew somewhat hysterical, feeling itself far from home, and began to run in an agitated manner, short bursts of speed striving to make up for more frequent laggarding. . . .

Light showed ahead. The weary Morris sighed with relief and edged to the pavement in front of a red-curtained house with a swinging sign.

"You can't expect her to run on two cylinders," said Holly, and got out. The professor followed him without a word.

"The Fisherman's Rest," kept by George and Jemima Postlethwaite, was no better and no worse than hundreds more of its beneficent kind. It had a bar and a bar-parlour and a pike in a glass-case, and the landlord his proprietary jest; for when asked about the stream whose existence was implied in his title he could say, "The river's a mile, or maybe a mile and a half away, so old William Warble, who caught that big 'un over there, needed his rest pretty badly by the time he got here. And so do other fishermen I find, mostly from thinking about what they might have had to carry. And now what can I do for you, gentlemen?"

Mr. Postlethwaite was a little, paunchy, self-satisfied man with a round white face and grey bushy hair. While Holly and the professor waited for food to be cooked—Holly had shyly suggested going apart to eat and the professor had brusquely told him not to be a fool—there entered a young man, tall and thin, with heavy brownish hair that the sun had bleached here and there to the colour of tow. He had a jaw grimly moulded, a truculent chin, gloomy eyes, and a twisted mouth. Having politely said "Good evening," he sat beside the fire, took a book from his pocket, and read. His hands were delicate and he wore defiantly shabby tweeds.

Holly's hands had already been stealing to an inside pocket, and when the young man took a book from his, Holly pulled out the largest flask that the professor had ever seen, and deferentially set it on the table. The professor unscrewed the top, and Holly fetched two tumblers from a dusty sideboard. Not knowing what he was to see, the professor poured. And out of the flask came a thin sapphire stream, indescribably attractive. Even before he tasted it Holly's storm-sullened face grew glad, and manliness returned to the dejected father whose thoughts had been miserably between a fleeing Joan and age coming fast towards him with a coffin on his rounded back.

"We have been defeated," said the professor.

"We have come far and done no good. We are stranded. But we are not the first who have been beaten one day, and slept, and waked again to win. I have had graveyard thoughts, Holly, but under blue skies I defy the grave. The world is a good place. God plants his healing leaves beside the nettle. There is always a remedy and the rainbow returns."

The professor swallowed his cocktail and Holly remarked, "The extra bit of shaking it's had hasn't done it no harm."

"The native thought of mankind is gratitude. The most significant noise of earth is the singing of birds," said the professor with determination.

"Fritinancy," declared the young man beside the fire.

"What's that?" said the professor.

"I said fritinancy. Which is the whimper of gnats and the buzzing of flies. You're talking nonsense."

Intellectually the professor was not at his best. Emotion had harrowed his mind and rain had followed the harrow. Rain and beer. And even good cloth shrinks in the wetting.

"Who are you?" he asked belligerently.

"My name is Neale. I am a painter."

"A good painter?"

"Very good," said Neale.

"Then why don't you stick to your last?"

"When I hear a man of your years and appearance of education twittering pernicious optimism it is my duty to protest. I object to the lying dogma of redemption and I detest, even above dogma, a suggestion of the Panglossian heresy. You, apparently, believe in both."

The professor scratched his chin, for at the moment he did; redemption being carried as a kind of stepney on the best of all possible worlds. Holly, without a thought of rudeness, offered Neale a cocktail which Neale refused.

The landlord made his timely entrance with a tray and untidily set their meal on the table.

"Getting acquainted, I see," he said chattily. "Now if you can persuade Mr. Neale to show you his pictures you've got a promiscuous evening in front of you. Not that I appreciate them properly myself, for I'm not what you might call a criterion, and you need to be very well educated to understand the painting they go in for nowadays. But I'm willing to believe that an artist's opinion is as liable to be correct as my own, and that his work may entitle him to obloquy when I am long forgotten. And a poet's too. You go and bring your pictures down, Mr. Neale, and I'll look after these gentlemen till you come back."

Neale obeyed willingly; Holly and the professor ate; the landlord regarded them contentedly; and continued.

"You don't see anything like 'His Dead Master,' or 'Two Strings to her Bow,' or 'Christmas in the Baron's Hall' being painted nowadays. And why? The reason, I take it, is that we're growing up. Pictures like that were the A B C of art, all very well for childhood, but not much good for the eye of adultery. Now the modern artist gives us something difficult so that we can realize how grown-up we are; a bit of mathematics, solid geology and the like, instead of a fairy-tale."

"I like fairy-tales," said the professor with his mouth full.

"Every man to his taste," agreed the landlord. "I'm becoming more and more laxative as the years go on, for lots of artists come here to paint and stay to talk, and I listen to them, and they talk so convictedly, that I find it difficult to disbelieve any of them, so in the course of years my ideas have become completely ostracized, you see."

"Very pleasant and proper," said the professor, and Holly picked his teeth suspiciously.

Neale returned with a pile of canvases and set up two or three of them on chairs. They were landscapes, chocolate and dull green, and grey slab-sided houses with awkward angles stood uncompromisingly in the fields. Obviously the work of a man who could draw and who knew his own mind, ruggedly composed, they somehow expressed disintegration rather than coalescence.

"Cézanne with a difference," said the professor.

"You're not so blind as I thought you were," Neale answered.

The landlord rubbed his hands and declared, "I do like a little good-humoured sodomy of an evening."

"Sodality, you fool," said Neale. And the landlord, looking puzzled, repeated the two words under his breath, comparing their flavour.

"Why does everything fall away like that?" asked the professor, pointing to a solid farm-house that threatened collapse and a solider hill that appeared unstable from its very weight.

"Because that is the way I see things," said Neale. "You look at the world as fixed and perdurable. You think of it as something big and important; something to be taken seriously. You respect the world. Well, I don't, and that's a difference between us. I don't see it solid, but jerrybuilt without plan or foundation. To me it's a shoddy contraption of deserts and barren seas and stinking towns. You think of the world as Oxford, and Green Park, and a Scotch grouse-moor. I see the Sahara and the North Atlantic and a London slum. Can you worship the creator of sterility and the passive observer of filth? You think the earth is a comfortable place, whereas not ten men in every million that crawl on its surface know what comfort is. Have you ever heard of Welsh miners? or of negroes in the lynching states of America? or slaves in Africa? or untouchables in India? or beggars in Moscow? or political prisoners in Central Europe? or peonage in Central and South America? Japanese cotton mills? or starvation in China? or brothels, poverty, prisoners, cruelty, disease, miners and dirty factories all over the world—clean factories, too, which are ten times worse, because they keep their slaves alive longer and persuade fools into thinking them good."

"He knows what he's talking about," said the landlord, impressed by so many words.

"Do you think that such a world is the reasoned creation of a reasoning creator? That all the stench and cruelty and ugliness were inherent in the first casting of the rocks and the first dribble of fecund slime that fell on them? Do you think that these things are meant to endure? I say they're not. I say the world is nothing but débris, planet-ash, swirling in space like a rotten boat in a whirlpool with wood-lice, rats, and an ultimately devouring sun as its companions."

"And what do you propose to do about it?" asked the professor.

"Teach the truth," said Neale. "Even you saw disintegration when my pictures showed it to you."

The rain beat on the windows and beyond them the tireless wind tore viciously at bending trees. The professor sighed and thought how foolish it was to ride out looking for adventure, and how unnecessary to meet an apostle of some combative and contrary creed.

"There is beauty in the world," he said.

"Circe's beauty," answered Neale.

"Courage."

"Which turns to cruelty."

"Hope—"

"For children."

"Loyalty."

"Or stupidity."

"Virtue."

"Only in the starkest truth."

"Do you believe in nothing, then?"

"In none of your toyshop idols."

"Then what do you believe in?"

"Negation and absurdity. Or, if you prefer a triune godhead. Buddhism, Birth Control, and Bathos."

"Ah!" said Holly. "Birth control!"

"Have you got anything to say against it?"

"I've got a whole lot of things to say against it. Just you listen to me. I don't know how many brothers and sisters you've got, but I had ten. Seven sisters and three brothers, and all of 'em older than me. Now what do you think would have happened if my old dad and my old mother had been birth controllers? Well, it's long odds that I wouldn't be here for one. And Nelly and Tom and Gladys and Marigold and Dick and Lottie and Lily—they were twins—mightn't have come either, so who would Henry and Mabel and Poppy have had to play with, without going on to the street and mixing with all sorts and kinds and conditions that you didn't know what they had in their hair? No one of us ever had ringworm or anything dirty like that, and I say that Nelly and Tom and Gladys— eight of us, at any rate—are eight good arguments against birth control."

"And what have you done to justify your mother's pains or to make you glad that you survived vaccination?"

"I've been bayoneted by a Prussian Guard and I've invented a blue cocktail," said Holly proudly.

"You have contributed to war and intoxication. A notable record. If you are married to a good woman your idiot's tale is complete."

"Is there anything wrong with your kidneys?" asked the professor.

"I have never been ill in my life," said Neale coldly. "Why do you ask?"

"I wondered," said the professor, "for I sympathize with your feelings but I can't accept your conclusions, and I thought nephritis might be the key to your philosophy."

A flush had slowly crept over Holly's face, occasioned not by Professor Benbow's indelicacy but by Neale's tripartite insult, the significance of which he had been slow to realize. He rose from his chair and stood in front of the painter.

"I'm not married, neither to a good woman nor to a bad one," he said bravely, "but I would have been if she hadn't preferred my Uncle Harry, he being younger than me, owing to our having a large family, and also more handsome in appearance. Now just you shut up! I've listened to you long enough and I don't like your voice."

Holly began hurriedly to take off his coat and waistcoat, and the landlord as hurriedly tried to prevent him, thinking that Holly was inciting either himself or Neale to physical combat.

"You go and sit down!" said Holly fiercely. "Go on now! And think of some other long words to gargle with."

He turned to Neale, who was looking bored.

"I'm going to show you something," he said. "You didn't believe me when I told you about the Prussian Guard, did you? They never do. Not even the newspapers didn't—they said it was Saxons—and they even believe in what's going to win the Derby. But what d'you think this is—eh?"

He pulled his shirt—it had pink stripes—out of his trousers and held it high in front of his face.

His voice came muffled from behind the curtain: "Look at that and then sneer if you like!"

Neale saw a long white scar running prettily over Holly's ribs—thin ribs that curved tightly upon a narrow chest—and up towards his left armpit.

"There are thousands of branded cattle in the world," he said. "Personally I would prefer a Tyburn T on my thumb."

"Now do sit down," said the landlord as Holly stuttered with rage. "The conversation was just growing interesting, I thought, when you interrupted it by getting incestuous all of a sudden."

"Incestuous yourself, you cock-eyed old poodle!" shouted the wrathful Holly, his shirt hanging down in front something like a sporran. The professor smiled pleasantly at the animated scene while Neale looked scornful and remote.

Then, before the landlord could reply, the door opened and a husky voice said, "'Oo's is that there motor-car standing outside of 'ere?"

The newcomer was a policeman, solemn, fat-cheeked, wrapt in a rain-streaming cape.

"It's mine," said Holly.

With a sombre eye the policeman considered his improper appearance. Then he turned to the landlord.

"Is this an orggy, Mr. Postlethwaite?" he asked.

"He was only showing us his wound," explained the landlord.

"Then let me see it too," said the policeman.

"What for?" asked Holly.

"Evidence," said the policeman.

Once more Holly pulled up his shirt while the constable examined his scar with interest.

"My wife's youngest brother's got a better one than that," he commented; and before Holly could retort added, "Now show me your licence."

Helplessly submitting to both the insult and exaction of authority Holly picked up his coat and took from a pocket-book his driver's licence. As the constable opened it a four-times folded piece of paper fell to the floor.

Holly dropped on his knees with instant knowledge in his heart and an imperative desire to read again those few lines, the half-dozen figures, that he had thought stolen and far away. He smoothed out the paper on the carpet and visibly adored, while the rain-spilling policeman and the little fat white landlord marvelled. He looked up, and with an eye moist and lambent caught the professor's curious eye.

"The recipe," he added huskily. "I've found it, sir. It's never been stolen at all. I've had it in my pocket all the time."

"So this has been a fool's errand from the beginning," said the professor.

"I'm sorry, sir."

"You're like many men, Holly, who leave home only to find what they already possess."

Neale laughed harshly.

"I expect Miss Benbow's been just as safe as my recipe," said Holly.

"I hope so. Probably she has been. Keith followed them very quickly. I suppose I could have trusted him."

The landlord and the policeman listened intently but without understanding; like performing seals.

"Do you want to look at the rest of my pictures?" asked Neale.

"I am eager to see everything," said the professor, "so long as you do not ask me to believe in all I see."

"Then here is an imaginative landscape, a mere in starlight. I shall print under it these lines of Yeats:

    'I would find by the edge of that water
      The collar-bone of a hare,
      Worn thin by the lapping of the water,
      And pierce it through with a gimlet, and stare
      At the old bitter world where they marry in
        churches,
      And laugh over the untroubled water
      At all who marry in churches,
      Through the white thin bone of a hare.' "

"Good God," said the professor, "what merriment is in the world! Mr. Neale, I shall soon be an old man if I am not one

already. Already I am inclined to reminiscence and my mind is
no better than a rocking-horse that swings back and fore with
only the illusion of progress. And yet my heart beats quicker
as it rocks, and stronger rhythms than yours arise in my brain,
and my memory, queasy and senescent as it undoubtedly is,
recalls more cheerful things than you look forward to. Now,
for instance, these lines come into my mind:

> 'When drop-of-blood-and-foam-dapple
> Bloom lights the orchard apple,
> And thicket and thorp are merry
> With silver-surfèd cherry,
>
> And azuring-over graybell makes
> Wood banks and brakes wash wet like lakes,
> And magic cuckoo-call
> Caps, clears, and clinches all. . . .'

"And this verse too, which is apposite to the occasion:

> 'I'll not be a fool like the nightingale
> That sits up till midnight without any ale,
> Making a noise with his nose.'"

"I don't drink," said Neale.
"I accept your apology," replied the professor.
The policeman wiped his moustache with the back of his
hand. It was a proleptic gesture.

CHAPTER XXVII

The storm grew gentler going south—as many things do—
and poured upon Downish without malice, so that on Monday morning the High Street was like a liner whose decks have
been newly washed; not, as might be feared, a dismal thoroughfare choked with fallen branches and ravished tiles, hens
drowned, dead dogs, and all the other wrack that tempest
commonly leaves behind it. The gutters were full, but the
water in them made a pleasant brook-like noise. On the house-
tops damp sparrows sat and roofs were shining wet, but already the sun was shining, primrose-pale and watery, and the
sparrows perked their invincible heads.

The wheels of John Jellicoe Judd's bicycle made a sibilant,
slurring noise on the drenched road, but his whistle rose shrilly
and he slung a bundle of newspapers into "The Pelican" with
the animation that older people reserve for rare and important
occasions.

George the Boots was waiting for it, and behind George
waited Maria and Bill and Herbert, while O'Higgins and Veronica were not far away. George looked important, Bill sceptical, Herbert gaped and gulped like a young starling waiting for
worms, and Maria in expectation of tragedy was ready with
tears to shed. O'Higgins and Veronica were discussing mutual
acquaintances.

"She may 'ave been boss-eyed," said O'Higgins, "but 'e was
no gentleman to go and marry 'er sister after what 'e'd led 'er
to expect."

"You're that stern, Mr. O'Higgins," exclaimed Veronica
blissfully.

And yet in spite of their apparent pre-occupation Veronica
and O'Higgins shared equally the excited expectancy of Bill
and Maria and Herbert and George. It was that excitement
which had sharpened their sensibility and made it remember
the Dido's fate of a cross-eyed girl. Since the previous afternoon
the kitchen of "The Pelican" had been like a cave of the winds
with blowing rumour and counter-rumour, theory and explanation, and cross-currents of doubt and perplexity. Saturday

Keith and his friend Mr. Cotton had vanished in a blue chara-banc. Joan Benbow had vanished; abducted, it was said. Nelly Bly who had always been half a mystery, had vanished, none of them knew how. Holly had gone. Lady Mercy and Mr. Wesson and Mr. van Buren had gone. Things had been stolen. Strange disorder had been discovered in Mr. Wesson's room. Docu-ments had disappeared. Scotland Yard had been notified. All the remaining visitors, in a state of barely-suppressed excite-ment themselves, had been conscientiously calm before ser-vants and so made the servants doubly sure that calamity of some kind had occurred. And nobody could suggest a theory that took account of all the circumstances they severally knew.

But the newspapers would tell them. It was sure to be in the papers. They were argus-eyed, sensitive to news as a micro-phone to the rustle of paper, omniscient and omni-explanatory. And with Lady Mercy and Saturday Keith, kidnapping, stolen documents, and a pirated charabanc to dazzle their eyes, de-light their ears, and occupy their brains, why, the newspapers would be full of the story. And so George and Maria and all the rest of them would find out— when the newspapers came— what had really been happening at "The Pelican."

Like rugby forwards, then, lined up for a throw-in, they waited for the bundle which John Jellicoe Judd would bring. And when it came they pressed forward eagerly.

"Never mind *The Times* and the *Telegraph*," said O'Higgins. "You've got to set a compass-course to find your way through them. Look for the *Daily Day*."

George, cutting the string which held the papers together, snorted and said sarcastically. "I thought you might like to read about it in 'Ansard first."

"What's 'Ansard?" asked Veronica.

"Parliament's *Comic Cuts*," said Bill. "'Ere, give me one too."

The *Daily Days* were handed round and for once nobody looked at the racing news. With the certainty that headlines awaited them they turned immediately to the centre page. Nor were they disappointed. For Lady Mercy had visited the office of the *Daily Day* as well as Scotland Yard, and Lady Mercy herself was news. "The Pelican" was Lady Mercy's pub, and Lady Mercy was Cotton's Beer, and Cotton's Beer (as the starry sky-signs said) was Britain's Beer. So across the principal news page of the *Daily Day* a full length streamer ran:

INN OUTRAGE:

CHARABANC COMMANDEERED TO CHASE CRIMINALS

A bright area at the top of the two left-hand columns was strikingly cross-cut with a succession of pneumo-privative headlines, and a brief précis of the story followed in a distinguished font. In this manner:

POET'S PUB PILLAGED

ABDUCTION OF PROFESSOR'S DAUGHTER

PRETTY CHAMBERMAID
PRECEDES POET
IN PURSUIT

LADY MERCY COTTON'S NARRATIVE

"An extraordinary outrage took place yesterday afternoon at Downish. 'The Pelican Inn,' which has become famous under the management of Mr. Saturday Keith, the old Oxford Rowing Blue and a poet of national repute, had its Sunday peace disturbed by the abduction in broad daylight of Miss Joan Benbow, who was there on holiday with her father. The kidnapper, who had also been staying at 'The Pelican,' is possibly a member of an international gang of criminals. His plunder included the manuscript of Mr. Keith's latest volume of poetry and a secret process for the development of the petroleum industry. A personal account of the outrage by Lady Mercy Cotton, the owner of 'The Pelican Inn,' who was an eyewitness, is exclusive to the *Daily Day*."

"Well, this beats Barnum!" exclaimed O'Higgins with a rich and juicy satisfaction.

"Just about what I'd been expecting," said George in a gratified voice.

"They 'aven't found the bodies yet," said Maria.

"Bodies!" protested Herbert and Veronica.

"There's always bodies," said Maria.

"Oh, shut up!" Bill complained. "Can't you enjoy yourselves quietly?"

The story, confined by now to column breadth, reopened as follows:

> "As if a bomb bursting, the old-world peace of Downish was ruthlessly destroyed yesterday afternoon by the discovery of a plot which involved the manuscript of an unpublished poem, documents relating to a new process for refining petroleum, and the person of Miss Joan Benbow, a daughter of the well-known author, scholar and critic, Professor William Benbow."

It continued in a vivid and arresting style to relate the succession of events so far as they were known; to emphasize the sinister aspects of Mr. Wesson—a book-collector of mysterious origin, an American and so probably a millionaire, a Croesus of the underworld, perhaps?—and to revel in the immediate pursuit of the kidnapper by the commandeered "Blue Bird." "Elizabethan Tactics" was what a subheading called the manuvre which had so offended Miss Horsfall-Hughes and her fellow Giggleswaders.

Nelly Bly's part in the affair was mentioned admiringly but briefly, for Lady Mercy had no personal acquaintance with Nelly and she was somewhat concerned for the safety of her Isotta-Frascini. Nor was the *Daily Day* in the secret of Helen Blythesdale's alias—the editor of the Women's Page being out of town for the week-end—and that revelation, which subsequently added greatly to the reputation of the *Day*, was necessarily reserved for a later instalment.

Lady Mercy's narrative followed in the adjacent column. The story as already related was, of course, based on the information which she had supplied, but to be able to report her own words, garnished with the personal authority of inverted commas, was a tribute to the importance of the *Day*. And whereas the left-hand column was conscious art, the right-hand one was simple word-of-mouth narration of personally observed incidents. It was a human document. And the readers of the *Daily Day* thought well of human documents.

> "The first indication that anything out of the ordinary had happened," said Lady Mercy, "was when Mr. Keith told me that the manuscript of '*Tellus* Will Proceed,' his new poem, had disappeared. It was the only copy in existence, for he had destroyed the earlier drafts, and naturally he was perturbed."

Lady Mercy conveyed the impression that the loss of Saturday's poem was a more serious matter than the theft of van Buren's papers. This was in accordance with van Buren's own wishes, for the time was not yet ripe to advertise his invention with any detail. Lady Mercy knew the advantages of publicity. She had realized immediately that if Saturday's fame as a poet grew, the reputation of her favourite pub would grow with it. Most poets were pleased enough if anybody borrowed their books, and here she had in her own service a poet who could actually get his work stolen. It was a superb mishap.

And so while expressing genuine anxiety for the fate of Joan Benbow she contrived to throw into higher relief Saturday's praiseworthy decision in immediately commandeering the "Blue Bird" for rescue work.

"His own anxiety," she said, "was clearly for Miss Benbow. The loss of his book was forgotten in the major claim which arose."

She had been tempted, but resisted the temptation, to stress the additional "human interest" dependent on Saturday's affection for Joan. It would have made a pretty picture. And yet it was perhaps better to leave the gold ungilded, better to represent him as a poet who would leap to instant action at the sight of anyone's distress.

"To think that all this 'appened 'ere!" said Veronica when she had read as far.

"That there Nelly Bly!" Maria commented. "Fancy 'er in the 'eadlines. An' calling 'er pretty too."

"Well, so she is," said Herbert. "I always told you that, and clever, ever since I first seen 'er."

"Lot you know about it! Anyway, I'm glad it isn't my motor-car she's gone off in. 'Er ladyship'll never see it again, I shouldn't be surprised."

"What I can't understand," said George, "is why a man like the guv'nor *wants* to write poetry."

"'E'll make money by it now," said Bill. "D'you see what Mr. Solomon Something-or-other says?" And he pointed to a subjacent paragraph which read:

"Mr. Solomon Pfennig, the managing director of Messrs. Pfennig and Fpunck, the well-known publishers, said in an interview last night: 'Mr. Keith is the author of two volumes of poetry, both of which have been published by my firm. In my opinion Mr. Keith is one of the most promising poets in England, and I am surprised that his merit has not been more generally recognized. It is news to me, I confess, that his reputation in America is so high that a book-collector should run the risk of imprisonment to secure an unpublished manuscript of his. But American bibliophiles are very enterprising, and there is in the United States a genuine enthusiasm for high-class poetry. I have been eagerly looking forward to Mr. Keith's new work, and there was little doubt in my mind but that it would win the favour of critics and public alike. I can safely promise that this, his third volume, will be published as soon as the manuscript so romantically misappropriated has been recovered. And I venture to prophesy a very large sale for it.'"

"'E'll make thousands of pounds," said Bill. "Thousands of pounds out of poetry!"

"And there's another piece about 'im on the opposite page," said Veronica excitedly.

There was indeed an editorial paragraph—following a leading article entitled "More Cruisers and Less Cringing!"—to which George gave his attention. But it was not very interesting. He read a few lines:

"Not since the discovery of the lost books of Livy was announced—erroneously, as it was subsequently found—has the public interest been so dramatically pointed to a work of

literature, ancient or modern, as it is to-day to Mr. Keith's new
and unpublished poem. . . ."

And then he said, "Pieces written on that page don't count
much. It's only journalists who've got too old to go and look a
fire in the face that write those pieces. Or else very young journalists, practising."

"It's funny there isn't nothing about 'Olly," said Herbert.

"He 'adn't nothing to do with it," said George.

"Well, 'e's disappeared, and that's just what the others did."

"An' the professor with 'im," Veronica added.

"I wouldn't be surprised if they've made a suicide pact,"
Maria suggested hopefully.

O'Higgins, who had read steadily on, began to laugh happily. His face grew dark red and his stomach shook.

"Turn over," he ordered, "there's the best bit of the lot on
the other side."

"Bodies?" whispered Maria.

"You and your bodies! No! But the old woman—Lady
Gawd 'elp us—as put 'er old man in quod."

"Go on!" said George.

"You look and see," said O'Higgins.

The papers rustled as they were hurriedly turned about.

"Right at the top," said O'Higgins. "There!"

"Scotland Yard at once became active on hearing Lady Mercy
Cotton's story. She was able to give them the number of her
son's motor-car in which Wesson is said to have escaped, and
this was broadcast to police stations all over the country. Between seven and eight o'clock it was reported from King's Lynn
that a car which answered to the description issued had been
stopped, and its driver taken into custody. The driver protested
vigorously against his arrest and asserted that he was Mr.
Sewald Cotton of Cotton's Breweries. After being questioned
and retained in custody for some time he succeeded in establish-
ing his identity as such, the friends whom he had been visiting
having been asked to come to the police-station. He was at once
released. Police enquiries elicited from Lady Mercy Cotton the

admission that she had made an unfortunate mistake when giving the number of her son's motor-car. Both he and his father,
she said, had Bentleys, and in her natural excitement she had
evidently remembered the number of the wrong one. The police
are still confident that the wanted car will soon be found."

"Gawd," said Bill, "I'd 'ave given a week's pay to 'ave seen
him."
A guffaw, a snigger, a giggle, and hoarse laughter declared
their enjoyment of Mr. Cotton's predicament. "Well, I never!"
they said. "Fancy that old Father Christmas in quod! Now that's
what I call a good 'un."
"I'd 'ave liked it better if it 'ad been that there Nelly Bly,"
said Maria.
"Chuck it, M'ria!" they said. "There's nothing wrong with
'er except what's in your nasty mind."
Maria sniffed, dissenting.

CHAPTER XXVIII

Nelly had slept very comfortably in a house which advertised by
a placard on the gate, "Teas, Bed-Sitting-room"; ambiguously
qualify them as "Moderate." She said afterwards that the house
was on the outskirts of St. Helens, which may have been true,
and that she chose it for cheapness and because she was too
tired to drive any further. There was a garage fairly near where
she left the Isotta before asking for a night's lodging; judging
that so expensive a car was not the appropriate vehicle for the
occupant of a moderate bed-sitting-room. She left the garage
wearing Lady Mercy's raincoat and carrying Lady Mercy's attaché case, which the *Intelligent Woman's Guide to Socialism
and Capitalism* and Saturday's portfolio insufficiently bal-
lasted. Her prospective landlady readily accepted her story, in
which the Isotta—safely out of sight—was re-christened Ford
and Nelly became a lonely tourist. The neighbourhood, said the
landlady, was attracting an increasing number of visitors.

Nelly slept too long and woke with an uncomfortable feeling that the day had got ahead of her. She dressed hurriedly, reassuring herself with the thought that Liverpool was not very far away, that Wesson's ship did not sail till two o'clock, and that her plan was to wait on the quay and watch for him among the passengers going aboard whatever ship might be sailing for America that day. When she had paid for her bed and breakfast, for the Isotta's accommodation and for some more petrol, she had one-and-threepence left.

She had been in Liverpool before and knew her way to the proper docks. It was a quarter to twelve when she came in sight of the Customs sheds, and between them a glint of water, and over their roofs thin masts, red and black funnels, and a slow spouting smoke.

She stopped and spoke confidently to a policeman, saying, "There's an Atlantic liner leaving to-day, I think, but I forget its name."

"The *Corybantic's* sailing at twelve," said the policeman. "There she is, just down there."

"At twelve!" said Nelly, "I thought it was at two."

"Twelve o'clock's her time," said the policeman.

And then she remembered, while hurriedly backing her car into a space among others that stood beside a tall wooden paling. Two o'clock was the hour at which the Glasgow ship was to sail. But Wesson hadn't gone to Glasgow. He had come here. Obviously she had no time to lose.

Bare-headed—for one-and-threepence had not been enough to buy a hat—and again wearing Lady Mercy's raincoat and carrying Lady Mercy's attaché case, she ran to a door in the wooden paling. Another policeman stood there.

"Sailing on the *Corybantic?*" he asked.

"Not exactly," said Nelly.

"Then you can't get in without a pass."

"Press," said Nelly impatiently; and showed her card with its *Daily Day* inscription.

The policeman stood aside.

The quay beside the towering black flank of the liner was almost empty. Visitors had left the ship and were grouped on an upper platform. Passengers lined the shoreward side of the promenade deck. Wesson was probably among them. A few men stood about the quay and hoarsely responded to an occasional command. There was that look of expectancy in the scene, that stripped appearance of imminent action, which immediately precedes the sailing of an important vessel. Two gangways protruded from immense vacancies in the hull. Men stood beside them, waiting for the order to haul them in.

Nelly ran to the nearer one.

"Passenger?" asked an official of some kind.

"No," she said, "but I must go aboard. I'm a press representative." And she showed her card.

"No good," said the official, "all visitors have gone ashore."

Nelly did not stay to argue. Her brain worked quickly, and shrugging her shoulders with the air of one casually disappointed, she turned away. The Customs shed was momentarily empty. In it she took off Lady Mercy's raincoat, pulled from one of its pockets the discarded apron of her uniform, and tied it round her waist. Then she ran to the other end of the shed and out of it to the farther gangway.

She tried to go aboard as if such were her right—and all the time she was conscious of ropes waiting to be cast off, of the liner straining to go—but again an official stopped her.

"Passenger?" he asked.

"Of course I'm a passenger," she snapped.

"Passport? Ticket?" He queried.

"Do you think I carry them round my neck? I've showed them to you once."

"How do I know that?"

Wesson—Wesson—Wesson, her brain was secretly repeating, but aloud she said with anger that there was no need to simulate, "I'm Lady Cotton's maid. Ever heard of Lady Cotton? She's up there now, watching you. She sent me ashore a minute ago—I went down the other gangway—to look for her attaché case which she'd left in the shed over there. Now will you let me pass?"

"Go on," said the man, "and tell her to get a brunette the next time."

The lower deck on to which the gangway led was dark and almost deserted. A couple of stewards looked curiously at her. With desperate feet Nelly raced up stairs, broad shallow stairs, endless stairs, stairs that curved and straightened again and split into two, branching either way. She turned to the right and faced a great embrasure that showed her the river, blue-grey and sparkling, a tug, a ferry, and in the distance like a smoky dry-point the Birkenhead shore. This was the wrong side. There were no people here.

She ran to the other, where passengers stood at the rail look-ing at the cherished land and the friends they were about to leave. A long row of backs confronted her, a double row, a confused uneven row of men's backs and women's backs, some of them bending, some straight, square shoulders and round shoulders, obtrusive rumps and rumps recessive, red necks, white necks, no necks at all; bare heads and hats, tweed hats, felt hats and women's cloche hats, hair ruffled by the wind, bald heads, square heads, shingled, bingled, bob-tailed heads. . . . How was she to find Wesson here? She had about five minutes to discover him, and she could not remember what the back of his head was like.

Feverishly she looked for his among the other occupants, sought his nape in the host of napes, and eagerly scrutinized croup and crupper. Where hope arose, as from an apparently familiar scruff, or a counter that might be his, she pressed for-ward to peer round the angle of a jaw, the corner of a brow, for proof in the construction of the face. In this way she saw pale, proud, and pimply faces; a happy face and a perfectly horrid face; family faces and I'm-here-all-by-myself faces; but never the face of Mr. Wesson.

Nelly reached the end of the line.

She was in a fine breathless state of determination. A vivid petal flared on either cheek and her eyes sparkled. There was a lounge, she remembered, and people sitting in the lounge; chil-dren, husbands, dowagers, and young men who looked like somebody's nephews. These glanced appreciatively at Nelly as she swept by with her keen Diana look and her red wind-tossed hair and her apple-green dress and her crumpled apron.

Out of the lounge a smoking-room opened; out of the

smoking-room, a music-room, out of the music-room a library; and out of the library a verandah café. In all of them people were sitting; reading, talking, counting their children, or merely sitting. At least a dozen men had Actæon's eyes for the red-haired Diana who hunted through them. But Wesson was not among them.

A deep shuddering blast shook the vessel and everywhere people put vain hands to their ears to shut out the intolerable noise. But Nelly stamped her foot and scarcely heard it.

"Where is the purser's office?" she shouted to a convenient young man.

"Straight down there and turn to your left," he shouted back.

She ran down stairs again, broad shallow stairs, two at a time. An impenetrable crowd of people stood round the office. With a minute or so to spare it was useless to wait for the purser.

"Where can I find the head steward?" she asked an under-steward.

He looked at Nelly with interest and said, "I can't just say for the moment, but if we were to walk along this way I shouldn't be surprised if we saw him about somewhere."

They walked along a seemingly endless corridor with narrow doors on either side. Cabin trunks obstructed it. Every few yards an electrically-lighted sign drew attention to the recurrent needs of gentlemen aboard ship. Nelly tried to increase their pace but the steward was inclined to loiter and showed a too-friendly curiosity. Underfoot, Nelly felt a throbbing, the vague and immense stirring of hidden power. The ship was coming to life. Its heart was beating.

With a sudden cry Nelly darted from the steward, swerved round a cabin trunk, and sped swiftly down the narrow way. She had just seen at a cross-roads in the corridor a figure which looked like Wesson. It had disappeared almost as soon as she caught sight of it. Her heart pounded as she ran.

She turned a corner. The figure was in sight, turning another. It did look like Wesson. She followed with painfully growing excitement.

On still more stairs she caught her man by the sleeve. He turned a dull and unfamiliar face. He had bushy eyebrows and

a pale round polished wart beside his nose. He appeared unfriendly.

"I'm sorry. I apologize. I've made a mistake," said Nelly, and
felt hollow and despairing. She gasped for breath, swallowed
two or three times, and fumbled for a handkerchief. But she
had no handkerchief. Nothing more comforting than the *Intelligent Woman's Guide to Socialism and Capitalism*, and the
manuscript of "*Tellus* Will Proceed."

The man with the shining wart grunted and left her.

For a moment or two Nelly waited on the companion-way,
her head drooping, leaning on the broad banister, dejected and
utterly at a loss. Another steward—there were hundreds of
them, it seemed— stopped in passing and said cheerfully, "Not
sick already, are you?"

The throbbing of the ship had grown louder. Nelly stared
blankly at the steward and without answering him ran on deck.

On the one side stretched grey-blue water, sun-flecked; small
black craft stood under their smoke and behind them, like a
dusty dry-point, was the shore. On the other side was more
water, grey-green, and a nearer shore. The *Corybantic* had gone
to sea.

"There's no need to be frightened," said Nelly to herself but
half-aloud. "There's not the slightest occasion for fear. I'm
doing my duty. Wesson must be aboard somewhere. I'll catch
him before we reach America. They can't do anything to me.
I'm perfectly sure they can't. I'm not a stowaway. They can't. . . .
I'll send a wireless message to the *Daily Day* and to Keith and
Quentin. There's no need to be afraid. Not a bit. But I wish I
had a handkerchief."

A kindly man, seeing her distress and her attractive features,
said to her, "Is anything the matter? Can I help you?"

"Tell me this," said Nelly, "when do we arrive in New
York?"

"New York!" exclaimed the kindly man. "Why, we're going
to Madeira!"

"*Where?*"

"To Madeira. On a fourteen-day cruise. Didn't your mistress tell you?"

"No. Did yours?" said Nelly wildly. "Oh, for God's sake take me to the captain!"

CHAPTER XXIX

Saturday woke to see through his window a blue sky over which white clouds were swiftly sailing. He stretched his arms upwards and his toes to the very foot of the bed. Oh, the luxury of slowly waking to a fine day and stretching every single joint under soft sheets! Blissfully he considered the ceiling, and between that virgin whiteness and the feather-smoothness of his bed he began to think of Joan.

About the same time Joan also woke and saw through her window another section of the same blue sky and some almost identical clouds. Blissfully she stretched her arms and blissfully her legs; more delicately than a man would do it but, it is probable, with as much satisfaction. Then she curled herself up very neatly and something like a shrimp, and thought about Saturday.

A little before this Quentin had wakened. There was blue sky beyond his window too, but he took no heed of it. Nor did he crack his several joints and luxuriate in smoothness and ease. He sat up immediately and hugged his knees and frowned at the nether bed-end. For he was thinking about Nelly, who was far away and under another sky. Quentin had dreamed a sinister dream of the Red Square in Moscow.

None of them thought about Mr. Wesson, who had been awake for several hours. Even more than the defeat of all his schemes did his present confinement irk him, for like most Americans he was accustomed to rising at an hour when all but the most unfortunate classes in England are still comfortably asleep. And so he walked up and down his room in a very bad temper. He could not walk far, for the turret room was small. And he had no clothes to put on. Nor a razor. Nor a toothbrush. Nothing indeed but very old pyjamas and a magnificent view from his lofty window. But for the present he was not interested in scenery. He wanted to get dressed.

There was no bell in the room, but he had knocked long and loudly on the door and succeeded in attracting the attention of a maid, who listened for some minutes to his request for clothes and hot water and a razor and—if there happened to be a new one in the house—a toothbrush. But she was unimpressed and finally told him to "Bide whar ye are, ye auld blather, an' haud y'ur wheesht." This conveyed no meaning at all to Mr. Wesson, but when he heard her going down the turret stair again he realized that his captivity must still endure.

About midday Joan and Quentin and Saturday met for breakfast, and in spite of Quentin's anxiety about Nelly Bly there was definitely a holiday atmosphere in the room.

"But I must telephone to father," said Joan. "I meant to get up early and do it, but it's so difficult to remember things where you're asleep."

Sir Colin came in with Bran the deerhound at his heels. Bran endured with patience the examination of his iodine-insulted face, and Sir Colin sat down beside Joan.

"I sent a telegram to your father a couple of hours ago," he said, "saying that you were all here, perfectly well and safe, and that van Buren's documents had been recovered. I asked him to repeat it to Lady Mercy. There should be an answer very soon."

"I'm going to put a trunk-call through to 'The Pelican,'" said Saturday, and went out.

"Have you seen the newspapers?" Colin asked. "You've become figures of national interest overnight."

The London papers had just arrived. The *Daily Day* was among them. "Comes to Castle and Cottage" was one of its well-known advertising mottoes.

Joan and Quentin were visibly shocked when they saw it. The hugeness of the type daunted them. It was like a threat delivered in the presence of two million witnesses. The black, intolerably black, square letters thrust themselves forward with the brutality of branding-irons. Joan turned white and Quentin red. They looked at each other, like soldiers half panic-struck, to see if their weakness was a common one.

"What shall we do?" whispered Joan. "We must go and hide somewhere."

Quentin held the paper in clenched fists. "'Pretty Chambermaid Precedes Poet in Pursuit,'" he read. "Pretty chambermaid! Joan, I love her! You didn't know—you don't know yet—the truth about Nelly. But I love her. And now two million, five million, God knows how many million people in Britain think of my darling as a pretty chambermaid preceding poets in pursuit of pseudo-pundits!"

"Why," said Joan, "I never guessed that you were even interested in her."

"I hid my feelings," said Quentin. "But didn't Saturday tell you?"

"Not a word. Does he know?"

"I told him something about her."

"And did you want him to tell me?"

"Of course I didn't. What I told him was in the strictest confidence. I thought he might have dropped a hint to you. That's all. But there's no need to whisper now, with this foghorn blaring to the world."

"Poor Quentin! You'll find her again."

"Not as she was before. This dreadful publicity may kill her. She was brought up in a convent, Joan."

Colin had listened to this conversation with some impatience.

"I don't think you should worry too much," he said. "Advertisement doesn't hurt people nowadays—except those who buy the pills. I expect this Nelly Bly will enjoy it all."

"You don't know her," said Quentin shortly.

"Well, if she doesn't, Saturday will."

"Saturday!" exclaimed Joan indignantly. "Do you think Saturday likes to have his name bandied about all over England? He's the last person on earth to enjoy publicity of this kind."

"Have you seen what Mr. Solomon Pfennig says?" asked Colin.

Joan read the paragraph which ended in a prophecy of large and remunerative sales for "*Tellus* Will Proceed."

"Of course, this may make a difference to his book," she said in an altered voice.

"I think they might have mentioned my novel too," Quentin

remarked. He had read the story over again and *A Nettle Against May* was unnoticed.

"It certainly is a striking testimonial to his poem," said Joan, "that anybody should want to steal it. Of course nobody did actually steal it, but the *Daily Day* creates that impression. Oh, Saturday, have you seen what the paper says about us?"

Saturday was inured to publicity after his three calamitous boat-races, but even he appeared to shrink a little when he saw the terrible black and white banner which proclaimed their adventure to the world.

"Did you get through to 'The Pelican'?" asked Quentin.

"Yes. There's no news of Nelly Bly. Your father's all right, Joan."

He read the history of "The Pelican" and the "Blue Bird" with a critical frown.

"I suppose you hate all this," he said to Joan.

"It is rather trying," she said. "But I'm glad they've mentioned your book."

"'Mentioned' is a frugal word," said Colin.

"It's magnificent advertisement for '*Tellus*.' Do you mind very much being mixed up in it, Joan? It's going to make a tremendous difference to my sales. You see what Pfennig says. And they've actually got an editorial note about it."

"It will go into three editions in a week," said Joan, "and father will give us his blessing with both hands."

"It seems a pity that the manuscript is lost," Colin observed.

A depressed silence followed his remark.

"But it's sure to turn up," said Joan. "I expect Nelly Bly has it."

"Why do you think that?" asked Quentin.

"She looked such a clever girl," said Joan sweetly.

"They had heard nothing from her at 'The Pelican.' She has simply disappeared. Your father and Holly got a car and followed us, Joan, but they were held up by engine trouble. Colin's wire was opened and copies forwarded to him and Lady Mercy. George says there's a large crowd outside 'The Pelican' and no room inside for anyone except reporters and policemen."

"I believe my mother has had something to do with all this," said Quentin, "she has a genuine talent for creating an audience."

In the afternoon they walked down to the bridge and looked with interest at Quentin's half-drowned car; and afterwards they sat and talked idly of returning to Downish. In front of them the lawn stretched green and smooth and then slid steeply down to the unseen river. Hills rose beyond, cup-shaped, giant hummocks pleasant with grass. Green hills as round as apples, and behind them dim ranges shading through olive and sage into tawny colour, into dove-greys and blue. There was still wind enough to bend the trees all one way, but the terrace where they sat was sheltered and warm in the sun.

Lady Keith had been out all morning. "Just looking at things," she said. "Little things like tits and finches. What shambling twilight horrors we human beings appear in comparison with birds!"

Joan, triumphantly emerging from adventure, was not inclined to depreciate her species.

"But there are such beautiful qualities in human nature," she said; "courtesy, and constancy, and love—"

"Those qualities are typically displayed by the widgeon and other ducks. From the marismas of Guadalquivir to the Arctic a widgeon and its mate fly side by side, hungry and steadfast and cheering each other on. I have seen flighting ducks shot. Always, if the shot bird is a female, its mate follows it down, attending the dead body with every appearance of distress and careless of its own danger. I assure you, my dear Joan, that you could find the germs of constancy and love in every duck's egg that was ever laid."

She and Saturday, thought Joan, Saturday and she would love each other to the death. . . . Old people spoke of death. It might or might not be a reality. Old people were so often mistaken. . . . Hand-in-hand she pictured her lover and herself walking from the marshes of Guadalquivir to a flower-lit Arctic Spring. Loving and constant and cheering each other on. Happily she sighed, and looked at the round hills beyond the river, grassy half-moons, green cantles vast and up-ended.

"How is your prisoner to-day?" asked Lady Keith.

They looked blankly at her till Saturday confessed, "I had forgotten all about him."

"When you were a little boy," said Lady Keith, "I once let

you keep a linnet in a cage, because you cried till you were sick
when I at first refused. You were a very little boy and I was
even more foolish then than I am now. And you are treating
Mr. Wesson to-day exactly as you treated that wretched linnet
twenty years ago. You caught him and now you have forgotten
him. Unfortunately you're too big for me to thrash you again,
but I am very angry with you. Go and release Mr. Wesson at
once."

Saturday obeyed.

With a kind of soft indignation Lady Keith addressed the
hills; or it may have been an invisible company of birds. "Children," she said. "Naughty children. That's all they ever are."

"I'm so sorry," said Joan.

"Of course you're sorry. Children are sorry at least one night
in three. But they forget about it in the morning."

In a little while Mr. Wesson appeared, hastily dressed in a
mixture of his own and borrowed clothes. He fingered his
unshaven cheeks, and while some distance away could be
heard complaining to Saturday about the manner of his imprisonment.

"Mr. Wesson," said Lady Keith. And Mr. Wesson was silent.

"We have decided to let you go free. No one has suffered any
serious loss as a result of your ill-considered action, and consequently I feel that to prosecute you would merely be an exhibition of petty spite. I am sure that I can speak for Mr.—Mr. van
Buren, is it? Thank you—for Mr. van Buren also. You are both
Americans, I understand, and naturally he would not want to
send a fellow-countryman to prison. Have you enough money
to pay for your passage home? In that case you had better get
something to eat and then I will have you driven to the station.
Does anyone want to add anything to what I have said?"

Nobody did. Colin looked out over the valley with the contented smile of one who listens to a favourite tune. Saturday
and Joan were slightly abashed. Quentin openly admired. And
nobody showed any wish to speak except the prisoner. He
cleared his throat significantly.

"Your ladyship," he began, "this is the gesture of a noble
heart. As your great national poet Burns has so rightly said,
'Ah, Freedom is a noble thing!'—"

"It wasn't Burns. It was Barbour," said Lady Keith.

The butler appeared.

"A trunk call for Mr. Saturday," he announced.

Saturday got up hurriedly.

"Take Mr. Wesson and see that he gets something to eat," said Lady Keith.

Mr. Wesson's eyes had meanwhile fallen on a copy of the *Daily Day* which lay open on a chair. A glow of happiness suffused his features as the enormous type shouted to him. His shoulders straightened. He braced himself like an actor taking his call.

"Your generosity has been so notable," he said, "that I am emboldened to ask you a further favour. May I take this newspaper with me? My little exploit seems to have hit the editor precisely where he lives, and this page will be a proud addition to my press-cutting album."

"You are welcome to it," said Lady Keith.

"I thank your ladyship. Good-bye, your ladyship. Good-bye, Miss Benbow. I shall treasure the recollection of our little journey together. Sir Colin and Mr. Cotton, good-bye. I'm very pleased to have met you."

Not without dignity Mr. Wesson suffered the butler to lead him away.

"Well!" said Joan.

"They are a resilient people," Colin observed.

"And would consequently suffer great distress in prison," said Lady Keith.

Saturday returned with a look of ineffable content on his face and a slip of paper in his hand.

"What's the news?" they asked him.

"Messages of congratulation from Lady Mercy, van Buren, and the professor," he said. "They don't matter for the moment. Listen to the important thing: 'Led astray by false clue indicating Wesson intended embarking Liverpool. Now aboard ship *Corybantic* proceeding Madeira holiday cruise. Your manuscript safe with me. NELLY BLY.'"

"Where did that come from?" Quentin demanded.

"From the *Corybantic* by wireless. The telegram was handed in to 'The Pelican' less than an hour ago. They repeated it and

I wrote it down. So now you know where Nelly is and I know where my poem is. Are you happy?"

"I am," said Joan.

Quentin reached for the slip of paper on which Saturday had copied the message. He read it word by word, balancing each as if it might contain a hidden meaning that would fall apart under scrutiny. He was still a slave to the Russian heresy.

"Why has that girl decided to go on a holiday cruise at such an awkward time?" asked Lady Keith.

"She was led astray," said Joan.

Quentin stared tragically into space and saw as in a pageant Nelly attended by gigantic perils. A field of snow, a procession of dreary prisoners staggering under their gaolers' whips, the cruel Oriental domes of Moscow; bright blue sea and a sunlit beach; palms; and over them, like a red phantom, the Sickle and Hammer of the Soviet.

"How far away is the station?" he asked abruptly. "Lady Keith, will you excuse me if I go now?"

He disappeared into the house with giant strides.

According to their mood they commented on the manner of his departure and waited for him to return and explain what he meant to do. They discussed the telephone message from Downish and were glad that "*Tellus* Will Proceed" was safe. And then they heard from somewhere behind the house the racing-roar of a motor-engine. And round the corner, on to the drive beneath them—steps led down to it—came the battered "Blue Bird." Mud-splashed, with sagging hood and a broken wing, the charabanc drove slowly past.

Saturday started up and shouted, "Where are you going?"

Quentin leaned out and shouted back: "Moscow!—I mean Madeira."

In a roaring crescendo of noise the "Blue Bird" leapt forward, a feather of gobelin-blue smoke flying under its mud-plastered azure stern.

THE END